If Only You

A BERGMAN BROTHERS NOVEL

CHLOE LIESE

BERKLEY ROMANCE
NEW YORK

BERKLEY ROMANCE
Published by Berkley
An imprint of Penguin Random House LLC
penguinrandomhouse.com

Library of Congress Cataloging-in-Publication Data

Names: Liese, Chloe, author.
Title: If only you / Chloe Liese.
Description: First Berkley Romance Edition. | New York: Berkley Romance, 2024. |
Series: A Bergman Brothers novel
Identifiers: LCCN 2023042086 (print) | LCCN 2023042087 (ebook) |
ISBN 9780593642450 (trade paperback) | ISBN 9780593642467 (ebook)
Subjects: LCGFT: Romance fiction. | Novels.
Classification: LCC PS3612.I3357 I35 2024 (print) | LCC PS3612.I3357 (ebook) |
DDC 813/.6—dc23/eng/20230928
LC record available at https://lccn.loc.gov/2023042086
LC ebook record available at https://lccn.loc.gov/2023042087

If Only You was originally self-published, in different form, in 2023.

First Berkley Romance Edition: February 2024

Printed in the United States of America
1st Printing

Book design by Kristin del Rosario

*For the hard hearts that bravely learn
to soften, and the brave soft hearts
that love them as they do.*

Dear Reader,

This story features characters with human realities who I believe deserve to be seen more prominently in romance through positive, authentic representation. As a neurodivergent person living with chronic conditions, I am passionate about writing feel-good romances affirming my belief that every one of us is worthy and capable of happily ever after, if that's what our heart desires.

Specifically, this story portrays a main character on the autism spectrum and a main character who receives a celiac disease diagnosis. No two people's experience of any condition or diagnosis will be the same, but through my own experience and the insight of authenticity readers, I have strived to create characters who honor the nuances of those identities. Please be aware that it also includes the topic of self-medicating with alcohol and substances, as well as past experience of a verbally abusive stepparent and abandonment by a parent.

If any of these are sensitive topics for you, I hope you feel comforted in knowing that loving, healing, affirming relationships—with oneself and others—are championed in this story.

XO,
Chloe

Broken hearts, unrequited love, and inconsolable misery are subjects which, most fortunately, I have only ever read in books.

—JANE AUSTEN,
Sanditon

ONE

Ziggy

Playlist: "Shame," Elle King

This just might be the perfect day. Except for one small thing: my underwear.

Standing beside my siblings, I smile for another wedding photo and try to focus on how magical this day has been instead of how far my panties are riding up my butt. I think about this gorgeous beachfront wedding that just went off without a hitch for my brother Ren and his now wife, Frankie, who's been like a sister to me for years. I think about the glorious tangerine sun glowing on the horizon, the luscious sea breeze that's kept me cool this afternoon, despite the heat weaving through our whole chaotic Bergman brood—my parents, six siblings, their partners, and my niece and nephew.

The camera clicks as my little gratitude exercise comes to a close, unfortunately leaving me no less aware of the wedgie from hell. I wiggle my butt to try to dislodge it and force my grimace into a smile as the photographer calls for one more take.

"Okay," Frankie says after the next click of the camera, brushing back a lock of dark hair from her face. "That's enough memory making. This bride needs a seat, five minutes of quiet, and a very large glass of red wine."

"Coming right up," the wedding planner says, jumping into action.

The tight photographer-staged ball of our family dissolves into easy mingling—quick laughter and steady conversation. Before someone can rope me into it, I scamper away across the sand, sandals hooked on my fingers, making a beeline for the elegant venue that boasts grand doors opened wide to the sights and sounds of the beach, the dwindling light mingling with ivory candles and floral centerpieces.

Trying to be circumspect, I follow the edge of the room, racking my memory for the nearest bathroom, though, at this point, I will take a closet, nook, the first private space available, to lose these horrible panties, because I'm about to crawl out of my skin.

Not everyone gets this upset about their underwear riding up their butt; however, I'm autistic, and I have a lot of sensory issues. Itchy seams, fabric bunched where it shouldn't be, send me spiraling if I don't address the issue promptly. I need to find somewhere to deal with my sensory misery *immediately*.

As I finally locate the restroom and stumble into the lounge area—an art deco ode to shell-pink velvet and bronze accents—I come to an abrupt stop, encountering the one thing that could distract me from the underwear from hell:

People talking about me.

"Don't get me wrong, Ziggy's sweet. She really is." I can't see her, but I recognize that voice. It's Bridget, one of our just-retired midfielders from the National Team, whose spot I filled on our starting lineup. "She's just so—"

"Young," offers a voice I recognize, too. Martina, another recently retired player and former starting defender.

"Exactly," Bridget says. "Frankly, I was surprised she made the roster at *all*. When Mal asked what I thought about her place on the team, I told him, she's talented, but she doesn't have the confidence, the . . . *poise* for a starting position, for the exposure and pressure that puts on you."

"She really doesn't," Martina agrees. "I mean, as soon as the camera's pointed her way, she goes silent and her face turns as red as her hair."

My hand goes to my hair. And my cheeks turn hot. My vision is starting to get blurry.

"Well, soon enough, Mal will see what a mistake he made."

Twin tears spill down my cheeks. My hands are fists, shaking as anger boils up inside me.

What Bridget and Martina said is so unfair. But it's also not unprecedented. I'm painfully familiar with this attitude, this perception that I'm juvenile and naïve, some delicate innocent who can't handle the real world.

My family babies me. My peers underestimate me. I'm tired of it, and I'm sick to my stomach thinking about what this perception, if it sticks, could cost me—what it already threatened to cost me, but for Coach Mal ignoring Bridget's warnings and putting me on the team anyway.

I'm mad that I have to deal with this nonsense on today of all days. I get why my brother Ren invited Bridget and Martina to his wedding. They're local high-profile professional athletes who partner generously with his charity. But still, right now I really wish he hadn't.

"All right," Martina says, her voice growing closer on the restroom side of the lounge. "That's enough preening. I want to get my hands on those hors d'oeuvres. They looked damn good, and they aren't going to last forever. This place is crawling with professional athletes; you know how much food they can put away."

Bridget snorts. "Yeah, I do. I've seen you eat."

Martina's echoing laugh grows closer. They're about to see me, and they'll know I've heard them. Desperate to avoid that, I spin and rush out of the room, right into my sister.

"Whoa." My oldest sibling, Freya, clasps me by the shoulders as I plow into her.

I duck my head, quickly dabbing my face, but Freya hasn't missed a thing.

"Zigs, what's wrong? Did someone upset you?" She curls an arm around me and tugs me down the hall. "Hey, talk to me. I can't help you if you don't talk to me."

"I don't need your help!" I wrench myself away as we turn the corner in the hall, thankfully hiding us from Bridget and Martina. "I don't need you to manhandle or womanhandle me or whatever, and I don't need you to stick up for me."

Freya blinks, her pale blue-gray eyes, just like Mom's, wide with surprise. Slowly she lifts her hands in surrender. "Okay. I'm sorry. I get in mama bear mode; you know that. I just want to take care of you. You're my baby sister."

I shake my head, scrunching my eyes shut. "I'm the youngest in the family, but I'm not a baby anymore, Freya. I'm a twenty-two-year-old woman." Huffing a breath, I stare up at the ceiling and try to calm myself. "I vote. I got my driver's license. I have a job and an apartment. I pay my rent. I take care of myself, okay?"

Freya lowers her hands, her voice quiet and hesitant. "Okay, Ziggy. I'm sorry."

Guilt turns my stomach sour. I've hurt Freya's feelings, and I didn't mean to. I meant to be honest, to tell the truth, but I didn't say it in a way that made her feel good.

So often, it feels like when I'm my true, honest self, I can't do anything right.

"It's fine. I'm sorry, too, I just . . ." Growling with frustration, I clutch my sandals tightly in my hand. My underwear's location in my butt crack is turning into my villain origin story. "I just need somewhere to lose these freaking panties!"

Storming down the hall and leaving my sister in my wake, I catch sight of glass doors opening out to a shadowy terrace, a steep roof shielding it from the last marigold streaks of twilight. Tall tropical plants cover the terra-cotta tiles and form a small, lush oasis, affording me plenty of privacy for what I need to do.

I drop my sandals and hike up my dress to reach the waistband of my underwear. With a sigh of deep relief, I hook my fingers on the waistband, then drag the offending fabric down my thighs. When it hits my ankles, I celebrate by flicking the horrible panties off my foot, into the air over my head. Then I spin around, prepared to catch them.

Except when I turn around, I see someone's beaten me to it. Someone lounging in the shadows, long legs outstretched . . . one familiar, tattooed hand, holding my panties.

I take it back. It's not the wedgie from hell or Bridget and Martina's gossiping or my well-meaning-but-suffocating family that's going to ruin this otherwise perfect day. It's the sight of my underwear dangling from Sebastian Gauthier's heavily tattooed index finger.

Heat crawls up my throat and floods my cheeks as my brother's best friend stares at me from the shadows. Slowly, he sits up and leans forward, elbows on his knees.

Then he gives my panties a little twirl around his finger.

Somehow, my cheeks get even hotter. I'm going to die of mortification.

"Lose something?" he asks.

It's the longest he's ever looked my way, the most words he's ever spoken to me. (We've bumped into each other a handful of times either at my brother Ren's place or after their games, which is when I've only ever been the recipient of a terse nod followed by a chilly *hello*.) Any other day, I'd probably stand here, tongue-tied, stunned that Sebastian's acknowledged my existence.

But today, I'm at my limit. I've been dealing with a noisy crowd, aggravating undies, petty fellow athletes, over-involved family, and I'm *done*.

Cheeks burning, fire in my veins, I take the two steps between us and reach for my underwear as he swings it lazily around his finger.

At the last second, Sebastian pulls back and does some confounding sleight of hand that makes them disappear. A soft *tsk* shivers through the air as he peers up at me, one dark eyebrow lifted. "Not so fast."

I glare down at him. "Give me my panties."

Gaze holding mine, he flashes a dangerously slow, sensual grin. And in that moment, I understand exactly how Sebastian Gauthier has managed to get away with being such a despicable human: He is despicably handsome.

I stare into those rare quicksilver eyes, cold and sharp as they stare right back at me. His dark hair rustles in the sea breeze, a few loose waves caressing his temple before they're blown back, revealing the full and unfair beauty of his face. Cool gray eyes framed by thick dark lashes. A long, strong nose. That unreasonably lush mouth, twin faint hollows in each cheek.

Slouching in his chair again, long legs sprawled out, he wears a booted Aircast on his right foot that I can only imagine sucked to wear out on the sand, though I'm not inclined to feel much of anything in the way of sympathy for him right now. Inked fingers with their silver rings drum on the chair's arms. He's dressed in a charcoal suit so dark it's nearly black, a white button-up undone way too far, revealing a deep wedge of golden skin and silver chains. From his collarbones down, every exposed inch of him is *covered* in tats.

In another world—in which he wasn't an unapologetic jerk—I could mistake him for one of those morally gray villains who star in the fantasy romances I've been reading since adolescence.

Dangerous and dark-haired, inked and angry. Villains who ultimately redeem themselves, revealing their true natures when they prove themselves to be deeply good, feminist, sacrificial heroes.

I know. It's called *fantasy* romance for a reason.

As he inspects me with that cool, sharp gaze, I set my hands on my hips and glare at him, profoundly annoyed.

He is literally *the* most beautiful person I've ever seen.

But while he looks like he could spread some epic Faery King wings and whisk me off across the night sky to his palace, he is *not* one of my fantasy romance heroes. He is someone who—according to a lot of deeply damning and corroborated news headlines—breaks not just promises and property but hopes and hearts. Which is why his devious charms have not and certainly will not work on me.

And also why I continue to be baffled that my second-oldest brother, Ren, the sweetest, most tenderhearted man, could be bonded to him so deeply.

Sebastian and Ren are teammates—both are star forwards for the LA Kings hockey team—but beyond that, what makes them so close is a mystery to me. Ren says there's good in Sebastian, that he just struggles to demonstrate it in observable ways. Now that I'm experiencing firsthand what a jerk Sebastian can be, I'm wondering if Ren sees in his teammate what he *wants* to more than what's actually there.

"Sebastian Gauthier," I say sternly, "give me my panties."

His cold gray eyes turn arctic as he peers up at me. He raises an eyebrow. "What panties? I don't see any panties, do you?"

I glare at him harder, my anger ratcheting up. "I don't see them, but I know you have them. I watched you do . . . something with them."

His smirk is wolfish and infuriating. "Better come find them, then."

Again, on any other day, I would probably throw up my hands

and walk off, enjoy bursting Ren's idyllic bubble by telling him that I'd appreciate it if he asked his *best friend* to cough up my panties the next time he sees him. But today is not that day. Today I am past my limit, and my rare temper is a wild colt free of its reins.

Without preamble, I step between the bracket of Sebastian's legs, wrap a hand around his wrist, and tug up his arm, slipping my other hand inside the sleeve of his suit coat. I fully expect the panties to be there, since that's the hand that was holding them.

He laughs, and the sound is so self-satisfied, so arrogant, I barely resist the urge to scream in frustration. "Try again."

Angry, I drop his wrist. "Where *are* they?"

If they're not up his sleeve, I have no idea where else my underwear could be. At this point, the only way I could possibly find out is frisking him.

When I glance up again and find that sardonic grin lifting his mouth, I have one of my little delayed autistic epiphanies: That's exactly what he wants me to do.

As if he's watched the light bulb *ping* to life over my head, Sebastian stretches out his impressive wingspan, grin widening. "I suppose you'll just have to pat me down."

I roll my eyes. But before I can come up with some witty retort, my brother Viggo's voice carries from somewhere inside: "Ziggy! Get in here! The chocolate fountain's running!"

Sebastian jerks in his seat like he's been electrocuted and bolts upright, suddenly standing beside me.

Very close beside me.

He takes me by the shoulder and spins me a quarter turn, until light from inside spills across my face. His eyes widen. "Fucking hell. *Ziggy?*"

TWO

Sebastian

Playlist: "Broken Boy," Cage The Elephant

I have a long history of truly terrible sins, but mentally debauching my best friend's baby sister while watching her strip off her panties just might take the cake.

To my credit, I didn't recognize Ziggy at first. My vision's fuzzy, thanks to my drunkenness, and she was backlit when she walked out onto the terrace, nothing but a stunning silhouette whose defining features were hidden. Then, when she stepped closer, and I had a chance of seeing her, her hair was down—it's never been down before—and in the dying light of sunset it was a sheet of molten bronze curtaining her face, nothing like the fiery red that Ren and his little sister share.

I didn't realize it was Ziggy I was mentally undressing until I heard someone inside yell her name and watched her answer to it. Now I stand, clutching her arm, drinking her in as she glows in the harsh brightness of the venue's lights. My stomach sours. The liquor I've been drinking since before the ceremony began crawls up my throat.

She looks only a little like Ren—the same long, straight nose and sharp, high cheekbones, and (now that we're in proper lighting) the same rich red hair—but mostly she looks nothing like him. Unlike his ice-blue irises, hers are wide, deep-set emeralds. And while I've noticed a few on Ren, her skin is scattered with freckles, a shower of cinnamon sparks splashed across her nose and cheeks, across her arm, which I'm still holding. That I can't seem to stop holding.

I think I just might be in shock.

I watched quiet, shy Ziggy Bergman viciously strip off her panties. And I thoroughly enjoyed it.

More than enjoyed it. Got very, *very* aroused, watching her hike up her dress, looking like some ocean goddess—long, wild hair whipping in the breeze, seafoam-green fabric dancing over pale, freckled thighs that kept going and going, leading to wide hips and two full curves of her ass—

Shit. *Shit.*

I'm mentally debauching her again.

"Sebastian." There's my full name again, scolding and authoritarian. Ziggy sounds like a chiding schoolteacher faced with a naughty little boy, a fantasy I'd enjoy much more if (a) it didn't involve my best friend's little sister, and (b) she hadn't used my full name. I hate when people use my full name.

"It's *Seb*," I tell her icily.

She blinks slowly, curiously, as if impervious to the frigid warning in my voice. As if she's not one bit intimidated by me, even when I stand to my full height, maximizing the two inches I have on her. She lifts her chin and stares right back.

The hairs on the nape of my neck stand up. The way they always do when my sixth sense kicks in. A warning.

I should be running the other way, putting distance between us like I have the past two years.

Since I joined the Kings and found myself inextricably tethered to her brother, I have kept my eyes, thoughts, hands, attention thoroughly away from Ziggy Bergman. Because Ren—the kind, good, always smiling captain of my team, a man who is truly my antithesis—is the one person I haven't been able to scare off, who's not only refused to be put off by my horrible reputation and merciless streak of misbehavior, but who's insinuated himself in my life to the point that we've become profoundly close, and like hell will I risk that friendship.

That means steering clear of the people he loves. Which there happen to be quite a lot of. Six siblings. *Six*.

It hasn't been a great challenge, given most of them are partnered, not that—let's be clear about the quality of my character—this has stopped me from seducing someone before. The remaining two who are unpartnered, I swore to myself I'd avoid entirely, no matter how attractive they are.

One has been easier than the other.

Viggo, his younger brother, wasn't hard to write off. While damn good looking, he's always waving around a romance novel, yelling about toxic masculinity and happy endings. I don't touch romantics, a lesson I learned the hard way after a few clingers refused to believe I'm really as disinterested in commitment as I told them.

Ziggy, on the other hand, has been trickier. Striking height and looks, but so demure and quiet, a delicious blend of contradictions that I've had to remind myself repeatedly I will not be exploring. She, I've had to *decide* to ignore. And I've done very well following through on that decision the past few years.

Until now.

"Be right there!" she yells inside, before rounding on me. I catch the whisper of a perfume that's soft and clean, so light, it could be only the scent of her skin, the soap she uses to bathe.

Christ. Now I'm thinking about her bathing. Bubbles frothing along those long, freckled legs, dissolving at the curve of her breasts—

"What was that about?" she demands, snapping me out of more debaucherous thoughts.

"I didn't know it was you."

Her eyes narrow. "You . . . didn't know it was me."

I turn away and stare out at the ocean, avoiding looking at her. God, I'm drunk. The world's tipping like I'm on a ship weathering sky-high swells.

"Yes," I say on a nauseated exhale.

She folds her arms. "We've seen each other easily a handful of times. I look just like your best friend—"

"That is patently untrue," I mutter, massaging my aching temples. My brain feels like sludge.

And like it does so often, my stomach thuds with a familiar sharp pain.

She snorts. "You really expect me to believe you didn't recognize me."

"Yes," I snap, rounding on her, making her take a fast step back as her eyes widen in surprise. "It's getting dark. You were backlit, and I'm drunk. Your hair was down, and it's never down. I didn't recognize you."

Now her eyebrows rise, twin cinnamon curves arched over those wide green eyes the color of wet glossy leaves like the ones surrounding us. "How do you know my hair's never down?"

"I don't pretend to know or care what it looks like," I tell her sharply, hoping it'll scare her off. "I mean, when I've *seen* you, it's never down."

She tips her head, arms across her chest. "I wasn't aware you even saw me when we *did* cross paths. You seemed to overlook the fact that I even existed."

"Yes, well, it's easy to overlook someone who obviously *wants* to be overlooked. If you've been hoping for a different response, I'd suggest revising that attitude."

Suddenly, her expression blanks. When she blinks, a sheen of wetness turns her eyes glassy.

That's when I realize I've done something even more unforgivable than mentally debauching my best friend's little sister: I've made her cry.

————

The past three weeks since I watched Ziggy run off on the verge of tears began as a typical self-loathing bender, but have culminated in a new, bleak low. With my reinjured foot propped up, I lounge on Ren's sofa, the recipient of a formidable scowl.

Frankie's.

My highly displeased agent sits in an armchair across from me in her usual head-to-toe black, her long dark hair curtaining intense hazel eyes. This, paired with her severe expression and her hand flexing menacingly around her gray acrylic cane, make her look like a pissed-off witch, ready to curse me. I think, one more wrong move on my part, and she just might.

"You," she says flatly, "are an ass of unfathomable proportions."

"This is not news." Shutting my eyes, I drop my head back on the arm of their sofa. Frankie jabs my thigh with the tip of her cane. Hard.

"Ow!" I whine. "Ren, Frankie hit me."

"Don't talk to him," she snaps. "He has no part in this conversation."

"So we're having this meeting at your house while Ren makes us lunch, why again?"

"So I won't murder you," she tells me darkly.

I swallow. Frankie's wrath is just about the only thing I'm scared of. That and losing my hockey career.

I might also be a teensy bit scared of finally having done something that could cost me Ren's friendship, too. Not that I'd ever admit that to anyone, especially Ren.

I glance toward the man in question, who still exhibits no signs of having written me off, considering he drove me to and from my most recent doctor appointment in his minivan and is now making me a meal. Still, he's got me nervous, standing with his back to me, focused on whatever's cooking on the range while he wears his theater nerd apron with *William Shakespeare* doodled all over it.

"Ren," I whisper-plead.

He gives me an apologetic glance over his shoulder. "Better listen to her. You know I'd step between you and anything, Seb, except my wife."

As he says that, Frankie's expression transforms from a scowl to a smile, which she beams his way. He beams a smile back.

Their mutual gaze is disgustingly affectionate.

"Stop doing that in front of me. It's making me nauseous."

Frankie cuts me another scathing glare and pokes me in the hip this time, making me yelp. "Sure that nausea isn't a response to your self-sabotaging bullshit finally coming back to bite you in the ass?"

"I know I fucked up. I told you, I understand, okay? Now it's your job to help me fix it. That's why I pay you the big bucks."

Frankie snorts, leaning back in her chair, and—thank God—dropping her cane beside her. "Seb, I am brilliant at my job. I am a damn good sports agent. But this is pushing the limits of even *my* abilities. If it were simply managing your image, that would be one thing—"

"Managing my image is exactly what I need you to do."

"No," she says flatly. "It's not. Your image does not need 'managing.' It needs a goddamn resurrection."

I frown. "It's not *that* bad, is it?"

Frankie blinks at me slowly, as bleak silence thickens the air. Ren bites his lip and keeps his eyes on the stovetop, stirring steadily.

"Yes, Gauthier," she finally snaps. "It is 'that bad.'"

Oh fuck. I've been Gauthier-ed. I'm in trouble.

"So I crashed my car," I concede diplomatically. "But it wasn't into anyone else."

"No," Frankie mutters between clenched teeth. "Just an *after-school outreach program facility*."

Ren winces.

"At least it was two in the morning? No one was hurt?"

"Oh, people were hurt," she says. "These kids don't have a place for their program until it's fixed; that hurts them. I have to figure out how to spin some tale justifying your reckless endangerment on the road and tens of thousands of dollars of property damage caused by wrecking a luxury sports car while driving with a busted foot, so that it doesn't finish off your career and make you look like a selfish, irresponsible prick."

"How about emphasizing that I wasn't drunk driving? I never drink and drive. I feel like I should get brownie points for that."

"There are no brownie points!" she yells, her eyes wide. "There is nothing redeeming about your behavior, Gauthier. You're sure as shit paying for all damages, but the facility is unusable until the repairs are made. Even throwing money at them, this will take time to fix, and the story will linger. If this were your first mis-guided offense, that would be one thing, but it's not. You already broke your foot in the world's most pointless of bar fights—"

"He took a swing at me. I had to defend myself."

"You didn't have to let it devolve to a full-on brawl with some-one wearing steel-toed boots, a James Bond–level chase across the bar, and you jumping off the bar's rooftop patio into a dumpster! I *thought* it couldn't get any worse," she says sharply. "But now, you, one of the team's highest scorers and most pivotal players, had to go and crash your car into a community service building and bruise your nearly healed foot again because you drove when you shouldn't have. You were about to start preseason conditioning and kick off a huge press junket."

"I hardly need preseason conditioning anyway," I tell her, plucking a piece of lint off my dark jeans. "I'll pick up right where I left off. And I'll be fine to do the press junket with my foot. It'll be healed up soon."

"I can't." Frankie stands slowly out of her chair, like always. She has rheumatoid arthritis, and transitioning from sitting to standing, I've observed, takes her a little longer than it does most. "I cannot with you. I've never throttled a client, but I am so close to it right now. Pazza!"

At being beckoned, her white-and-black Alusky, Pazza, bounds down the hallway, straight toward me, and jumps onto my throbbing foot.

I grunt in pain as I shove the dog away. She pivots back, licks me from chin to forehead, which is *disgusting*, then twirls, chasing her tail a few times. Finally, she parks her ass in front of my face and blows a violently loud, foul fart.

"Good girl." Frankie snaps her fingers, yanks open the sliding door to their back patio, which Pazza bounds onto, then slams it shut with surprising force.

A painful, echoing silence ensues. Ren clears his throat, stirs whatever's in the pot one more time, then sets down the spoon he was holding.

After crossing the open-concept space from his kitchen to the couch, Ren drops onto the chair Frankie vacated and leans forward, elbows on his knees. "Seb, you know I love you like a brother."

I shut my eyes. "Ren—"

"And you love me like a brother."

"The only thing I love," I remind him pointedly, "is—"

"Hockey," he says, a smile in his voice. "Yes, I know. Even

though you have this funny way of doing loving things that protect me and look out for me, like that check late in the season that got you concussed, which you threw yourself into so I wouldn't get hit—"

"I tripped," I say offhandedly.

"Uh-huh. The fastest, most agile skater in the league 'tripped' into a concussive hit. Sure. My point is this: Though you clearly cannot stand to admit it, you are capable of good things. You aren't beyond redeeming yourself."

A hot, sharp pain carves down my chest as I meet his eyes. "That's where you're wrong. Even Frankie thinks so."

"Nah." Ren stands, then gently squeezes my shoulder. "She didn't say you're irredeemable. Frankie said that fixing this is going to be hard, that it's going to take time. Good things, healing things, that lead to growth, are often like that. Victories are won with patience, endurance, and tiny, incremental steps. You know this already, Seb. You've lived it. Yes, you're talented, but you're also profoundly dedicated—look at how hard you've worked, day after day, for two *decades*, to become the elite hockey player you are, to get where you are professionally. You're telling me you don't think you're capable of that personally, too?"

That sharp pain's hotter and deeper, burrowing dangerously close to the shriveled-up organ in my chest that's best left unacknowledged. "Is there a point to this motivational speech?"

When Ren speaks, his voice is unusually somber. "My point is, Frankie can help you as much as possible, but ultimately, this is up to you, your motivation, your belief in yourself. You've got to dedicate yourself to making the changes that will turn this around, Seb."

I groan and rake both hands through my hair. "Yes, I know."

"I think you need to cut back on drinking," Ren warns. "Or preferably, stop entirely."

I grimace. "That seems a little extreme."

"And no carousing."

"Carousing?" I snort. "What is this, the nineteenth century?" I'm walloped with a pillow. "Fine," I grumble. "No 'carousing.'"

Ren stands, arms folded across his chest. "If you keep to the straight and narrow for a while, heal your foot, give Frankie some time to figure out a way to rehab your image, you'll be back in the team's good graces in no time—"

"And my sponsors'," I remind him. "Let's not forget the sponsors."

He rolls his eyes. "You'd be fine money-wise, even if you lost a few sponsors."

"Ah, yes, but then how would I afford another hundred-thousand-dollar car to wreck?"

Ren's eyes turn a rare icy cold.

"Joking," I tell him, sitting up. "That was a joke."

"Too soon," he mutters, turning back toward the kitchen. "You could have seriously injured yourself or someone else."

I slump back on the sofa and stare up at the ceiling. Ren's right. To get myself on the team's and my sponsors' good side, I have to appear to behave myself for a while, to have turned over a new leaf. And I do mean *appear*. I'm not actually going to change, of course.

If I don't put on a good show of having cleaned up my act, I might really lose the only things that matter to me. Hockey. The rare friendship that's burrowed its way into my existence. The lifestyle that brings me the indulgent pleasures I so thoroughly enjoy.

Stretched out on Ren's sofa, I rack my brain, wondering for the first time in my adult life how I could possibly pull off the ruse of being a decent human being.

I don't have the faintest idea where to begin.

THREE

Ziggy

Playlist: "Body of Mine," Liz Brasher

Sunday family dinner used to be my favorite part of the week. All the local Bergmans, and when they're visiting, the Washington State siblings with their partners, seated around the long, worn wooden table at my parents' place. Laughter and conversation over a spread of my Swedish mother's family recipes and flickering candlelight.

But now Sunday family dinner is just another place where I feel trapped in a role that fits like old clothes after a growth spurt—too small, aggravatingly tight. And I don't know exactly how to change that. I know I've outgrown the labels I used to wear, but I can't for the life of me figure out what I want to put on now, what will feel right.

I guess I wish that my family of all people could make a little space for me, act even just a *little* open to the possibility of my growth and change, while I figure that out.

I'm sitting with my niece at the kids' end of the table, surrounded by coloring books and tiny Squishmallows, to give you a sense of how far that wish is from coming true.

Don't get me wrong, my niece, Linnea—Linnie, as we call her—is adorable. Three and a half, highly verbal, she's so precocious, she has me worried she's going to give my mischievous brothers, Viggo and Oliver, a run for their money.

However, while we eat a delicious meal, candles down at the

other end of the table so they're out of her reach, I'm keenly aware that I've been listening to Linnie's poop and fart jokes—albeit very clever poop and fart jokes—for the past twenty minutes, while my parents sit at the other end of the table, deep in conversation with the rest of my local siblings and their partners. Linnie's parents, my sister, Freya, and her husband, Aiden, who burps their infant son, Theo, on his shoulder, sit across from my brothers Viggo and Oliver, and Ollie's partner, Gavin. Beside them are my sister-in-law, Frankie, and my brother Ren. They all lean in, elbows on the table, heads close, glasses of wine and beer in hand as dancing candlelight illuminates their faces.

While I sit down here, with a cup bearing a lid and a straw, because apparently Mom still thinks I'm nine and prone to spill. Sighing, I move a tiny Squishmallow off my niece's Pokémon coloring book and start to shade Pikachu's big pointy ear.

Linnie leans in, those ice-blue Bergman eyes locked on me. Her dark wavy hair, like Aiden's, is half out of its bun, which bounces as she wiggles her eyebrows. "I got another joke, Aunt Ziggy."

I force a smile and wipe a streak of sauce off her cheek. "I'm all ears."

"What are a clown's farts like?"

A sigh leaves me. "I don't know. What are they like?"

She wiggles her eyebrows again and says, "They smell funny."

I wrinkle my nose dramatically, knowing it will please this kid who loves to gross people out.

"Ewww."

She lets out a goofy chuckle and stabs a bite of cut-up meatball. "That's my new favorite." As Linnie shoves the meatball in her mouth, I catch the tail end of Ren's sentence:

"Thankfully he only bruised his foot, but he's still out for at least another two weeks."

"The one he broke this summer?" Freya, who's a physical therapist familiar with injuries like his, and the work needed for their recovery, grimaces at Ren's nod. She takes a fussing Theo from Aiden, and lifts some secret flap in her shirt, then cuddles him into her arm to nurse again. "That's rough."

"A banged-up foot is the least of his problems," Frankie mutters. "His public image is in much worse shape. He crashed his damn— sorry, darn," she amends for Linnie's benefit, "car right into an after-school outreach program facility. While recklessly driving with a broken foot. The optics are terrible."

Gavin frowns thoughtfully. Like Ollie, he's a professional soccer player, though he's now retired. "His sponsors dropped him?"

"Like a hot potato." Frankie takes a deep drink of her wine. "And he's—sorry for the pun—on incredibly thin ice with the Kings' management."

"I'm worried about him," Ren admits. "Seb's always had a reckless streak, but this latest slipup seems more serious than before."

"It *is* more serious than a slipup," Frankie says. "It's rock bottom."

My stomach knots. I shouldn't care two figs about Sebastian Gauthier. But hearing that he drove his car into a building and hurt himself even more, knowing he's fallen out of his sponsors' good graces and is in huge trouble with the team, makes me inexplicably sad.

I've seen Sebastian when I've been to Ren's games, flying across the ice. The man comes *alive* when he plays. If he feels for hockey even close to what I feel for soccer, he has to be miserable with himself right now for jeopardizing his career.

I try to move my thoughts along, past empathizing with someone who's managed to destroy so cavalierly what few dream of ever attaining, someone who really is despicable. But the truth is, my thoughts have been on Sebastian Gauthier a lot the past few weeks.

Because he treated me differently, as no one else has. Not just at first, when he didn't recognize me, when he teased and provoked me, but when he recognized me, too. Even then, he treated me like a grown woman who could handle his assholery, not some fragile, delicate thing to handle with care. He didn't let up. He dug in. He said something that cut and burrowed deep: *It's easy to overlook someone who obviously* wants *to be overlooked. If you've been hoping for a different response, I'd suggest revising that attitude.*

I almost told him, *I know, for crying out loud—I* know *that if I want to be seen differently, I have to* do *things differently. I just don't know how to do it.* Except frustrating tears tightened my throat, and the words wouldn't come.

That's how I've felt so often lately, like I'm on the cusp of telling a lot of people a lot of things that are long overdue, but the truth is a knot in my throat that I can't untangle, the force to tug it free something I can't yet find inside myself.

I *want* to discover that courage and those words. I want to stick up for myself and say that I deserve the chance to grow into who I'm capable of being—on and off the pitch. I want to be recognized as a grown, desirable, bisexual woman, a concept that seems wholly foreign to my social circle and siblings, despite the fact that a lot of them have single friends who are interested in dating. I want a damn open container and a glass of wine with dinner. I want to be seen, not as the baby at the end of the table, but as someone with a mind and a voice in our family.

I want to push myself, to stretch and reach and shine a little bit. And I want my family to believe in me, to be the first people to see that possibility.

Is that too much to ask for?

"Absolutely not." Dad's voice ruptures my thoughts. It's unusually serious and low, like thunder rumbling through the air.

I glance toward the other end of the table, where Ren and Dad engage in a quiet stare-off.

Dad's where Ren and I get our red hair, though my father's is now silvered at the temples, streaked with white. His green eyes, which he gave me, are narrowed on my brother.

Ren's face leans toward Mom's bone structure, but he's built so like Dad: broad, solid, and tall. Also like Dad, Ren is a giant teddy bear of a man, which is why it's very odd that they're holding each other's gaze while tension radiates between them.

"What's going on?" I ask.

Mom glances my way, hesitating before she says, "Don't worry, *älskling*. It's just a bit of an ongoing conversation about family . . . decisions."

"Ongoing?" I frown. "Why don't I know about it?"

Oliver, the sibling closest to me in age, who I'm closest to emotionally as well, gives me a guilty look that makes me feel like I've been kicked in the stomach. He's known about whatever this is, and even *he* hasn't told me.

"It's nothing you need to worry about," Dad says, sitting back in his seat as he wraps a hand around his beer. "That's why."

My cheeks heat, and the first warning of tears pricks my eyes. "It's about our family, and I don't need to worry about it?"

No one seems to process how hurtful that is. Mom sets her hand over Dad's and pats it softly.

Freya is almost Mom's twin beside her, with their shoulder-length white-blond hair; her pale blue eyes locked on Dad in concern. Theo pulls away from nursing and starts to cry. Aiden gently takes him from Freya, then stands, bouncing Theo in his arms, though not before softly squeezing Freya's shoulder, his thumb brushing tenderly along her neck.

Frankie sets a hand on Ren's back and rubs.

Gavin's arm stretches protectively across the top of Ollie's chair.

Viggo is uncharacteristically quiet, picking at the label on his beer bottle.

"What's going on?" I ask, my voice sharp. "Why is everyone acting weird?"

Linnie stops coloring and looks up at me. "Who knows. Adults *always* act weird."

"*I'm* an adult!"

Linnie frowns and tips her head. "You are?"

God, out of the mouths of babes.

Tears well in my eyes. I know I'm sensitive. I know I might be overreacting, but I'm so tired of feeling like this. I'm hurt that, once again, I'm being treated as less than a full member of this family. I'm sure my parents and siblings mean well. And I imagine whatever's going on must be so difficult, they want to shield me from it.

That last thought is the only thing that keeps me from exploding, after bottling up this frustration for far too long.

I blink away almost-spilled tears and force a smile my niece's way. Appetite ruined, I scoot my plate of half-eaten food aside, then draw the Pokémon coloring book closer. "What color are Pikachu's cheeks, Linnie?"

As she answers me and I fill those circles bright cherry red, the room settles around me, the predictable order of our family's world restored.

At least, I imagine, that's how my family sees it.

I, on the other hand, make a promise to myself, that somehow, someway, I'm going to make sure that soon, finally, my family, my team—*everyone*—will see just how much has actually changed.

———

Turns out, that resolution was easier said than done. The past five days since the disastrous family dinner, between practices, conditioning, and diving back into a comfort reread of my favorite fantasy romance series, I've been trying—and failing—to figure out what comes next.

I want people to see me differently, but how do I get them to? I know that *inside*, I have changed. But as I look at my reflection in a shop front's window not far from my apartment, I'm confronted with the fact that on the outside, I really don't look like I've changed at all.

Which is pretty darn frustrating, considering how much I've grown in just a few years. Since graduating from UCLA this past spring, after an accelerated three-year track on a full ride, thanks to my grades and my athletic scholarship, I've been more independent than ever. I scoured listings fastidiously and—all on my own—secured a sunny studio apartment that's just a short walk to the beach. I chose my agent without anyone's input besides Frankie's, but she's in the field, so I was only doing my due diligence. I made the starting lineup on the women's national soccer team, then I signed with LA's Angel City. I even finally got my driver's license, after hours of practice in Viggo's beloved beater, Ashbury.

And yet I still look like that quiet, awkward teenager who left the social nightmare of high school for cyber school and never looked back. The girl who sat at the back row, end seat of every lecture, not wanting to be seen or called on because speaking articulately on the fly is not my strength, and when I feel eyeballs on me anywhere except when I'm on the field, I turn tomato red.

I watch my reflection as a hefty sigh leaves me, before the sound of a cheering crowd draws my attention. Turning toward the noise, I spot an open patio restaurant with TVs playing sports highlights and watch Dodger Stadium erupt at the sight of a home run before footage cuts back to the sportscasters in their newsroom. The late August evening breeze picks up, and with it comes the enticing scent of hot, salty French fries.

My stomach rumbles, reminding me I haven't eaten since before practice today. Maybe some food in my stomach will get the creative juices flowing, help me figure out my first step in what I've decided to call Project Ziggy Bergman 2.0.

There's a small two-top nestled in a corner of the restaurant patio that gets some evening sun, and I ask the host for that one. Once I'm seated, I scour the menu before deciding on a grilled chicken sandwich and a plate of fries. At the last second, I order a boozy strawberry milkshake.

Halfway into the boozy milkshake, my chicken sandwich long gone, I drag a fry through a glob of ketchup and stare up at the TV. I am nowhere closer to knowing my first step in Project Ziggy Bergman 2.0.

I am, however, a little tipsy.

Which is the only explanation for why seeing Sebastian Gauthier appear on TV in full hockey gear, soaring across the ice, makes me blush, swift and hot.

Alcohol always makes me rosy-cheeked. It's a coincidence that the heat from the booze in my milkshake happened to find my face now, when this sports news program started covering hockey phenom Sebastian Gauthier's fall from grace.

Eyes glued to the screen, I bring the fry to my mouth but pause, watching Sebastian weave past his opponents, the puck so tight on his stick, I'd swear it was glued there. I watch him pass it to Ren, who fakes a shot, spots their teammate Tyler Johnson cutting toward the goal, passes it to him, then cheers when they score. Even though I know this is a replay, even though I'd remember if Ren had been hurt from this, so I can only conclude the hit isn't going to happen, I can't help but brace myself as I see a goon from the other team wind up for what promises to be a brutal high stick to my brother's face, only for Sebastian to skate in, freakishly fast, and shove the guy back, though not fast enough to avoid the hit himself. The stick slams into Sebastian's face, sending his head snapping back.

The fry drops from my hand, landing with a *splat* in the ketchup on my plate. I watch blood well from Sebastian's nose as he shoves the guy hard, then mutters something through his mouthguard that sets off the goon, who starts swinging at Sebastian. A crowd of players builds from both sides, piling into an epic brawl that Sebastian escapes only because my brother grabs him by the collar and yanks him back.

My stomach churns at the sight of thick crimson rolling down Sebastian's face. I push away my plate of fries and ketchup and swallow back a wave of nausea as the newscasters talk about the high-sticking player, who's got a reputation for this kind of foul. They talk about him in the same breath as Sebastian, pointing out that Sebastian's always in the thick of these brawls, too.

And yet. Didn't they see what I did? Someone who stepped in and protected someone who matters to him? It doesn't seem so, as they go on about his recent car crash, his broken foot.

They call him the names that are the backbone of his terrible reputation: reckless, troublemaker, bad boy.

Bad boy.

Inspiration dawns on me, a light bulb illuminated on a mega-watt *ping*.

My stomach churns even harder now, but this time it's not from nausea—it's from excitement. Heart pounding, I drop enough cash on the table to pay for my meal twice and stand, before rushing out of the restaurant.

It's not hard to find Sebastian's address through a quick internet search. Like the rest of the team, he lives in Manhattan Beach, and he's gotten himself in the news enough that his property's location is no secret. I put it in my map, make sure I'm headed the right way, then start to power down the sidewalk, destined for the last place I'd ever expect to show up to, let alone unannounced.

This might be the most foolish, ridiculous thing I've ever done. Or it might be an absolute stroke of brilliance. But I refuse to let that uncertainty stop me from giving it a shot. *Finally*, I have an idea for Project Ziggy Bergman 2.0.

Involving a certain fallen-from-grace hockey star who has exactly what I need, and who needs exactly what I have to offer:

A public image overhaul.

FOUR

Sebastian

Playlist: "Shine a Little Light," The Black Keys

Until Frankie figures out how to get me back on everyone's good side, I am under strict instructions to stay in my house and out of trouble.

For once, I'm doing what I'm told.

Granted, if Frankie saw me right now—and I'm very glad she hasn't—she'd probably disagree.

I sit on my second-floor balcony overlooking the Pacific Ocean, wearing nothing but bed head hair and black boxer briefs, my bruised foot free of the boot but propped up on a cushioned deck chair. My stomach hurts, the pain somewhat dulled by the joint I take another long drag from, its pungent smoke curling into the air. I glare at the horizon, resenting the low, dying light as it spears my eyeballs and stabs my thudding brain. I drank a lot of whiskey last night.

No, Frankie definitely wouldn't agree that I've been doing as I'm told. But technically, I have. I've stayed in and stayed out of trouble by misbehaving in private, thanks to a highly sophisticated security system.

Relaxed, confident in that, I shut my eyes and hold in the smoke from my joint, feeling its acrid sweetness burn my lungs. And then I promptly choke it out at the sound of feet landing on my balcony.

I sincerely hope I'm hallucinating.

"You're not," Ziggy says.

She's either a mind reader or I said that out loud. Either way, she's no hallucination.

Ren's little sister stands on my second-floor balcony, the sea breeze tugging her hair loose from its braid, fiery ribbons dancing across twilight's fading blue. Her cheeks are flushed, glowing pink as the dwindling sun. If my heart weren't about to pound right out of my chest from being caught so shockingly off guard, I'd be fixated on that blush that I recognize from our little terrace encounter at Ren and Frankie's wedding.

Not that I've thought about that night at Ren and Frankie's wedding since then. Or Ziggy's blush.

At all.

She stands, staring at me, hands on her hips—whose supple curves I most absolutely do *not* notice, thank you very much. She's in nondescript athletic gear—dark blue soccer shorts, matching lace-up high-tops, a loose dark green athletic shirt that makes those emerald eyes jump against the peach of her skin, the fiery freckles splashed across her nose.

I've never had a thing for other athletes, but right now, hypothetically speaking, I could appreciate how the sporty look might be attractive.

To someone besides me. Because I am most definitely not even *contemplating* being drawn toward Ren's sister, who's on my balcony while I sit here, in my underwear, stomach aching, smelling like an overripe corpse with a dubious relationship to alcohol.

Just fantastic.

It isn't that I give two shits what Ziggy or anyone, for that matter, thinks of my lifestyle choices—I gave that up long ago—but I do have a vanity streak a mile wide. No one's seen me looking this disgraceful since I was born.

Pinning the joint between my teeth, I reach for the nearby black cashmere throw and drape it across my lap, then rake my fingers through my hair, smoothing back my messy waves until I can restrain the top half of them with the hair tie on my wrist.

Then I slump back in my chair, taking a long drag from the joint. "Ever heard of knocking on the front door, Ziggy dear?"

"I had a sneaking suspicion that if I did, it wouldn't be answered." She leans against the balcony railing and nearly gives me a heart attack. I lunge forward, wrap a hand around her wrist, and yank her my way.

Her eyes are wide as saucers as she stumbles toward me, coming to a stop at my feet. "What was that for?"

"You infiltrated my property and scaled my house. You don't get to ask questions right now."

I realize I'm still holding her wrist. That it's soft and warm, and the faintest scent of strawberries clings to her skin. I let go.

Ziggy folds her arms across her chest and peers down at me as I try to settle myself with another hit of this very expensive, very smooth marijuana, and says, "Should you be doing that?"

I raise my eyebrows, holding in the smoke, then slowly exhale. Ziggy watches me, her expression a delightfully compelling blend of fascination and wholehearted disapproval.

"This is Frankie-approved." Smirking, I lounge deeper in my chair. "Weed is about the only thing she and I agree on."

"Frankie uses it for pain management," Ziggy points out.

I'm not about to admit that my stomach's in agony. I gesture with the joint to my bruised foot. "Ouch. I'm in pain."

She rolls her eyes.

"So." I bring the joint to my lips again, annoyed to see Ziggy making herself at home.

She plops down on the chair across from me and stretches out her long legs, arms folded across her chest. "So," she offers.

I gesture around my patio, exhaling. "To what do I owe the pleasure of having my privacy invaded?"

Her blush deepens.

The sight reminds me of the moment she hiked up that dress on the terrace, dragged off her underwear, and glanced over her shoulder—

A memory that has a very inconvenient effect on my body. Thank God for the blanket, which I tug tighter over my lap. I draw up my uninjured leg to obscure what's started happening.

This is what I'm reduced to when I have to swear off "carousing." I'm so keyed up, I'm half hard from the sight of a blush.

Shutting my eyes, I revisit the last time I saw my mother and stepfather. That very quickly puts an end to the trouble that just started in my briefs.

"I'm here . . ." Ziggy continues, then pauses.

Dammit, somehow it's even more arousing when my eyes are shut, hearing the rasp at the edge of her voice, the upswing in her pitch at the end of each phrase.

I crack open an eye and glare at her, thoroughly annoyed by this. "You're here? Spit it out already."

Her jaw clenches. She sits up, arms still tight across her chest. "I'm here because . . ." She takes a deep breath, and now I feel like an utter ass. Her mouth works, but words don't come out, as if they're caught somewhere between her brain and her tongue. She scrunches her eyes shut and turns away, until she's sideways on the chair, the sea breeze unfurling more hair from her braid. I watch those strands jump and dance on the wind like flames, before they wrap around her head, hiding her face.

Her shoulders lift, then fall. A deep breath, as if shoring herself up.

"I have an . . . idea. A plan, I mean. That will help us both get out of our current . . . situations."

I lift my eyebrows in surprise. Of all the people to have a plan for helping me out of the mess I got myself into, Ren's little sister was the last person I'd have ever considered. "Why would you want to help me? Last time I saw you, I harassed you, insulted you, and made you cry."

And I hated myself for it.

"You didn't make me cry," she says evenly. "I mean, you kind of did. They were angry tears, though. You ticked me off. But . . ." Silence stretches between us, before she says, "Just because you were a jerk about it doesn't mean you were wrong. If I want to be seen, I need to take ownership of that. Which is where you come in."

I stare at her, curious. "Go on."

She bends her head as the wind pins her hair against her face, hiding her from me. Her fingers knot in her lap. "You need to repair your public image."

"'Resurrect' is the term I believe Frankie used."

A soft, huffed laugh leaves her. Involuntarily I smile at that sound.

She shrugs. "Same thing."

"It's really not, but I'll hear you out."

Another silence stretches between us as she smooths her hands down her thighs and sits straighter. "I want my image . . . smudged up a little. Matured, if you will."

A frown tugs at my mouth. "I don't understand."

"We each have what the other wants. I have a good-girl reputation. You have bad-boy notoriety. If we were seen together, those public images could rub off on each other. I'd be taken more seriously. You'd look like you cleaned up your act."

I blink at her, stunned by the implication of what she's saying. "Are you suggesting we pretend to *date*, because there's not a chance in hell that I'd—"

"No!" She shakes her head. The wind shifts, tugging her hair back in slim, copper strands.

"Not pretend to *date*. Just pretend to be . . . friends."

The word drops like a stone in the still, frigid well of what little feelings I have and ripples out, an unwelcome disturbance. I can't help but fixate on how she said that word—"friends"—like it's as strange to her as it is to me.

While someone like me doesn't deserve or desire friendship, why the hell wouldn't she?

A dull ache echoes through me. That ache is a bridge too far. I drag on the joint and hold in its smoke, calming myself, telling myself that ache's only there because she's Ren's sister. Because the one good person in my life, who I haven't managed to scare away, loves her fiercely and protectively.

"Friends," I repeat on my exhale.

The wind whips back her hair, revealing her profile—that long, straight nose, a cascade of cinnamon-spark freckles. She shrugs. "Yes. Friends."

"What would you tell your brother? He's not going to be suspicious that suddenly I'm friends with you, too?"

Ziggy bites her lip. "I'll think of something. It would have been recent, obviously. Maybe it started when you and I talked at the wedding, which isn't a lie. We did talk."

I am not thinking about the fact that we *talked* on that terrace. I'm thinking about watching her lift up her dress like a dream come to life, sinking her hands into the fabric—

Don't think about her taking off her panties. Don't think about her taking off her panties.

I growl in my throat and massage the bridge of my nose.

"We bonded over . . . something," she continues, oblivious to my suffering. A frown wrinkles her nose. "I'll figure out what to tell him, he'll believe me because he's Ren, and that'll be that. Friends. Totally plausible."

A sigh leaves me. "Ziggy, I don't exactly bond with people. I'm not the 'friend' type. I'm not sure how 'plausible' that would be."

I watch her frown deepen in profile, seeing as she still won't look at me. Her eyes stay on her knotted hands. "You're friends with Ren."

"Yes, but that's because your brother is a saint with a complex about saving unsavable things."

"Then it won't be so implausible that I could view you the same way. Besides, you're not unsavable," she says matter-of-factly. "No one's unsavable."

There's that ache again. An anxious band squeezes my lungs. "You're very wrong, Ziggy dear."

"I'm not. But I'm also not trying to save you. I'm just trying to leverage what's advantageous in your terrible reputation, and I'm willing to barter with my spotless one."

The panic tightening my ribs loosens. I know I disappoint Ren, even though he hides it well. I know he still hopes for me to redeem myself from the shithole existence I've dug myself into. And while I appreciate that it makes him stick with me, the truth is, knowing I'll fail him one day like I've failed everyone else is a burden.

But with Ziggy, there's no such risk.

Ziggy Bergman has on her shoulders a surprisingly level head. In two sentences she's conveyed that she sees me much more realistically than her brother ever has.

And since that's the case, since there's no danger of my disappointing—and thus hurting—Ren's little sister, who am I to say no to her when she's offered me the perfect solution to my very pressing problem?

Slowly, I sit up and ease down my aching foot, bracing my elbows on my knees. "So . . . we'd pretend to be friends?"

She shrugs. "In a nutshell, yes."

"You'd want us to be seen. Out and about."

"Exactly. We do some things that polish your image, some things that rough up mine. When we're both satisfied with the results, we'll stop pretending and just act cordially."

Cordially. It's like one of Ren's words, like *carousing*. I smile but hide it behind my hand, dragging my knuckles across my mouth. "Well, then. I'm in."

"You mean it?" she asks.

I'm not someone whose word means anything. I've made promises and broken them. I've lied and sworn up and down I was telling the truth. But here, there's no promise I can't keep. I'm not vowing to change, knowing I'll backslide. I'm promising only to *look* like I've reformed, to pretend to have experienced a positive transformation while she pursues her own.

Still, I'll have to be careful. Putting myself regularly in Ziggy Bergman's company, agreeing to deliberately dirty her name while letting her clean up mine, is going to require a considerable amount of care and effort on my part so I don't do her any lasting damage.

I don't make a habit of caring or exerting effort in anything except hockey. And fucking. And occasionally, drinking to incredible excess. But what else do I have to do for the next few weeks while my foot heals? Sit around in my underwear, waiting for my public image crisis to magically resolve itself?

Pretend friendship has a nice ring to it. I don't have real friends, besides Ren, and I don't plan to find one in Ziggy. I don't let others in, only for them to realize how much I'll disappoint them. I don't allow myself to care about people, because it's too easy for them to disappear when I need them most.

Ziggy threatens none of that. She won't be my real friend. I won't let her in. And I certainly won't care for her. It'll be easy, once we have our plan in place—a transactional, mutually beneficial publicity stunt, nothing more.

So it's with supreme confidence, easing back in my chair, that I tell her, "I mean it."

I'll never forget this—the long, silent moment she absorbs my words, as if waiting for me to draw them back, before she turns and, finally, fully looks at me.

The last golden streaks of dusk pour down on her, liquid gold transforming her hair to living fire, her eyes to blazing emeralds, every freckle to amber embers lighting up her skin.

Air whooshes out of my lungs more violently than after the most brutal check I've ever taken into the boards. In that moment I see it. I *feel* it. The spark of what's forged inside her—a spine of steel, a white-hot intensity, simmering beneath that seemingly sweet, serene surface.

Her eyebrow arches as she looks at me, and a slow, dawning smile warms her face. Her hand reaches out toward mine. "Then you have yourself a deal, Sebastian Gauthier."

Ziggy

Playlist: "bad guy," Billie Eilish

I think I might have made a massive mistake.

Sebastian clasps my hand, and heat seeps into my skin. I feel my heart sprint in my chest.

I was very sure that I could do this, that we could pull this off. But maybe that was the boozy strawberry milkshake talking.

I stare at Sebastian, his face all sharp, lean angles, cool silver eyes, and warm golden skin—the stranger I thought I had a handle on, whose desperation I could leverage to counterbalance my own.

But now I'm sitting here, smelling weed and whiskey titrating out of his system. I'm seeing purple smudges under his eyes and a pale, thin scar slashed across his left eyebrow. A freckle at the base of his throat.

Now he feels . . . human. Formidably, terrifyingly human. Humans are hard for me. To read, to learn, to understand. Looking at him, I'm wondering if I bit off way more than I can chew.

And I'm also feeling how strong he is.

His grip is *very* strong.

I stare down at his hand covered in intricate webs of ink, numbers, and signs, fragmented words twisted around his fingers, curled down his wrist to his arm.

Heat floods my cheeks. It's better to stare at his hand, considering the tats on his hands have nothing on what's stretched across his bare chest, beneath those silver chains. I've always stared longer than I should when I'm curious. And I'm very curious about what's inked across his torso. I don't want to stare at Sebastian Gauthier—his torso, or otherwise. At all.

A growing sense of dread seeps through me. I could not be more his opposite. How the heck am I going to pass as this guy's friend? How are we going to convince anyone that we're actually people who share the same world?

"Ziggy." Sebastian's voice is rough at the edges, ragged from what I imagine to be some combination of smoke and sleeplessness and too much alcohol. He sounds dangerous and daunting.

And yet, I still glance up, meeting those sharp silver eyes, telling myself to be brave. "Yes, Sebastian?"

He draws his hand away and folds his arms across his chest. "*Stop* calling me that."

"Why?"

His eyes narrow. "I told you this already. You infiltrated my property. You don't get to ask questions."

"But we're friends now," I remind him, smiling sweetly. "Friends tell each other these things."

"We're *pretend* friends. Pretend I told you."

"Hmm." I tap my chin. "Maybe it's our 'friend' thing. I call you Sebastian. No one else does. Yeah, I like it."

His hands come to his face, scrubbing it. "I need a drink."

"Pretty sure you've got a couple still sloshing through your bloodstream."

His hands drop, and he flashes me an exasperated look, chased by a wolfish smirk. "Never stopped me before."

"But now that you're on the path to self-improvement, it will."

Sebastian's eyes scour my face, before he leans in, bathing me in the sour scent of weed and whiskey. I wrinkle my nose. "Let's get something very clear here . . ." He tips his head. "What is *your* full name? It's not just Ziggy, is it?"

My stomach knots. "I don't go by my full name."

"Neither do I," he points out. "But that hasn't stopped you from using it."

I sigh, annoyed. "Fine. But you can't tell *anyone* else." Extending my pinkie, I lift it toward him. "Promise."

His eyes crinkle at the corners. His tongue pokes into his cheek. "A pinkie promise? Is that what I'm being held to?"

Undeterred, I offer my pinkie. "I mean it, *Sebastian*."

His expression turns frosty. "Go on, then." His finger hooks mine, hard, jolting me.

"It's Sigrid," I blurt out. "Sigrid Marta Bergman."

Like Ren, whose full name is Søren, after Dad's beloved Søren Kierkegaard, I used to get teased about my full name in school. I dropped it in upper elementary school and took the name Viggo gave me as a preschooler when he couldn't say Sigrid. It started as Siggy, then became Ziggy, until the whole family called me that.

I have a lot of bad memories tied to the name Sigrid. I should be the first person to honor Sebastian's request not to call him by his full name. Maybe he has bad memories tied to his full name, too. But pettily, I've wanted something on this man who, even in his disheveled, haggard state, displays the kind of nonchalant composure and confidence that I frankly envy.

"Sigrid," he says quietly, eyes dancing over my face again. "It's . . . unusual. But sweet. In a . . . cardigan-wearing, prim-librarian sort of way—"

I shove him, because with as many brothers as I have, physical retaliation after being teased is a reflex.

He smirks, self-satisfied, and flops back in his chair. "I wasn't done, you know."

"I don't care." Standing, I walk away from him and face the ocean, already kicking myself for tethering my life to this schmuck for the next however long, until we both get what we want out of each other.

Glaring out at the ocean, feeling the dregs of my little milk-shake buzz dissolve just like the sun on the horizon, I sigh heavily.

And then I feel him, warm and close behind me. "I was going to say . . ." His voice whispers across my neck, the sound of midnight smoke and starlight dancing down dark alleys. "This librarian . . . by day, she's very well behaved. Proper, quiet, sweet . . ." His breath brushes my ear, and I shiver. "But by night, she's a dominatrix, a wild animal finally let out of her cage."

My eyes widen. Heat floods my cheeks.

And then he's gone, the deck set between us as he sinks back into his chair. "You're fun to scandalize."

I whip around, glaring at him. "And you're an incorrigible jerk."

"Guilty, Sigrid. Guilty."

My teeth clench.

Sebastian picks up the joint he let die out and brings it to his lips, pawing around for the lighter. "Now, if you'll excuse me, oblivion awaits. I'll let you know when I'm ready to start this pretend friend ruse—"

"We start *now*." My voice is strong. Flint.

I hardly recognize myself.

But that's the point of this, isn't it? There's a voice that's strong inside me. I've just spent a long time not listening to it, not believing in it. Since I went to college and stepped fully into my independence, I've sworn to myself that I'd nurture that voice, heed that voice, little by little, more and more.

No turning back now.

I'm not some dominatrix like he teased me, but dammit, there *is* something fierce and wild inside me, clawing at its cage. Time to start acting like it.

"We start now?" Sebastian lowers his joint, staring at me appraisingly. "Says who?"

Purposefully, I walk toward him, standing to my full six feet and one inch. I pluck the joint from his hand, smash it in his empty whiskey-reeking glass, and tell him, "Me."

SIX

Ziggy

Playlist: "Love Myself," Olivia O'Brien

"If I get in trouble with Frankie for leaving the house," Sebastian mutters, using the keypad to lock the door leading from his home to his garage, "I'm blaming you."

I pluck the keys hanging from his black jeans' back pocket and toss them up in the air, catching them with a shrug. "If she gives you grief, let me know. I'll tell her you were craving something nourishing while you're drying up, and I obliged."

He arches an eyebrow. "You're going to lie to Frankie?"

"It's not a lie. It's just . . . not a truth yet."

A snort leaves him. "I'm *not* drying up."

"You're going to need to at least look like you have." I start across the interior of his massive garage, past sports car after sports car. Finally, I find the one I want, which matches the fob on his key ring.

"*Fuck* no," he says as his Bugatti's lights wink at us. I smile, hitting the button again to lock it. "Gotcha."

I could never in a million years handle being behind the wheel of a car worth that much, not when my driving is passable at best and my anxiety makes me a white-knuckled driver.

He glares at me. "Little jokester, are you?"

"Jokester?" Moving past the Bugatti, I settle on the least-intimidating vehicle, which is still a sleek red Porsche Cayenne.

"I've never thought of myself that way. Put up against my brothers Viggo and Oliver, I seem very tame."

"That's a disturbing thought, seeing as you got past my security system and scaled my house. You still haven't said how you did that, by the way."

"How? Oh, easily." I open the driver's door of the Cayenne. Sebastian pushes it shut. I open it again. "I have five exasperating brothers and a very stubborn sister, Sebastian. I could do this all night."

"Seb," he corrects me, shutting the door once more. "Tell me how you got into my house."

"Tell me why you don't like it when I call you Sebastian."

Muttering to himself, he turns away and starts around the hood of the car. When he spots his reflection, he stops, grimaces, then fusses with his wet, dark waves.

Wisely, he decided to shower before we left, considering he smelled like death. When I was about to follow him in after he stood up with the black blanket wrapped around his waist and made that announcement, Seb stopped, pressed a finger into my shoulder until I took a step back, and locked me out on the balcony. Then he told me through the glass that if I could get myself up there, I could certainly get down.

Jerk.

Wincing at the bruise on my butt that I acquired upon landing in his yard—climbing my way up onto that balcony was definitely easier than coming down from it—I slip into the driver's side and turn on the car.

"All right." Seb presses a button on his phone that makes the garage door slide up. "What painfully wholesome establishment am I being dragged to?"

"Betty's Diner," I tell him, pulling out.

I can do this. I can drive this very expensive SUV and not crash it. I am a confident, capable driver.

"Betty's Diner?" He frowns. "Why does that sound familiar?"

"Ren probably mentioned it at some point."

"Ah, that's it. He and Frankie go there a lot, don't they?"

I smile as I flick on my turn signal and ease onto the road. "Yeah. It's their spot now. It used to be where Ren took me when . . ."

My voice dies off as hard memories of that time in my life come rushing back. Back in high school, undiagnosed autism meant profound social struggles and sensory issues that led to massive burnout. My anxiety was a vortex, spiraling me into bleak thoughts, and I became deeply depressed. While I'm grateful that recognizing those struggles led me to a life-changing diagnosis, to learning how to know and care for myself, that time wasn't happy. It was hard. And lonely.

"When . . . ?" he repeats.

"When I was in high school."

"Why do I get the feeling there's more to that story?"

"Because there is."

"Well." He slouches lower in his seat, flicking down the mirror to inspect his hair again. "I've got time."

"So do I. Doesn't mean I'm sharing."

The mirror snaps shut. "I thought we were bonding, Sigrid. Talking, as friends do."

"*Pretend* friends, as you've so helpfully reminded me. So *pretend* I told you."

A huff of air, the shadow of a laugh, leaves him. "Touché."

Uncomfortable quiet settles between us. I shift, wincing because of the bruise again, and glance in the side-view mirror. I need to get into the left lane for my next turn. Glancing in the mirror one more time as I change lanes, I catch my appearance and feel my stomach knot. My hair looks like a windblown flame. There's a blob of strawberry milkshake on my shirt.

Suddenly, I am keenly aware that, having showered and changed, Sebastian Gauthier now looks much better than I do.

Not exactly a good start to Project Ziggy Bergman 2.0, if we're seen when we're out—which is the whole point—me drab and messy in my athleticwear, Sebastian sharp in black jeans and a soft chambray button-up that he changed into before letting me inside his house, then herding me toward his garage.

I shift in my seat again, uneasy. "Maybe we should make a stop first."

He glances my way, eyebrows arched. "What kind of stop?"

"At my place."

"Why?"

"I need to wear something different."

His gaze slides down my body like an X-ray. "And why's that?"

"Because maybe, now that you're wearing more than your underwear and don't smell like the walking dead, I feel a little underdressed."

"And what are you going to change into? Another pair of soccer shorts? A new athletic shirt? It's not like you wear anything else."

I scowl, hating that he's right. All I wear are workout clothes. Ever since I grew another inch and filled out right when I started at UCLA, when all I did was hustle between soccer games, practices, conditioning, and classes, replacing the not inexpensive sensory-friendly street clothes I'd outgrown seemed pointless when I knew I'd barely have time to wear them.

"Do you even *own* anything besides athleticwear?" He's pressing right into one of my sore spots. It's hard to dress a six-one female body, let alone one with a ton of sensory aversions to seams, tags, and numerous fibers.

Heat hits my cheeks. I grip the steering wheel so tightly, my knuckles ache. "Yes," I say coolly, taking the turn that will get us to my apartment. "I have throw blankets that I wear when only underwear doesn't cut it."

His mouth drops open. "A sarcastic dig from the angelic Sigrid?"

"I'm *not* an angel."

"That's certainly clear, after that zinger." His voice is lower now, tinged with something I don't recognize.

I glance his way as I stop at the red light and catch him staring at me. "What?"

Eyes pinned on me, he leans an elbow against the window, knuckles dragging across his mouth. "Just . . . realizing what you've been hiding under that sweet, shy surface this whole time."

"I knew I was on to something with the prim librarian bit." Sebastian shuts the door to my apartment behind him, eyeing up my bookshelves.

I throw him a glare as he pointedly steps around the pile of books I don't have room for yet, at least until I assemble my next bookshelf. "I'd say make yourself comfortable," I tell him, "but I'm not terribly concerned for your comfort right now."

He throws me one of those sardonic smirks, leaning a hip against my tiny kitchen's one counter. "I'm plenty comfortable here."

"Delightful." Walking toward my dresser, I drag the curtain that I've anchored to the ceiling around me, giving me a makeshift bedroom and privacy to change. "Okay." I tug off my shirt, then my sports bra. "Hypothetically speaking. What would a . . . badass gal wear to a casual meal?"

It's quiet. Too quiet. I lean back past the curtain so just my head is stuck out. Sebastian's back is to me now. He's staring at my bookshelves. "Sebastian?"

"What?" His voice is tight, and he doesn't turn around.

"I asked what I should wear."

"Whatever the hell you want," he snaps.

"Geez," I mutter.

A heavy sigh leaves him. "You should wear something that makes you feel good."

"Yeah, but I want to *look* good, too. I don't know how to do that."

There's a long pause. Another heavy sigh. "Do you have clothes on?"

"Uhh . . ." I stare down at my bare boobs. "No," I answer slowly. "Why?"

"Put something on. A robe at least."

"You're bossy."

"I'm *hungry*. Someone interrupted my bender, and now that my stomach is empty of liquor, it's painfully aware that it's empty of food, too. I'd like to eat sometime tonight."

"Robe's on, crankapotamus."

I hear the thud of his Aircast boot across my parquet floors, then the curtain whips back. He stares at me, and his jaw clenches. I tug my robe tighter. Suddenly the soft white waffle cotton that comes halfway down my thighs feels like a deeply insufficient amount of material.

Brushing by me, Sebastian yanks open my dresser drawers, riffling through them. "No. No. No. Jesus, woman, do you own anything that isn't ninety-five percent Lycra?"

"You're real funny, Gauthier."

"I'm supposed to find something edgy that you can wear from this selection? It's like asking Monet to paint with peanut butter."

I bite my lip so I won't laugh. That was kind of funny.

"Ah-hah." Sebastian yanks out a black double-strap, low-impact sports bra that I wear for yoga and tosses it onto my bed.

He digs around the same drawer some more, until he finds a

white racerback tank top that I sleep in, so soft and worn, it's semi-sheer now. "That," he mutters. "And . . ."

Shooing me back, he drops onto the edge of my bed so he can reach the lower drawers and riffle through them, too. He finds a pair of faded jeans—the only pair I've ever owned and actually liked the feel of—that I sadly had to give up after my last growth spurt. They still fit my hips, though they're more formfitting than they originally were, but they're too short now, an odd length that aggravates my ankles.

Holding up the jeans, he inspects them. "These."

"They feel weird."

He arches an eyebrow. "Then why are they in your drawer?"

"Because they're nostalgic."

"Nostalgic. What the hell is there to be nostalgic about when it comes to jeans?"

"Just give me those." I try to yank them from him, but Sebastian yanks back, sending me tumbling onto him, both of us collapsing onto my bed.

I stare down at him, wide-eyed, frozen. My legs straddle his hips. My pelvis presses right into his.

Sebastian is very . . . hard. Everywhere. I feel lean muscle. The bones in his hips. I didn't pay close attention to his body when I was on his balcony because, well, I was trying very hard *not* to, but now I can't help but feel proof that he's clearly thinner than he typically is, not leaned up in the healthy way like Ren gets when they ramp up conditioning before the season. The harmful kind. The I-drink-and-don't-eat kind.

It's like the moment I saw the smudges under his eyes, saw his hair sticking up funny before he smoothed it back. I feel how human he is. And I feel this inexplicable urge to hug him. To drag him to Mom and Dad's and shove a massive plate of Swedish comfort food in front of him.

"Ziggy." His voice is tight as he pulls his hips back. Thanks to gravity, mine follow suit, shifting in tandem with his. It's how I'd move if I were on top for a wholly different reason, if there was nothing between us, a lazy, long roll of my hips. Unfortunately, because I have only panties on—this pair's actually comfortable— I feel much more than I'd like, the thick length of him, tucked inside his jeans, rubbing right against me.

I scramble off frantically, nearly falling on my butt. "Sorry. I . . . Sorry." I clear my throat.

Seb eases upright on the bed, still holding my jeans. Then he stands, his gaze pinned on mine. With how small my "bedroom" area is, we're left standing nearly chest to chest.

He blows out a slow breath and stares down at my jeans in his hands. "Why do they feel weird?"

I don't want to tell him. I don't want to give someone who's so far proven entirely unworthy of my trust this confession about my sensory needs.

But something about his expression as he peers up beneath those thick dark lashes makes the words melt out of me and spill into the air. "They itch my ankles. They used to fit, but then I had a growth spurt, right before college, and now they're too short. But they just felt so good. They're the only jeans that have ever felt good."

He studies my face, quiet, shifting my jeans in his hands. Then he glances down, again, examining the interior, the seams, the label stamped on the fabric. "And if they were shorts?"

I frown. "Shorts?"

"It *is* eighty degrees outside, Sigrid. It's this season right now called summer—heard of it?"

"Says the man wearing pants." I poke his armpit, a classic tickle spot that seems to work, because he swears and twists away.

"Easy does it, Sporty Spice."

For that little moniker, I go for his other armpit, but this time he catches my hand, clasping it hard. I stare up at him, heart pounding in my chest. His thumb, it's sliding along the inside of my palm, in steady, lulling circles. Circles I'd enjoy very much, elsewhere on my body. My nipples tighten. Heat spills, low in my belly, and settles into a soft, pulsing ache.

I knew I was in over my head with him. Sucking in a deep breath, I press my thighs together and will that ache away.

"How would you make them shorts?" I'm wildly proud of how steady my voice comes out.

Sebastian lifts an eyebrow. "Got a pair of scissors?"

I pull my hand away, and this time he lets go. I take my sweet time finding the scissors in my kitchen drawer to cool myself down, then offer them to him, handles first. Sebastian lays the scissors on the counter, then steps closer to me.

Staring at him, I tell my heart to stop speeding up. "Can I help you?"

"Yes. By standing still."

And then he kneels. My stomach plummets at the sight.

"Step in," he says, holding the jeans open for me.

"Step in?"

He peers up. "To wear them while I do this. Unless it'll bother you too much. Having you wear them will help me figure out where to cut them, but I can hold them up against you instead and figure it out that way, too. It's less accurate, though."

I just need him not to be down on his knees in front of me anymore, his head right at my pelvis. I'd suffer a dozen jeans that feel weird at the ankles to get this over with before my libido hijacks my brain again and makes my thoughts devolve into a full-on fantasy about what it might be like for Sebastian Gauthier to kneel in front of me for a very different, much more pleasurable reason.

"I can do it." Clutching the counter, I step into the jeans quickly, then take over from him when he lifts them past my knees. Our fingers brush, and I jolt. Sebastian drops his hands away sharply, pressing them against his thighs as he sits back on his heels. He looks away, staring at my bookshelves.

Waiting for some snide comment about my reading preferences, I tug the jeans up higher, under my robe, before I get them zipped and buttoned.

"Okay," I tell him.

He lifts his eyes, sharp silver. His throat works. "Can you part your robe over your jeans, so I can see where to cut—"

I lift the robe, bunching it at my stomach.

He clears his throat. "Pen?"

Reaching past him, I open the small drawer in my kitchen where I keep pens and pencils.

"Pen."

He doesn't say anything, just takes it and starts to draw a line across my thigh. A yelp jumps out of me, which sends the pen zig-zagging down the fabric. He gives me an exasperated look. "This is going so well, with you wiggling."

"It tickles!"

Sighing, he grips my thigh *hard*. The heat of his hand seeps through my jeans. "Be still, and I'll be quick."

I bite my cheek while he drags the pen around my leg, hand holding me tight, before he switches and does the other one.

"All right." His gaze dances up to mine from where he kneels. He clears his throat again, then glances away. "Take them off."

I start to shimmy the jeans off, but they stick as I roll them down. Sebastian brushes my fingers away, wraps his hand around my ankle, then yanks away one jean leg, then the other, in two swift, efficient tugs.

Oh boy. He's very good at removing clothes.

I scrunch my eyes shut and tell my lusty brain to can it.

Sebastian stands with my jeans, holding them in front of him, but this kitchen is small, and once again, we stand close. Too close.

I feel achy and flushed.

"I'm just going to go, uh—" Clearing my throat, I throw a thumb over my shoulder. "Brush my hair."

Sebastian makes a noncommittal grunt, focused on my jeans. He turns so he's right up against the kitchen counter and lays them out, before making the first cut with the scissors.

Safely distanced from him in the bathroom, I get my hair untangled, swearing foully in Swedish while I comb out every wind-induced knot. By the time my hair's smooth and freshened up with dry shampoo, tugged into a sleek high ponytail, there's a knock on the bathroom door.

I ease it open. A pair of shorts hits me in the face. "Thanks?"

He doesn't even answer me as he tugs the door shut.

"Somebody's moody."

"Hungry!" he calls. "Hurry the hell up."

Muttering to myself in Swedish, just in case Sebastian can hear me complaining about him, I yank on the shorts, then whip open the door, storming past him for the bra and top he picked out and left on my bed. I yank the curtain around me, change into the bra and shirt, tug on socks, then wedge my feet into the black-and-white Nike high-tops that he must have set out, too, before I tug back the curtain. "Was that fast enough for you?"

Sebastian turns from where he's been standing with his back to me, arms folded across his chest. The tiniest pull at the corner of his mouth, a flicker of light in those cool, gray eyes, is all the change in his expression. But it's something. And it makes me feel good.

Taking his sweet time for someone who was just harassing me about hurrying up, he strolls my way, somehow still graceful, even with that Aircast boot thudding on the floor.

"Well?" I ask. "How's it look?"

He's quiet for a moment, his gaze roaming my face, trailing down my body. Then he says, "Turn around."

"Why?"

"Sigrid. Just turn around."

Sighing, I do as I'm told and face my reflection in the wall-mounted mirror. I look . . . exactly how I wanted to. Me, but with an edge.

The tank is threadbare, but not too sheer, the shadow of my black bra hinted beneath it.

Sebastian not only cut the jeans into shorts but also managed to mildly distress them, the occasional slash across the fabric but not cut clean through, the bottom edges frayed so they're soft but not ticklish. They're short, yet not *too* short, enough to show off my legs without making me feel like my butt's going to pop out when I sit. My white high-tops with their black accents and laces match my bra and top. It's perfect.

"Now," he says, his voice warm on my neck. "*You* tell me how you look."

I bite my lip against a smile, meeting my reflection's gaze. "I look badass."

Sebastian's eyes lock with mine in the mirror as he stands behind me. His expression is blank, but his gaze is sharp, piercing. "Come on, then, badass. Time to eat."

———

Sebastian looks comically out of place in Betty's Diner as we sit in a shiny retro vinyl booth, oldies playing on the jukebox. This six-three, dark-haired Adonis with his tats and silver chains and rings, wearing his expensive-looking clothes and a severe expression, reads the menu surrounded by families with babies banging on tables and senior citizens digging into apple pie.

I nudge his knee under the table. He lowers the menu just

enough to reveal those cold quicksilver eyes, one dark arched eyebrow. "What?"

Setting my elbows on the table, I lean in, voice quiet. "We're supposed to be passing as friends. Not two strangers stuck in a booth at a diner you wish was a club instead."

He sighs, lowering his menu fully, then mirroring me, resting his elbows on the table, lacing his hands together. The lights wink off his silver rings, drawing my attention to his fingers and the ink woven over them.

"It's not polite to stare, Ziggy dear."

"Does it hurt, when you get them?" I point to his hands. I'm too riveted to acknowledge how annoyingly condescending that *Ziggy dear* is.

"Yes," he says simply.

I glance up, searching his eyes. He takes a sip of water. "Is it a good hurt?"

Sebastian chokes on his water, then wipes his mouth, frowning at me. "What the hell does someone like you know about a 'good hurt'?"

"'Someone like me' would be a twenty-two-year-old bisexual woman who knows more than you think." I glare at him. We engage in a little stare-down. "I'm not a nun, Sebastian. Stop acting like it."

"You"—he leans in, voice low—"are my best friend's baby sister. That's *exactly* how I'm going to act. Do you understand?"

I lean even closer, then whisper, "No."

"What'll it be?" Our waiter, Stevie, breaks the moment. Pulling apart, we pointedly do not look at each other. When I place my order, Stevie, who knows me from my late-night diner runs with Ren over the years, gives Sebastian a very obviously appreciative glance, then throws me a wink and mouths, *Wow.*

Once he's gone, Sebastian says, "This might be a problem."

"What?"

He slouches in the booth, one hand's worth of inked fingers drumming across the table. "People will assume we're fucking."

My eyes nearly bug out of my head. "You can't say that word in Betty's Diner. Also, *why*?"

He smirks. "Because that's what I do best, Ziggy dear. Besides hockey. And when I'm seen out with anyone besides people on the team, that's what the tabloids—reasonably, I might add—assume."

I decide to study the menu so I won't have to look at Sebastian while he talks about this. I'm turning bright red. "Well, then . . . it'll just be another way that you're showing you've reformed. You made friends with someone who you're not trying to . . ."

He leans in, an elbow on the table, his face propped in his hand. "Go ahead. Say it."

"Sleep with," I finish timidly.

He *tsks*. "Honestly, Sigrid. You could say it. *Fuck*."

"It's a family establishment. You can't keep saying that here."

Rolling his eyes, he slumps back in the booth again. I glance around, hoping we haven't been loud enough for people to be offended by Sebastian's foul mouth.

That's when I realize while nobody looking at us seems scandalized, there are definitely a lot of patrons looking our way. A couple of them not-so-subtly pick up their phones either to film or take a picture.

There are a *lot* of eyes on us.

My pulse starts pounding in my ears. My legs start to wiggle under the table. I pick up the menu again despite already having ordered.

Memories from high school, the creep of anxiety as I walked into classrooms, the cafeteria, the locker room, make me shut my eyes and suck in a deep breath.

This is why I've done my best to go unnoticed for so long. Because the last time I felt seen, I was an awkward girl with incapacitating anxiety, a total inability to make friends, and a perpetual fear of saying the wrong thing—of saying *anything*, for that matter.

"Shit," I whisper, exhaling shakily.

"*Sigrid.*" Sebastian sounds delighted. "Is that a swear word I finally heard?"

I throw him a glare, or try to, but the world feels a little fuzzy. I'm having a hard time taking a deep breath.

Sebastian's sly smirk dissolves on his face as he takes me in. "What the hell's wrong?"

A thick swallow works down my throat as I clutch the menu for dear life. "I think this might have been an epic mistake."

SEVEN

Sebastian

Playlist: "Don't Let It Get You Down," Johnnyswim

I should be thrilled that Ziggy's second-guessing this nonsense. Considering how things went in her apartment, I should jump at the chance to end this ridiculous stunt before it's even begun.

Because what I felt—watching her naked silhouette through the curtain separating us before I spun away and shut my eyes; after that, kneeling at her feet; then, standing behind her as she looked at herself in the mirror—is bad, bad news.

I'm painfully attracted to her. To this delicious contradiction of shy quiet and sheer courage, tender feeling and tenacious fire. She's a goddamn knockout, and she has no fucking clue. She doesn't know that sheer white top draped across her dewy skin is jaw-clenching torture, that her hips sway when she's feeling confident, and the freckles on her legs dance as she walks.

She will *never* know that from me. Because that kind of conversation is never going to happen with my best friend's sister.

Who only wants to *pretend* to be my friend.

And who's very obviously on the precipice of losing her shit in this syrupy-sweet diner.

Her legs bounce frantically under the table. I wedge a knee around each of them and pin them together, making her legs go still. She glances up and takes a deep, slow breath, something like relief warming her eyes. Her shoulders settle from where they'd crept up to her ears.

A rare, bone-deep satisfaction pours through me, better than the best high, more potent than the smoothest whiskey. I did that. I made her feel better. Fuck, could I get hooked on the rush it gives me.

Even more reason to agree with Ziggy that this idea was an epic mistake. I should throw down some cash, drag her outside, and put an end to this.

But instead, inexplicably, I say instead, "Why?"

Ziggy slides her fingers around the edge of her menu. Her hands are shaking. "The whole idea of this was to be looked at, to be seen. I'm not used to that, though, being noticed. It freaks me out."

"You're six-one with flame-red hair. How the hell are you not used to being 'noticed' by now?"

She bites her lip and ducks her head, so her ponytail becomes a curtain of hair that shields her from the curious eyes turned our way. "You said yourself, I'm good at hiding in plain sight."

My chest aches. My jaw creaks, I'm clenching it so hard. Who the fuck made her feel like this? What made her decide it was best to hide herself away and dim her fire?

She glances past her hair, inspecting the room, then winces. "I can't do this."

"The fuck you can't."

"Watch your mouth," she whispers, glaring at me. "Some public-image overhaul you've got underway, dropping all these f-bombs in a family restaurant."

I lean in and tell her, "If I'm expected to look like I've reformed myself and talk like a good little boy, you can sit tall and let people see you."

She shuts her eyes. "It's hard. Change takes . . . time for me. I can't just snap my fingers and make myself suddenly comfortable with that."

I stare at her, a sharp knot forming in my chest. "Then let's take a step back. Ease you into it."

Her eyes meet mine, curious and guarded. "Ease me into it?"

I lift a hand to grab our waiter's attention, holding Ziggy's gaze.

Stevie, as he introduced himself, is at our booth *very* quickly, as if he's been waiting for this moment. "Need something?" he asks.

"We've decided we'll take our food to go," I tell him. For Ziggy's benefit, when she widens her eyes at me, I flash Stevie a grin that's gotten me exactly what I want more times than I can count. "*Please.*"

Ziggy watches Stevie blink at me and turn bright pink. "S-sure," he says, tucking back a lock of brown hair behind his ear. He pushes his glasses up his nose, from where they've slipped. "Absolutely. No problem."

Ziggy's eyebrows rise as Stevie turns, walks into a table, then slowly steps around it, fidgeting with his hair again, throwing me a dazed smile over his shoulder. "That charm, Gauthier," she mutters bleakly. "It's a dangerous thing."

I smirk as I slouch back in the booth. "Don't I know it."

"Man, this is good," Ziggy moans around her food. "I didn't even think I'd be that hungry—I already ate dinner—but there's something about Betty's burgers." Another happy moan leaves her as she chews, then swallows.

Ketchup seeps from the burger, landing with a splat on her thigh. "Oops," she mutters.

I watch her slide an index finger across her skin to wipe up the ketchup, then bring it to her mouth, licking the ketchup clean off the tip of her finger with one swift flick of her tongue.

I bite the straw stuck in my milkshake so hard, it cracks.

It's bad enough that I've had to sit right beside Ziggy, listening to each appreciative groan as she bites into her burger. Now I have to watch her lick her fingers.

I need to get laid.

But that's pretty damn impossible when I'm on virtual house arrest and under strict instructions from Frankie not to fuck around with anyone. My hand's been getting a workout, and it's barely taken the edge off. It was that way even before I got myself into this latest bit of trouble. I've been restless, annoyed, frustrated. No one's pleased me, no one's drawn me in. There hasn't been a single person I've enjoyed debauching in weeks.

Now, sexually frustrated, stuck in the longest abstinent streak of my adult life, I have to listen to Ziggy moan over diner food on the hood of my car.

Fucking hell.

"Oodonikeurs?" she says around her bite.

I raise an eyebrow, sipping from my chocolate milkshake, which Ziggy's helped herself to at least half of. "Believe it or not, I didn't quite catch that."

She swallows, then says, "Sorry. You don't like yours?" She nods toward my barely touched BLT.

I stare down at the sandwich, my stomach tightening. Before this one, I hadn't had a BLT since the day my dad left. He loved them. I have few memories of him before he walked out on my mom and me—he was a professional hockey player, often on the road for games, but I remember the smell of bacon and toasted bread, eating a grilled cheese at the table while he chowed down on his beloved BLT. I've hated the sight and smell of BLTs ever since. But after I, for some inexplicable reason, asked Ziggy as we walked into the diner what she liked to eat here, and she said their BLT was the best she'd ever had, I ended up telling Stevie I'd take one.

The worst part is Ziggy's right. It's fucking good. I stare at the sandwich, then pick it up and take another bite. This bite's even better than the last, the thick-sliced tomato having softened the crisp, toasted bread; smoky bacon mingled with rich mayonnaise, still a bit of crunch from the romaine lettuce.

I hate it. And I love it. Shit, I need a drink.

"It's good," I admit to her, dropping the sandwich back in its carton, brushing off my hands. "I'm just . . . slow finding my appetite."

She turns my way, sharp green eyes examining me. "Sort of like me being seen in the diner, you and nourishing yourself, huh?"

I stop chewing, my chest tightening as I remember what she said about being seen in the diner, being comfortable with it.

It's hard. Change . . . it takes time.

Staring down at the sandwich, I shrug. "Maybe."

"When you have hockey, it's easier to make good choices, isn't it? But when it's off-season, you don't make those good choices, because you don't think you deserve good things. You only do it because that makes hockey possible."

I throw her a look, and say around my bite, exasperated, "All right, Freud."

"You can blame my therapist, not Freud, for that one." She shrugs, eyeing up her burger. "That's how it is with me and soccer. I can play in front of a stadium packed with people, and I'm fine. But take me out of soccer, and I can't do it. I feel worthy of that kind of attention and respect when I'm Ziggy the soccer player. Anywhere else, any way else . . ." She sighs, forlorn, as she stares at her burger. "Not so much."

I stare at her, biting my lip. "Look at you, chattering away, Sigrid. I didn't know you had it in you."

"Yeah, well," she mutters. "Try being the last of seven kids and see if you ever cultivate the habit of trying to get a word in edgewise."

"Talk as much as you want around me. You know, if that's what you'd do around a . . . friend. I can stare moodily into my sandwich and pretend to listen while you do."

I feel her gaze on the side of my head, a thick silence before I'm shoved halfheartedly.

A little throaty laugh leaves her. "Seb Gauthier." She shakes her head, then licks off another drop of ketchup that's landed on her hand. "Only you could be both sweet and a total jerk in the same breath."

"I'm not sweet," I warn her. "I told you, it's just for show."

She nods, eyeing up her burger. "Mm-kay."

I stare at her, my tongue pressed into my cheek. "You called me Seb."

She's about to bite into her burger when she glances my way. "You don't like being called by your full name, so I figured I'd stop torturing you with it."

Shrugging, I bring the milkshake to my mouth and draw a gulp through the straw. "Sort of feels weird now, you calling me something besides Sebastian."

I fiddle with the straw, avoiding her eyes.

Ziggy's quiet again, but her hand wraps gently around the milkshake and tugs it toward her. I can't seem to let go, so I let her fingers tangle with mine, let her strength tug me close.

I shut my eyes as I list toward her, smelling her soft, clean scent, feeling her hair lift on the wind and whisper against my skin. When I open my eyes, she's right there, sucking from the straw, eyes on me.

She sits back and licks her lips, peering at me thoughtfully. "'Sebastian' it is."

"I still reserve the right to tell you to fuck off when you annoy me with how you say it."

A snort-laugh leaves her. "I'd expect nothing less." Then she takes another bite of her burger, chewing as she stares thoughtfully out at the parking lot, elbows braced on her knees.

She looks fucking perfect.

I lift my phone and take a photo. The moment she hears the synthesized sound of a shutter, her head whips my way. "Wawas-dat?" she yells around her bite.

I bite back a laugh. "Settle yourself, Sigrid. I'm documenting your badassery, that's all."

She glares at me, then with surprisingly fast reflexes, yanks the phone out of my hand, rotating it so she can see the photo.

Her chewing stops. She swallows thickly, a painfully large bite, judging by how hard her throat works.

"What is it?" I ask.

She shrugs, sniffling. "I like it. A lot. I really do look badass." She sniffles again and clears her throat.

"Don't cry, for shit's sake."

She shoves the phone into my chest and shoves me, too, for good measure. "I'm not crying. The onions on the burger make my eyes water."

"This response came on suddenly, rather late into your burger."

"Shut up, Gauthier." She tugs my phone back and with one hand starts typing.

"Sigrid."

"Sebastian."

I rest back on my elbows, watching her. "What are you doing with my phone?"

Hers dings in her back pocket. "Texting my phone from yours. Now you have my number and I have yours."

My heart rate spikes. "What the fuck for?"

"Because friends have each other's numbers, genius." She tosses the phone on my lap and narrowly misses nailing me in the dick.

I give her a wry look. "You didn't have to make up that excuse to get my number, Sigrid. I'd have given it to you."

"You're such an arrogant piece of work," she mutters before biting into her burger again.

The self-satisfied smirk I flash her way fades a bit as I watch her having another foodgasm with her burger.

As a car pulls into the parking lot, I glance over my shoulder, then swear under my breath when I see who, of all people, has just showed up.

Ziggy nudges my thigh with her knee. "What is it?"

None other than the Kings' owner steps out of a vintage sports car, followed by two gangly grandkids, smiles on their faces.

"That's—"

She sets a hand on mine. "I know who that is. He's obsessed with Ren."

"Of course he is," I mutter. "Ren's every owner's dream athlete—excellent, dependable, minimal injuries, well behaved." I sit up, raking both hands through my hair. "This is it. He's going to see us, and if we tell him we're friends, it's going to get back to Ren, the team . . ." I clench my jaw, pulling my hand away. "You don't need to do this, tangle yourself up with me—"

Her grip tightens, stopping me. Then her fingers thread gently through mine. "I want to."

"Ziggy—"

"Mr. Köhler!" she calls, dropping her burger in its container to wave brightly.

I swear under my breath again.

"Quit with the swearing," she says through that wide smile.

Art Köhler walks toward us, an arm around each grandkid, who I recognize from when he brought them around the team for autographs. Art's smile is warm as he says hello to Ziggy, introducing his grandkids. It cools but remains polite as he looks at me. "Gauthier."

"Mr. Köhler." I nod toward the diner's glowing neon sign. "You picked a good place for a late-night bite."

He arches an eyebrow. "Betty's Diner doesn't seem like your kind of haunt."

"First time for everything," Ziggy interjects. "Seb was even generous enough to treat me."

Mr. Köhler glances her way, puzzlement starting on his face as if he's finally piecing together that Ziggy's with me and I'm with her. "And what's a sweet girl like you doing with trouble like Seb Gauthier?"

Before Ziggy can answer, one of his grandkids says, "I think Seb's cool."

Mr. Köhler gives me a censorious look. "That's exactly the problem."

Regret gnaws its way through me. I'm a lost cause, but this kid isn't. He has vital years ahead of him to make better choices than I have; I don't want him emulating me.

"It's cool," I tell his grandkid, "to work hard and go after what you want. And I have done that. I'm where I am in this sport because I worked my a—" Ziggy's knee hits my thigh sharply, right before I almost swear. "My *butt* off. But . . ." I glance toward Ziggy, who's watching me intently, then back to Mr. Köhler's grandkid. "I've also done a lot of things you shouldn't admire me for. That aren't cool at all."

Ziggy gifts me a small, approving smile, which I shouldn't be so damn pleased about receiving.

But I am. I bury my face in my milkshake so I don't have to look at her or Mr. Köhler, who's staring at me curiously.

Then Ziggy says to Mr. Köhler, "To answer your question, Sebastian and I are hanging out here because we're friends."

"Friends?" Mr. Köhler frowns.

"Yep," Ziggy says. "Friends. He and I connected over angry yoga."

I almost choke on my milkshake. *Angry yoga?*

"Angry yoga?" Mr. Köhler's voice echoes my incredulity.

"Mm-hmm. Want a fry?" She offers our shared carton of fries to the grandkids, who both help themselves. "You know they're good when they're tasty even after they've cooled off. But anyway, yes, angry yoga. It's yoga that makes space for complex, often negatively connotated emotions, with the goal of using mindful movement to process them constructively with an ultimate goal of healing."

"Cool," the other grandkid says.

Ziggy smiles. "I'm doing it to tap into my anger and let myself feel the tough emotions I tell myself I shouldn't. Seb's going because he's realized he needs a healthier conduit for all his existential angst." She slaps a hand on my thigh, and I barely hide a glare. She's taking this a *bit* too far.

"Well." Mr. Köhler folds his arms across his chest, staring me down. "I'm very glad to hear this. That sounds . . ."

"Almost unbelievably healthy of me?" I offer.

Mr. Köhler chuckles, clapping a hand on my shoulder. "I hope it's a change that sticks. Take care, Gauthier. And, Ziggy, say hi to my favorite player."

"Will do!" She waves and smiles as they start to turn toward the diner.

As soon as the door of the diner shuts behind them, I round on her. "*Angry yoga?*"

She flashes a smile my way. "Look at me, thinking on my feet! Being conversational! I was amazing."

I roll my eyes. "Angry yoga, Sigrid. Of all the things."

"What? It'll be fun." She opens up her phone and shows me an Instagram account with videos featuring lots of people who look like me—pissed, tattooed, flicking off some unseen higher power. "There's a studio nearby that offers classes, and I've wanted to try it for ages, but I never felt like I'd fit in. Now, with you, I totally will. I gotta reserve us a spot ASAP so we have evidence to corroborate what I just said."

"You mean the *lie* you just told?"

She hushes me, slapping my thigh gently. "It's not a lie, it's just—"

"Not a truth yet, I know, I know." Scowling, I reach for the milkshake but realize it's in Ziggy's hands, her loud slurp heralding the end of it.

"Ooh, they have a morning class tomorrow," she says happily.

"Ziggy dear, I can't just go to a yoga studio tomorrow morning. It'll be mayhem."

She rolls her eyes. "Your ego."

"I'm serious. I can't just go places. If we do angry yoga, angry yoga has to come to us."

She frowns. "Really?"

I press my tongue into my cheek, a little annoyed by how unbelievable this seems to her. "You don't know how people react to me in public? My widely known sexual appeal and erotic exploits? What kind of rock do you live under?"

"The rock where I don't give a flying fart about your alleged sexual appeal and erotic exploits?"

"Well, time to start giving that flying fart because it's going to impact you, *friend*."

She lets out a frustrated growl. "How are we going to be seen together as 'friends' if an alleged mob of horny people are tripping over themselves for you all the time?"

"It's not *everywhere*. I mean Betty's Diner was a safe place to come. Then again, you saw Stevie walk into a table when I smiled at him. Stick this handsome, twenty-seven-year-old pansexual specimen of sensual glory in a yoga studio with a bunch of people in their prime, and what do you think's going to happen?"

She snorts as she types something on her phone. "To have even a fragment of your ego. Fine. I left a message with the studio, but I doubt I can get an instructor to come to us at such short notice, seeing as it's eight at night—"

"Mention my name, and you'd have a damn good chance."

That earns me a flat, annoyed look. "You're a hot hockey player, Gauthier, not Justin Bieber."

"First, nice to know you think I'm hot."

She sighs wearily. "Sebastian."

"Second, I deeply resent the implication that I am not on par with Justin Bieber."

"Sorry to have offended," she says, not sounding sorry at all. "Back to the matter at hand. Here's the plan, unless this instructor miracle happens. I've got us registered to log in online and participate virtually, two spots at the six a.m. class. We can take some photos as we do it, post them to Instagram, knock it out before breakfast, and then I can head to practice."

"*Six* a.m.?"

Ziggy gives me a withering look. "I'm sorry, Sebastian, do you have some other pressing engagement at that time? Wallowing? Waking and baking? Trying on a different color cashmere throw blanket as your outfit of the day?"

"Fine! I'll do it, all right?"

"Excellent. We'll log in for yoga—"

"At *my* place. If I have to wake up at the ass crack of dawn for this, then your perky little morning-person self can come to *me*."

"Fine," she grumbles. "Yoga at six a.m. Post some photos to

Instagram. Then we go get a breakfast smoothie or something afterward, to be seen. How's that sound?"

"Yoga with a sore foot hours before I'm normally awake? Sounds
terrible." Groaning as pain knifes through my stomach—this is
why I don't eat, because every time I do, it fucking hurts—I ease
off the hood of my car. "However, since you backed us into this
little corner of a fib with Köhler, I'll do it." I tug the milkshake cup
out of her hands and shake it meaningfully. "You owe me one of
these, by the way."

EIGHT

Ziggy

Playlist: "Angry Too," Lola Blanc

The smug look in Sebastian's eyes when he opens his door almost makes me turn around and walk right back out. Before I headed over, I texted him that the instructor responded after all; Yuval will be here at 6:00 a.m. sharp. I was hoping by the time I got to his house, he'd be past the point of gloating.

I was wrong.

"Told you," he says, shutting the door behind me.

I roll my eyes and walk past him with my yoga mat under my arm, straight down the hallway toward the smell of coffee. "You're annoying."

A satisfied sound rumbles in his throat as he follows me, though it dies away abruptly as I yank off my tunic-length hoodie. I glance over my shoulder, confused.

As he clomps in his boot across the kitchen, Sebastian scowls at the coffeepot like it personally insulted him.

"What's your deal?" I ask.

He grunts, pouring two cups of coffee, sliding one across the counter my way.

"Sebastian."

"Sigrid. Drink your coffee."

"Listen, *friend*." I pour a hefty glug of milk into my cup, which he was surprisingly considerate enough to leave out. "Yuval is going to be here in five minutes, and they're not going to buy our friendship if you're grunting and glaring at me."

Sebastian sips his coffee and transforms his expression into a smooth, cool glance. "I'm not glaring."

"You were. And you were grunting."

He pulls his cup away and flashes that sharp smirk. "Who? Me?"

"You're impossible."

The doorbell rings. Sebastian and I tip our heads back, shot-gunning our coffees in tandem.

"Well, Ziggy dear," he says, gesturing for me to walk ahead of him. "Ladies first."

Yuval is clearly here for one person and one person only. To Sebastian's credit, he's been polite to them but firmly professional, not at all flirtatious. Who knew he had it in him?

Loud, angry music blares in his workout room, and after a gentle warm-up sequence, Yuval cranks up the volume. The sound vibrates in my chest, which I'm surprised I enjoy. I've always struggled with complex noise, and I assumed heavy metal would similarly bother me. Who knew I'd love it?

After standing, I walk off my mat and reach for my water. I take a long drink, mentally kicking myself for chugging so much coffee this morning, but I slept terribly, so it was that or be a zombie for angry yoga.

When Sebastian's voice fades from his conversation with Yuval, I glance toward him, finding his gaze on me. He lifts his eyebrows, a smirk on his mouth.

He's so darn aggravating, sitting there in his black joggers and a muscle-hugging silvery sage-green shirt that brings out his eyes. His dark hair's tugged back, just the pieces that fit, the rest falling onto his already sweaty jaw and neck.

I'm frustrated with myself, with how aware of him I am. He's my *pretend* friend, mercilessly egotistical, self-absorbed, and he only sees me as his best friend's little sister, who's only worth his time because I've proved myself useful for this season in his life. That's all this is. I just need my body to get the memo.

"Right," Yuval says, stretching their legs wide on their mat. "Ready to move on?"

Sebastian nods.

I force a smile as I plop back down on my mat. "Yep."

"We'll keep it low impact, since Seb's healing his foot, and, Ziggy, you'll be exercising lots later on today." Darn Yuval, being nice, making it harder to resent them for flirting with Sebastian.

Not that I care who flirts with my pretend friend.

When Yuval instructs us to begin with breathing exercises that involve lying down, I flop onto my back and glare up at the ceiling.

"And you were lecturing *me* about grunting and glaring?" he mutters out of the side of his mouth.

"I'm just tired," I hiss-whisper.

"You're pissed, is what you are."

I glare at him.

Sebastian points a finger at me. "See? Pissed."

"I'm *fine*."

"The fuck you are." He rolls onto his side, facing me. "The whole point of this is for you to find that spine of yours and be your badass self, so how about you do it for goddamn once?"

"Everything okay?" Yuval asks, eyes darting between us.

"Not quite, Yuval," Sebastian says. "If we could get right to some of those anger-release exercises, I think we'll be in better shape, though."

Gracefully, despite his bruised food, he stands, then extends a hand to me.

Yuval smiles at him. Of course they do. "Sure. Fine by me. So, you can face each other, and this can be an exercise of mutual support and presence as you process whatever you need to, or you can face away—"

"We'll face each other," Sebastian says, holding my eyes.

My throat feels thick. I don't know why. Why it feels like a pinch in my heart and a perfect hug—hard, squeezing, tight. Why, when I take Sebastian's hand and he yanks me up, I feel a rush of something comforting and safe.

"Deep breath," Yuval says. "We'll go through a sun salutation, using ujjayi breath. You're familiar with sun salutation?"

We both nod.

Yuval tells Seb, "I'll model a modification of each pose that could strain your foot as we go, okay?"

Seb shakes his head. "I'll be fine doing the traditional sequence. I need to move my ankle around. It's too fucking stiff."

Yuval seems nervous about that, but under the spell of Seb's charming smile, they settle for saying, "Well, just please be careful." First bringing their hands to their chest, they then lift their arms wide overhead. "Remember, in through your nose, out through your nose. If breathing becomes groaning, grunting, sighing, cursing, let it. Just let it all out."

I lift my arms, feeling my chest open, an ache sharpening in my heart. My eyes prick with warning tears. I blink them away, then fold over, my nose touching my knees. A hitch catches in my breath as I do a halfway lift. The hitch becomes a groan as I fold back down.

Back up to a halfway lift, I open my eyes, trying to blink away tears, and find myself face-to-face with Sebastian, something fierce tightening his expression.

I blink my eyes as tears well in them, dropping into a full plank.

"Fuck," he mutters, gritting his teeth as we lower our plank.

Yuval says, "That's it. Let it out. Now, cobra."

We both push up, arms extended, chests out, faces much too close as we breathe in, filling our lungs.

Sebastian's gaze roams me, his exhale rough as we move back into a plank, then downward dog, a halfway lift. My breathing is getting rougher, the knot tighter in my throat as I roll my spine up, standing to my full height.

By the time I've straightened, I'm trying so hard not to cry, it's nearly impossible to breathe. Which is, I realize, counter to the entire point of angry yoga, but like I told Seb, change is easier said than done. I hate crying. I hate feeling the dam break inside me, that loss of control that was so familiar as a teen, the flood of emotions so intense, I was terrified I'd drown in them.

I haven't learned how to feel the way I need to without being scared it's going to swallow me whole. But right now, unless I want to pass out from lack of oxygen, I don't have a choice.

On my next inhale, I lift my arms over my head and let out a single groaned "Fuuuck."

Sebastian's arms are high, too, his own "Fuuuck" not far behind. His sounds—unlike my rage-filled cry—are pained, exhausted, spent. And yet, knowing he's there, that this cool, aloof man is feeling something, too, confessing it with raw weariness in his voice, makes me feel so much less alone, so much less afraid to groan out another gut-deep curse as I fold over.

Yuval's turned up the music, and its tempo builds. My heartbeat pounds in my ears. I feel like a decade of pain has parked itself beneath my ribs, and unless I scream it out, it's going to crush me.

"Breathe deep," they remind us both.

I hear Sebastian's strong inhale, his groaned exhale as we rise up halfway and our eyes meet, faces close again.

His gaze searches mine with an intensity that just might be concern, etched into his perfect features. I feel like he sees every single thing I'm about to scream out as I suck in air and straighten my body, swinging my arms upward.

A noise I have never made before, a broken, animal howl, leaves me as my chest opens. The pressure in my chest, the knot in my throat, dissolves as I yell, as the pounding music echoes in the room and swallows up my sounds.

As the last trickle of air leaves me, I gasp, sucking in a breath. Sucking in a breath again.

I'm crying. *Hard*.

Then, I'm crumpling to the ground—

Well, I was. But now, I'm falling into arms. Lean, sweaty arms wrapped around me, crushing me to a lean, sweaty chest.

God, he smells good. Like he did last night after his shower, only *more*. Cool and clean—snow-covered pine branches, frost-kissed sage leaves rubbed between my fingers. I bury my nose in his neck as another sob rips out of me, and I clutch his shirt, the damp fabric clenched in my fists. The music's so loud, thumping through my body, yet all I can hear is the pound of Sebastian's pulse in his neck against my ear, the steady rise and fall of his chest as he presses me into it.

I scrunch my eyes shut, feeling so much, that familiar flood of intense emotions, a torrent of thoughts. But they're not drowning me, not stuck in my throat or filling my lungs like cement. Instead, each breath is a little easier, each sob becomes softer.

I don't know how long we stand like that, only that at some point, by some mutual agreement, our grips loosen, and we pull apart.

Slowly, I peer up at Sebastian and meet his eyes. I'm flushed and sweaty, and I'm sure my face is blotchy from crying. I do not give a single damn. He saw me scream-cry and fall apart. He held me while I put myself back together. My ruddy exercise complexion and cry face are the least of my indignities right now.

"Honestly, Sigrid," he whispers, wide-eyed. "You didn't have to sell the angry yoga angle *that* hard."

I blink at him, biting my lip.

His mouth tips to the side in a faint, uncertain smile. "I'm just joking," he says, his eyes tightening with concern. "Ziggy, I didn't mean that, I was just trying to make you—"

A laugh bursts out of me, hard and throaty. I double over, one hand clutching his arm as I laugh even harder, joyful lightness bubbling through my body. "You're such an asshole," I cackle, wiping my eyes.

"Well, now you're catching on," he mutters, taking my elbow and pulling me back up, into his arms. He cups the sweaty nape of my neck with his hand and squeezes gently. "I know that crying's good, that you needed it. I just selfishly . . ." He exhales heavily. "I just couldn't take it anymore. So I tried—very poorly, clearly—to make you laugh instead."

Another burst of laughter leaves me as I drop my head to his shoulder. "That was plenty of crying for me. Laughing . . . laughing feels good."

He doesn't say anything for a moment. His hand still cups my neck, massaging it gently.

"Well . . . good."

I glance past him, chin resting on his shoulder, and realize the music has faded; there's no Yuval anymore.

"Where'd they go?" I ask, pulling away, blotting my eyes with the heels of my hands.

Sebastian's quiet at first, as he softly scrapes his fingers through my hair, pressing back every flyaway that's stuck to my tear-and-sweat-soaked face. "I gave them a nod, and they stepped out."

I search his face, confused.

He reads my expression, those cool silver eyes turned warmer, liquid mercury, bright and alive. "Some things aren't for just anyone to witness, Sigrid. This was one of them." He squeezes my shoulders gently, then steps back. "Come on, let's get you home."

"But our outing, being seen—"

"We don't need to go on that outing when you feel like this."

I shake my head, wiping my nose again. "Sebastian, I'm okay. I mean . . . I'm okay to do that. I *want* to."

He looks skeptical, maybe even . . . worried. "Ziggy—"

"I promise. I'm not just saying it." I exhale slowly, peacefully. My chest feels like a weight's gone from it. I feel both tired and energized, like I could curl up in a ball just as much as I could run a dead sprint. "I need something in my stomach besides coffee anyway—I'm jittery. And I'm low on groceries. I don't have anything at my place to eat besides granola bars, and I need way more than that if I'm going to eat my feelings, which I fully plan to."

He seems to deliberate before finally reaching for his boot, ripping open the Velcro, and sliding it on. "Then let's get you some breakfast, after all."

NINE

Sebastian

Playlist: "Mountain to Move," Nick Mulvey

Ziggy's been quiet on our drive to the café, one of those places where people go to see and be seen. There's a long, roofed balcony with tables that are highly visible. It's the perfect place to be photographed from, which is what Ziggy insisted she wanted, even after what happened at yoga.

She and I take our seats at the table, still in workout clothes, though I changed my shirt, since it was sweat soaked, and Ziggy's wearing her hoodie now—lightweight sage green, draped just past her hips, the one she was wearing when she walked into my place. It's the same color as the dress she wore to Ren and Frankie's wedding.

When I saw it this morning, tantalizing memories of her from that day flooded my thoughts, memories I've tried hard to unsee, but watching her strip it off in my kitchen is what sent me over the edge, free-falling into a terribly erotic fantasy. That long, red hair, drifting between my fingers. My mouth tasting every freckle as I kissed my way down her spine—

I grit my teeth, hating myself for how incapable I seem to be of stopping this—thinking about her, wanting her. I have no business wanting Ziggy, not just because of who she is to Ren, not even mostly because of that, but because she is *good*.

And I am not. There is no world where I'd be worthy of her.

Not that my fantasies involve anything . . . serious. If I had Ziggy, it would be once—no, one *night*—a deliciously long, sleepless night. And then, like every other person I've sexually enjoyed, she'd be out of my system.

It would be a simple release. An itch scratched.

Except, when Ziggy clears her throat, opening her menu, her eyes still a little puffy from crying, a sharp twinge tugs in my chest. I've never felt that way, looking at someone who was an itch to be scratched.

I've never felt that way looking at *anyone*. And I certainly haven't tried to make them laugh. Avoiding the temptation to look at her, I focus on my smoothie options, determined to move past this uncomfortable tug in my chest, the twitch in my hands to reach for her the way I did in my workout room.

"Sebastian."

I jolt, hearing my name in her voice, that tinge of husky smoke at its edge, the way I can only imagine it is after she screams her way through an orgasm, breathless and hoarse.

I make a fist with one hand beneath the table, so my rings will cut into my fingers. A lick of pain to punish myself for where I let my mind wander again.

Forcing my expression into cool neutrality, I glance up from my menu.

But fuck if there's nothing neutral about what I feel when I look at her, those deep green eyes locked on me, her face serious.

"Sigrid?" I say quietly.

She bites her lip, worrying the napkin between her fingers as she stares at me. "Thank you."

My heart jumps in my chest. But I keep my expression blank. "You don't need to thank me."

"I do," she whispers, biting her lip harder.

"Stop." I nudge my chin toward her lip pinned between her teeth. "You'll hurt yourself."

She lets her lip go, but arches an eyebrow, planting her elbows on the table and leaning in.

"Says the guy who's been on a self-harm bender for . . . how long?"

I arch an eyebrow back, my heart pounding. Who the fuck does she think she is, calling me out like that? "Careful."

"Of what?" she asks, tipping her head. "Touching a nerve? Saying something to your face everyone else is too scared to say?"

"They're not scared," I tell her, leaning in as well, my expression still cool and smooth, even though there's something hot and jagged tearing its way through me. "They're resigned. They've given up."

Her eyes hold mine. She leans in a little closer. "Then you need to find yourself some new people, Sebastian Gauthier. Everyone deserves to have someone in their corner who believes the best in them even when they're at their worst."

"I could find a hundred people if I wanted, Ziggy, but everyone gives up eventually. As they should. Too many vices, too many mistakes, too many unforgivable sins."

She's quiet, searching my eyes. "What have you done that's so terrible?"

"Why should I tell you?"

"Because, *friend*," she says without missing a beat, "I just lost it in front of you during angry yoga and got all vulnerable. One good turn deserves another."

I drop my menu, then fold my hands on the table, warring with myself. Part of me wants to tell her to fuck right off, that I owe her nothing.

But another part of me wants to tell her everything, both aches and fears, to pour it out, only to watch disappointment tighten her face, to watch her realize, like everyone else has, that once you know the real me, I'm not someone you want to know anymore.

I *should* tell her, knowing that's how it'll go, to scare her off and get myself out of this ridiculous situation, spending this much time with someone I swore I'd never let myself want, who, with every minute I spend with her, I just want more.

"I have stolen," I tell her.

"Stolen what?" she asks evenly.

"Money."

She frowns. "But you have tons of it."

"I didn't always, not when I was a teen."

My mom and stepfather didn't trust me with any more money than I could make on my own, and with hockey dominating my life every waking minute outside school, there was never time to work. So of course, to spite them, and in a self-fulfilling prophecy, I took matters into my own reckless hands.

"Teenager shenanigans." She waves her hand. "You paid them back, though, once you were an adult."

I glare at her. What is she, some mind reader? "Doesn't matter. I took money from people who counted on my honesty. I betrayed their trust. I've betrayed lots of people's trust." Gritting my teeth— why is this so hard? I've never batted an eye before when stating plainly who I am, what I've done—I tell her, "I've done more than that, too. I've slept with people who were with other people. I've ruined relationships."

"That took two people; you didn't ruin those relationships on your own."

"It was still wrong."

"Yes," she says simply. "It was. You just don't get to take all the responsibility."

"I've punished those who got on my bad side, fucked with the people who mattered to them, reeled them in, seduced them, then ghosted them. I've lied, cheated—"

"Sebastian."

I stare at her, jaw hard, furious. Why is she still here? Why is she still looking at me, that beautiful, striking face still calm, still . . . gentle?

"What?" I ask, trying to snap, to make her flinch, to finally see what's good for her and pull away.

But she doesn't. Instead she stares at me, her expression serious. "Did you apologize?"

"For the sake of hockey only, and on pain of death threatened by Frankie, I made tangible amends, when possible. Paid back what I stole and cheated, set the record straight where I'd lied. Distanced myself from relationships I'd been a part of undermining that were trying to recover. That was my apology."

"That's good," Ziggy says. "Reparative action is important. But I still think you need to actually *say* sorry."

"It's a little late for saying sorry."

"That's the beauty of saying sorry, though—you can always say it. It's never too late."

"People I've crossed don't want my apologies, Ziggy. Unlike yours, my mistakes aren't petty human errors, which people don't mind forgiving and forgetting because they haven't actually cost them anything. They're not interested in forgiving truly terrible things."

She stares at me, so intensely. "That . . . can't feel good. But it's also okay. Your apology, it's as much for you as it is for them. It's their choice whether or not they receive your apology and forgive you. Your choice to be genuinely sorry helps you, whether or not you have their forgiveness."

"'Helps' me how, Ziggy dear?"

Her eyes hold mine. "It helps you forgive *yourself.*"

My jaw clenches. "You're getting very Freud on me again."

"It's called therapy, Gauthier. You should try it."

"Fuck no—*Jesus*." I wince, rubbing my shin in the wake of Ziggy's kick.

"Watch that mouth," she says between her teeth as she forces a smile. "You're reforming, remember?"

I feign a smile, too. "Well, with how much you've been beating me, at least one of us is following through on our public image overhaul."

A genuine smile lifts her mouth as she sips her water. "Sorry. It's a habit. My siblings are very physical. Just existing in the Bergman household is a contact sport."

"Yeah, well, I'm not a Bergman."

"You're right. I'm sorry. I won't beat you up anymore. But we need some kind of signal to stop you from being such a potty mouth. How about a word?"

"A word?"

She shrugs. "Like a code word. Something you wouldn't normally say." Frowning, she peers up in thought. "*Zounds?* How about that?"

"*Zounds?* That's one of Ren's words." My eyes widen. "Wait, are you in his nerdy little theater club—"

I'm kicked *again*.

A groan leaks out of me as I rub my shin. "Sigrid, we *just* talked about this. You can't beat me—"

"*You*," she says pointedly, her voice hushed, "cannot talk about that. It's a secret."

"Then it's the most un-secret secret I have ever known."

She sighs, exasperated with me. "If there *were* a Shakespeare Club, and if I *were* a member of it—hypothetically—I still wouldn't admit that to you, after you called it a 'nerdy little theater club.'"

"I was joking."

"Hmph."

I stare at her, rubbing my knuckles across my mouth. "In all seriousness—"

"I didn't know you were capable of that," she says airily.

"Harsh, but not undeserved. In all seriousness, I think that club is a good thing for Ren. It's important he has a place and friends to be himself with, to nerd out and loosen up, free from the pressures of the team, with his public image."

Ziggy stares at me, her gaze sharp. "Would it appeal to you for those reasons, too?"

Just a few days ago, I'd have laughed that off, made some asshole remark.

But something about the way Ziggy looks at me as she asks that, soft morning sun lighting up those vivid green eyes, makes me pause, makes me consider it. Oddly, a group situation that isn't just a glittering shell of vapid interaction sounds almost . . . appealing.

Especially if Ziggy were there. She's turned my shins black and blue, and she has an annoying tendency to psychoanalyze me, but she's also . . . How can I describe what it's like, sharing space and time, even just a facsimile of a friendship with someone so far above me, who doesn't make me feel like shit for it?

It's . . . water on a desert-dry throat, air after diving far too deep—a gulp of grace that defies sense.

And I can't say no to it.

Besides, friends would share this sort of thing with each other, invite each other to an activity they liked, wouldn't they?

"Maybe," I finally answer her. "It might go some way to improving my image, at least."

Ziggy tips her head from side to side. "It might. But it's not like we could broadcast it. Remember: This is a secret club."

"The most un-secret secret club," I remind her. "Regardless, my image could use all the help it can get, even if it is only via rumors. For once, at least they'll be positive rumors."

"Well, then you should come. It's a lot of fun. But first, you have to memorize some of your favorite Shakespeare, then recite it for at least two members. If you do that genuinely and prove you have good intentions with the group, you're initiated."

I drum my fingers on the table. "That's not hard."

She seems surprised. "Really?"

"You're looking at the lead heartthrob in our tenth grade English class's dramatic reading of *Romeo and Juliet*."

"Wow—I'm in the presence of high school theatrical greatness."

I lift my water in cheers, then take a drink.

Ziggy rests her chin in her palm, eyes crinkled at the corners, dancing and playful. "I bet you were good. You have a flair for the dramatic, after all."

"Oh, fuck off—"

"Zounds!" she hisses, eyes wide in warning. "Sebastian, you and that mouth!"

A deep laugh cracks out of me. I have no idea why it delights me—whether it's the sweetness of her reprimand or the absurdity of an Elizabethan oath being yelled my way—maybe both. I bury my face in my hands as I laugh, my shoulders shaking.

Ziggy's laugh catches in her throat, like she's trying to stop it. "It's not funny. You have a very serious cussing problem, Gauthier."

A wheeze leaves me as I laugh harder. Ziggy's laugh pops out of her like a firework, all sparkle and smoke.

Then our waiter steps up to the table and puts an end to the moment. Instantly, their gaze snags on Ziggy. Annoyance crawls through me, watching them appreciate her bright smile, the pink in her cheeks that bloomed as she laughed.

I clear my throat loudly, startling them. They glance my way, but only for a moment before they're focused on Ziggy again, telling her the specials, answering her questions.

Ziggy bites her lip, deliberating as she peers back down at the menu. "I think I'll take the strawberry banana smoothie and also . . . a ham and cheese omelet. Oh, and can I have extra cheese, please? Thank you. Wait! Sorry. And a blueberry muffin. That sounds good. Thanks." She hands them the menu, then turns toward me, smiling.

Somewhere in our laughing, that tug in my chest from watching her cry dissolved. Looking at her now, I feel something new, something there's room for only since I cussed my way through yoga beside her in a space that felt big and real enough to hold my mess. Since I told her things I was so sure would cost me even this farce of a friendship. Since I laughed in a way I haven't in as long as I can remember.

That something new, weighty and warm, spreads through me, a hunger for . . . What did she call it last night? Nourishment. Something filling, sustaining.

Something good.

Slowly, I lift my menu, scouring it with fresh eyes.

With thorough satisfaction, I watch surprise strike Ziggy's expression as I tell the waiter, "I'll have what she's having, but for the smoothie and muffin, scratch the berries, make it chocolate."

This time, Ziggy doesn't have to remind me. As I hand the waiter my menu, I add with a smile: "Please."

"You're not walking me back to my place," Ziggy says, the car's engine ticking in my garage as it cools.

"Why the hell not?"

She raises her eyebrows.

"I just said 'hell,' *Sigrid*, in the privacy of my own home. Relax."

"It's a habit, though, *Sebastian*, and you're trying to break it."

"'Appear' to break it," I remind her.

She sighs wearily.

It makes me wonder how long it'll take before my stubborn intractability pushes her away, makes her realize I'm not even worth a fake friendship.

"It's broad daylight," she says, opening her door. "Nothing's going to happen to me."

"How do you know?"

"I walked to your place yesterday evening and this morning and lived to tell the tale."

Now it's my turn to sigh. I rack my brain, searching for some justification for the jaw-clenching need to see her home safe. I shouldn't need to see her home safe. But I do.

It's because she's Ren's. Because, while she's with me, I'll be damned if she's ever not safe—from me, from the world, from anything that could hurt her. For once in my life, I'm determined to see this situation through with a spotless record, to be able to look Ren in the eye and tell my best, my *only*, friend that I had nothing but good intentions with his sister and nothing untoward ever happened.

"Sebastian." Ziggy's voice pulls me from my thoughts. I glance over at her where she stands, arm draped across the driver's side door. Her hair's mostly out of its braid, fiery wisps framing her face. She looks so fucking lovely, it's obscene.

I swallow roughly. "I should walk you home," I tell her. "Because . . . the reformed Seb would."

"But your foot—"

"Fu—I mean, forget my foot. It's fine. It hardly hurts."

That's a lie. It aches a good bit from how I pushed it at yoga. But that's nothing to the discomfort I'll feel, sitting here on my ass, stomach knotted, waiting like some anxious, hand-wringing boy for her to text that she's back safe.

Ziggy arches an eyebrow, skeptical. But surprisingly, finally she says, "Fine."

"Well, Sir Seb, thank you for your escort."

I frown at Ziggy. "*Sir Seb?* What on earth did I do to deserve that name?"

She smiles, swift and bright. It feels like a punch to the gut, it's so lovely.

Don't look at her like that, an admonishing voice hisses in my thoughts. *You don't even deserve her smiles, let alone her friendship—fake or not.*

I glance down and brush some lint off my joggers.

"It had a nice ring to it, 'Sir Seb,'" she says. "You were being chivalrous."

"Chivalrous." I roll my eyes. "Okay. Get inside. Drink some water. You're dehydrated and delusional."

Ziggy's quiet for so long, I can't keep my gaze down anymore. When I peer up at her, my heart skips a beat. Her head's tipped, those piercing green eyes fixed on me. I have the uncomfortable sensation of being seen right down to my marrow.

"I'm starting to wonder," she says, "if Ren wasn't totally off the mark. If you're kinder than you want to admit you are, Sebastian Gauthier."

"Ziggy—"

"Hug," she says, wrapping her arms around me.

God. Her smile was a gut punch, but this hug is a blow that knocks the wind right out of me. I stand rooted to the pavement outside her apartment building as she holds me, not a drop of air in my lungs.

"Hey." She squeezes tighter. "Where's my hug? You hugged me at yoga, why can't you hug me now?"

"That wasn't a hug," I mutter into her hair, because the wind's slapped it into my face, and fuck, does it smell good—like sweet, clean water, a purifying pour of goodness that I don't deserve. "It was a . . . supportive . . . hold."

"A supportive hold." She snorts, an adorable sound in the back of her throat, chased by a bright, bubbly laugh. "Okay, sure. Well, it didn't kill you, and this won't kill you now. Besides, friends hug."

"Not this friend."

"C'mon. Hug me. Don't leave me hanging."

Sighing, resigned, I wrap my arms around her waist. She's so strong . . . and yet so soft. I feel the long, hard muscles in her back and torso, the smooth curve of her hips. My teeth clench.

"Thank you," she whispers against my ear.

A shiver runs through me that I barely suppress, but if Ziggy notices, she doesn't let on. She just pulls away, flashing another one of those smiles that rips out the air I've just managed to draw in.

"Your turn," she says, pulling her keys from her leggings' pocket.

"My turn?"

"To come up with something friendly to do."

I frown. "What would I know about that?"

As she opens her door, Ziggy smiles her widest yet. "You'll figure something out. I have faith in you."

TEN

Sebastian

Playlist: "Good Luck," Broken Bells

Ren looks as surprised to see me as I am surprised to be at his doorstep. Damn Ziggy and her parting words.

I have faith in you.

I stood outside her apartment, as aggravating, frustrating urgency crawled through me. I tried to shake it off, to lose it, as I turned from her place, hoping walking away from her would wrench me free from it, pull me back into my old self.

But instead, I got to my house, showered, and walked the short distance to Ren's.

Because absurdly, I seem to want to deserve Ziggy's faith in me. And apparently, that starts with paying a confessional visit to the person who led me to her.

"Seb?" Ren's expression morphs from puzzled to pleased as he opens his front door and steps back. "Come in."

"Thanks." I shut the door behind me and follow Ren, grateful Pazza doesn't seem to be around to harass me. That dog lives for my torture. "Sorry for coming by without a heads-up."

"You're always welcome, Seb." Ren smiles over his shoulder as he leads me into the kitchen. "Something to drink? Water? Tea? Coffee?"

"No, thanks." Drumming my fingers on the counter, I grit my teeth. I hate this. Caring. Trying. It makes me feel like I've unzipped my skin and let it drop to a puddle at my feet, leaving me unnaturally, terribly exposed. I'm long past deluding myself that I don't care or try with Ren, even in my limited capacity. So, I do my best to breathe through my discomfort and search for the right words. "I need to say something," I finally grit out.

Ren turns slowly, his expression growing pensive as he faces me and searches my eyes. "Okay. I'm listening."

Clearing my throat, I stare down at the ground, then force myself to look up and meet his gaze. How do I say this in a way that's honest but doesn't betray Ziggy's trust and reveal her plan? "At your wedding . . ."

Ren tips his head, and the gesture's so like Ziggy, I squeeze my eyes shut, then scrub my face with my hands. "Ziggy and I bumped into each other, and . . . talked . . . in a way . . . we haven't before."

So far, this is entirely honest. Am I leaving out crucial details? Like the fact that our talking at all was a novelty, since I'd pointedly avoided more than a cool *hello* since I met her? Or that as I watched her hike up that dress, all I could think was how much I wanted to fall to my knees, spin her around, and bury my face in those freckled thighs? Or that when I dragged her into the light, and her eyes locked with mine, there was a moment I nearly wrenched her into my arms and kissed her?

Yes. I am leaving out those details.

Not because I'm trying to get around a truly uncomfortable confession—well, not *primarily* because of that—but because they'd undermine our pretend-friend ruse, and more importantly, they're irrelevant; I will *never* act on those impulses.

I will never have her all the ways I've fantasized about having her. I will never taste her, kiss her, until I'm light-headed from favoring her soft, lush mouth over the intrusive need for air. I'll starve those unspoken truths inside me until they wilt and die. No need for Ren to know something that will one day be obsolete.

Ren's quiet, watching me, waiting, kind, patient, steady, as always, as I search for the words to further explain myself. "Since then, we've . . . sort of hit it off."

The terrible truth is that's not a lie either. I've only spent an evening and a morning with her—cornered on my rooftop patio, eating beside her on the hood of my car, undeniably bonding with her somehow at yoga, seated across the restaurant table for breakfast—but we *have* hit it off. I like her, dammit. Worse, I think she likes me, too. At least, the version of me that's trying to appear to behave myself.

"Only as friends would hit it off," I add, very deliberate in how I phrase that. It implies we're friends without explicitly saying we're friends. I haven't lied to him.

Ren leans a hip against his kitchen counter, arms loosely crossed over his chest, and smiles. "Seb, that's great."

My stomach knots. "I wasn't sure you'd think that."

A furrow settles between his eyebrows. "Why wouldn't I think that?"

"Because I'm a jackass with a horrible reputation and Ziggy is . . . the opposite. She's kind. Good. Angelic."

Ren snorts a laugh, pushing off the counter before he strolls to his fridge, pulls out a seltzer, and offers me one. I shake my head. "My baby sister"—he cracks open the seltzer—"is the kindest. And certainly good. But 'angelic' is pushing it. She's capable of some formidable pranks, has terrifyingly accurate tickle-dar, and not only can out-sprint every single one of us but has zero problem gloating about it."

I feel a smile lift my mouth and drop my chin, staring down at the ground so he won't see that. "I've experienced the tickle-dar. It's brutal."

Ren laughs again. "Right?"

Forcing my face into cool blandness, I peer up and hold his

gaze. "I want you to know . . . I respect how much she means to you, how protective you are of her. I won't forget that."

Ren's smile deepens. His eyes crinkle at the corners. "I know you won't, Seb."

I hate how much that means, to have his trust in this. And I can't deny how much it means either. "Thank you."

"So," he says, "the pictures of you two at Betty's Diner, then at breakfast today, and the angry yoga story online are making a lot more sense."

I stare at him, wide-eyed. "There's something online already?"

Ren nods. "I've got Google alerts set for my family. Popped up about half an hour ago."

"They named Ziggy?"

He shakes his head. "No. They named you."

"I'm not . . ." My voice dies off. "I'm not your family."

"To me you are," he says, scrolling through his phone, like he hasn't just dropped an existential grenade at my feet.

I can't risk the obliterating impact of that statement, so I don't touch it. Instead, I pull out my phone and scour the first article I find. "'Yuval Burns,'" I read, "'founder of angry yoga, was seen leaving Seb Gauthier's home, not long after followed by Seb himself and an unknown redhead driving his car, most likely due to his injured foot, which would prohibit safe driving.

"'Seb and his companion were then seen at Café du Monde, laughing and enjoying a hearty breakfast. Is she his minder? Friend? Something more? We'll report back when we have details.'"

Groaning, I drop my phone on the counter. "'An unknown redhead.' She's going to love that."

Ren frowns. "Ziggy's never been comfortable stepping into the spotlight. I doubt she'll mind having flown under the radar."

A weird pinch in my chest stops me from saying more. It's odd and unreasonably satisfying to know something about his sister that he doesn't. The Bergmans clearly don't recognize how much Ziggy *wants* to be seen. Somewhere along the way, the people who loved her best lost sight of the fact that just because you've lived one way for a time doesn't mean you want to live that way always, that your struggle to evolve isn't an indicator of a lack of *desire* to evolve. It just means . . . it's hard. And it might be a hell of a lot easier if the people around you saw your possibility.

Fierce, piercing pride floods me. *I'm* that person for Ziggy. At least, I can be. Not just someone whose tough image can roughen hers up. But someone who shows her that he recognizes her possibility.

"Maybe that's changing," I hedge, pushing off the counter, pocketing my phone. "I'm going to head out."

"You sure?" he asks. "Want to stay for lunch? Frankie will be back soon."

Oh Christ, not Frankie. She'll have gotten a whiff of that yoga story, seen the pictures of Ziggy and me, and while I'm confident I can navigate this dynamic with Ren, Frankie has a terrifying ability to sniff out my bullshit and scare the hell out of me for it.

"That's okay," I tell him. "I'm still full from breakfast."

He frowns. "Well, all right. Let me know if I can pick you up soon, maybe we can . . ." He shrugs. "I don't know, catch up a bit. You've been lying low because you're healing and Frankie's . . . trying to figure out how to fix things for you, but I miss seeing you."

When I first got to know Ren, this staggeringly honest communication, the emotional openness, made me deeply uncomfortable. That's not how my family works, not how I was raised. But since becoming close to him in the past few years, I've come to admire the bravery that requires. That he can look at me and tell me he misses me, that he can admit his needs and wants, so freely, without fear.

"I've—" I clear my throat. "Same here. I actually, uh . . ." I clear my throat again. "I actually was wondering if maybe . . . That is, I was thinking . . ."

Ren's smile is faint and amused. He lifts his eyebrows, waiting.

"I was thinking . . . maybe I could join your Shakespeare Club."

The smile on his face shouldn't be humanly possible, it's so bright. "Seriously?"

I shrug. "Seriously. Ziggy didn't admit to there being a club, but she said that *hypothetically*, if there was a Shakespeare Club, it was a damn good time. And I could use that. Some fun that isn't . . . empty."

Ren smooshes me into a hard backslapping hug. "I'd love it, Seb! You'll love it, too. All you have to do is—"

"Memorize and recite some of my favorite Shakespeare for at least two members of the club. If they agree that I perform genuinely, I'm invited to be a part of it."

He nods as he steps back from our hug, still smiling. "She told you, then, good. Okay. Cool. Well, lucky for you, our next meeting is two weeks from now. Saturday, six sharp, my place, so get memorizing."

Shit. That escalated quickly. "Uh. So soon?"

"It'll be great," he says. "You'll be great." I'm hugged once more as I'm about to argue, make up some excuse to buy me a little more time, but the look Ren gives me, his excitement and happiness, stops me.

After promising to be there, I see myself out. I take my time as I walk, watching the sun climb higher in the sky, feeling the sea breeze cut through my hair, whipping it back.

When I get to my place, I wander around, until my hands find their way to the bookshelves lining the small back room that I keep tucked away, private, just for me. Sliding my fingers along the spines of the books, I find the volume I want, tug it out from the shelf, and sink down into my chair.

The sharp, aching pain that's become more frequent lately, nearly after every time I eat, claws into my stomach. I suck in a breath and tuck up my legs, gaining some relief in the pressure of wedging a pillow against my stomach, tight between my chest and thighs.

The pain's bad. Bad enough that I'm starting to think this isn't something I should keep ignoring any more than I've been ignoring the throbbing body aches, the thick fog wrapped around my brain, turning my thoughts sludgy and slow.

I should get myself checked out, get to the bottom of this. Especially now that I'm so close to coming back to hockey. The idea of trying to skate, to play at full capacity, when I feel like this—it seems impossible.

And yet, I'm so tempted to keep avoiding it. I don't want to know what could be wrong, what could come between me and my identity as a healthy, active person, let alone someone who relies on that for my career and the one thing I love—hockey.

Gritting my teeth against the pain, I let my eyes settle over the words, and I think about saying them in front of Ziggy. The pain doesn't dull, but I'm distracted, even if only briefly, by a calm sense of contented purpose.

It's strange. And sort of lovely.

Glancing up, seeing my reflection in my windows, which looks so much like my piece-of-shit father, I'm reminded swiftly, brutally, what this little foray into allegedly reforming myself is, all it can be—

A performance that will have to come to an end.

ELEVEN

Ziggy

Playlist: "Sheets of Green," Cat Clyde

"'An unknown redhead'?!" I growl at my screen, squeezing my phone so hard, my sensory-friendly bubble-backed case makes a series of ominous pops.

"Easy does it." Charlie, my best friend and teammate, plucks the phone from my grip and slips it back into my bag, which is shoved at the base of my cubby. "Let's go take out our anger on a soccer ball and let your phone live to see another day."

"'An unknown redhead'!"

She grips me by the elbow and drags me toward the exit of our locker room. "Yes, I heard you. Just breathe. Get yourself out on the field, and we'll deal with this."

My heartbeat's pounding in my ears. I barely register our trek out to the field, where Charlie salutes Karla, our Angel City coach, and then proceeds to jog out across the field. Stopping at the cluster of balls that sit in its center, she one-touch boots a ball my way, forcing me out of my head.

It's like she knows me or something, that only a soccer ball flying toward my face could wrench me out of my spiraling thoughts. I one-touch it back to her, cracking the ball hard.

An audible grunt leaves Charlie as she takes my pass—or more accurately, line-drive—to the chest and drops it to the ground, then sends it flying across the field to me. I run onto it, then dribble her way. Stopping at Charlie's feet, I set my foot on the ball and meet her eyes, hands on my hips. "Sorry."

"It's fine." She tugs her short, dark hair into a ponytail at the top of her head. "My boobs haven't been bruised in a while. They were overdue."

I snort a laugh, scrubbing my face. "I'm mad."

"Understandably so." Charlie pokes the ball away from my feet and starts to juggle it. "You are not an 'unknown redhead.' You are Ziggy Freaking Bergman, and it's about time the world knew it."

"I'm trying, Char."

Charlie lifts a tiny hand (she's pocket-size and has tiny everything), frowning up at me, hazel eyes narrowed. "You're doing great. I'm not blaming you. I'm blaming this sexist news machine that fixates on male athletes and traditionally masculinized sports. You are one of the most promising, talented, highest-performing midfielders soccer has ever seen. You were a high scorer your entire career at UCLA, and you're starting both this and the National Team. The tabloids *should* know who you are, and you shouldn't have to do this ridiculous publicity stunt with that good-for-nothing Seb Gau—"

"Shhh," I hiss, glancing around. "Charlotte, do not make me regret telling you that."

"Simmer your soccer shorts. I said it quietly."

"Charlie, I'm serious, if the truth gets out, it will undermine and ruin everything we—"

"*We?*" she says emphatically. "You're a 'we' now?"

I clear my throat. "Everything *I* am trying to do."

"Uh-huh." Charlie folds her arms across her chest. "You're not throat clearing your way past that one. Since when are you and that urchin a 'we'?"

"We're not a 'we,' it was just linguistically efficient to say it."

Charlie raises her eyebrows.

Sighing, I gesture to the soccer ball at her feet. "Can we kick a ball around, please? Before we get yelled at?"

Charlie scowls but relents, flicking the ball up and juggling between her feet, then passing it to me. I juggle it up onto my thighs, down to my feet, before I drop the ball to the field and dribble far enough away to buy me space from Charlie's mind-reading tendencies.

I love having a friend who knows me this well—except when I'm trying to hide some slightly murky feelings about a certain very complicated, badly behaved fake friend who keeps surprising me with tiny moments of goodness that threaten to make me actually *like* him. And given how attracted I am to Sebastian Gauthier, that is a very bad idea.

I'll get a handle on it. I'm working on reining myself in. Until then, Charlie *can't* know I'm torn about Sebastian. And if I stick too close, let her do her mind-reading, best-friend wizardry, she definitely will.

Charlie is my oldest friend, my only friend from when I was little and we still lived up in Washington State. We sent each other letters and doodles for years after my family moved down to LA for Dad's job as an oncologist at Ronald Reagan Medical, but when I started struggling socially in middle school and my mental health suffered, I got really bad at keeping in touch.

Charlie and I never stopped talking, but it spaced out for years, until she reached out and told me she was going to USC.

Our schools might have been rivals, but it did nothing to keep us apart—we started reconnecting then, building back closeness. Since we both signed with Angel City, the bond between us is strong as ever, and I'm so grateful for it. I've never really been good at making friends—too much social anxiety about trying to get to know new people, too much family to fill in my time and keep me busy so I never got too lonely or hungry for more than that. Charlie is the sweet spot—someone I had a foundation with and didn't have to overcome profound anxiety to get close to, who's known me nearly as long and as well as my family does but exists outside their chaos so I can turn to her when they're driving me up the wall.

Charlie is my person—I can go to her for anything. Except for help with Project Ziggy Bergman 2.0.

Because Charlie *hates* publicity and loves being a nobody. Then again, if I grew up the child of two of the biggest celebrities in Hollywood at the time and was dragged across the tabloids for the better part of a decade during their tempestuous on-again, off-again relationship (I mean *tempestuous*—her parents have so far married and divorced each other three times), I'd want to be a nobody, too.

Charlie loves her private, peaceful life, and her partner, Gigi, who she met freshman year at USC. Gigi is a former child TV star turned celebrity stylist who loves flying under the radar, living behind the scenes now, too. Gigi and I were there when Charlie was weighing even going pro with soccer, knowing it would lead to increased visibility. But her love of the game won out, and the work of years in therapy made her feel prepared to handle the exposure signing with Angel City might lead to. Even then, it hasn't been easy for her.

On top of her antipathy to being in the spotlight, she'd be the last person to know how to help me toughen up my image—Charlie is infinitely sweeter and better behaved than me. She's always been like that.

When we met in Washington State, where she lived with her mom during her parents' first acrimonious divorce, Charlie was the kindest, gentlest little kid in the eye of a truly terrible storm, unlike her older brother and sister, who processed the trauma of their childhoods by being absolute terrors. Harry was volatile—loud

and angry, constantly getting into trouble and lashing out. Tallulah, on the other hand, was deceptively quiet and deeply unnerving, like the silence right before an earthshaking storm.

Then there was Charlie—always warm and friendly; she smiled
lots and gave hard hugs and loved tromping through the woods.
Charlie was my age and got what it was like to be the baby in a social sphere where everyone was older than you. She was happy to
disappear with me into imaginative worlds and be faery queens and
brave maiden warriors; to make soup from flowers, leaves, and mud;
to befriend baby birds and adopt the family of bunnies that demol-
ished my mom's vegetable garden at the A-frame, our family's get-
away home, which became a refuge for Charlie, too.

Charlie has always been so good to me. Knowing what she's
been through, how she's learned to cope and live in a way that makes
her happy, I could never ask her to go through anything that made
her miserable like she was when she was in the spotlight as a kid.

I think Charlie knows this, that I didn't ask for her help, even
in the ways she could, because I'm trying to shield her from what it
would expose her to. When I told her what I was doing, she didn't
disapprove of my plan to put myself out there a little more, get noticed, and take the chance to change my image. But she *definitely*
disapproved of my plan involving Sebastian.

"Listen," she says, jogging up to me, breathing heavily. My mind's
been spinning in place, but Charlie and I have been running, sending long, hard one-touch passes to each other across the field. "Fact
is, I don't trust that guy. That's all there is to it. He is—"

"Despicable," I finish for her. "Yes, I know. You've told me,
Charlie, and I've told you I'm aware of his reputation. That's *why*
I'm doing this with him."

Her scowl returns as she squints up at me. "I know you're leaning on him because you don't feel like you can lean on me, and I
hate that—"

"Charlie—"

"No, listen. I also selfishly appreciate it. I am not ready to put myself in the spaces you want to be in right now, and you and I are secure enough in our friendship that we can both own our boundaries as well as honor each other's. I know you don't resent me for not being able to do this for you. You've just outsourced."

I bite my lip. "I really do think he's a good outsource."

"Oh, on paper, heck yes. But the thing you have to be careful of is not to count on him for *anything* beyond that. People like Seb Gauthier don't change, Ziggy. Ask me how I know." She lifts her eyebrows. "My parents are self-absorbed, self-destructive, and reliable for one thing: their unreliability. Sebastian's cut from that same cloth."

I swallow the questions that are burning in my throat: How does she know that? How and when can anyone decide they have a fundamental read on a person's character, let alone know that character is immutable?

I don't ask Charlie those questions, because it's territory we don't venture into. It would come dangerously close to sounding like I question her view on incredibly difficult parts of her past. I can't do that. So I'm quiet, waiting for what comes next.

"I can't go out with you," Charlie says, wiping sweat from her forehead, eyes narrowed against the sun. "But I can certainly help make sure you aren't 'an unknown redhead' for much longer."

I frown down at her. "How?"

Charlie smiles, slow and just about as close to wicked as I think she'll ever come. "Come home with me after practice. We'll let Gigi work her magic."

Charlie's got me covered, all right, but just barely, if we're going by the dress she hooked me up with. I stare at my reflection in the mirror, specifically the dress's hem, which is dangerously close to revealing *everything*. "If I so much as sneeze," I tell her and Gigi, "I'm going to flash the whole place."

Gigi chuckles as she plucks a pin from between her teeth and slips it along the hem of the dark green dress that she raided from her closet. "Wardrobe malfunctions are great publicity."

I wrinkle my nose. "How?"

Charlie stands behind me, arms folded across her chest as she watches Gigi work. "You know what they say. No such thing as bad publicity."

"I'm no expert, but I think there is absolutely bad publicity, and it would definitely be bad publicity if my first identifying moment in a major news outlet was exposing myself."

Gigi sits back on her heels, head tipped as she examines the hem and its precarious location at the edge of my butt cheeks. "Okay, maybe you're right. This is a little short. I'll take it down."

A sigh of relief leaves me as she starts to take out pins and lowers the hem.

"So," Charlie says, walking around to face me. "Let's recap and talk strategy."

I nod. "Okay."

"First of all, this is your move, your moment. Remember that. *You* took charge, and this Friday is *your* night. The charity event's after-party is the perfect sweet spot for being a little naughty but still classy."

"Kudos to Seb for coming through with that on such short notice," Gigi says.

Charlie glares at Gigi, but it's tinged with affection and lacks heat. "Of course he came through. Parties like that are brimming with hypocrites like him and are a dime a dozen. Rich people wearing expensive clothes, pretending they give a shit about people who aren't rich and can't afford expensive clothes, after donating a paltry amount of their wealth to a cause, when, if all those fancy fools simply donated the money they spent on their clothes for these events and after-parties, the very issues they raise money for would be eradicated."

"That's . . . bleak," I mutter.

Gigi snorts. "Welcome to the life of the rich and famous."

I *was* surprised Seb came through so quickly after I texted him, with the news he had an event that would work this coming Friday. But now it sounds like maybe that was silly, to be surprised, given how prevalent Charlie and Gigi said these sorts of functions are.

"On to logistics," my best friend tells me. "At both the event and the after-party, the two of you shouldn't spend any time alone, not in a corner, not on a couch, not on the dance floor. That's too couple-y. Either join a group together and stick with them, or divide and conquer, mingling with others, got it?"

I nod.

"Next. Be very careful what you say or how you behave and how it could be taken out of context. You have to think about the worst possible way you could be perceived, then work backward from that to avoid it. You want your image to have an edge, not fall clean off the cliff of decency."

I snort. "The cliff of—" I sober, seeing how seriously Charlie's staring at me. "Sorry. Go ahead."

"She sounds like a chaperone in an Austen novel," Gigi says as she takes another pin out of her mouth and slides it along the hem, "but she's right. It's a fine line to walk. Our cultural narrative paints women, especially those in the public eye, with one of two brushes—sinner or saint, nothing in between."

"Exactly." Charlie meets my eyes in the mirror. "What you're trying to do is exist in a space that the tabloids, let alone society, don't generally recognize, so just . . . be careful."

I set a hand over my pounding heart and rub it, trying to calm myself. "I will."

"Also, if that creep so much as *looks* at your butt in this dress," Charlie growls, "I will break his eyeballs."

Feeling my cheeks heat, I glance over my shoulder at my backside, which, like my hips, filled out in college, transforming my beanpole frame to a pear. "Is the dress . . . is it too tight on my butt?"

"Hardly," Gigi says, chuckling. "It's perfect. Now I'm just making sure everyone will see that."

Swallowing nervously, I glance back at my reflection, the dark green fabric, soft and stretchy, hugging every curve of my body. "Okay."

"Go ahead and take it off," Gigi says, leaning back.

I step into her walk-in closet and slip off the dress, marveling at the sheer volume of clothes surrounding me. Gigi says she has more designer samples and castaways than she knows what to do with, and it sure looks like it, even after she and Charlie raided her closet for me. After trying on options and deciding what I liked, I've got a black stretchy romper for Friday's event, a few colorful sundresses for future use, and this dark green number for the event's after-party, which, with a few minor alterations, should be a perfect fit.

"Don't get dressed," Gigi calls from her room, where I already hear the sewing machine whirring. "Just grab a robe from in there. Fixing this hem won't take more than a few minutes, and I'm going to have you try this on again once I'm done."

I glance around, finding a robe of pale peach silk covered in scarlet roses and dark green vines, and throw it on. There's no sash to tie it, so I tug it tight around me, then step out, arms pinning it to my waist.

Gigi does a double take when she glances up from her sewing machine. "Oooh, I like that on you! Take it."

"I—no." Peering down at the fabric, I shake my head. "I can't take this from you."

"Please take it," Charlie says. "Her closet is about to burst, she's got so much stuff."

Gigi throws Charlie a playful scowl before she smiles my way again. "It's never going to get used. Those aren't my colors, and they're definitely yours. Take it. But first—" She stands, holding up the dress. "Try this on again."

Dress back on, I stand in front of the mirror. Gigi is just a few inches shorter than me and has the same size feet, so I'm wearing a pair of her kitten-heel tan pumps, which miraculously don't pinch my toes. I stare at my reflection and grimace. "It's a lot of skin."

"Beautiful skin," Gigi says. "Freckles are very in right now."

Charlie tips her head, examining me. "You do look uncomfortable. And that's not what we want."

"Wait!" Gigi grabs the peach silk robe from her bed and slides it up my arms. "But it's a robe," I tell her.

Gigi grins. "It's not a robe, sweet pea. It's a wrap. And it's perfect for this. You can take it off if you eventually feel comfortable showing more skin, or you can just wear it all night. You'll look sexy and edgy either way."

I peer at my reflection, warming to what I'm seeing. The dress's scoop neckline is low, but I don't have much in the way of breasts, so it sits flat against my chest, revealing just a shadow of cleavage, which feels good to me. With the silky wrap draped over my shoulders, down my arms, I'm more at ease—a little out of my comfort zone but not too much.

I catch Charlie's scowl in the mirror's reflection and stare at her, puzzled.

"You look amazing," Gigi tells me. "And now you feel like it, don't you?"

I nod, a smile winning out. "Yeah, I do."

Gigi swats Charlie's shoulder. "Hey there, Miss Sunshine. Be happy for her."

Charlie's scowl deepens. It's unsettling to see my always-happy friend looking so bleak. "You look like a million bucks," she says, meeting my eyes. "And I'm happy for you."

"So you're frowning, why?" Gigi asks.

Charlie steps back and folds her arms across her chest again. "She's about to go dancing with the devil. *That*, I don't have to be happy about one bit."

———————

I'm nervous as I let myself into Ren and Frankie's house the next morning. I'm overdue for this conversation with my brother, and that's because I've been avoiding it. Because the brother I've trusted with some of my hardest truths is the one I'm about to come pretty close to lying to.

I'm going to try my best to be as honest as possible.

Frankie must still be sleeping, because I see only the top of Ren's head through the sliding glass doors leading out to their deck. After doctoring up a cup of milky coffee, I step out onto the patio and find my brother sitting in a deck chair, feet on the railing as he stares out at the ocean and Pazza, who streaks by on the sand, chasing after her ball. He glances over his shoulder and smiles, then stands to give me a hug. "Hey, Zigs."

"Hey, Ren." After our hug hello, I ease into a chair beside him and sit, legs crisscrossed.

Pazza bounds up the steps to me, wet with salt water as she drops the ball at my feet and pants happily. I give her a good rub behind her ears, then, after she snatches it up again, I take the ball from her mouth and lob it back out onto the sand. "So."

Ren glances my way and smiles. "So."

"I, uh . . . may have poached your friend."

Ren's eyes crinkle as his smile deepens. "I've heard."

Thank God I have my coffee mug in front of my mouth, because there's no other way I'd manage to hide my shocked, dropped-jaw expression. Burying my face in my mug, I finally take a gulp of coffee. By the time I've swallowed and glanced up, I've made sure my face is relaxed.

Sebastian talked to him about us? "What did he say?"

Ren sips his coffee, glancing back out at the ocean, tracking Pazza as she chases her tail, then flops onto the sand and rolls around in it. "Oh, not a lot. Just that you two hit it off at the wedding—as friends. That he knew how much you mean to me and he wanted me to know that you're safe with him."

My jaw clenches. *Safe.* Like I'm some fragile thing to handle with care. "Safe, huh?" I mutter into my coffee, before gulping down some more.

Ren's brow furrows. He angles himself toward me, head tipped. "Are you upset about that?"

Exhaling slowly, I set my mug on the arm of my deck chair. "I'm a little tired of being talked about in such . . . protective, bubble-wrap terms. I'm not an innocent little girl anymore, not a struggling teenager, either. I'm strong and capable, and I can handle being friends with Sebastian Gauthier without you two needing to have some patriarchal chat about my 'safety.'"

Ren blinks at me, brow furrowing deeper. "I . . . take your point. I hadn't considered it in that way. I saw it as Seb owning that he's frankly pretty careless with most things in his life, and wanting me to know, as someone who loves you, that you weren't going to be one of them. The content of what he said was reassuring, yes, but much more so, it was the fact that he made a point of saying it at all."

I tip my head. "What do you mean?"

"I mean that I know Seb well enough to have been a little anxious when the conversation began and your name was in the mix, because I've seen the kind of trouble and hurt that he gets tangled up in. While I would never expect him to *intentionally* tangle you up in that, too, the truth is his past dictates that you could have been inadvertently hurt along the way. So I appreciated him telling me he's being intentional about keeping you safe from *that*.

"Even then, my biggest relief was that he came to me and spoke so openly about becoming friends with you. Talking like that is hard for Seb, and yet he made a concerted effort to do it anyway. That means a lot."

I sip from my cup, mulling this over, warmth spreading through me that has nothing to do with the fresh, hot coffee I just swallowed. Framed that way, I think maybe what Sebastian did means a lot to me, too.

Cradling my hands around my cup, I tell my brother, "Thanks for explaining it. That . . . helps."

Ren stares at me, searching my face. "I'm sorry if I've ever made you feel overprotected, Ziggy. I just want to be there for you."

"I know, Ren. I'm beyond grateful for all the ways you've been there for me when I needed it. I just . . . want you to be there for the me who's here *now*, not who *was*. Make sense?"

He nods slowly. "Yeah, it does."

I stare out at the ocean, a smile tipping my mouth as Pazza barks emphatically, scaring off a seagull. After she bounds my way with her ball again and I throw it out toward the surf, Ren and I sit side by side in companionable quiet, drinking our coffee. While I turn over this little insight into Sebastian.

I'm trying hard not to let fuzzy warmth wrap itself around my heart like a fire-warmed blanket, but it's hard. It's hard not to feel good, knowing even while we're just *pretending* to be friends, that Sebastian cared enough to talk to Ren openly, healthily, that he made a promise to his best friend that he and I won't get mixed up in things that could hurt either of us. He wouldn't lie to Ren—he loves him too much, that's obvious, even if he tries to hide it—which means Sebastian Gauthier, for all his huffing and puffing about not *actually* reforming himself, just might be reforming a little after all.

Pazza's bark startles me and pulls me from my thoughts. I catch Ren watching me curiously, a small smile on his face, before he whistles softly and calls Pazza back when she starts to go too far down the sand.

"So." I clear my throat. "Part of why I wanted to tell you about me and Seb, you know, being friends, is I'm going to the roller race fundraiser Friday night. With him. As his guest."

Ren blinks rapidly, clearly confused. "But it'll be chaos, Ziggy. You hate events like that . . ." His voice dies off as he looks at me, searching my expression. "You . . . *don't* hate events like that?"

I shrug. "It's not my ideal environment, but part of what I've been sorting out since I started college is how I can enjoy those kinds of chaotic environments sometimes. I like your teammates. I love kids. I think it's an incredible initiative. So, I figured out how to make it accessible for me. I've got it covered."

My brother peers into his coffee mug, frowning thoughtfully. "I never invited you to it before because I thought you'd feel pressure to come, or feel like I didn't know what's difficult for you—"

"I know." I set my hand on his arm and squeeze gently. "I know you meant well."

He sighs, rubbing across his shut eyes. "I feel like a really crappy brother right now."

"Ren, no." I set aside my coffee cup and throw an arm around him, resting my head on his shoulder. "You're a wonderful brother. Years ago, I would have felt that way, had you invited me."

"But people change," he says quietly. "And it's important to remember that." He glances my way, then rests his head on mine as we both peer out at the ocean, lulled by its steady roar. "I'm sorry I forgot."

I swallow against the lump in my throat and squeeze his shoulder harder. "I'm sorry I didn't speak up for myself. I'm learning. I'm trying to do better."

"I'll do better, too," he says quietly, then after a moment, "I'm glad you're going. Frankie will be *delighted*."

I smile. "We'll be earplug twins." Like me, Frankie is autistic and struggles with complexly noisy environments—she's the one who turned me on to earplugs for that very reason years ago.

He laughs softly. "Yeah. You will."

After one last squeeze to his shoulder, I ease back and settle into my chair, cupping my coffee in both hands again. A muscle in my back twinges as I shift, and I wince.

"What's up?" he asks, observant as always.

"Oh, just tweaked a little something in my back during angry yoga. Sebastian and I went real hard on those *chaturangas*."

Ren nearly drops his coffee mug, then catches it. "Whew. Too much caffeine." He sets the mug on the ground beside him. "So, uh, this angry yoga. How was it? I mean, how'd that go?"

I meet his gaze, searching his face for some clue as to whether or not Sebastian told him how far I lost it, but there's nothing I can read in Ren's expression, just a sort of odd curiosity. "I said a lot of swear words and got out some repressed feelings. I haven't really processed all of what that was, but I just know it felt good to get it out."

Ren nods slowly. "Right. So . . . was it, like, a partner thing? You know, where you do poses together?"

"Yeah. Well, kind of. We did the same flow, facing each other. It was a 'supported practice,' Yuval called it."

A quiet hum leaves Ren as he bites his lip, just like I tend to when I'm thinking something over, and he glances toward the sand, eyes on Pazza. "Do you two . . . plan to do it again?"

I nod before sipping my coffee. "Yeah, this Wednesday, actually. Why do you ask?"

A beat of silence stretches between us but for Ren's fingers tapping on the arms of his deck chair. A furrow forms in his brow. "Just wondering."

TWELVE

Sebastian

Playlist: "Outnumbered," Dermot Kennedy

My stomach hurts like hell, and I'm telling myself it's nerves. Because for the first time in my career, I'm actually attending one of our team's mushy-gushy, feel-good fundraisers, and I'm doing it sober as a saint.

It's not that I don't like my teammates or that I don't support raising money for childhood cancer research. I do. No, I don't get cuddly and socialize with them, but we get along fine; and privately, I make sure a good portion of my income goes to a number of philanthropic outlets—I just make sure that shit never leaks.

Because if I did regularly show my face at these events, if I did publicize where my money went, it would nudge my dastardly public image into precariously positive territory. And I can't have that, when every way that I fuck up shows my stepfather I don't give two shits about his disapproval and humiliates my father, who walked out on my mother and me and who has his own professional hockey legacy that I'm determined to tarnish as much as possible by association with his no-good son.

This has been my plan for years, and I've stuck to it. Well, until recently, when I realized it was about to cost me hockey. And now I'm on this bizarre detour, digging myself a little out of the hole I purposefully made, just enough to get my place on the team secure again, to keep my grip on hockey safe and secure.

Me being seen at this team-run charity event, our annual Roller Race for Research of Childhood Cancer, will go a long way in hopefully repairing my standing with the Kings' management, and Ziggy will get her moment in the spotlight at the event, then have a place to be a little wild, at the after-party at Tyler's. It's just right for both our agendas. And yet I have the funniest feeling it's going to go all wrong.

As I finish buttoning up my shirt, I examine my appearance, making sure everything's in place—the silver chains I always wear, no buttons off my chambray shirt, sleeves cuffed to my elbows.

In front of the mirror, I fuss with my hair more, adjust the collar of my shirt again. I check the line of my scruff that I shaved along my neck to keep it neat.

A jaunty whistle of "You're So Vain" suddenly echoes in my bathroom, and I startle. Thank God I don't still have the razor at my neck, because if I did, I'd have risked slitting my throat.

I spin around, heart pounding from surprise.

And then my heart's pounding for an entirely different reason.

Ziggy stands framed in the doorway. Black strappy romper, legs for days, a pair of rainbow high-top Nikes. She wears colorful, dangly tasseled earrings that jingle softly when she walks closer.

Jesus Christ, she's gorgeous.

"Have you heard of knocking?" The words leave me, hoarse and thin.

Ziggy stares at me, her cheeks turning progressively pinker as she bites her lip and shrugs. "Why knock when I know how to get in?"

I tear my gaze away, because I can't take looking at her one more second. "A basic respect for private property. Come on. We'll be late if we don't leave soon."

I brush by her, leaving her in my wake as I stroll across my bedroom to the dresser, gathering my wallet, the key for the Cayenne, which I've kept on me for her to use, since she seemed comfortable driving that last time.

Even after I've made sure I have everything I need, she's quiet. Too quiet. Turning, I see her standing in my bathroom, staring at her reflection in the mirror, eyes wide.

Concerned, I walk her way, until I stop right behind her.

Our eyes meet in the mirror. A slow deep breath lifts her chest, like she's trying to calm herself. She swallows thickly. Then I feel it . . . she's trembling.

It's like that moment at the diner, when I saw her white-knuckle the menu and realized something was very wrong. Except this is much worse. Now I know what scares her, what makes her breathing tight, makes her freeze up in fear.

It happens before I process it, my body stepping closer. My hands settle on her shoulders, and warmth seeps to my palms. I squeeze gently and feel her shoulders fall, tension seep out of her posture.

A rush of relief crests through me, knowing it helped. Already an addict, I go for my next fix, slide my palms down her arms, over warm, satin-soft skin, and squeeze her forearms, too. Her hands drop from fists to slack fingertips.

Another wave of relief knocks into me, seeing how it soothes her, reassuring me that I can keep going. Even if I shouldn't. I *know* I shouldn't. I don't deserve to touch her, comfort her, offer her anything of me. But I am selfish and greedy, and I want this moment to know that even in all my undeserving, I can give her this.

Our gazes hold as I press my hands lower, until our palms run over each other's and our fingers link. Her eyes fall shut. Her head lists back against my jaw.

I stare at her because it's safe to while her eyes are closed, drinking in the tiniest details, the freckles dusting her nose, across her cheeks and throat, the soft strawberry tendrils of hair at her temples, curled around her ears. The dark auburn roots of her lashes, burnished to gold tips.

I have never been this close to something this unspeakably good. I have never wanted more to be worthy of it.

And I never will be. I wouldn't even try, risking failure with someone like Ziggy, who, in just a week's time, has shown me how deeply she feels, how deeply my disappointing her would hurt. And I *would* disappoint her.

I'm not capable of everything she deserves. But maybe I'm capable of a little . . . to a small extent. Maybe I could earn my place as her *actual* friend, someone lucky enough to exist in her orbit, without ever drawing too destructively close.

As her hands tighten their grip in mine and a soft smile lifts her mouth, I have the faint, desperate hope that this dream I've allowed myself could become real. That for once, I could have something a little good, be capable of a little good myself, too. Just for the chance to have a sliver of her.

"Thank you," she whispers.

I squeeze her fingers back, then force myself to let them go. "Don't thank me."

Her eyes flutter open. She lifts her head from where it's rested against mine and tips it in curiosity. "Why not?"

My fingertips find hers again, dancing against them—one last, swift indulgence. "I don't want to be thanked, like I've done you some favor."

She wrinkles her nose. "But you did. You helped me feel calmer."

Freeing a piece of hair that's caught beneath her romper's strap, I avoid her eyes. "Just let me do those things, knowing that I want to, that I've done a lot of shitty things in my life, and the few good ones, well, they're the least I can do, especially when they're for you."

Her confused expression deepens. "Seb—"

"Sigrid." I clasp her hand, tugging her gently across my bedroom. I keep my back to the bed, doing everything I can to lock down my thoughts. I'm not going to think about how it felt when we tumbled onto *her* bed the night we stopped at her place and I felt her, warm and snug, against me. I'm not going to indulge the fantasy of tumbling with her down to my bed, pulling her over me until she falls, hips heavy on mine, long, thick hair an auburn tapestry shutting out the world, until it's only her hands and mine, mouths meeting, tongues touching, our bodies moving slow, then fast, aching and hungry.

Ziggy doesn't help anything. She glances toward my bed and blushes. Her eyes widen as she spots the prostate vibrator I inadvertently left on my nightstand after trying to work off this edge I can't seem to shake. "What *is* that—"

"Nothing." I slap a hand over her eyes and drag her out of the room.

"That was definitely not nothing!" Ziggy says as we start down the stairs.

"It was none of your business, is what it was, Sigrid."

A laugh jumps out of her. "Not even if I play the 'friends would tell each other' card?"

I fight a smile, walking ahead of her. "Especially if you do that."

At the bottom of the stairs, Ziggy turns toward my coat closet, where a garment bag hangs off the top. Carefully, she unzips it. "Before we go, and since you have quite the eye, Mr. High Fashion, I wanted your formal approval of this for the after-party. Thoughts?" She tips her head, stepping back, shoulder to shoulder with me as she peers at the outfit. "Oh, and picture this with tan heels, not my rainbow high-tops. Obviously."

I blink, staring at a dark green dress that makes my mouth water, just picturing it hugging her curves. Over it, a silk wrap that shimmers orange one moment, blush the next, the soft peach-pink of sunset spilled across bare skin and rumpled sheets. The fabric's covered in roses the same rich red as her hair, winding vines that match her eyes. I can see her in it, picture how she'll look—achingly beautiful.

I glance from the garment bag to her, marveling at her lovely profile while she frowns in thought at her outfit.

"Absolutely perfect," I tell her.

She turns her head my way, beaming. "Yeah?"

Don't look at her, that voice inside me snaps. *Don't drink her in. Don't want her.*

I can't help it any more than I can help the need to breathe. I'm so completely fucked. Swallowing roughly, I glance away, back at the outfit. "Yeah."

Satisfied, she strolls back to the closet and zips up the garment bag, then unhooks it from the door and throws it over her shoulder, a wide smile warming her face. "Well, if Sir Fancy Pants approves, then I can rest easy."

"I'm not a fancy pants," I mutter, opening the door that leads to my garage. "I just have sartorial standards."

"Ooh, *sartorial*." She stops right at the threshold, bracketed beneath my arm, so close I can see every freckle splashed across her nose. "What a great word."

Her gaze dances down me, then back up, a blush on her cheeks. "Speaking of sartorial standards," she says quietly, adjusting the bag draped over her shoulder, "you look handsome, Sebastian."

Goddamn her. It's so sincere. And sweet. So . . . her. It makes my pulse slam like a drumbeat, the way only filthy words spoken in the dark, in the most depraved whispers, should.

I take the bag from her shoulder, then nudge her across the threshold. "And you look like a fucking goddess. Now let's go."

Ziggy smiles as she drives, but as we get closer and closer to the rink, it becomes more of a grimace. "So, uh—" She clears her throat. "How are we going to play this?"

"Just be yourself. Give me shit when I deserve it, smile your fantastic smile, and I'll be there, trying my best not to be an asshole. We'll tell people we're friends, and act friendly. That's it."

She sighs. "It's just this is the first time we've had a live audience, besides Köhler. I don't want to give us away or make a mistake. *I know we're not really friends, but no one else does. We have to make sure it stays that way.*"

We're not really friends.

Those words shouldn't feel like a gut punch, but they do. I breathe through their impact, spinning my rings on my fingers.

"Where's this coming from?" I ask. "We've done fine so far. We'll do fine tonight, too."

"Group settings are a different animal for me, Sebastian. They're chaos; they defy patterns and predictability, and I tend to rely heavily on patterns and predictability when it comes to human interaction."

"What do you mean?"

Ziggy glances at her side-view mirror, before easing into the passing lane. "Has Ren told you . . . anything about me?"

"What do you mean?" I frown. "Like personal stuff? No. Just funny family anecdotes."

"Right." She nods. "Because I, uh . . . didn't know if he'd mentioned I'm autistic."

I blink at her, brow furrowed. I don't know much about autism, have no personal experience of it with anyone in my own life. "No," I finally tell her. "He hadn't."

Ziggy tugs her lips between her teeth. "Well, I am."

"Can you . . . explain it to me? So I can understand? Is that all right to ask?"

She nods, blowing out a long, slow breath. "Yeah, it is. And I can." After a quiet moment, she says, "I have a lot of social anxiety because people . . . are strange to me, more than they are to someone like you, unless you're neurodivergent. I shouldn't assume."

I shake my head. "I'm not, far as I know, at least."

She nods, eyes on the road. "So . . . when *you* meet someone, it's easier for you to read their nonverbals, to pick up on their tone, to read between the lines of what they say, to engage and understand them. In fact, someone like you is probably amazing at it. You're very . . . charismatic with people."

"Manipulative, you mean."

She shrugs. "I don't know you well enough to say that, Sebastian. I don't plan to hold against you what the world's said about you."

My heart thuds in my chest. "Why not?"

She's quiet again for a moment, tugging her lip with her teeth, before she finally says, "Because I believe we all deserve the chance to be seen for who we are in our present, not for who we've been in our past. Because I believe that while you can't rewrite life's previous chapters, you have every present moment to do something new, something better, and I hold on to hope that anyone who wants to can shape their life into a story they're proud of."

I stare at her, knuckles grazing my mouth, panicking.

I have never wanted to believe in someone's belief so much. I have never wanted to kiss someone so much. I want to tell her to pull the car over, and I want to drag her across the console, crush her onto my lap, and learn every corner of that soft, sweet mouth.

I want to soak up and breathe in whatever's inside this woman that charges the air and makes my atrophied, frozen heart want to grow and warm and heal and fill with things it hasn't in so long.

But that's not what this is. That's not what she wants or deserves, and I've made a promise—to myself, to her brother, and in my own way, to her, too—that I won't hurt her, that I'll keep her safe.

And goddammit, for once, I'm going to keep my word. I'm going to do the right thing. Even if it just might kill me.

THIRTEEN

Ziggy

Playlist: "Over the Rainbow," Ingrid Michaelson

"Well." Sebastian clears his throat, knuckles grazing his mouth as he stares out the window. "I hope you don't just believe that for other people."

I glance his way quickly, before retraining my gaze ahead, as I make the turn into the designated parking area for players and their guests. "What do you mean?"

He shrugs, his thumb spinning a silver ring on his index finger, eyes fastened out the window. "This . . . project of yours, it's all about how you're perceived, right? Wanting to take control of that. But let me tell you this, which I've learned from experience. There's only so much you can do about how others perceive you. You can't control it. You can only be yourself and be true to that. If they can't see what an incredible—" He clears his throat, lifting his shoulder. "If they can't see you as you really are, that's not your fault. They can fuck right off."

I bite my lip as I ease into a parking space and set the car in park. "Don't you think . . . I mean, aren't relationships more complicated than that? They're messy grayscales, not black and white."

A noncommittal grunt leaves him. Apparently, he disagrees? I don't know about any of Sebastian's relationships beyond his friendship with Ren, or if he even has any. I'm starting to wonder if that's telling. If it's not just that we haven't been doing this fake-friend thing for very long, but more to do with how he views relationships.

"It's simpler with my teams," I tell him. "National and in the city here. It's not their fault they don't see a person I haven't shown them. Now's my chance to stop acting like the girl I was and advocate for myself as the woman I've become. With my family, it's complex—they've known the old me, loved and protected the old me. I don't want to resent them for holding on to the idea of a person they've known and treasured and taken care of when I really, really needed it. I just . . . want to show them who I am, and I want them to embrace that. If they can't . . ." I shake my head, unable to process the possibility that my family wouldn't welcome what I show them with open arms. "I'll deal with that then, but I won't let it stop me from figuring out how to be and show the people who matter to me who I've become."

He glances my way for only a second, but I feel its impact like a snap of bracing air—the kind during a Washington winter that hits your face and makes you gasp, fills your lungs with cold, clean peace, as you gaze out at the vastness surrounding you.

He glances back out the window, then says quietly, simply, "Good."

I smile at him. "That was nice of you to say. Look at you, expanding your repertoire beyond snarky quips and bone-dry sarcasm."

He swallows roughly as he glances back my way. His eyes dance between mine. "It's your fault. You're rubbing off on me."

My smile deepens. "Sorry I'm such a terrible influence."

"Not forgiven," he mutters, back to staring out the window, his gaze traveling the rink. "We got sidetracked again. You were . . . explaining what it means for you, being autistic."

I pick up his keys where they sit in the console and turn them over in my hands. A few players and their guests are leaving their cars, joining up with each other. Talking, hugging, laughing. I suppose we could join them, too, but I don't want to get out yet. I want to tell Sebastian. I want him to know this about me, because I can't do this anymore—judge him the way the world has and use that judgment to hold him at a distance. I have to decide for myself, based on what he shows *me*, how I'm going to see him. And trusting him with this part of myself will certainly be the litmus test. He'll either be a jerk about it, or he'll be . . . the way I hope he is, the way he's shown me he *can* be. Curious. Kind. Caring.

The way he was when he comforted me as I fell apart at yoga last Saturday and when I started to spiral tonight, no words, no pressure to do anything except stand there and let him offer me grounding, strong touch, a sure, steady presence.

Maybe this is all just pretend, what he and I are doing. But just because something's pretend doesn't mean it can't hold within its deceptive shell a kernel of truth. That's why I love Shakespeare Club, why I read books, because those made-up worlds contain some of the tenderest, scariest, most beautiful human truths, navigated in the safety of imagination, whose wisdom and hopes I take with me bravely into my own life.

Maybe when this is done, Sebastian won't look back twice, won't see me as anything beyond his best friend's little sister who served a purpose for a time, who made him suffer through angry yoga, kicked his shins for swearing, and hogged his chocolate milkshake. Maybe I'll do the same and look back on this with fond memories of the foulmouthed, sardonic man obsessed with his hair, who had a penchant for surprising me with kindness, yet ultimately who was never meant to be a lasting part of my life.

But right now, while we're doing this, I want truth. I want trust. I want it to be real, when we're here, sharing space and life, however brief that is.

So I take a deep breath and tell him. I explain, "I have a lot of social anxiety, and I don't find it intuitive or . . . particularly straightforward to learn and understand people. That means I don't make friends easily. I've been able to figure out how to get along with my teammates, and I have my best friend, Charlie. But mostly, I just focus on my family and soccer, and that's it. On top of that, busy events can overwhelm and overstimulate me. So tonight, I'll have to pace myself. I might be a little awkward, a bit quiet; I might disappear briefly to reset before I can return to the action."

He's watching me with that way he has—knuckles grazing his mouth, silver eyes locked on me, his expression inscrutable. "Is it . . . hard, spaces like this? Is that why you don't normally go to them?"

My heart's sprinting in my chest. I can't read him, can't tell if there's judgment hiding beneath the surface of his curiosity. "Yes. They are hard. I have a lot of sensory issues that I have to navigate in busy settings. Different sounds overlapping each other— complex noise—they hurt my brain. Flashing or harsh lights make me nauseous. If people touch me when I don't expect it or in ways that I don't like, I start to feel like my skin's crawling with fire ants, and I can't breathe well. With strangers, I get nervous I'll say the wrong thing—and honestly, I often do—so I get so quiet, it's uncomfortable for people. In short, I'm terrible at this kind of thing."

His jaw clenches. He drops his hand. "Then why the fuck are we doing it?"

"Zounds!" I yell. "No f-bombs tonight, you hear me?"

He doesn't blink, doesn't acknowledge me. "This is not happening. I'm not taking you in there, not somewhere that upsets you like that."

"Sebastian, I agreed to this event for a reason. I can handle it. I know the team, so it won't be talking to strangers. I love kids, and I can focus on interacting with them. I'll let you do the conversational heavy lifting, the small-talking and being charming. And I have . . ." I reach for my purse and pull out my saving grace. "Ear-plugs." Gently, I wedge them into my ears. "They'll help with the auditory issues. And it won't matter that I might talk a little too quiet and then a little too loud, since I can't hear myself well, be-cause it'll be chaotic in there anyway. Everyone will be talking over the music and other people's conversations, having to repeat them-selves anyway, right?"

His mouth rises at the corner, a hint of a smile. His eyes travel my face. "That's right. So there's the conversational aspect, the overwhelming sound. Now, the unwelcome touching?"

I ease out my earplugs. "I usually just keep my space from people."

"Not at a roller race you don't," he says, adjusting his rings on his fingers. "Well, at least, it won't be easy. But I'll manage it. No one will touch you who you don't want to. It might involve . . . me staying close, though. Is that all right with you?"

A swallow works down my throat as I stare at him, as he stares at me, spinning that ring on his fourth finger over and over. "Yes." My voice is faint, cracked. "That's all right with me."

"Well, then . . ." He leans in, brushing back my hair from where it's fallen around my face into a curtain, my familiar hiding place. Carefully, he smooths it away until it's behind my shoulders, spill-ing down my back. "No hiding tonight, Sigrid. Time for you to shine."

FOURTEEN

Sebastian

Playlist: "Too Late to Say Goodbye," Cage The Elephant

"Look who it is!" Tyler, my teammate, wraps Ziggy in a hug and squeezes her close.

My hands are fists in my pockets as I watch her for any sign that this hug is unwelcome, but goddammit, to my annoyance, she hugs him back, smiling at me over his shoulder and mouthing at me, *I'm okay.*

I nod tersely.

"Seb!" Another teammate, Kris, slaps me on the back. I glance his way and offer a hand, which he takes. "You actually came."

"Shocked?"

He grins, then wrinkles his nose. "Kinda, yeah. But I'm not mad about it."

I glance around at the roller rink we've secured for the event, decorated to be colorful and bright, clearly with kids in mind. The music isn't too loud and the lights aren't terribly bright, which is good for Ziggy. The crowd's noise is low as players mingle with their guests, the staff, and the kids who are our guests of honor.

I snag glances with Frankie, whose gaze snaps from Ziggy to me. She gives me a scary intense look. Note to self: Avoid Frankie tonight.

"You gonna hit the rink?" Kris asks. "Skate for the cause?"

I shake my head. "Foot's still iffy. Doc said no rinks for another week."

He peers down at my boot, which I now have medical permission to take breaks from. Tonight, with a bunch of rowdy, oversized men trampling around, did not seem like the time to expose my finally almost healed foot, though, so I stuck with the boot. "That sucks, man."

"It's my own damn fault," I admit. "I was a reckless ass. I'm lucky I didn't hurt myself worse."

Kris frowns thoughtfully. "Well, I'm glad you'll be better in time for the season. We need you. ASAP. Dryland conditioning is miserable without you giving Lars those arctic glares and muttered roasts when he tells us we have another set to do because we 'aren't going hard enough.'"

"God, I loathe that man. He's sick."

"Definitely a sadist," Kris agrees, glancing to where Ziggy laughs at something Tyler says. "So, uh . . . you and Bergman's little sister, huh?"

"Just friends," I tell him, staring at Ziggy.

Just friends. That's it. She's not mine. Not even my real friend, let alone something more.

Even though when I watch Tyler knock shoulders with her and laugh as she does, I want to fucking break something.

"Seb!" Ren throws an arm around my shoulder, squeezing tight. "I'm so glad you're here."

"Yeah, me too." I set a hand on his back in greeting, before we step apart. "So can I just ask a favor?"

Ren turns and faces me fully, his expression serious. "Of course, Seb. Anything."

"Keep your wife far from me tonight. She looks like she wants to find the nearest sharp object and impale me with it."

Ren grimaces, scrubbing at the back of his neck. "She may not have taken the news well that you and Ziggy were coming together, even though I stressed it was only as friends."

"Yeah, that's not surprising. She doesn't trust me to behave myself, let alone with someone she cares about. I don't blame her. I've given her no reason to."

He frowns. "Seb, it's not—"

Someone calls Ren's name, making him turn quickly. It's a kid who's a fan, waiting for his autograph, and like the softie he is, Ren immediately takes their Sharpie and crouches so they're eye to eye, engaging them in a conversation. Another kid tugs on Kris's sleeve and draws his attention, as well. Those two are veteran players on the team and well loved, for good reason.

"Seb!" Tyler yells, making me spin his way. "You gotta skate."

I point to the boot. "Can't."

He sighs, shaking his head. "Come on, man. This would be pure gold—the ice-cold bad boy skating his heart out to eighties classics."

"Next year," I tell him, shocking myself not only with making that promise, but with the realization that I actually mean it.

"Fine," he sighs, before turning to Ziggy. "Zigs. You gonna join?"

Zigs? My jaw clenches.

She smiles and shrugs. "Yeah, sure." Without preamble, she turns, then strolls off. Thierry Arneaux, who notices her passing, turns and follows her on a jog until he catches up, pointing toward the other end of the rink. Presumably to help her get a pair of skates.

Better be all he's helping her with.

I stare after her. Arneaux keeps his hands to himself, and Ziggy tugs down the hem of her romper's shorts. I don't stare at her ass as she walks.

Too long.

"So." Tyler claps an arm around me. "Zigs. Isn't she the best?"

I force myself into that familiar cold, numb place that I rely on when I want to keep my shit in check and I'm dangerously on the verge of losing it. "Yeah. She is. You two seem—"

"Close?" he offers.

"I was going to say 'acquainted.'"

He grins. "Oh, we're way more than acquainted."

Fuck, I'm going to strangle him. Ziggy would have told me if she'd been with Tyler Assclown Johnson, wouldn't she?

No, dipshit, she would not have. She owes you nothing of her dating or sexual history. Why would she tell you that? You're not dating. You're not even real *friends.*

"We go back years," Tyler explains, nodding to someone who walks by and shaking their hand, before turning back to me. "Trying to think, when did I first get to know Zigs? I guess it's ever since she joined—*ouch!*" He glares at our teammate Andy, who's stepped behind him and issued some kind of painful warning, given how Tyler rubs his arm.

"Easy does it, Johnson," Andy mutters, raising his eyebrows meaningfully in my direction. "He's not in—"

"The least-secret, secret Shakespeare Club that's ever existed?" I offer.

"Shhh!" they both hiss.

"Oops," I deadpan. "I said that out loud."

Andy and Tyler look at me warily, uncharacteristically quiet given those fools never shut up. "You . . . know about the club?" Andy finally asks.

"I gotta be honest, if you've actually been trying to keep it a secret, you're doing a shit job."

Tyler groans, raising his fists dramatically. "'See, we fools! Why have I blabb'd? who shall be true to us, When we are so unsecret to ourselves?'"

"*Troilus and Cressida*?" I grimace. "That play is such a downer."

Their mouths fall open in tandem, shock painting their faces. "You actually *know* your Shakespeare?" Tyler asks.

I shouldn't be offended. I certainly haven't made it a point to share much about myself with these guys. They have no reason to know I'm way more familiar with the Bard than I ever wanted to be. But with an oppressive stepfather obsessed with breaking my "headstrong will," I got to spend Saturdays under his authoritarian eye, reading classics from ancient philosophy to Shakespeare, essays from the Enlightenment, gothic novels, twentieth-century writers, like Whitman, Capote, and Hemingway, who took themselves way too goddamn seriously. I was tasked with reading them, writing about them, then being thoroughly berated when I always somehow managed to get it wrong. Nothing was ever good enough for Edward. According to him, I was stupid, illiterate, lazy, insubordinate.

On the outside, and from my mom's perspective, Edward was just trying to raise me to be a man of culture worthy of his old blue-blood family name that he so "graciously" adopted me into at my mother's request. On the inside, it was hell. As he chastised me, shamed me, verbally tore me apart, I learned to go into that cold, numb place and leave myself. Edward knew exactly how to hurt me so Mom wouldn't see. And Mom never asked questions about how sullen I was before and after those lessons because she didn't see it—all she saw was a moody, angry boy with daddy issues who resisted a bond with the man she'd chosen to step into my absent father's place.

I tell myself that's how it went, because I have to. The alternative—that she saw how he hurt me, how fucked up he was, and did nothing anyway—is something even I'm not able to numb myself enough not to feel something about.

Realizing I've been quiet for too long, I clear my throat and shrug as I answer them. "I'm familiar, yeah."

"Prove it," Andy says, folding his arms across his chest.

Ren stands from chatting with his small fan, and turns, rejoining our conversation. "Prove what?"

"That Gauthier here didn't just pull a wild, lucky guess out of his ass," Tyler tells Ren. "He recognized a *Troilus and Cressida* quote."

Ren frowns, glancing between us and looking thoroughly confused. "What?"

As Andy and Tyler catch up Ren on what he's missed, I watch a small crowd of people part.

Ziggy walks past them, smiling, roller skates clutched by the laces in one hand. Her rainbow earrings swing as she walks, and she winces a little when the new song comes on louder than the last one. Subtly, she slips her finger to her ear beneath her hair and wedges her earplug tighter.

Something snaps inside me, like a band stretched too far. I want to hold her. Press a hand to her ear and clutch her to my chest and seal out the world, until everything is as quiet and calm as she needs, as peaceful and perfect as she deserves for it to be.

"Tyler quoted the play," Andy tells Ren. "So I told Seb to prove he's not blowing smoke up our butts and actually knows his—"

"'Sweet, bid me hold my tongue,'" I recite, loud enough for them to hear, my gaze fastened on Ziggy. "'For in this rapture I shall surely speak the thing I shall repent.'"

Andy gapes. Tyler blows out a heavy breath, then says, "Poor Cressida. She was down bad for Troilus."

Ren smiles, clapping his hand on my shoulder. "Seb! You did it! You're in."

"Did what?" Ziggy asks, her voice so quiet, they all lean in, cuing her to repeat herself. This time she's a little louder than she normally would be. With the music's volume and other people's conversational sounds to contend with, no one makes anything of it.

I just stand there, fighting a smile.

Because as I stare at her, I see that moment in my parked car all over again, those earplugs wedged in her ears as she explained their purpose in this adorable half whisper, and that hard, cold place inside me melted and ached and wanted in a way it hasn't in so long.

"Seb just recited Shakespeare," Ren tells her, not loud enough, given she has earplugs in, but she seems content to read his lips and lean in, eyes narrowed as she concentrates.

Her eyes widen, then she turns to me, her mouth parted. "You said it without me? I missed it!" She grabs my arm and shakes it a little. "You stinker."

I fight another smile, inordinately pleased that she cares. That she's touching me, even if, *shit*, is her grip rough, almost painful. "I'll throw a line your way at some point," I tell her. "Promise."

She gives me a narrow-eyed glare. "Hmph."

I hook my finger on her roller skates' laces, then lift them from her hands. "Come on. Let's get you ready to race."

FIFTEEN

Ziggy

Playlist: "Meadows," Wild Child

Sebastian's been gone for a while. I scan Tyler's gorgeous three-story great room, with its floor-to-ceiling windows overlooking the Pacific Ocean, and frown. I still don't see him.

"One more selfie." Tyler's girlfriend, Sofie, takes our photo and, with my permission, posts it to Instagram. A fellow professional athlete, she plays for New York's women's soccer team.

We've spent the whole after-party talking about our professional soccer careers, about her and Tyler's long-distance relationship, my hope for building some brand partnerships, all while tucked in a quiet corner away from the rowdier bunch at the other end of the great room. I think I just might have made a new friend.

"Ziggy." Sebastian steps up to me, then nods Sofie's way. "Hey, Sof."

She smiles. "Hey, Seb."

He rakes a hand through his hair. "We should go."

I frown, confused. "Everything okay?"

He shrugs. "It's late."

I peer down at my phone. He's not wrong. "Okay." Turning to Sofie, I hug her good night and exchange numbers, then let Sebastian more or less drag me out of the room, barely letting me wave goodbye to anyone.

"I can't drive," I tell him as we turn the corner into the hallway.

"I'm not drunk, but I did drink a cocktail just now pretty quickly, so I'm not sober, either."

"I can drive," he says. "I haven't had a drink the whole night."

"But your foot—"

"It's fine."

I point to the boot. "It is definitely not fine."

"It is. I'll take off the boot—I just had it on to protect my foot from the crowd. It's more than fine enough to drive."

"Then why have I been driving you around, Miss Daisy?"

He takes me by the hand and tugs me with him down the hall-way. "Because Frankie would castrate me for being behind the wheel any more than strictly necessary, but more so because you seemed to like driving the Cayenne."

"Well, you misread that one, big-time. I'm a white-knuckled driver."

Sebastian frowns at me as we walk to his car. "That's why you drive so slow?"

"I don't drive slow. I drive *cautiously*."

"Sorry. I . . . I should have asked."

I stop at the passenger's side, turning to face him. "I liked that you didn't. No, you aren't the most . . . communicatively thought-ful person I've ever met, Sebastian, but it gives me a chance to speak up for myself in ways I suck at. You don't have to feel bad about that. I could have suggested we get where we needed some other way, but I wanted to try driving. This is all part of the plan. I'm trying to be brave."

Sebastian stares down at the ground, brow furrowed as he pops the trunk and sits on its ledge, changing from boot to shoe. He seems distracted as he opens the passenger door for me, then shuts it after I'm settled in.

The drive is quiet as he pulls out and accelerates gradually down the road.

I'm trying to piece together a puzzle whose picture I don't know. Is Sebastian upset? Why has he withdrawn? As he drives, I almost ask him a dozen times, but I keep reminding myself what this is—*pretend* friendship. I have no right, no reason, to ask him to open up to me, not when none of this is real.

And yet, when I see him making the turn to take us to my place, panic sets in. I don't want to leave him alone like this. I don't want to be left alone like this, either.

"I don't want to go home," I blurt out.

He frowns at the road. "Why not?"

I stare at him, biting my lip.

Because I just did something wild and brave tonight. Because while I loved how empowered it made me feel, I think I loved the minutes with you that took me there a little bit more. Because I think you're sad, and I don't want to leave you alone in that.

Because I'm still reeling from what just happened, and I don't want to be alone in that, either.

I don't say any of that. My bravery has its limits, and this moment is one of them. Instead, I lean across the console, my fingertips sliding over his rings, playing with them as they shine in the streetlights overhead. "I just . . . need some time to process tonight. I don't want to be by myself while I do that."

Sebastian slows the car, as if he's deliberating, before he speeds up and takes the turn back toward Manhattan Beach and his house. I slump in my seat, sighing with relief.

"What do you need to process?" he asks. "Did something happen with Sofie?"

I glance his way, my head swiveling against the headrest. "Nothing bad. Just . . . a lot. What about you, where did you disappear to?"

He sighs heavily. "A skeleton fell out of my closet. And I had to deal with it."

"That . . . sounds super sinister."

"It was. Or at least, it started out that way. I bumped into someone I'd hurt in the past. They got upset with me. We talked it through. I . . . apologized. They actually forgave me." He sighs moodily. "It sucked."

I turn in my seat, facing him. "Sebastian, that sounds like it turned out well."

He shakes his head. "This is my life. Everywhere I go, there's someone I fucked over or fucked up with. This is who I am, what I've done. I haven't cared about other people or the impact of my actions on them."

"Sebastian, you've told me this. I understand."

"No, you don't!" His eyes are wide, his hands tight on the steering wheel. "Because I barely understand it myself."

"Understand what? I'm so confused."

"Makes two of us," he mutters, flicking on his turn signal. "I swear to you, Sigrid, up until now, I could have told you without blinking that I didn't give a good goddamn about my past." He makes the turn down his street, hitting the button inside the car for his garage.

"*Didn't?* Meaning . . . you do now?"

"Christ," he grits out. "Yes. I feel sick to my stomach. I . . ." He shakes his head, like he's in shock. "I wish I could undo it. I fucking *care* that I can't undo it. I *care*."

"You sound angry about that."

"Of course I am!"

I stare at him, heart pounding. "Why?"

Sebastian's silent, his jaw clenching as he pulls into the garage. He kills the engine, then slumps back in his seat, scrubbing his face. For a long silent moment, I wait, hoping for an answer.

But instead, all he says, hands falling from his face, is, "Come on. Let's go inside, get you settled until you're ready for me to take you home."

"Sebastian—"

I'm cut off as he pushes open his door and shuts it.

Circling the car, then opening my door, he's quiet, his expression cool, back to the stranger who used to silently brush me off, who barely even acknowledged me.

Well, that's not happening anymore.

I step out of his car, head held high as I lead the way to his door, which he unlocks with the code, before letting me in. The door slips shut behind me, and I walk into the kitchen, plopping down on a seat at the island. Sebastian strolls past me toward the kitchen, pointedly not looking my way.

I sit there, and I wait. Because I know something about needing time to find the right words.

Time to feel safe to say them.

I sit there, hands folded, watching him drag open the door to his balcony, welcoming in the sea breeze. He keeps his back to me in the kitchen and starts to open cabinets, then bang them shut when he doesn't see what he seems to be looking for.

"Tea?" he asks. Another cabinet opens and shuts. "Warm milk?" The refrigerator door this time, open, then shut. "What wholesome nighttime drinks do people enjoy?"

"Sebastian—"

He rushes past me, out on to the balcony.

"Sebastian!" I don't yell his name, but I'm not quiet, either. I wait until he slumps against the railing of his balcony, then turns his head my way, eyes down.

"Don't do this," I tell him, trying to keep my voice steady. "Don't do what you used to, what everyone else has, and brush me off, look past me, treat me like someone you can dismiss—"

He pushes off the railing, turning toward me. "Ziggy—"

"I'm speaking!" I walk right up to him until we're chest to chest. Sebastian's silent as I wait him out, until he glances up.

When his eyes meet mine, my heart free-falls to my feet. He looks . . . terrified. He looks like I did in the mirror earlier, before we left tonight, frozen with fear.

So, like he did for me, slowly, gently, I brush my fingertips against his, until our palms brush. I squeeze hard.

"Sebastian, I want you to answer my question. I don't want to be shielded or coddled. I want you to do what you've done for the past week and not hold back with me. I want your honesty."

His eyes search mine. "No," he whispers, "you don't."

Anger pulses through me, heats my cheeks. I step closer, my chest brushing his. "Don't do this. You don't tell me what I do or don't want. You've been . . . you're supposed to be . . ." My voice dies off. "You're supposed to be different. You *were* different."

"Oh, I'm different, all right," he says hoarsely. "I'm a fucking piece of shit, is what I am, Ziggy. I'm not your wholesome brother Ren or your wholesome other brothers or your wholesome sister married to her wholesome college sweetheart with their perfect kids or your precious parents who are still madly in love. I am a fucking *wreck*. I have bent my life around revenge and spite to the point that I'm so contorted, I don't even know what it's like to live without hurting myself and others. And then you—" He clasps my face, his thumbs sweeping my cheeks. "You just . . . had to bust into my life, quite literally. Standing on my balcony while I was at my lowest low, seeing . . . *something* in me, a tiny chance I could do something good, something good for you—"

"For you, too," I whisper. "Something good for you, too."

He shakes his head. "No, Ziggy, I'm un—"

"'—savable.' I know what you think of yourself." I wrap my hands around his wrists, my thumb sweeping over his pounding pulse. "And you know what I told you."

He stares at me, his jaw clenching. "No one's unsavable."

I smile. "And I believe that. I meant what I said. And I meant it when I said I'm not here to save you, either. But I'm asking you, for as much as you seem to believe in me and my possibilities, to believe in yourself, too." I stroke his pulse with my thumbs, searching his eyes. "Don't give up on us, not when we've barely even gotten started."

"I want to," he mutters through clenched teeth. "But for some fucking irritating reason, I can't. I *can't*." His eyes search mine. I hold his wrists to steady myself as his thumbs sweep along my jaw.

He leans in, his mouth a whisper against my ear. "I've spent so long, numb to everything, I forgot what it was like to feel. But now there's you, banging around, being scared and brave and determined and curious right up in my face, making me feel all this shit I haven't wanted to. I've been *pretending* to be someone who matters to you for a week, and this is what happens? Thank fuck you didn't ask for an actual friendship. Who knows how much worse off I'd be."

I lean into the warmth of his breath at my ear. His scruff brushes my cheek, making me shiver. "Would the effects of being actual friends really be so bad?"

He lets out a rough, tight sound, his nose drifting to my hair. "Ziggy, they would be *devastating*. So don't you dare—"

"Be my friend," I whisper, nuzzling into him, emboldened by hope and a warm sea breeze and the dregs of crisp champagne fizzing through my system. "Feel some feelings. Get messy with me. Be my friend, Sebastian."

His hands drift gently into my hair, massaging my scalp. An effervescent warmth better than the best bubbles, the softest sea breeze, spills through me. I'm in very dangerous territory. But for once, I don't mind it—no, I *like* it. Because this is who I am, who I'm becoming. Ziggy who's brave. Ziggy who takes chances. Ziggy who reaches for what she wants, rather than stopping herself, frozen by her fear of rejection, of failure, of getting it wrong.

Because if I've learned anything this past week while being wild, taking risks, trying new things, it's that getting it wrong, stumbling and falling apart along the way, isn't the end of the world. It's just . . . part of living. And I'm strong enough to weather those hard moments, pick myself up, dust myself off, and keep going.

Sebastian pulls back enough to look at me, piercing gray eyes searching mine; rough, calloused thumbs brushing tenderly along my neck. "Friends? With me? You can't actually want that."

I clutch his shirt at his hips and shake him. "Don't tell me what I can or can't want." I search his eyes, my voice softer as I hold him tight. "I'm telling you I want to be your friend. Believe me."

For a moment it's nothing but the quiet of the night, the roar of the ocean beyond us, the snap of the breeze whipping my wrap away from my body. Sebastian sighs. His gaze travels my face. "As long as you promise to keep yelling Shakespeare at me when I swear," he says, a hoarse, cracked edge in his voice. "And stealing my chocolate milkshakes and driving me around ten miles under the speed limit—" I pinch his side, making him grunt, his grip on my hair tightening. "I suppose . . ." he says quietly, his eyes holding mine, "we could be *actual* friends."

I smile wide, throwing my arms around his neck in happiness, making us stumble sideways.

He laughs, husky and deep. His hands settle on my hips, steadying me.

Slowly we grow still.

And suddenly, the courage I had to find to ask him to be a friend feels like the slightest, most inconsequential drop in the bucket of what I'll need for what I want to do right now. What I'm *about* to do right now.

My hands drift down his chest. His muscles tense beneath my touch, and I stop my hands, resting them over his pounding heart. "Do you want me to stop touching you?" I whisper.

Sebastian's grip tightens on my hips. He stares at me, eyes bright and shimmering. "No."

My fingertips graze his sternum, the hard jut of his collarbone, the silver chains warm against his skin. "Do you want me to stop this?" I ask, leaning in, my mouth a whisper away from his.

Air rushes out of him as my hands travel up his neck, into his hair; thick, silky strands cool in the night air. "We shouldn't, Ziggy—"

"That's not what I asked," I whisper, nuzzling his nose. I can't believe I'm doing this. I can't believe I've lasted this long *not* doing this.

"You know I don't want you to stop," he whispers back, his thumbs sweeping over my hips. "I just . . . I promised myself I wouldn't."

"Then *I'll* do it," I tell him. "I'll take full responsibility for what's about to happen."

"'What's about to happen'?" he asks roughly. I trace his mouth with my fingertips and stare at his lips parting for me.

"You really don't know what this is? I find it hard to believe, that you, Sebastian Gauthier, don't recognize a kiss when it's about to happen."

Sebastian exhales roughly as I brush my lips to his cheek, the corner of his mouth. "I'm no expert on friendship, Sigrid," he says shakily, pulling me closer, "but I don't think friends do this."

I smile against his scruff, pressing a featherlight kiss to his jaw. "Sure they do. It's called 'friends with benefits.'"

"Ziggy," he whispers, turning his head.

Our mouths brush while my name's still on his lips.

"Sebastian." Slowly, softly, I press my lips to his, and God, it's perfect. Warm and delicate, curious and careful, before he opens his mouth, then breathes into me a hoarse, aching groan.

Heat floods my body as I sink my fingers deep into his hair, as I lean into our kiss.

Sebastian draws in a rough breath, wrapping his arms around me, crushing our bodies together. His hands splay across my back, traveling my ribs. His thumbs graze my breasts. I gasp and press my body into his as his tongue finds mine, with hot, silken strokes that make me lean in and ache for more.

A needy sigh leaves me as he tips my head tenderly, then deepens our kiss. I kiss him back, desperate for his taste, to discover every corner of him, to make him fall apart the way he's making me fall apart, only to realize it's somehow managed to put us both back together.

I open my mouth against his and suck his tongue. Sebastian lists sideways, like I've stunned him. He lands half on a chaise and I ease over him, smiling as he tugs me down, until I'm straddling his hips, my legs on either side of him, right where I want to be.

His hands sink into my hips and tug me close. I throw my arms around his neck and kiss him like I've never kissed someone before—wild, uninhibited, my body moving with his.

I never want this to end.

But, of course, as soon as I think that, Sebastian tears his mouth away from mine.

SIXTEEN

Sebastian

Playlist: "She's So High," Paratone

Air heaving in my lungs, I press my forehead to Ziggy's, willing my-self to regret what I've just done. But with each second that passes, the echo of her soft sighs fresh in my memory, the warm sweet taste of her lingering on my tongue, I can't. I can't regret what I did.

And that's all the proof I need that I am as unworthy of her as ever. I didn't deserve what she just gave me. I can't have that ever again. I can't allow myself to be that selfish, that greedy, not when it would only hurt her in the end.

I can be just a *little* selfish, just a *little* greedy. I can be her friend. I can laugh with her and do yoga with her and share diner milkshakes and watch her become everything she wants to be-come. And I'll be lucky simply to witness that.

What I can't do is drag her down onto the chaise and rut into her like an animal in heat, which I've just come dangerously close to doing.

"Was it bad?" she asks quietly, peering down at me. "Is that why you stopped?"

A smile I can't help lifts the corner of my mouth. I let my head fall back on the chaise and smooth away those fine, fiery hairs from her face. "It was *good*. That's why I stopped."

A swift, pink blush heats her cheeks as she smiles, and a shiver dances through her body. "That doesn't make any sense."

"It does, Sigrid." I sit upright and pat her hip, trying to signal that I want us—no, *need* us—to stand, to place vital distance between our bodies. "Let me take you inside. You're shivering."

Another shiver racks her as she shakes her head. She doesn't budge. "I'm not shivering."

"Yes, you are, now . . ."

She leans back, tugs off the wrap that she's held tight around herself all night, and throws it into the wind. Before I can finally process the reality of her body in only that tight dark green dress, she leans in, clasps my neck, and brings my mouth down to hers.

Oh God, I try. God, do I try to resist. But I can't. I can't resist her. Even though I have to. I *have* to.

"Kiss me," she whispers against my mouth as mine falls open, a gust of air leaving me. "If you want to kiss me, kiss me. Don't talk yourself out of it."

That's exactly what I should be doing—talking myself out of it. But fuck, I don't want to. I want to touch her, taste her, please her. Just this last time. Once more.

I unleash everything I held back last time, dragging her close until she's right there, warm and snug, tucked against me, where I'm hard, so goddamn hard for her. She sighs and her eyes fall shut with the kind of pleasure that, in my weakest moments, I've dreamed about giving her. Clasping her jaw, I tilt her head until our kiss can deepen and her tongue meets mine, wet, hot glides and seeking strokes that make my hips arch up into hers. "Never again," I promise her. "This is the last time. Never again after this, I swear."

"Not if I have anything to say about it," she pants against my mouth. A sweet little moan leaves her as I drag a hand up her thigh, to her hip, and haul her against me, feeling her hips start to move. Fuck, she's perfect—strong and soft, her body tucked against mine, every single part of us lined up like we were fucking made for this.

She feels like everything I never knew I could hope for, let alone have. A long-ago prayer answered, a forgotten dream come to life, too unbelievably *good*.

Her fingers delve into my hair, scrape down my shoulders, as my hands glide up her back, traveling the smooth warmth of her shoulders, bare to the night air. She wraps her arms around my neck, tugging me tight against her, and I groan as our hips start to move together, so perfect, so fucking perfect.

"Sebastian," she mutters against our kiss. "I want—*hiccup!*" It's a short, sharp squeak, but it's more than enough to make me wrench myself away.

I can't help but think about what caused that hiccup—the cocktail I watched her drink at Tyler's.

She's tipsy, influenced by alcohol, and I took advantage of that. Dread seeps through me.

Jesus Christ.

Ziggy frowns. Hiccups again. "What—*hiccup!*—What's wrong?"

"You're intoxicated, that's what's wrong."

She laughs. Laughs! "Sebastian, I've had more to drink at a Sunday family dinner than I had tonight. I was tipsy before we drove back but only because I drank it fast. I'm fine now. I have been. I'm safe."

No she isn't. She hasn't been safe at all. We kissed. We started doing more than kissing, too.

In the light of day and with a clear mind, she's going to regret that.

I have to salvage this. I have to show her I can be her friend, not a depraved, dry-humping ass.

A frown forms on her face. "What's wrong?"

She leans in. I lean back. Her eyes widen, filled with hurt. Slowly, she sinks back from my hips and slides onto the chaise. I tug my good foot back quickly, spinning so I sit sideways on the chaise, my face buried in my hands.

"Sebastian, talk to me. I can't . . . I can't tell what's going on, what you're thinking. It's hard to read you, and that makes me so anxious. Please just say it, whatever it is, whether you're mad at me or you're regretting it, just—"

"Hey." Turning, I tug her into my arms and hold her tight as I tuck her head against my shoulder, just the way I wanted to when I saw her at the roller rink. Ziggy sets her arms around my waist and turns toward me, too. Slowly, I feel her relax into me.

"Why did you pull away?" she whispers.

"Because that shouldn't have happened. And I needed to be sure it wouldn't happen again. That's why I pulled away."

Ziggy pulls back enough to peer at me, her head tipped, hurt tightening her eyes. "Why shouldn't it have happened?"

I smooth back her hair as the wind drags it across her face, so her eyes can find mine while I tell her the truth for once: "Because you asked me to be your friend, Ziggy, and I'm hardly worthy of that, but I'd like to be. Don't ask more of me, please, not when . . . not when I could never . . ."

Never be enough, never deserve more of you, never be worthy of more than this.

She stares at me, confusion tingeing her expression. I can't make myself finish that sentence, can't make myself speak that damning admission into the air between us. Even if it's true. Even if I know myself—that while tonight shook me up, and I do know I want to find a different way forward, to focus more on the good in my life, I'm so marred by my past, so inexperienced at trying to be anything but selfish and spiteful, there are so many ways I could fail her if I ever tried to be anything more to her than this.

"So . . ." Ziggy swallows, biting her lip. "Friends?"

I shrug, brushing back another wisp of hair from her temple. "Despite what a giant pain in my ass you can be—"

She pokes my armpit, trying for a tickle spot, and relief rushes through me. There's that fiery playfulness, a faint, sweet smile warming her mouth.

"Yes," I tell her. "Friends."

"Like how we started?" she asks quietly. "Like . . . when it was just pretend?"

"No. Not how we started. How we ended up. Real. Real—" It takes two tries to get it past this sudden, sharp lump in my throat, to tell her the lie we're both better off believing. "Friends. If you still want even that from me, after all this."

Ziggy stares at me in that keen, incisive way, her body entirely still, but for the wind whipping her hair. Finally, she stands from the chaise and tucks those long copper strands behind her ears, glancing around the balcony until she finds her wrap. She leans down and picks it up, turns it over in her hands, but she doesn't put it on. God, I wish she would. Now that I've seen her in that dress, I'm very grateful she had it wrapped up all night. I wouldn't have been able to carry on coherent conversation at the party. Every single person there would have known just exactly how bad I have it for her.

Slowly, Ziggy glances my way, then offers me her hand. "Well, friend . . ." She says the word gently, kindly. A smile tips her mouth as I wrap my hand around hers and squeeze, the way she likes, the way I know she'll squeeze right back. "Got a pair of sweatpants I can borrow?"

"So." Ziggy pops another spoonful of strawberry ice cream into her mouth and looks at me, eyes narrowed from her end of my sofa.

She's wearing one of my black Kings hoodies, a pair of my gray sweatpants, and her hair's braided down past her shoulder. I want depraved, delicious things from her.

Which is why I'm sitting seven feet away, at the other end of my sofa with a pillow on my lap.

Eating pretzel after pretzel scraped through my pint of rocky road, I've been trying to talk down my erection by remembering the last time Kris—who I do *not* find attractive—streaked across the locker room, singing Cher's "Believe" horribly off pitch at the top of his lungs.

It's not working. "So," I offer.

"We," Ziggy says after swallowing her bite, "need to talk about the fact that you went to Ren like this is some Regency romance and reassured him that my virtue was safe."

I almost choke on my mouthful of ice cream and pretzels. "I said absolutely nothing about your virtue."

She spears the spoon back into her ice cream and carves out another bite. "It's implicit in what you said. You told him I was 'safe.'"

"Because I do want you to be safe with me. Your body. Your emotions. All of you. And given what a reckless piece of work I tend to be, it was important for him to know that I was committed to that."

Ziggy pauses, spoon heaped with ice cream hovering at her mouth. She takes a lick and stares at me. "I understand why you wanted to tell him, to make sure your friendship with him doesn't suffer while we do this."

"Exactly."

"Well, I just wish the focus hadn't been so much about protecting me, ya know?"

I pause, pretzel wedged in my ice cream, holding her eyes. "I hear that. I could have said it differently. I leaned into the idea of protecting you rather than stressing what I should have—my commitment to being a decent person for you to be around."

She smiles. "I appreciate that. And I do want to say, I think it's pretty great that you talked with Ren directly. Just a week into this little project of ours, and look at you, using your feeling words with your best friend. That's growth, Sebastian."

My eyes narrow in annoyance, but my mouth kicks up at the corner, a lost battle against a smile I can't fully overpower. "Don't act like this is some defining moment in my journey, Sigrid."

"I would never dream of it." She slips the spoon into her mouth, then pulls it out with a clean *pop*. I wedge the pillow harder on my lap and try not to watch her lick ice cream lingering at the corner of her mouth. "I'm just saying . . . maybe, *maybe* our friendship isn't the only thing that's gone from pretend to real in such a short span." She leans in and steals a spoonful of my rocky road, smiling wide. "Maybe reforming your ways is turning out to be not so pretend, too."

"Even if it was, I couldn't reform *too* much, not when I have your image to keep roughening up." I lean in to steal a scoop of her strawberry ice cream, but when I stick my spoon into her container, Ziggy uses it to tug me toward her, sending me right into her space.

Our mouths are a breath away. Ziggy tips her head and smiles. "How magnanimous of you, *friend*."

I pull out my spoon and sit back, scowling. For someone so sweet, she's a damn good flirt when she wants to be. "Speaking of being friends, when's your next game?"

Ziggy's eyes widen. "My what?"

"Your next game," I repeat slowly.

"Oh. Uh." She tugs on her ear and clears her throat. "Why?"

"Because I'd like to see you play."

Ziggy bites her lip and ducks her head. I watch her cheeks turn as pink as the ice cream she's eating. "You want to see me play?"

"I just said that, didn't I?"

"Well, okay." She shrugs. "So, uh . . . there's my Angel City game. This Sunday is away, but next Sunday is at home. You could come to that."

"Perfect." I set the lid back on my ice cream and shove aside the pretzels. Leaning back, I clench my jaw and draw up my knees. The sharp, nagging pains have started in my stomach again. I really do need to get myself seen. I'm an expert avoider, but even this is too much for me to ignore anymore.

I catch Ziggy frowning at me. "Something wrong?" she asks.

"Just need to lie down so I can bask in my brilliance."

She snorts. "What brilliance is this?"

"How many image-rehabilitating brownie points I'll get for showing my face at a women's soccer game."

Ziggy picks up a couch pillow and smacks me in the face with it. "You're a jerk. Women's soccer deserves more coverage, and I really cannot stand that you are one hundred percent correct. You'll be seen as some benevolent deity blessing us with your presence, rather than someone lucky enough to have front-row seats when we kick Chicago's butt."

I tug the pillow away, combing back my hair, which got fuzzy from being walloped. "Who says I'm getting myself front-row seats?"

Settling back into her corner of the couch, Ziggy rolls her eyes. "Please, Sebastian. I've known you for a week, and I already know exactly where you'll be sitting at that game—front and center, for everyone to see."

SEVENTEEN

Ziggy

Playlist: "Gold," Sister Sparrow

"Doorstep delivery." I set Sebastian's car in park right in front of my apartment building and kill the engine.

Turning toward him, where he sits, clutching my party clothes in his arms, I hold his eyes. "Thanks for tonight."

He huffs an empty laugh and glances out the window. "Don't thank me for that. It was rocky at best."

"It wasn't. I know . . . things got complicated for you at the after-party, and I'm sorry. But the roller race was fun. I had a good time. I think maybe even you did, too."

Sebastian shrugs. "You *are* pretty fun to watch roller-skating. You go as slow skating as when you drive."

I shove his shoulder. "I was skating with *kids*. Of course I went slow! I left the skate racing to the guys who do that for a living. Sometimes knowing how to graciously hang out in the wings is a *strength*, Gauthier."

A soft smile tugs at his mouth. Finally he glances my way. "Fair enough."

A beat of silence hangs between us. That small smile fades as Sebastian peers down at my clothes in his hands. "Ziggy, I just . . . want you to know you really can back out whenever. I feel like an ass, that I didn't consider this when I agreed to our publicity scheme, that this is how it goes for me. Being out in public, I bump into people I've fucked up with." He sniffs, tugging at his rings, spinning one. "I just want you to know, at any point, I'll understand if you don't want to deal with that anymore, if the impact of the skeletons that'll keep falling out of my closet outweigh what you were hoping to get out of this—"

"Sebastian—"

He shoves open his door before I can say more. Then he rounds to my side, drawing open my door after I begin to open it.

Sighing, I ease out of the car. Sebastian shuts my door, and we walk side by side up to the front of my building, then stop and turn, facing each other.

I step close and take my clothes from him, then tuck them under one arm. With my free arm, I find his hand and squeeze it tight in mine. "You keep hopping out of cars, very determined not to listen to me, but I made myself heard earlier, and I'm going to make myself heard now: This is worth it to me."

He stares at me, face tight. "What is?"

"Being friends. It's worth it, whatever it is that you think will make me back out or not stick with you. *You're* worth it. And I'm not going to be spooked by a couple skeletons."

"Yes, well, I have a lot of them," he mutters, massaging the bridge of his nose.

"I know." Letting go of his hand, I slip the key into my apartment building's door, then glance over my shoulder. "And I like you anyway. Good night, Sebastian."

He peers up at me from the sidewalk, gray eyes pale and glowing in the darkness. "Good night, Sigrid."

———

Legs dead, body spent, I walk up to my apartment door, grateful that the past forty-eight hours since the fundraiser and after-party have been a blur. Early rising yesterday, flying out for our away game. Practice, team meeting, team meal, talking with Charlie in our hotel room about the event and after-party—carefully omitting those kisses Sebastian and I shared. Then Sunday's exhausting but victorious game and rushing to catch our flight home. It's all been so mercifully busy, I haven't had much free time for my mind to play a loop of those kisses.

Because when it *does* have free time, that's exactly what it does: replays every moment, every kiss, every touch, over and over.

I have never thought this much about kissing someone. Or about the outcome of those kisses: Sebastian asking if we could just be friends.

Ouch.

Now, without the away-game hustle to occupy my brain, I need to find something else to keep my mind busy until I leave for the National Team's international friendlies the day after tomorrow. I plan to hide in a book this evening, always a sure way to distract myself from real life's complications. Then I'll just have to figure out some other mind-occupying coping strategy until I'm focused on soccer again, and I can push the memory of those kisses right out of my head. For good.

Quiet moments like I have right now, rooting around for my keys, are the problem. My empty mind wanders, and all I can see or think of or feel is Sebastian brushing back my hair from my face as he peered up at me from that chaise, the way he looked at me when he saw me home and we said good night . . .

That's when I get myself into trouble.

At least, until I open my apartment door, confronted with a new kind of trouble, and a very disconcerting development:

My fortress has been breached.

Standing on the threshold, I take in the sight of my brother Viggo's long jean-clad legs stretched out from my reading chair, his face hidden behind one of my favorite fantasy romance novels.

I glance to my right, where my tiny kitchen is located, and there's my brother Oliver, peeling a string cheese.

"Well." I shut the door behind me. "I guess I should be grateful I outlasted you this long."

"Truly impressive," Oliver agrees, dropping a strand of cheese into his mouth. "Definitely the longest any of the siblings have managed to keep us from breaking and entering."

Viggo drops the book only far enough to peer over the top of it. "Wow. Faery smut is good."

"Told you." I drop my keys on the kitchen counter and let my duffel bag fall to the floor, too.

"So." Leaning a hip against the counter, I open my arms wide. "To what do I owe this honor of you lords of mischief breaking in?"

Viggo glances at Oliver. Oliver glances at Viggo. One of their silent eye conversations seems to ensue.

I watch them with a growing sense of annoyance. It's hard not to be jealous sometimes, of how deep their bond runs, the way it makes me feel a little like a third wheel. In our family's birth order, Viggo and Oliver are the youngest besides me, born so close in age, they act like twins and look like it, too. Both of them are a similar blend of Mom and Dad, slightly favoring Mom's sharp bone structure and her pale blue-gray eyes. Oliver got Mom's blond hair, which he shares with Freya and my brother Ryder, and keeps his facial hair to a neat, golden stubble.

Viggo's chocolate-brown hair is like our oldest brother Axel's, his beard thick and dark, tinged with auburn.

While as kids we played together a lot, he and Oliver have always had this frustrating habit of closing ranks and huddling up, just the two of them, when they're getting themselves into mischief.

Which they definitely are right now, paying this visit, even if I'm not sure what that mischief is. Yet.

Silent eye conversation with Oliver concluded, Viggo snaps the book shut and pops up from my reading chair, tall and rangy, ball cap tugged low over his messy brown hair. "What kind of greeting is that?" he asks. "We can't pay our little sister a simple courtesy visit?"

I glance at the clock. "At eight at night? On a Sunday? Don't you have better things to do with the final hours of your weekend than hunker down in my poorly air-conditioned apartment at the sweltering end of August and wait around for me?"

Viggo tugs rhythmically at his shirt, which is indeed clinging to his perspiring chest, fanning himself. "No other way I'd rather spend my Sunday night. How about you, Ollie?"

"No other way," Oliver says, peeling his string cheese. "Even if I was just about to relax with my boyfriend in his new hot tub, minding my own damn business when you corralled me—ouch!" Viggo sidles up next to Oliver with a not-so-subtle elbow to his ribs and rips half of Ollie's string cheese away.

"Hey!" Oliver shoves him. "That's my string cheese."

"Technically, it's *my* string cheese," I point out.

"Too right, Zigs," Viggo says. "And let's be honest, Oliver, I'm doing you a favor, cutting your dairy intake in half."

Oliver glares at Viggo. "Believe it or not, I can handle my dairy intake without you rationing me, Viggo. Besides, Gavin got me supplements that help me digest dairy better."

"Sure they do, honey bunch."

Oliver reaches for the string cheese again. Viggo yanks it away. And as is typical when they don't see eye to eye, they devolve into a scuffle that I'd probably find entertaining—my two giant brothers banging around in my tiny kitchen, fighting over half a string cheese—if I weren't already so annoyed.

"Hey!" I holler. Abruptly, they stumble apart. "I love you both. You know I do. And I'm sure in some warped, twisted, brotherly way, you mean well. But you either need to say what you're here for or get the heck out of my apartment. I'm tired. I'm hot. And I'm hungry. Also," I add, "there's a reason you don't have keys to my place anymore. After you abused that privilege, your key access was revoked."

"Aw, c'mon," Oliver says. "That was a really good prank. And we owed you after the marshmallow fluff stunt you pulled on us at our birthday party."

"Our *birthday* party," Viggo reminds me, like I'm supposed to feel bad about this or something.

I sigh. "Guys, it's not my fault you taught me basically every devious thing I know and the pupil became the master. My point stands—you forfeited your keys, and you weren't supposed to help yourself to my space. I really don't appreciate having my apartment broken into."

"Coming from the woman who's been known to do some pretty stealthy breaking and entering herself," Viggo says, dropping the string cheese half in his mouth. Watching him, Oliver makes a strangled, infuriated noise in the back of his throat.

My cheeks are hot as I blink at Viggo. Is he spying on me? There's no way he's seen me get into Sebastian's house.

He smiles smugly. "That's a guilty look on your face, Zigs. Care to share what you've been up to lately?"

Now I'm making a strangled, infuriated noise, too. "Good grief, Viggo, stop being so . . ."

"Brilliant? Observant? Cunning?" He opens my fridge door, like he's honestly going to help himself to something else in there. I slam it shut.

"*Annoying*, is what I was going for. Mind your own business."

He moves to the snack cabinet next and beats me to it when I lunge to stop him, pilfering a chocolate chip granola bar and slipping out of reach. "We both know minding my business is not one of the many skills I've cultivated—"

"Well, you really should," I snap, glancing between him and Oliver. "Also, you two have a lot of nerve forcing your way into my home, acting all chummy, when the last time we were together as a family, it was very clear *you* knew something I've been kept out of."

"Crap," Oliver mutters.

Viggo has the grace to look a little ashamed as he chews a massive bite of granola bar, scrubbing at the back of his neck. "Yeah," he says around his bite. "About that . . ."

"We're sorry," Oliver adds. "Mom and Dad, they were worried it would upset you, so they asked us not to say anything, but then Dad did that thing he does every couple of years, where he actually loses his temper a little bit, and he snapped at Ren because Ren was in rare form that night, too, and pushing the topic, then the keep-it-on-the-down-low aspect was sort of shot to shit."

"Very shot to shit," I agree, folding my arms across my chest. "Now. How about you tell me what's going on?"

Viggo and Oliver glance at each other, having another silent eye conversation.

"It's money," Oliver finally explains. "Our college loans, specifically."

"Which Dad insists on paying," Viggo provides. "To the detriment of his and Mom's retirement savings—"

"So Ren asked to pay them. Well, he asked on behalf of the siblings, if each of us could."

I suck in a breath, my chest suddenly tight. "Why would you keep that from me?"

"One, because as a fellow anxious soul, I know that you're a worrier," Oliver says, "and you'd worry about Mom and Dad's retirement."

I am indeed worrying about Mom and Dad's retirement.

"Two," Viggo adds, "you have no student loan debt, because you're an overachiever who got a full ride."

"I still deserve to be included. Plus, I'm good with Dad. He listens to me. Have you ever seen me ask Dad for something and heard him say no?"

Viggo scratches his jaw. "Come to think of it, no. But you don't ask for much."

"That's the key," I tell them both.

"Wow." Oliver sighs. "We're brick heads for keeping you out of it."

"I know. And guess what? I could have insinuated myself and helped out, despite your best efforts to keep me in the dark, had I not been stuck at the kids' end of the table with my sippy cup and Pokémon coloring book."

Viggo bites his lip. "I thought you liked it down there."

Oliver gives me big, sad puppy eyes. "Yeah, me too."

"Well, I don't. I'm a grown woman, and I'd like to be treated as such in our family, okay?"

Viggo slumps against the kitchen counter, scrubbing at his beard. "Sorry, Zigs. We'll do better about that."

"I'm sorry, too, and I promise I'll do better," Oliver says.

"I'll own I could have stuck up for myself. I could have said, 'Love ya, Linnie, but Aunt Ziggy's going to join the adults for this one.' I'm going to do that from now on, so just . . . yeah, don't be weird about it when I do."

"Ziggy." Oliver sounds genuinely hurt. "We would never."

"Really, Zigs." Viggo steps closer, holding my eyes. "We're always on your side. The three amigos, right?"

I smile and swallow against the lump that's knotted in my throat. "Yeah. Three amigos."

"Sandwich cookie hug?" Ollie throws open his arms.

"Sandwich cookie hug," Viggo agrees.

Sighing, I step between them and let them squish me like filling in a sandwich cookie, how they always have. I pretend I hate it but secretly love this—the pressure of them, the comfort of their familiar scents and voices. I love my family, even when they're annoying me. And right now, I feel a bit of the icy anger I've been harboring since that Sunday dinner thaw inside me.

"Nice as this has been," I mumble, "get off me, and get out of my apartment."

"Fine," Viggo sighs. "But first, how about you explain why you and Ren's bad-boy bestie have been photographed rubbing shoulders the past week?"

"I mean, only if you want," Oliver says diplomatically. "There's no pressure. Tell us in your own time—"

Viggo swats him from the confines of our group hug. "Oliver, what did we talk about?"

Oliver swats him back. "And by 'What did we talk about?' you mean, 'What did you tell me you were going to do that I firmly disagreed on?'"

"My dudes, I'm right here."

I'm ignored.

"You have a better idea for getting to the bottom of this?" Viggo hisses.

I shove my way out of their building physical animosity and reach for the door. "Both of you, out!"

They turn my way, frozen in a tableau of tangled, hostile limbs. "Ziggy," Viggo says sweetly, "we just want to make sure you're okay."

Oliver shoves Viggo away and steps close to me. "We love you, Zigs, and we respect your privacy. It's just . . . weird for us not to know what's going on, let alone when you've started hanging out with someone really . . . unlike you."

I grit my teeth and force a smile. "Sebastian is a friend. That's it. He might seem very different from me on the surface, but there are parts of him . . ."

I think about the tiny ways in just the past week Sebastian has shown me that there's deeply caring goodness beneath his tough exterior, that—even though I don't know exactly why or what caused it—he's someone who doesn't connect with a lot of people and struggles to know how to do better.

"There are parts of him that are more like me than you think," I finish. "Now, get out of here. Go relax with your boyfriend," I tell Oliver. "And go back," I tell Viggo, "to whatever not-so-stealthy shenanigans you're trying to be stealthy about down in Escondido."

Viggo gapes at me.

"Yeah," I say with a smile, herding both of my brothers toward the door. "I'm not quite as oblivious as you think. Goodbye, you two. Love you."

Oliver scrambles for my fridge door, then grabs a new string cheese on his way out. Viggo frowns as I nudge him backward. "But—"

I pick up the fantasy romance novel he was reading from where he abandoned it on my kitchen counter, then shove it into his chest, pushing him over the threshold. "And next time you want to 'stop by for a visit,' knock first."

EIGHTEEN

Ziggy

Playlist: "Somewhere in Between," Morningsiders

There's a knock—at least, I *think* there's a knock—on my door as I sit curled up in my reading chair with an abandoned book in my lap. I frown at the door, waiting to see if I hear it again, but I don't, so I go back to talking on the phone with Charlie, who was absent from practice today, out sick with a cold.

She and I haven't connected since we got back from our away game last weekend and I had to hit the road—well, the air—with the National Team for a couple international friendlies. I just got back last night, then dragged my butt out of bed for Angel City practice this morning, but Charlie was out sick, so we're getting caught up now.

"So," she says. "You kicked butt during your international friendlies and got some great press coverage of it, which is incredible. Your news hits and social media stats are still trending upward, meaning more visibility and public image clout—that's good, too. The speculation about you and the gremlin, however, is less than ideal, but unavoidable, I suppose."

She's talking about the latest social media buzz from photos of Sebastian and me after our most recent angry yoga morning. Before I left for my friendlies, Sebastian surprised me by initiating plans for another session early in the morning, before I caught my flight—roaring, cussing, sweating our way through a fast-paced flow set to blaring punk rock.

Surprisingly, I got so into yoga and then my massive breakfast (I was starving), that I didn't think about the kisses *too* much. After our quick breakfast at the same spot as last time, we parted ways, both of us in a rush, without even a platonic hug goodbye. It doesn't matter, though.

As Sebastian predicted that first night at the diner, there's been ongoing conjecture that he and I might be more than friends.

Knowing how much Charlie disapproves of Sebastian, I decide to sidestep that remark. "I can't complain," I tell her. "Rory"—my agent—"says I have some promising new sponsorship opportunities that she's vetting, but best of all, I'm telling you, it was different when I was with the National Team, the whole time. Not just during the games, with how well I played, but traveling, practices— I even did an interview and only stumbled over my words a little. No one's ever been unkind or unwelcoming to me on the team, of course, but this time I just felt . . . seen and respected in a way I never had before. It felt *good*."

I hear the smile in Charlie's voice. "That's great, Zigs. You deserve it. I'm glad this is working how you wanted."

"Thanks, friend, I—"

There it is again. Definitely another knock. I frown, because no one should be knocking on my apartment door. I haven't invited anybody over.

If this is Viggo and Oliver trying to be cute after that break-and-enter they pulled last weekend, it's not cute. It's annoying. Is it such a crime to want a cozy Saturday night in, enjoying a chat with my best friend and the comforting predictability of rereading a favorite romance novel?

"Sorry, Char." I ease up from my chair, crossing my apartment to the door. "Someone just knocked. Going to go see who it is."

"Don't just open the door. Check the peephole. You're a celebrity now. Who knows who's out there."

I snort a laugh. "I'm not a celebrity."

"Well, you definitely aren't 'an unknown redhead' anymore, either."

I stop short of the door, leaning against the wall. Whoever it is can wait a minute while I wrap up with my friend. "I'll be careful. Promise."

"Good. I'll sign off and let you go. I need to take more antihistamines and sit in the shower again to deal with this sinus pressure. My head feels like a foot."

I smile. Charlie's full of funny sayings like that. "Good idea. Take care of yourself. I'm sorry you feel so crappy, Char."

"Ah, that's okay. This is what happens when Gigi and I babysit her niece. I always get some crud from her. But she's cute, so it's worth it."

I smile, thinking of my niece and nephew, little Linnea and baby Theo, who have definitely shared a couple bugs with me, after evenings of babysitting, snuggles, and cuddles. "Take it easy, and get some rest," I tell her.

"Will do. Good luck tomorrow. Sorry I'll be leaving you high and dry in the midfield."

"Well, I'll let it go this once, but after tomorrow, no more abandoning me. I'll miss you out there. Talk after the game, okay?"

"'Kay." She sneezes loudly and, by the sounds of a *clunk* followed by her far-off voice, drops the phone. "Bye, Zigs!"

The call disconnects, and I pocket my phone, then step up to the door, peering through the peephole. Good thing I'm not holding my phone anymore, because I'd drop it, too.

Sebastian Gauthier is on the other side of my door. Leaning against the opposite wall, he looks like he could be sleeping—head back, eyes shut, hands in his pockets.

He was quiet those couple of days after our big night, minimally communicative when scheduling angry yoga. And then he dropped off again after Wednesday evening, when I texted him the link to a really positive write-up about him. It featured photos of Sebastian with the attending kids and his teammates at the roller rink fundraiser, as well as of the two of us smiling at each other over breakfast after angry yoga, saying it seems he's finally turned over a new leaf—a huge PR win.

And what did he do?

He tapped back a double exclamation point and hasn't said a word since. Damn tapbacks: where in-depth text conversations go to die.

So why is Mr. Tapback and Go Radio Silent here?

Curious, I unlock the door, then open it. "Sebastian?"

His eyes snap open as he jolts, then pushes off the wall. Clearing his throat, he rakes a hand through his hair, not the way he does when he wants to fix it, but in the way I've already learned means he's uneasy. "Hey, Ziggy."

I stare at him, as butterflies burst to life in my stomach and flutter right through my limbs.

My fingertips tickle. My toes curl.

He's a little rumpled—faded blue jeans that look old and loved hugging his powerful hockey player legs, even leaned up from his obvious weight loss. His pale gray-green T-shirt—the one that I love, the one that makes his eyes jump—is wrinkled and drapes too loosely on his shoulders. There's so much ink to look at, more than I've ever seen, weaving up his arms and biceps, peeking out at his collarbones.

I'm blushing. I have to be, knowing how hot my cheeks feel. Clearing my throat, I hold open my door. "Do you, uh . . . want to come in?"

He seems to hesitate, halfway between the wall and my door. "Yeah. If that's okay."

"Sure. Of course. Yes." I lean behind the door and hide for a second as I open it wide for him, grimacing at myself. Could I be more awkward?

Stepping into my apartment, Sebastian moves past me, out of the way, so I can close the door. He stands almost unnaturally still, like a cat ready to bolt, tension coiling his body as he shoves his hands into his pockets. There's nothing of the nonchalant, sardonic man who breezed into my place just a few weeks ago, cut my jeans into shorts, and busted me about my whole wardrobe being athleticwear.

"What's wrong, Sebastian?"

The words are out of my mouth before I can stop them, but often, that's how things go with me. I'm honest to a fault, not just in what I share but what I ask. Frankie says it's damn refreshing, but then again, she's autistic, too—she appreciates my candor. Not everyone does, though. I've learned that the hard way.

Slowly, Sebastian glances my way, his gaze traveling my face up to my hair. I am suddenly reminded my wet hair is twisted into my favorite dragon-print towel turban. My hands reflexively go there as Sebastian stares at it, the corner of his mouth rising. "Dragons, huh?"

I clear my throat, letting my hands fall. "They're my favorite reptile."

His smile deepens, and my heart kicks in my chest. "I didn't know imaginary creatures were fair game for favorites."

"Who says they're imaginary?"

He presses his tongue into his cheek. "Science?"

"There's no science disproving the existence of dragons."

"Except the fact that we've never seen one."

"Just because we haven't seen something doesn't mean it doesn't exist." I fold my arms across my chest and prop a foot on the wall as I rest against it. "Some of the most beautiful discoveries have come from the persistent pursuit of a possibility most people were too ready to give up on."

Sebastian leans his hip into my kitchen counter, eyes dancing over my face, up to the towel turban again. "Fair enough."

"So." I push off the wall and brush past him into my kitchen, before opening my glasses cabinet. "Want a drink? You know, water or something? It's hot as heck out there. I bet you're thirsty. Did you walk?"

He turns, watching me, then shakes his head. "No, I'm out of the boot. I drove. And no, thank you. I'm okay."

I lower my hand from where it's been heading toward the cabinet. "Right. Sure."

"I . . . brought the roller rink clothes you left at my place." He glances over his shoulder to my duffel bag. "Rainbow earrings, black romper, high-tops, and fuzzy ankle socks. That was everything, right?"

"Yeah, it was. Thanks."

Sebastian stares at me, shifting his weight, leaning harder into my counter. Finally he says, "I'm sorry I've dropped off the radar a lot the past week."

My heart flip-flops. I wasn't the only one who noticed, then, who felt there was a significance to our silence. That shouldn't matter to me. But it definitely does.

"Oh." I shrug, turning and leaning against the counter, too, stretching out my legs. "That's fine. I mean, you know. Friends do that."

He stares down at his hands, spinning one of his rings. "Well, I don't know about that. Maybe some do. I'm no friend expert. But . . . I don't think that's the kind of friend I want to be to you."

I bite my lip. "It's really okay, Sebastian—"

"Don't do that," he says, peering up at me. "Don't go easy on me. You never have before. You're different. *We're* different. Just like you told me."

At the mention of what I said last weekend, the memory of our kisses feels so tangible between us, it's like for a moment it's a third person in the room, bursting through, all color and heat and sparkle. But then I remind myself what he said afterward, even though he said our kisses were good, even though his enthusiastic response seemed to indicate he enjoyed himself as much as I did:

"*. . . you asked me to be your friend, Ziggy, and I'm hardly worthy of that, but I'd like to be. Don't ask more of me, please.*"

I told myself I'd honor that request. And I mean to, even if I've thought a *lot* about just what exactly "more" could mean.

Pushing aside kissing thoughts, I clear my throat and meet Sebastian's gaze. "Okay. Well, in that case, I was worried about you."

A muscle in his jaw jumps. He nods.

"And I . . . sort of missed talking to you."

His eyes hold mine. "Yeah. I . . . missed that, too."

I try not to smile, hearing that, but I fail. Twisting my mouth, I try to hide it. "Is that why you're here? Or was it just to drop off the clothes?"

A heavy sigh leaves him. Sebastian brings his hands to his face and scrubs it roughly. "I think so, yes. I mean . . . it wasn't just the clothes. It wasn't even mostly the clothes." His hands fall. "Fuck me, I don't know—I don't have experience with this. I'm flailing around, trying to find my way. I want to be around you without being a depraved asshole who only teases you or is sticking his tongue down your throat, but clearly that's not a skill set I've spent a lot of time developing."

I almost tell him I really don't mind the teasing, because Lord knows I like giving it right back to him. I almost tell him I wish he'd stick his tongue down my throat again already. That I have thoroughly missed that—*all* of that—everything that I feel and experience when spending time with Sebastian.

But he told me his boundary. He told me what he wants. *Friends.* Nothing that compromises his friendship with Ren. Nothing that makes him feel like he's crossed the line with me into a place he's uncomfortable with.

I'm going to respect that.

Even if I'm pretty sure I've stumbled into a pretty serious crush on Sebastian Gauthier. Even if I feel possibility crackle in the air between us, a magnetic pull right in the center of me, drawing me toward him.

"Well . . ." I push off the counter. "We did fine at angry yoga, before I left. No depraved assholery. Or . . . tongues down throats."

Sebastian blows out another heavy breath. "Yeah."

"Sure, things got quiet here and there, but that took two of us. We're just figuring this out, Sebastian. There's bound to be bumps on the road. Now you're here. I'm here. And we both missed talking. So let's go sit and . . . talk."

Sebastian glances toward my reading chair, the only seating I have. It's oversized, enough to fit two average-sized people. He and I, however, are not average-sized people. Sebastian clears his throat. "I'll stand."

"No." I start past him, taking his hand and tugging him with me. "I can sit on the floor, stretch out on the rug. I need to do my nighttime stretches anyway—"

Suddenly my hand is tugged, and I'm wrenched back toward Sebastian, making me stumble into him.

He stares at me, his thumb circling my palm. "Sorry. I . . ." He shakes his head. "Sorry. I just think I . . ."

Standing still, I search his eyes. "You think . . . ?" I offer gently.

"I think . . ." His hand slides up my arm, drawing me closer. "I might need . . . a hug. If you're, uh, comfortable with that."

A smile lifts my mouth. That's all he needed? I wonder why it was so hard to ask.

Then I remember how he stepped back as soon as I walked out the door from our breakfast spot earlier this week, how I barely caught that nonverbal cue in time to hide the fact that I was about to open my arms and hug him goodbye. I lifted my arms for a stretch over my head, complaining about how Yuval had kicked our butts.

He didn't want a hug then. And yet he wants one now?

Maybe because the last time you put your hands on him, you practically threw yourself at him? Maybe because he wasn't sure he could ask for a simple hug without you trying to maul his mouth with yours again?

Right. Well. This is my chance to show him that I can hug him, just as friends.

"Of course you can have a hug," I tell him. Thinking platonic thoughts, I wrap my arms gently around his neck. Sebastian lists into me, but slowly, almost as if he's resisting it.

He doesn't seem like he has much more knowledge of platonic hugs than he does of friendships. So I wait, giving him time to feel it out. Carefully, hesitantly, he wraps his arms around my back and pulls me close. Our chests touch, hearts beating against each other.

And then, little by little, I feel his body relax, tension leave his shoulders as they lower, air fill his lungs slow and easy.

"There," I tell him, scraping my fingertips gently across the nape of his neck and the curl of his hair. "You got the hang of it."

"Fuck," he mutters against my neck. "Hugs are good."

I smile into his shoulder. "Yeah, they are."

For a while, we just stand there, Sebastian with his arms around me, mine around him, chins on each other's shoulders. "Sorry," he whispers.

I comb my fingers through the ends of his hair again. "You don't need to be sorry for needing a hug, Sebastian."

He squeezes me a little, tucking me closer, and exhales heavily. "Well, I'm also sorry I showed up uninvited at your apartment. You have a game tomorrow. I shouldn't keep you up." He starts to pull away. "I should go."

"Wait." I lock my arms around his neck, holding him there. "Just . . . slow down."

He sighs against me and gradually tightens his hold again. But he doesn't say anything.

"*I* don't want you to go unless you want to go," I tell him. "Do *you* want to go?"

He hesitates, then after a few seconds, shakes his head.

"So stay. Talk to me."

He pulls back a little, his hand lingering on my hip, the sweep of his thumb across my waist sending heat waving beneath my skin.

Clearing his throat, Sebastian takes an awkward step back, nervously raking a hand through his hair.

"Come on," I tell him. This time he lets me thread my fingers through his and tug him into the living room area of my studio. "Sit." Gently, I push his shoulders until he drops into my reading chair.

I firmly push past the memories that evokes, of him falling onto a different kind of chair—the chaise on his deck—of me straddling his lap.

We're definitely making the right choice, sitting in two different places.

Sinking to the floor, I sit, too, and settle my legs into a wide straddle. "You sit and talk. I'll stretch and listen."

Sebastian stares at me as I lean forward in between my legs, reaching both my toes and pulling on them until I feel a nice tug in my hamstrings. He brings his knuckles to his mouth and sighs. "I've been feeling like shit."

I freeze, holding his eyes, keeping quiet, listening like I promised him I would.

"So," he sighs out, "I talked with Dr. Amy"—she's the team's lead physician—"had some tests run. That's part of why I've been quiet this week—I had all these appointments and diagnostics to get through."

Horrible, horrible fears streak through my brain. He's sick. There's something wrong with him. My heart does a terrible, constricting twist and starts to crumple in my chest.

"Since I was a kid," he says, still rubbing his knuckles across his mouth, "my stomach, it's always . . . I've always had these episodes where it just hurt like hell. Sharp, stabbing pain. Sometimes they were frequent. Then they'd go away for days, weeks. I'd get these aches all over, this dull, persistent headache. It was like a fog settled into my brain, and everything hurt. I'd just wanted to curl up in a ball and sleep. My stepdad, he'd tell me to toughen up, stop whining and lying around, said I was faking it to get attention, which was not fucking true . . . But I learned to push through it, ignore it, accept it.

"When I was in high school, I figured out weed helped the pain. Alcohol was a nice addition, just . . . numbed me right up." He sniffs, dropping his hand, playing with his rings. "But lately, it's just been so bad, I knew I couldn't ignore it, so I told Dr. Amy all this, and she had a bunch of bloodwork done, some other tests, and turns out I have, of all the fucking things, celiac disease."

Air whooshes out of me. I drop my forehead to the floor.

"Ziggy?"

I suck in a breath and sit up, blinking away evidence that I was on the verge of tears. "I thought you were about to tell me you were dying."

He frowns at me. "Well, I mean, I *might* die of disappointment that I'll never be able to eat another Milky Way again, which is one of about a million fucking things I can't eat anymore. I won't lie, I'm a little devastated. I fucking love Milky Ways. But no, I'm not dying."

"Okay," I breathe out, swallowing past the lump in my throat. "Excellent. Good. Great. I mean, it's not *great* that you have celiac disease—that really is crap—but it's, you know, good, that you're not . . . dying."

Sebastian leans in, elbows on his knees, his mouth tipped up at the corner. "Are you . . . crying?"

"No," I tell him, reaching for my right leg and bending over it, which conveniently hides the fact that I might have a few tears about to leak out.

His foot nudges mine. I narrow my eyes up at him. That jerk's smiling. For the first time, he's really, truly smiling, all bright white teeth and long, deep dimples. It *transforms* him. Tiny crinkles at the corners of those lovely gray eyes, a slight dimple in his chin.

Of course, now is when he unleashes that devastating smile on me, when I'm having a crisis.

A crisis that I've only known this guy for two weeks, half of which we've spent mostly bickering, in firm agreement that we weren't even *real* friend material, and yet I was about to lose my mind that something was seriously wrong with him.

"Sigrid," he says, nudging my toe with his again. "You really catastrophized there, didn't you?"

I clear my throat, shifting my stretch to the other leg, refusing to look at him. "Maybe."

"Well, you don't get to eulogize me quite yet."

I glare up at him. "That's not funny."

Sebastian stares at me, his smile fading. "You've known me for two weeks. What would you have to miss?"

"Plenty of annoying things," I tell him, nudging his foot back. "Your vain obsession with your hair. Your habit of deflecting authentic, honest communication with self-deprecating humor and sarcasm. Your . . . irritating tendency to surprise me with kindness when I had you all figured out as a self-absorbed jerk."

His eyebrows rise. He stares at me. "I'm still a self-absorbed jerk," he finally says. "Now I'm just a self-absorbed jerk with an autoimmune disease that fucks up my stomach."

I sit on the palms of my hands, staring right back at him. I'm learning Sebastian.

Learning that words are his sword and shield. That he wields them fiercely to hold healing at bay. I see in him what I've seen in myself plenty over the past few years—a desperate desire to change, to heal and grow, and an even more desperate fear of what that takes, what it will look like . . . all the ways I might get hurt while I try.

So I don't say anything in response to that familiar self-condemning comment. I can't win this battle of words with Sebastian Gauthier. But maybe I can one day win the war through *showing* him I don't believe what he says about himself, by showing him the good I see in him, through the simple act of time and presence, until I can only hope, one day, Sebastian sees in himself what I see, too.

"I'm sorry," I tell him. "Celiac disease, it sucks. I mean it's good that you know now, so you can hopefully feel a lot better. But just because there's a clear path for dealing with it going forward doesn't mean it's easy or fun or you can't feel sad about not eating Milky Ways."

"Or decent pizza," he mutters, flopping back in the chair, picking up the novel I'd left there and fanning through the pages. "Or donuts. Or baguette. Or chocolate silk pie. Or a brioche bun." He sets aside the book and rakes his hands through his hair. "It's ridiculous that I'm this miserable about all the foods I can't eat anymore. It's just food."

I nudge his toe with mine. "Food isn't just food, though. It's comfort and memory. It's family recipes and meals shared with friends. Food is a fulcrum of socializing and relationships, and now you don't get to just show up to that. You have to think ahead and tell people your dietary needs and explain them again when they're lunkheads about it or, worse, well-meaning, but very poor at understanding it. You'll probably end up accidentally eating something that hurts you every once in a while, and going to a restaurant will sort of suck until you find places that have nice gluten-free options. It's a big deal. It's a disease that's interrupted and fundamentally altered your lifestyle, impacted your relationships. It's very valid to be upset about that."

He glances down at me and sighs. "Well, at least the 'impacted relationships' part isn't at play, seeing as I don't have any."

"The hell you don't," I tell him, standing up, putting my hands on my hips. Sebastian stares up at me, eyes searching mine. "What am I, then? And Ren?"

Slowly, he sits up, too, and clasps the tips of my fingers. "Anyone ever told you that you've got the whole badass Valkyrie thing going, when you get fired up?"

"Stop deflecting, Sebastian Gauthier."

He traps his lip between his teeth, still looking up at me. "But I'm almost as good at deflecting as I am at hockey."

I arch an eyebrow.

He sighs, his fingers still sliding along mine. "You're right," he says quietly. "I just didn't want to talk about it, because I don't like feeling . . . knocked back on my heels, powerless, like there's something wrong with me."

I turn my palm, sliding our hands together. "Yeah. I hear that. It's okay to feel that way, you know? I'm not great at it myself, but I'm working on it with my therapist. To let myself feel things, even when they're hard."

"I don't feel like it's okay," he mutters, peering down at our tangled hands, taking mine in both of his and tracing my fingers. "I don't know how to do that. Be okay with not . . . being okay."

I watch him as he examines my hand, then I do something my lizard brain clearly told my other hand to do, because before the much more sensible, rational part of my brain can tell it what a bad idea this is, my free hand glides softly through his hair. "You learn by practice and more practice. Like anything you want to get good at. Little by little. Baby steps."

His thumb slides along my index finger and a sweet, hot ache settles low in my stomach. My fingers being touched should not turn me on like this.

Sebastian leans into my touch as I softly comb through his hair. "How do I do those baby steps?"

"Well, I think it's different for everyone. For me, I let myself acknowledge my 'not okayness,' my difficult feelings, which can be really, really intense. It's hard for me. Then, if they start to feel like they're too much to stay with, and generally they do, I use what my therapist calls 'distress tolerance.'"

"Distress tolerance?" He turns his face just enough that the words are whispered against my palm, hot and damp against my skin.

A shiver runs through me. "Something that helps you navigate intensely difficult emotions or situations. Often, they'll be distractions. Pleasurable distractions. Comforting distractions. *Healthy* distractions, preferably."

He groans into my palm, and I arch reflexively, just a little, hopefully not enough that he notices.

I think he notices. And I think, maybe he's a little wound up like I am, too, because he turns his face, until his lips graze my palm. "Distractions, huh?" he breathes against my skin. "Pleasurable, comforting distractions?"

I swallow thickly, combing my fingers through his hair, way too keyed up from simply his mouth brushing my hand.

Sebastian leans closer and sets his forehead against my hip on a heavy exhale. "Healthy distractions," he whispers, pressing his forehead harder into my hip, blowing out another breath. "Right."

"Happy distractions," I whisper. My voice comes out hoarse and uneven. Somewhere in the past ten seconds of this . . . whatever this is, my eyes fell shut, and they stay that way. All I know is soft, sweet darkness, the weight of his head against my stomach, his fingers tangled with mine.

"I think . . ." He clears his throat roughly. His voice is hoarse and uneven, too. "Happy and healthy distractions might be diametrically opposed with me."

"That's not true."

Slowly, he pulls back. I open my eyes gradually, dazed as I peer down at him. I force my hand to leave his hair, but not before my thumb grazes his ear. His eyelids flutter for a heartbeat.

"How so?" he asks.

I smile, setting my hands on his shoulders. "Hockey. Makes you happy and healthy. And if it's anything like soccer is for me, considering its demanding, consuming schedule, I'd say it functions as a distraction, too."

His brow furrows. "Huh. I never thought of it like that."

"How did you think of it?"

He tips his head back, all smirk and silver eyes, but there's something different about it, something soft at the edges of how he looks at me. "As something I'm fucking amazing at."

I roll my eyes, but a laugh still sneaks out. "Well, reframe it. It keeps you busy, and it's something that clearly brings you joy, that's very good for you. Happy, healthy distraction. Soon, you'll be back at it, but it's not available to you tonight, so . . . want to try something else?"

His hands settle on my hips, rocking me closer. "Something else?"

I stare at him, warring with myself. I want so badly to push him back, straddle his lap, settle my hips over his, and kiss him breathless all over again.

Friends! the voice of reason reminds me. *He only wants to be friends!*

Friends. Right. I can do this.

"Something . . . relatively healthy," I explain. "It does involve a lot of sugar, but it won't make you sick. And it involves chocolate, too, so I think it's going to make you pretty happy."

His eyes light up. "I'm listening."

NINETEEN

Sebastian

Playlist: "Transatlantique," Beirut

"This is . . . wild." I take another bite of flourless chocolate cake and savor it, butter-rich and bittersweet, melting on my tongue. "It's gluten-free. And it doesn't taste like ass."

Ziggy grins my way as she swallows her bite of (gluten-free) berry muffin. "Pretty darn good, right?"

I stare at her as she turns back to watching the sunset from my second-floor balcony, enjoying the dramatic irony of sitting here with her when just two weeks ago she was staring me down while I moped in my underwear. "Pretty darn good," I agree.

"I'm glad you like it." Ziggy takes another bite of her muffin, chewing thoughtfully.

"Rooney, my sister-in-law—the one I texted earlier who sent the gluten-free kitchen essentials list—she's the one who recommended this bakery. She said, eating this way is really manageable, so long as you make sure you're stocked up on good substitutes, and that includes a good substitute bakery."

"My belly thanks you, and soon my kitchen will, too."

Ziggy smiles. "Online grocery shopping is a beautiful thing."

"Usually I'd agree, but I wasn't anticipating it being beautiful. I figured I'd be scouring every goddamn item for proof of being gluten-free. You, however, saved the day."

I use my fork to cut into the cake, then stretch my hand toward her, a big chocolatey bite poised on the fork's edge. "Want a taste?"

She smiles my way, eyes lighting up. "Thought you'd never ask."

"Well, as our chocolate milkshake history dictates, it was offer you a bite or have the whole thing pilfered from me."

She laughs as she leans in, clasping my hand to guide the fork into her mouth. A groan leaves her. "Wow, that's good."

I stare at her mouth as she shuts her eyes, savoring her bite.

God, I'm torturing myself watching her, but I can't stop. Wanting her, denying myself her, it's the kind of pain that consumes me like the hardest practice on the ice—muscles shaking, burning lungs, sweat pouring down me. It's what Ziggy called it that first night at the diner. A good hurt.

"One more bite," she mutters, guiding my hand with the fork, breaking off another piece of chocolate cake, then bringing it to her mouth. I sneak a swipe of my thumb across her hand, just to feel her skin, warm and soft.

"Why didn't you get this, too?" I ask. "You like chocolate, obviously."

She shrugs, sitting back as she sets her feet on my deck railing. "Chocolate's too rich for me to want all of a chocolate something. I just like little tastes."

"Not what your consumption of my chocolate milkshakes and breakfast smoothies indicates."

She rolls her eyes. "Oh, come on, I don't drink *that* much of them."

"Verily, Sigrid, you do."

"Verily!" She laughs. "Now who's talking like a nerd?"

I laugh, too. "Maybe I am a giant nerd, and you just didn't know it. I'm a man of many mysteries."

Ziggy glances my way, her expression changing to something

soft, something curious. Something that makes me want to kiss her. Very badly. "I know you are."

I stare at her, telling myself to do what I promised myself I would—stay strong, keep my hands to myself. I won't let myself wrench her onto my lap and kiss her until her hair and the sky are the same breathtaking fiery color, until all I know is that flame-bright beauty wrapped around me, the sea breeze mingling with her sweet clean scent and the warm satin softness of her skin beneath my hands.

Steeling myself, I exhale slowly, steadily. But it's hard to do that, let alone think straight, when Ziggy stares at me, too.

Slowly she leans in. I hold my breath, telling myself I won't let her kiss me—*if* she's going to kiss me. God, I want her to kiss me. God, I shouldn't want her to kiss me—

She swipes her thumb across the corner of my mouth, then brings it to her own and sucks it clean. "See?" she whispers. "Just what I like. A little taste."

I couldn't speak if I wanted to. I can barely breathe. Sunset bathes her face in tangerine light, makes her eyes sparkle. Ziggy blushes, a pink-peach blossom on her cheeks as she stares at me.

And then she leans in again. I . . . well, I lean in, too. Because I'm weak. So fucking weak for her.

We're closer, closer—

And then my phone blasts, my security app emitting a sound that means my doorbell's been rung.

I swear under my breath and duck my head. Ziggy springs out of her chair so fast, she nearly drops her muffin to the deck, juggling it a few times before she catches it firmly. "Groceries are here!" she says brightly, darting past me toward the doors that lead inside.

I slump back into the deck chair and scrape my hands through my hair.

Generally, I'm a deep lover of grocery delivery, the fact that all I need to eat, for a small fee and tip, can be delivered right to my doorstep without my leaving the comfort of home or having to brave the public.

Right now, I have never hated grocery delivery more.

"Well, Sigrid." I fold flat the last paper bag from our grocery delivery and set it on my kitchen counter. "I'm impressed."

"Impressed? Why?" She slides a box of gluten-free cornbread mix onto my pantry shelf, then reaches for the gluten-free pasta boxes on the counter beside her.

"Just . . . how much you know about gluten-free eating. What brands are good, which ones are shit. Look at all this. I have everything I could possibly think of, and then some."

She glances over her shoulder, smiling at me. "I told you, it's all Rooney. It's her list. She's the true gluten-free expert. I only added a few things of my own that I've picked up along the way, stuff I've noticed has met my brother's culinary standards."

"*His* culinary standards?"

"Axel's the meal maker in their family," she explains. "Rooney can't cook to save her life."

"And Rooney's the one who has celiac?"

"No." She lines up the gluten-free pastas by type, straightening out the boxes. "She has ulcerative colitis. They just figured out that it helps with her symptoms, eating gluten-free."

"Really." I open up my freezer to add the gluten-free pizzas that Ziggy swore by.

"Lots of people eat this way. It's a lot more common than it used to be, so that's a silver lining. More yummy options for you than for people who got diagnosed even a couple years ago. And you can afford them."

"Yeah, that's a fact. This shit's expensive."

She turns, fishing around the counter for something. "Sebastian, I didn't want to pry earlier, when we were at the bakery getting our treats, and you asked if I knew anything about gluten-free groceries, not just baked goods, because I was more than happy to help, but . . . wouldn't your personal chef handle this for you? Your assistant? You can ask them for help with this, you know."

I come so close to swallowing the words, keeping them to myself, but dammit, she has this infuriating power to yank out my honesty like there's a hook she's sunk inside me and all it takes is a little tug on her end to reel it right out.

"I don't like other people in my house. It's my safe space, and it doesn't feel safe when people are traipsing around it all the time. I don't have an assistant. Or a personal chef."

She blinks at me, clearly surprised. "Oh . . . okay."

"Surprised Mr. Fancy Pants doesn't have a minion for every possible need? Shocked I don't pay someone to wipe my ass?"

She lobs a bag of gluten-free rolls at my head, which wouldn't be too big a deal, if they weren't frozen. "Christ, you have an arm on you."

She glares at me, but it's playful. "You have to admit you emit a very bougie, fancy pro-athlete vibe."

"I admit that," I tell her, picking up the rolls and reading the ingredients. Apparently there are twelve different grains that go into making a decent gluten-free baked good. And xanthan gum.

Everything has xanthan gum.

Ziggy closes the distance between us and takes the rolls from me. "I was just teasing about it being bougie, having a chef and PA. Those seem like reasonable needs for someone as busy and active as you. Maybe you should look into one, a chef at least."

I shrug, sorting through the rest of what's on the counter into pantry, freezer, and fridge items. "I like cooking sometimes. I make big batches of things, then freeze them."

"Well, I already asked Axel to send me his best recipes, so I'll forward those your way when I get them."

I glance up. "You did? When?"

"When you drove us to the bakery."

"You just . . . asked your brother about that . . . for me."

She gives me a funny look. "Yeah. Is something wrong? I didn't say who it was for, just a friend. I respect your privacy, Sebastian."

"No." I shake my head. "No, I wasn't worried about that, I just . . . That's kind of you. To do that. Thanks."

"Oh." She shrugs. "No problem." Turning back to the shelves, she adds the pantry items she's lined up, clearly with some organizational system in mind.

"So Rooney, Axel's wife, she feels better?" I ask. "Eating gluten-free? Like consistently feels better?"

Ziggy nods. "Yep. Hopefully you will, too, soon. Hey, do you have the gluten-free flour over there?"

I move aside the gluten-free chocolate chip cookie dough ice cream Ziggy recommended, then pick up a large bag of gluten-free flour that promises to be an easy cup-for-cup substitute in place of typical flour. "Here."

"Toss it my way."

I lob the bag Ziggy's way, then turn back toward the remaining freezer items just as I hear an audible *pop*, followed by her gasp.

When I turn back, Ziggy's covered in flour.

Covered.

"Holy shit." I round the island, grab a hand towel, then bring it to Ziggy, where she stands, eyes scrunched shut, her mouth open with surprise. "Hold still. I got you."

I wipe the flour from her face as best I can, enough that she can blink open her eyes. She peers up at me. "I said *toss* it, Sebastian, not yeet it at my face."

"I didn't yeet it at your face!"

She starts to laugh, the sound smoky and soft in her throat. "Clearly, you don't know your own strength."

I bite my cheek, trying not to laugh, too, as I brush flour from her hair. "You're a mess, Sigrid."

"Thanks to *you*." She pokes my side, glaring at me.

I duck her next poke, giving her a warning look. "How was I supposed to know it was going to explode on you?"

"Oh, I don't know, maybe because it obviously had a hole in it?" She points to the flour trail that follows the arc of how I threw the bag. Then she lifts the bag where she dropped it on the counter, pointing to the rupture in it.

"I didn't see that, I swear."

"Sure you didn't." She sets aside the bag and glances down at the flour on her hand, then toward me, a devious smile brightening up her face. "I should get you back. It's only fair."

I peer down at the flour in her hand, then up to her. "Ziggy. Don't even think about it—" A soft pat to my face silences me. Flour puffs into the air.

I gape. "You just slapped me! With *flour*!"

"I tapped you," she says, bringing her other hand to the other side of my face. Another puff of flour blooms in the air. "And now you're symmetrical."

"Ooh, woman, you're in trouble." I feign reaching for the flour past her, and she shrieks, darting away, circling the counter. Whipping around the island, I catch her by the waist and yank her toward me.

"Sebastian!" she yells, chased by a smoky laugh. "That tickles—"

"Tickles, huh?" I smile as she shrieks a laugh and thrashes

when my fingers dance down her sides to her hips. "A brutal tickle is the least you deserve after that—"

"You're the one who threw flour at my head!"

"By *accident*!"

She yelps as I try for her armpit, then spins in my arms before I can keep her pinned to me and dives in for my waist. I catch her wrists and hold them, lifting them away from my sides. "I'll give you this, Sigrid, you have fast feet, but when it comes to hand-eye coordination—" I shake my head, breathing heavily. "Don't even try to best me."

She's breathing heavily, too.

We're two professional athletes. We have no business sounding this winded after a quick chase and tickle wrestle around a kitchen island.

"Something you hockey players don't understand," she says, pressing into me until our fronts touch and I fall back against the island counter's edge, "that soccer players *do*: There's more to a winning strategy than hard hits and brutal speed." I suck in a breath, barely holding back the impulse to arch my hips and rub myself right into her. "It's all about timing and pacing. Patience until that perfect moment opens up and you have the perfect shot. Like . . . this."

I've been lulled by her words, distracted, my grip slack on her wrists. She spins her arms, deftly freeing herself, before her hands fly into my armpits.

A string of curse words leaves me, and it takes five seconds, which is five seconds too long, before I manage to catch her arms again and stop her from tickling me.

Bending, I throw her over my shoulder, making her shriek. "Sebastian! What are you doing?"

"Being the bigger person. Throwing you in the shower."

"I don't need a shower," she protests.

"Respectfully, Ziggy, you do."

"Sebastian, be careful of your foot! I'm not small. Put me down—whoa, you're strong."

I take the first leap quickly up the stairs, holding her tight. "My foot's fine. I'm insulted you're this surprised by my strength."

"I'm just saying, I don't know many people who can chuck a six-foot-one woman over their shoulder and walk up the stairs, let alone with a barely healed foot."

"Well, this person can, so get used to it."

"Oh? Is the fireman carry going to be a new staple of our friendship?"

God, I wish. I could get used to throwing Ziggy over my shoulder and hauling her upstairs, tossing her onto my bed, kissing my way up her body—

I shake my head, banishing those thoughts from my mind. I promised myself and her that we weren't going there. I just told her I was being the bigger person, and I want to be—my best self, for her, *with* her.

"If you're this stubborn in the future," I tell her, "and you plan on trying that tickling shit again, then yes, the fireman carry is definitely going to stay."

Gently, I crouch, lowering her to her feet in the guest bathroom. "I'll bring you a towel and some clothes to change into, okay?"

She peers at me, a small smile tugging at her mouth.

"What?"

Her smile widens. "You look really funny."

"*I* look funny? Sigrid, have you seen yourself?"

She turns, peering at her reflection in the mirror, then immediately busts out laughing. "Oh boy. It is worse than I thought."

Her hair's powdery white, flour still dusting her eyebrows, lashes, and clothes.

"See? I told you that you needed a shower." I tear my gaze away, because if I stay here, I'm going to do something I'm not supposed to, like spin her around and press her against the sink, then kiss her until she's sighing and pleading, until we're fused so close, flour covers me the way it covers her.

"Be right back," I tell her.

After grabbing a towel and washcloth, a pair of sweatpants and a T-shirt, I step back into the bathroom, freezing as she peels off her hoodie, then tosses it aside. Her T-shirt's slipped off her shoulder, revealing a splatter of freckles painting her skin. She brings her hands to her hair and starts to tug out her ponytail.

"Here you go." I drop everything beside the sink, then start to drag the door shut.

When I hear a yelp, chased by a muttered string of Swedish, I freeze. Ziggy only seems to mutter in Swedish when she's really upset.

"You okay?" I ask.

"This hair tie is just . . . really knotted, and it's tugging my hair. I'm fine. I'll get it out."

"Do you . . ." I open the door a little wider, looking at her. "Do you need me to help?"

She bites her lip. "Yeah. Maybe. Just please don't tug. I'm . . . really sensitive."

I step behind her, gently taking over where the hair tie's tangled in her hair. "I'll be careful."

We're both quiet while I work. Ziggy dusts herself off more, brushing the flour from her face over the sink, shaking it out of her hair as it comes free of the hair tie. I focus on gently loosening each strand, taking my time, careful not to pull her hair as I do.

Finally, the hair tie's free, and I set it on the counter. "There."

Her hand reaches out and finds mine, then clasps it. She gives me one of her firm Ziggy squeezes. Slowly, she turns and faces me.

She looks almost like herself now, most of the flour gone from her hair, brows, and lashes. "Thank you." Her hands come to my face, brushing the flour from my cheeks, bristling across my scruff.

It's very hard to stand here, our bodies almost touching, her hands cupping my face. "Don't thank me," I say quietly.

"Too bad. Already did." She reaches up for my hair, brushing flour from that, too.

I clear my throat roughly, fighting the ache to press myself into her, to push her against the sink and taste her mouth again. I've gone a week without kissing her, and I'm nearly mindless with wanting to do it again.

I can't kiss her again. I *won't*.

I try to make myself pull back, but I'm weak and desperate, so instead I turn my face into her hand like I did earlier tonight. Christ, I'm practically nuzzling her. "Did you get flour in my hair, too?"

Her touch lingers for a moment in my waves before she drops her hand. "A little. But mostly, it got wild in the tickle wrestle. I was just fixing it how you like."

It's suddenly silent in the bathroom but for the faint, steady *plink* of water dripping from the faucet. I stare at her, feeling a tug right between my ribs, drawing me in. I want to hold her close. I want to touch her and taste her, learn her and earn her satisfied sighs. I want to feel the strength and softness of her body and kiss every freckle splashed across her skin.

Ziggy lists toward me. I list toward her, too.

Her hands settle on my elbows, mine on her hips. Our heads bend, coming closer. Our noses brush. I clench my jaw, fighting white-hot desire's pull that pulses through me.

You can do this, Seb. Be strong. Be the friend you told her you want to be.

Slowly, carefully, I ease my arms out of her grip, then wrap them around her, holding Ziggy in a bear hug to my chest. "Thank *you*," I tell her.

I feel her smile against my shoulder. "For what?"

"For letting me crash your night. For stealing a rather large bite of my chocolate cake—hey!" I shove her hand out of my side, where she's poked me, trying that tickle shit again. "For online grocery shopping with me. For helping me. And, uh . . . for the hug earlier. That felt good."

Turning her head, she sets her chin on my shoulder and squeezes her arms around my waist. "This is a pretty good hug you're serving, too, ya know."

"I've learned from the best."

She smiles against my neck, then slowly pulls away, staring at me. I stare at her, too. Our eyes hold as my hand starts circling her back, as hers drifts along my side. I don't know who does it first, but our hips brush, then our chests. Our mouths are so close.

Ziggy's throat works with a swallow. Mine does, too.

You promised you wouldn't. For once, let your promise mean something.

Gently, I ease back, even though everything in me screams to lean in and kiss her until we're both collapsing on the floor, mindless, breathless, lost in each other.

"You're a good friend, Ziggy Bergman."

Ziggy bites her lip, then gives me a wide smile that feels like something's missing in it, a lost piece in a puzzle I can't quite put my finger on. "I know you don't think it, but you are, too, Sebastian Gauthier."

Rather abruptly, she steps out of my arms, smoothing back her hair. She turns and looks in the mirror, inspecting herself. "I think I should just head home now. I'll shower there."

I want to argue, tell her to take a shower here, relax, wear my clothes, lie around and eat all these gluten-free snacks with me.

But then I think about how hard just the past five minutes have been, how much more torture I'll put myself through, hearing her shower, picturing all that pale freckled skin, naked and wet, soapy bubbles and beads of water sliding down her throat, over her breasts, her stomach, right to—

God, the heat that blazes through me, just thinking those words. She should *definitely* go home and shower there.

I clear my throat, then open the bathroom door wide. "Sounds—" My voice is gravel. The state of affairs beneath my fly is painfully tight. I clear my throat, then finally manage to tell her, "Sounds like a good idea."

TWENTY

Sebastian

Playlist: "Fire and the Flood," Vance Joy

I'm working off of three measly hours of sleep, after lying in bed most of the night, once I dropped off Ziggy, rock hard, refusing to touch myself because I knew it would be to the thought of her, and I'm determined not to let myself go there anymore. I won't let my attraction to her change what's grown between us, won't let myself jeopardize the trust and comfort we're building.

That said, I find it hard to sleep when highly aroused, and my mind was wandering with thoughts that I had to keep dragging back into the platonic lane, where they belonged. So while I've made it to her Sunday home game as I said I would, I'm definitely feeling and looking the worse for wear, the bags under my eyes hidden firmly behind sunglasses, an iced coffee cool in my hand as I sit under the warm September sun.

The stadium's slowly filling up, but I've been here for a while, trying to get myself together while sipping my coffee, soaking up the Sunday sunshine.

My leg bounces, nerves for Ziggy zipping through my limbs. I'm always cool and unfazed when I play, but the idea of watching her bear that pressure and expectation makes my chest tight.

I pull out my phone, debating texting her. But I shouldn't.

Should I?

A friend would text.

Wouldn't they?

What the hell do you have to say that she wants to hear? She doesn't need your good luck wishes. She doesn't need you at all.

Right. I pocket my phone, then sip my coffee again.

"Gauthier." Frankie's voice snaps through the air, and I startle so badly, I nearly spill coffee all over myself.

My agent plops down beside me in her first-row stadium seat, because of course, once I told him I was going, Ren made sure we had seats together.

Frankie looks formidable as always, badass business incarnate. Black V-neck sleeveless top, black linen shorts, her ubiquitous black Nike Cortez sneakers with their silver logo along the side. She's got her dark ponytail threaded through an Angel City black ball cap bearing the pink angel logo, and big, black sunglasses hiding her eyes. Settling into her seat, she nestles her cane between her legs and flexes her fingers across the handle, making the rock she wears on her fourth finger flash right in my eyes. How can one person be so terrifying?

"What," she says under her breath as she stares out at the field, "the *hell* are you up to?"

I've been waiting for this. It was only a matter of time before she cornered me and threatened to cut my balls off if I fucked this up—with my reputation rehab, with Ziggy, with all of it.

Sipping my coffee, gathering myself, I settle deeper into my seat, eyes out on the field. "I'm attending my friend's soccer game."

She snorts, still gazing out on the field, then smiling as the team walks out and she spots Ziggy. I'm watching Ziggy behind my sunglasses, too. She looks fucking incredible in her white home uniform, tall, serene, completely confident as she jogs out and starts to warm up. Her hair's in a tight braid down her back, and she smiles as one of her teammates leans in, saying something to her.

My chest aches from just looking at her. Fuck, it aches.

"Your 'friend,' huh?" Frankie arches an eyebrow and throws me a sidelong, disbelieving glance. "How did you two become 'friends'?"

"Yoga has a way of bonding people."

Frankie whips her head my way. "Did you say *yoga*?"

"Yep," I tell her, still watching Ziggy, who passes the ball to her teammate, then turns and does some high knees. I weigh my words, trying to figure out how to avoid the truth without telling Frankie a lie, either. "We bumped into each other at your wedding and talked. Then we . . . connected over angry yoga."

"'Angry yoga,'" she repeats skeptically. "What even is that?"

"I'm surprised you haven't heard of it. For how much you love yoga and for how pissed you've been with me basically since I signed with you, I'd have bet you found it years ago."

Frankie grips her cane, drumming her fingers on it. "I haven't been pissed at you, Seb." She peers back out at the field, her expression serious. "I've been disappointed."

That word hits me hard. It would have felt less terrible if she'd slapped me.

I've been disappointed.

I'm so familiar with that phrase, all the ways I've "disappointed" people—my stepdad, my mother, my teachers and coaches—when I was angry, acting out, frustrated, desperate for some kind of release and relief from everything bottled up inside me. I got so tired of trying to be good, only to lose it, then disappoint people, I stopped trying at all. Then, when I figured out disappointing people—particularly my dad and stepdad—gave me power over them, there was no going back.

"Well," I sigh, raking a hand through my hair. "That's even worse."

Her mouth tips up at the corner. "I know. But it's true. Sometimes, yes, I'm angry with you. But most of the time, I just feel really fucking sad that you have this incredible gift, a name and legacy you're building and . . . this is what you do with it. Hurt yourself. Hurt other people. I want better for you." She shrugs, adjusting her glasses so they're tighter against her eyes. "Because I care about you."

I stare at her, dumbfounded. "You do?"

"Yes, you ass." She pokes my toe gently with her cane. "Eyes on the field. Your friend's spotted you."

My head snaps toward the field the second I process that, my heart tripping in my chest.

Ziggy stands near the sidelines, hands on her hips, smiling at me.

The sun bursts through the clouds right then, spilling down on her, turning her hair to scarlet fire, casting a golden sheen across the top of her head, just like a halo.

I sigh heavily.

Her smile deepens, before her gaze finally darts to Frankie, who she waves to and blows a two-handed kiss, before turning and running back onto the field, where her teammates have circled up.

"So." Frankie slants me another glance. "This . . . angry yoga. Talk to me about it."

I clear my throat, tearing my gaze away from Ziggy. "It's a practice that makes space for processing repressed and difficult emotions. I'm using it to handle my shit in a more constructive manner than mindless benders and reckless behavior. Ziggy . . . she's got to let herself feel that shit in the first place, and it helps her do that. It's good. For both of us."

Frankie lifts her eyebrows. "Well. That sounds . . . healthy. And . . . platonic, I suppose."

I rub my knuckles across my mouth, remembering our first angry yoga, what it felt like to hold Ziggy, someone I realized in that moment I cared about, without relying on flippant seduction to deflect or diffuse it. It didn't feel like anything I've shared with someone before, friend or otherwise. It felt new and rare and . . . bewildering. But good. Very, very good.

And then I think about the past two angry yogas we've done, her colorful Swedish curse words, the way she challenged me to do more chaturangas than her when Yuval had their eyes shut and couldn't give us shit for breaking the sequence of their yoga flow. How she made a goofy-ass face when Yuval gave us a hard-as-hell pose that made Ziggy's back audibly crack.

I smile against my knuckles, my gaze fixed on her.

"Friends," Frankie muses, watching Ziggy on the field, her fingers drumming on her cane. Ziggy *is* my friend. In just a couple weeks' time, we've experienced and shared more at an emotional level than I have with anyone, even Ren. She's seen me looking like hell and feeling like hell. She's helped me reach with both hands for a better future. We've grocery shopped, done yoga, shared hugs and meals and milkshakes. We've bickered and talked. Whether that's a good friendship or that's simply Ziggy's goodness imbuing our friendship, I know it's nothing I've ever known before. I know it's good—no, the best—and I wouldn't trade it for anything.

"Yeah," I tell Frankie. "We're friends."

Frankie's quiet for a moment, staring at me even as Ren settles into his seat on her other side and reaches past her, squeezing my shoulder in greeting. I nod his way but hold Frankie's eyes in a silent stare-off behind our glasses.

"For some asinine reason," she mutters, "and against my better judgment, I actually think I believe you."

I hold her eyes. "If you believe anything, believe this: I have nothing but her best interests at heart."

Frankie's silent again for a beat, before she nods slowly. "Good."

Suddenly there's noise around us beyond the hum of folks filling the stadium to an impressive degree. They have damn good attendance for what I know to be a sport the country's lagged in supporting, especially when it's come to the women's league. I glance up and feel my stomach drop. "Oh, Jesus."

A stream of very tall, very Bergman-looking people stroll toward us. Frankie grins. "Baptism by fire, Gauthier. Brace yourself."

"Excuse me, pardon me, excuse me." Viggo, who I recognize as he comes closer, with his rangy limbs, thick brown beard, and messy hair curling up beneath his ball cap, steps nimbly over Frankie and her cane, but manages to knee me in the thigh, then step right on my recovering foot.

I groan, shutting my eyes as he plops beside me and offers a hand. "Seb, pleasure to see you again."

I offer my hand, knowing what's coming. A hard, bone-crushing squeeze. "Likewise." I squeeze back to offset the very real chance that he's about to break my dominant hand.

Viggo's smile switches to a grimace as he registers what I'm doing. "We good?" I ask.

"Excellent," he says as we mutually, silently agree to stop trying to break each other's fingers and let go. One of Ziggy's other brothers, Oliver, and the man I remember is his partner and retired soccer icon, Gavin Hayes, step past us next. Oliver smiles politely; Gavin gives me a curt nod behind dark Ray-Bans.

"Hayes."

He grunts, "Gauthier."

They drop beside Viggo before Oliver leans in, offering his hand. "There were a lot of us at the wedding, so I'm just going to reintroduce myself. Oliver Bergman."

"Don't worry," Frankie mutters from my other side. "Ollie's too nice to try to break your hand."

"Good to see you again, Oliver." I shake Oliver's hand, relieved to discover Frankie was telling the truth.

"That shouldn't be an issue in the first place," Ren chimes in, giving Viggo a meaningful look. "No one has any reason to break my friend's hand."

Viggo slumps down in his seat sulkily and tugs his ball cap low. "Except apparently he's Ziggy's *friend* now, too."

"And?" I ask.

Viggo throws me a quick side-eye. "It doesn't add up. What would someone like you want with someone like her?"

On the other side of him, Oliver groans as his head falls back.

"I'm not sure what you mean," I tell him.

Viggo rolls his eyes. "Come on. You're a classic rake. And she's a classic wallflower. A rake *always* has an angle when they rub shoulders with a wallflower."

"How am I a garden tool? And what the hell's a wallflower? Some kind of plant? If this is a metaphor, it's a bad one."

He sighs wearily. "Someone doesn't read historical romance."

I stare at him, a little stunned he even has to say it. "*Obviously.*"

"It is absolutely obvious. Dubious reading habits aside, I'm here to let you know I'm on to you. She's innocent and kind, and you're debaucherous and tortured, and while that trope's cute in fiction, it's not at *all* cute in reality, when my sister's heart is on the line, when she's too naïve to see what's really going on."

Fierce, reflexive anger pulses through me. How dare he think about Ziggy that way, *talk* about her that way? It's condescending and infantilizing. It's everything she's trying so damn hard to move beyond and leave behind. And here he is, just . . . reveling in it.

"What you just said," I tell him, setting my elbows on my knees and leaning in, my voice cold and hard, "how you characterized her, it's like you don't even see her. In fact, that's exactly your problem. You don't trust her to be a grown-ass woman. Ziggy isn't 'innocent,' though she is kind. She's got a level head on her shoulders and a big heart. She's no blithe, pie-eyed optimist. She *chooses* to see the best in people, knowing full well they could disappoint her or prove her wrong. But she believes in them anyway; she takes a chance on them. She's empathic and gracious toward people who frankly don't deserve it, and yes, I count myself as one of those lucky people, but don't for a damn minute condescendingly misrepresent that as naïveté. She knows what the hell she's doing. And I do, too. She's my fucking friend, and that's that, do you hear me?"

Oliver's mouth drops open.

Gavin's eyebrows rise above his sunglasses.

Viggo stares at me, eyes narrowed. And after a few tense, silent seconds, the oddest thing happens. A slow, satisfied smile lifts the corners of his mouth. Then he sits back, propping one foot on his knee. "Splendid."

Splendid?

I glance over my shoulder at Frankie. "What the hell just happened?"

She peers curiously at Viggo. He's sitting with a smarmy fucking smile on his face, legs bouncing as he cups his hands around his mouth and cheers loudly, hollering Ziggy's name.

"I'm not sure," she says, still staring at her brother-in-law. "But I don't think I like it."

"Makes two of us," I mutter, facing back out toward the field.

I've just found Ziggy again when I'm patted gently on the shoulder. I glance back and startle when I see a little person with curly dark hair, pale blue eyes, and a smile identical to Ziggy's.

"Linnie," Ren says, arm stretched across the back of Frankie's seat. He takes her tiny hand gently and gives it a squeeze. "This is my best friend, Seb Gauthier. You remember him from the wedding? Seb, you met her then, too. She was our flower girl. This is my niece, Linnie."

I was drunk as shit at his wedding, though I do have a vague memory of this little girl, now that I think about it, wearing a sunshine-yellow dress, twirling and throwing flower petals across the sand. My memories later into the night are fuzzier, except for every moment on the terrace with Ziggy. Those are burned into my brain, crystal clear.

I had *some* self-control and kept myself to only a buzz at first, sipping from a flask right up until the ceremony. I watched Ren stand with his brothers, counting down the seconds until it ended and I could chug the rest of my flask, numb that hollow ache that gaped open like a cracked scab when I couldn't help but witness Ren drinking in every moment that Frankie walked toward him, tears filling his eyes, when I caught Frankie smiling at Ren like she smiles for no one else, and I realized I have never known that. That I have no reason to believe I ever will.

Blinking, leaving those thoughts, I nod the little girl's way. "Hi, Linnie. Nice to see you again."

"Your name's Seb?" Linnie tips her head, the movement again a dead ringer for Ziggy. "I thought your name was Trouble—"

A hand claps over her mouth as she's tugged back. I peer up and see a blond woman who I recognize is Ren's older sister, Freya, settling Linnie in her lap. A pink blush warms her cheeks, and *that* reminds me of Ziggy, even though otherwise they don't look too much alike. Maybe a little in the wide set of their eyes, their high, pronounced cheekbones. But that's about it. Freya has nearly white-blond wavy hair to her shoulders, a silver septum ring, and ice-blue eyes like Ren. She smiles a little nervously and says, "Sorry about that."

"She's not wrong." I shrug. "I'm not offended."

"Well, look who it is." A warm, booming voice puts an end to our conversation. I glance up as Ren's dad—Dr. B as everyone calls him—joins us. He's tall and broad, a handsome guy who's clearly responsible for Ren and Ziggy's red hair, though his is threaded with white and silver. He has one of those smiles that's impossible not to find charming, and he claps me on the shoulder, then squeezes, just the way Ren always does. "Seb," he says, squeezing once more, then letting go. "Good to see you again! How you been, son?"

I feel a weird twinge in my stomach, being called that. It's not bad, it's just . . . foreign. My dad walked out on us when I was six. My mom married my stepfather, Edward, when I was seven. Despite my mom's wishes, I never called Edward "Dad," and he never called me "son." I have no memories of ever being called "son," actually.

I clear my throat and force a smile, trying to cover up the fact that I've been quiet longer than I should have. "I've been all right, Dr. B, thank you for asking. Behaving myself for once."

He grins. "Well, that's good. But hopefully not *too* much. Being on your best behavior all the time makes things awfully boring."

"Hey." Frankie turns and smacks his arm gently. "Don't encourage him."

He lets out a warm, booming laugh, then turns when his wife, Elin, settles in her seat beside him, holding a baby who wears electric-blue noise-canceling headphones over fluffy hair as white blond as hers. Dr. B takes the baby, propping him up on his shoulder, and pats his back. "So, Seb, what brings you here?"

Elin smiles my way, and *that's* where Ziggy gets it—coy and curious, a Mona Lisa smile.

She glances out toward the field and spots Ziggy. Her smile deepens as she waves.

Glancing back toward Dr. B, I tell him, "I'm actually here . . . Well, that is, I'm—"

"He's Ziggy's *friend*," Viggo supplies over his shoulder, arching his eyebrows at his father meaningfully.

Dr. B glances at Viggo, one eyebrow arched right back. "Speaking of behaving, what do you have to say for yourself lately, Viggo Frederik?"

Viggo blinks innocently, bringing a hand to his chest. "Who me?"

"Yes, you," Dr. B says, shifting the baby on his shoulder and bouncing him gently when he starts to fuss. "You haven't been around much. Your mother's and my kitchen hasn't looked like a flour bomb went off in weeks."

The image of Ziggy, powdered with flour, blinking up at me, how close our mouths were, floods my memory. I clear my throat and shift in my seat, feeling like a despicable human for thinking erotic thoughts about Ziggy and flour when surrounded by her family.

"Oh, ya know, I've been busy." Viggo shrugs. "A little of this, a little of that."

"Mm-hm." Dr. B doesn't seem satisfied, but he's distracted by the entrance of another member of the family—a man I recognize as Freya's husband, Aiden, who scoops up his daughter and gives her a kiss on the cheek, then blows raspberries into her neck, which makes her squeal.

"Daddy, this is Trouble!" she yells, pointing my way.

Freya slumps down in her seat and digs her palms into her eyes. "Why does she hear *everything* I don't want her to?"

"Hi, Trouble," Aiden says. A laugh leaves me. It's unexpected and kind, a bit conspiratorial, the way he smiles as he says it and offers his hand, which I shake. "Good to see you again. We didn't get to talk at the wedding—"

Because I was drunk and sulking on the terrace. God, I was such an ass that night. "I'm a big fan," he says. "You and Ren, out on the ice together, it's a thing of beauty."

"Thank you. I appreciate that."

"So." Aiden sits, settling Linnie on his lap and offering her what looks like a reusable fabric bag filled with pretzels, chocolate chips, and dried fruit. "What'd I miss?"

The family falls into a conversation whose rhythm and rapidity speaks to their closeness, a concept wholly beyond me. I turn back, facing the field and realizing it's empty, that they've cleared it, presumably getting ready in the tunnel to be formally announced.

I watch the team walk out, then line up, the starting players forming a neat row, shoulder to shoulder. I find Ziggy and feel my heart do a terribly unreasonable kick in my chest.

"Seb." A nudge to my shoulder makes me glance Ren's way, once again reminding me of the many reasons I have to ignore that tugging ache when I look at Ziggy. With his familiar, kind smile, my best friend says, "I'm really glad you're here."

Not that I'm surprised, but Ziggy Bergman is a goddamn joy to watch play the game of soccer. I have only a cursory understanding of the game, but I know enough to appreciate that she's brilliant at it. As a midfielder, she's running a huge stretch of the field nonstop, unlike the defenders behind her, who stay back, protecting their end of the field, or the forwards on her team, who work the top, pressuring their opponent.

Ziggy's as fast as Ren said she was, bolting across the pitch, her braid like a fiery comet stark against the green grass as vivid as her eyes. She's wildly agile for someone so tall, her touches fast and precise, her movements so quick, she's left players from Chicago stumbling on their heels as she flew by them.

She seems to swap places often with another midfielder, moving between the sideline and the center of the field, which is where she shines, controlling the ball, threading lightning fast, right-to-feet passes to her forwards. I watch her have one assist, then another, the team piling up in celebration on her and a compact striker with short purple hair who's scored both goals.

It couldn't be more obvious to me that she's poised to be the heartbeat of the team. I hope they see what I see. On the National Team, whose Instagram Reels I thoroughly stalked, it's obvious from the footage including her that she's just as vital to their success, becoming just as pivotal to them, too.

"Yay, Aunt Ziggy!" Linnie yells behind me as Ziggy wins the ball off her opponent in the center midfield, then soars up the field. With a perfect deke—well, that's what we call it in hockey; who knows what it's called in soccer—she tricks her defender, getting them to follow her fake to their right, while Ziggy nimbly switches directions and cuts with the ball past them on their left.

She's bearing down on the goalie now as the last defender sprints across the field and slides into her with a tackle worthy of the dirtiest American football. Ziggy's knocked to the ground and lands with a hard bounce on her shoulder, followed by her head, which slams to the grass.

My stomach turns into a block of ice. My heart's pounding. Because right now, she's not moving.

Every single Bergman around me sucks in a breath.

"Studs up!" Viggo yells. He stands from his seat. "What the hell is that? Where's the yellow, ref?!"

"V." Oliver yanks him back down to his seat by the T-shirt. "Settle yourself. The ref's gonna call that."

Frankie clutches her cane hard. "That was a nasty tackle."

Ren sits forward, elbows on his knees, and sighs heavily. "Yeah."

"She's fine," Elin says from behind us, hands clasped between her knees. She's staring at her daughter, her voice even as the trainers jog out to the field, those icy eyes she gave so many of the people surrounding me locked on Ziggy, as if, by sheer force of will, she can make her daughter move.

Viggo mutters something under his breath, tugging his ball cap low.

"She'll get up," Elin says. "She always does. Besides—" She lifts her eyebrows, her gaze still pinned on Ziggy. "She's taken worse tackles from her brothers, playing football up at the A-frame."

"That," Viggo says, turning around and giving his mother a wide-eyed, exasperated look, "was a long time ago. And why isn't Freya included in this shame-fest?"

"Uh, because I never slide-tackled my little sister so hard, I knocked her out cold?" Freya snaps, taking the baby from her dad and cuddling him, which seems to be more for her benefit than for the baby, who, I would assume in part thanks to those noise-canceling headphones, has slept in his grandpa's arms through most of the second half.

"Okay, you know what?" Viggo says, glaring at Freya. "I did that once, and nearly had a heart attack because I thought I'd killed her." He turns back to his mother. "And I apologized."

Elin nods, still watching Ziggy. "I know you did. I'm not saying it to make you feel bad, *älskling*, I'm simply reminding you that your sister is tough. Give her some credit."

"C'mon, Ziggy Stardust," Dr. B says quietly. "Get up, honey."

"Is Aunt Ziggy gonna be okay?" Linnie asks.

Freya's voice sounds a little thick when she tells her, "Yeah, sweetie. She'll be okay."

I stare at Ziggy, locking my hands together so tight between my knees, my rings cut into my skin. I have to ground myself somehow, find some way to keep myself in my seat. Because I am having very irrational thoughts right now, fighting the bone-deep need to hop over the drop from my seat, my finally healed foot be damned, and walk—no, run—out onto that field and have some damn words with Sigrid Marta about getting the hell up and being okay.

I *need* her to be okay.

The moment that thought unfurls in my mind, Ziggy eases up onto her elbows, then flops onto her back, setting a hand over her eyes. The team's nearby now as she, to my relief, talks with the trainers, while their captain, who I've been told is Gina, the short purple-haired striker, gives the ref a piece of her mind. The ref puts up their hands, backing away. I don't think they need any convincing as they tug a yellow card from their waist and raise it high in the air at the defender who had it in for Ziggy.

It's a home game, so the dominant crowd's response is a wild cheer.

"Damn right," Gavin grumbles. "Just inside the box, too. She gets to take a penalty."

"*If* she can take the penalty," Ren mutters, rubbing the side of his face anxiously.

Frankie snorts as she sets her hand on Ren's back and rubs circles. "You know that woman's temper. She's pissed right now. Nothing's going to come between her and a penalty shot."

"Gina might," Oliver says, pointing his chin toward the team's captain. "She's not going to want Ziggy to take it after she got her bell rung like that."

"Who says she got her bell rung?" Viggo asks sharply.

"Our eyeballs?" Aiden says from behind me. "Did you see how hard her head hit the pitch?"

Slowly, Ziggy rolls onto all fours, then stands, a little less steadily than I'd like, and submits to her trainers' inspection. Once she seems to have reassured them that she's safe to continue playing, given they're now jogging off the field, she turns and smiles at the ref, then takes a deep breath, resting her hands on her hips as she answers them next. Her captain comes by and takes Ziggy aside as the ref walks toward Chicago's goalie in preparation for the penalty kick.

I watch Ziggy talk with her captain, frustration tightening her face. She hesitates for a moment, biting her lip, then steps closer to Gina and points to the center of her own chest. I watch the words on her mouth: *I'm taking the damn penalty.*

I grin, bursting with pride. "That's it, Ziggy," I say quietly.

She turns away from Gina, who looks about to say something, surprise widening her eyes as Ziggy strolls off without once looking back, headed toward the line on the field where it seems she'll take the penalty.

The stadium quiets to a hush. Ziggy picks up the ball, spins it three times, then sets it right on the line. Then she steps back lazily, slowly, like she's got no cares and all the time in the world. She glances up, stares right into the goalie's eyes, and smiles.

Then, after a gentle jog right up to the ball, she strikes it so damn hard, on a thundering *crack*, and nails the ball into the back left corner.

Every single person I'm surrounded by flies out of their seats, screaming their heads off.

Somehow Linnie ends up piggyback-style on my shoulders, clinging to me, then scaling me like a monkey into my arms as she screams her head off, too.

"Plug your ears, Linnie."

She claps her hands over her ears and smiles, wide and excited. I set my thumb and middle finger in my mouth and let out a loud, piercing whistle that makes Linnie shriek with delight.

"Do it again, Trouble!" she screams. "Do it again!"

I let out another whistle that makes Linnie explode in laughter, bouncing against my side as I hold her tight. "Again, again!" she yells.

That's when Ziggy pulls back from the pile of her teammates who've swarmed her, beaming with pride. Her gaze snaps straight to us, dancing across her family, until it settles on me.

As our gazes hold, Ziggy's smile shifts to something soft and knowing. Something delicate, and dangerously tender, blooms in my chest as I look at her, as I give her a smile of my own, soft and knowing, too.

A smile only for her.

TWENTY-ONE

Ziggy

Playlist: "You Go Down Smooth," Lake Street Dive

I've been trying very, *very* hard not to acknowledge a very, *very* big problem: I like Sebastian Gauthier. Not only do I like him, but I like him more than I should, given (1) we're only supposed to be friends, (2) I've only really known him for a couple weeks, and (3) we're only supposed to be friends.

I'm repeating myself, but the reminder bears repeating.

And so I keep repeating it to myself as I watch him in the stands surrounded by my family, my beaming niece tucked in his arms as she waves and he smiles at me in this sweet, gentle way, in a way Sebastian hasn't before.

I repeat it to myself after the (victorious) end of our game, as I hustle to the locker room and shower off, then meet my family. As usual, when they make it to my game, I'm lavished with hugs and congratulations, and of course, concerned questions about my shoulder and head, which are both fine. But this time there's someone else waiting, a little distanced from everyone else.

Someone I shouldn't be having what feels dangerously like heart palpitations at the sight of.

Sebastian.

He hung around. He waited to see me.

Because that's what friends do, Ziggy. And that's what he is— that's all he wants to be: your friend.

Still, I can be happy. I can enjoy this. Sure, my heart's never jumped in my chest before with a friend, but then again, I don't have a vast history of friendships to work from. Maybe this is just how friendship goes with Sebastian.

Or maybe it's something more.

It doesn't matter if it is, though, does it? Not when we are situated squarely and interminably in the friend zone. Not when he's told me this is what he wants, and when I know, rationally, this is all I should want, too. Even in my small degrees of change and bravery that I'm reaching for, I'm always going to be *me*. Sebastian seems to enjoy me and my goofiness, my prim lectures, my sensory needs and preferences, as his friend, for now, but that doesn't mean he'd want something from me beyond that—

But he kissed you.

More like *I* kissed *him*, though . . . he did kiss me back. Very enthusiastically.

It was just a kiss. Well, kis*es*. And good ones, like he said. It still doesn't mean he wants more from me, or that I should let myself want anything more from him beyond friendship.

Friends. *Friends.* I'll just keep saying it to myself, like a mantra. Yes, I'm attracted to him. No, he's not nearly as sinister as I thought he was. But that doesn't have to change that we've agreed to be friends, and that's that. I can do this friend thing.

Clearing my throat, I walk toward Sebastian.

He pushes off the wall, his eyes fixed on me, and smiles the same way he did after I scored the penalty. "That," he says, "was one hell of a game."

I shrug, smiling back. "I know."

His smile deepens into a handsome, long-dimpled masterpiece that does funny things to my stomach. "You doing okay? You took a hard hit."

"I'm okay, yeah. I just felt a little stunned for a minute. It knocked the wind out of me. That's why I didn't get up."

"So your head's all right?" he asks, stepping closer. His hand comes up toward my face, but he stops halfway there, then shoves it in his pocket. "You got it looked at?"

"Yep, trainers took a look before they let me go. My head's fine."

His eyes dance between mine. "Good."

Smiling, I shift my bag higher on my shoulder. "Thanks for coming."

Sebastian shoves his other hand into his pocket and peers down at the sidewalk, nudging a pebble with the toe of his sneaker. I realize that his shoes are the exact pink of the Angel City logo. "I was glad I could be here," he says.

"Nice kicks."

He peers up, frowning. "Don't tell me you think I can't pull off the pink, because we both know I damn well can."

"I would never dream of giving Mr. Fancy Pants fashion feedback." My gaze drifts up his body—he's wearing faded black jeans and a soft-looking, but clearly high-quality, heather-gray T-shirt that hugs those inked arms and ties to the silver stripes along his pink shoes. It all goes in that way everything Sebastian wears always inexplicably goes. He looks like he walked off the set of a fashion shoot.

I clear my throat, hating that I can feel a blush warming my cheeks. "How's the foot feeling? You said you expected Lars to make you suffer yesterday."

"Ahh." He shrugs again, hands still in his pockets. "Yeah, it was okay. I'm a little out of shape, but I'm getting back into it. Back on the ice tomorrow. Hopefully I'll be ready in time for our first preseason game."

"Oh." I feel a little tug of selfish sadness. Now that he's fully recovered, that means he'll be busy again, back at his job of getting ready for preseason—dryland, PT, on the ice, doing preseason press with the team again. I know how consuming that schedule is. I've watched Ren live it for years. I know it means our spur-of-the-moment, spontaneous meet-ups for publicity that only had to accommodate my less-demanding schedule are history. I know it means less time with him. And I'm inordinately disappointed by that.

Which is exactly why this development is a good *thing. You shouldn't be this disappointed that you'll see less of him. You shouldn't be feeling this much of* anything *about Sebastian Gauthier.*

Well, I can feel one thing freely, without guilt or worry, and that's excited for him, that he'll be back to doing what he loves. "I'm happy for you," I tell him. "I'm sure you're eager to get back on the ice."

He nods, staring down at his shoes again. "Thank you, I am. I . . ." He rakes a hand through his hair and tugs. "I actually wanted to talk to you about that. Let you know, that is . . . I'll be pretty busy with that this week, so I'm not sure I'll be around much for . . ." He glances up and past me, I think to gauge if we're far enough away from others to speak honestly. His gaze slides to where my family stands, talking in their noisy circle, of which Linnie is the center, dribbling around with her tiny Angel City soccer ball that I brought out for her after the game. His eyes meet mine. "I won't be around much to get out and be seen for our publicity."

For our publicity. Right. I'm bad at reading subtext, but it's not hard to notice what he hasn't said—not a single word about seeing each other as *friends.*

"But, uh—" He shrugs. "I thought maybe we could—"

"Seb!" Ren calls, strolling our way. I swallow a groan, frustrated by our being interrupted. "Why don't you stick around? We're heading to my parents' for family dinner. Come join us."

"We'd love to have you," Mom adds.

Sebastian opens his mouth, then shuts it. "Oh, uh . . . Thank you, but I can't. I have . . . I've got plans."

Ren frowns, which is rare. "You sure?"

"Yeah." Sebastian flashes one of those glittering grins my family's way, one that I've realized is a shiny surface hiding much rockier terrain beneath. "I really do appreciate it, though. Good to see you all."

"Bye, Trouble!" Linnie yells.

A dry laugh leaves him, but it's off, the tiniest slip, like a wrong note in a song that I can't quite put my finger on. Sebastian waves to Linnie, then turns back to me. "I've got to go now, so . . ."

His gaze meets mine. Then, suddenly, his arms are around me, tugging me against him.

Reflexively, I let my bag drop to the floor and wrap my hands around Sebastian's waist. "Sebastian, what were you trying to tell me—"

"You were fucking brilliant out there," he says against my ear quickly, quietly. "Not just how you played, but how you stood up for yourself. I saw you hold your ground and tell Gina you were taking the penalty, even when she didn't want you to. Proud of you."

I swallow as a lump forms in my throat. "Thank you, Seb—"

He's gone before I can say another word, releasing me so abruptly, I nearly stumble back, then waving over his shoulder as he jogs toward his car.

I stare after him, brow furrowed, and feel Frankie join me as we stand shoulder to shoulder, her hand dancing on her cane. "He's acting weird," I tell her.

Frankie stares after Sebastian, too, from behind her big dark sunglasses, and nods. "Yeah, Ziggy. He definitely is."

———

"So." Ren pockets his phone, then leans in to put the final touches on his Toast Skagen, delicately placing dill garnish on the *skagenröra*.

"So?" I wipe down the counter with a towel so it's clean and ready for when we set out all the other food we have in the fridge and on the stovetop.

"Just got a text from Andy. He's puking his guts out."

I wrinkle my nose. "Ew. But also, poor Andy. That stinks."

"Indeed." Ren brushes off his hands and steps back, frowning at the Toast Skagen. He steps in again and adjusts a piece of dill. "It's less than ideal, since I was going to have him read Benedick. I thought you two would do great together."

"Ah, darn." I'm reading Beatrice, the other main character and Benedick's nemesis turned love interest. "Well, this is why we keep it low-key and ask everyone to read the play in its entirety ahead of time. It won't be hard to have someone else step in. We've still got enough numbers to read all the parts, right?"

Ren nods. "We do. But, you know, Benedick is a main role, and while I love every club member, not everyone's going to get all they can out of the humor and wit in Benedick's lines."

"True." I mist a greasy spot on the counter with more spray cleaner, then go at it with the towel. "So who are you thinking should take Andy's place?"

"Well." Ren steps back from the Toast Skagen again, and this time seems satisfied with the results of his food fussing. "I was thinking Seb could do it."

I slide sideways with the towel so hard, I nearly fly right off the counter's edge. Spinning, I save my literal slip—at least, I hope I do—and throw the towel over my shoulder as I lean against the counter, then ask casually, "You don't say?"

Ren's got his back to me now, stirring the Swedish meatballs, which, if absent, Tyler will literally cry about. "I thought it would be a nice way to bring him into the group—show them that he's got some acting chops, that he can commit to a role like that and do it justice."

My cheeks are bright pink as I snap the towel off my shoulder and start twisting it between my hands. Benedick and Beatrice have a *lot* of sexual tension. Creating that kind of dynamic with Sebastian seems like a very bad idea, given how things have gone since our conversation after my game.

I've spent the past five days trying not to fixate on what he was about to say when Ren interrupted him. I've tried to ignore the ache inside me for his voice and his hugs, the simple nearness of his body, when we couldn't even manage angry yoga this week, our schedules were so conflicting. I've tried hard not to mull over how much I miss our feisty back-and-forth as much as the quieter, kinder moments we seem to stumble into sometimes.

I don't think it's a good idea to spend two hours creating sexual tension—even if it's only pretend—with my *friend* who I'm definitely hung up on.

But if I make a stink about his choice, Ren's not only going to be hurt, he may also be suspicious about my true feelings when it comes to Sebastian. Because I'm sure Ren would wonder, if I just saw Sebastian as a friend, what would be the big deal about reading Benedick and Beatrice together?

"Ziggy?"

I blink, pulled from my thoughts. "Huh?"

Ren stares at me, a curious smile lifting his mouth. "You got quiet on me there. Everything okay?"

I peer down at the towel that's twisted so tight, it's nearly folded in on itself. I let go and it unspools with a flourish. "Yeah," I tell him, forcing a smile. I set the towel on the counter and throw a thumb over my shoulder. "I'm just, uh . . . going to splash my face before everyone shows up. Got hot, working in the kitchen."

Ren's still smiling when I dart out of the room.

———

"Bergman!" Tyler hollers. "The meatballs. They're giving me life."

Ren smiles his way. "Glad to hear it, Tyler. Eat as much as you want."

"Don't tell him that," Millie grumbles, swatting Tyler's hand away when he reaches with the spoon for another serving. "He'll eat the whole damn crockpot."

Millie is a former LA Kings' administrative assistant, and one of the few seniors in our group. Petite and spry, with short silvery hair and spectacles that magnify her eyes a little bit, she's wearing a white, long-sleeved T-shirt bearing in typewriter black letters a Shakespeare quote from *As You Like It*: "Though I look old, yet I am strong and lusty."

Tyler pouts at Millie. "I don't eat *that* many."

"I got two measly little meatballs after you'd wreaked your hungry havoc last time, you bottomless beast," she mutters, hip-checking him aside. "Now scoot. You can come back for your third helping later."

Tyler wanders off with his tail between his legs and plops down on the sofa beside Mitch, Millie's beau. Mitch is also a sort of grandfather figure to my brother Ollie's boyfriend, Gavin, who's been playing poker with Mitch and a group of rowdy seniors for years. Gavin normally joins us for Shakespeare Club, too, but this month he's gone with Oliver, who's traveling for the Men's National

Team international friendlies. Oliver has major flight anxiety, so Gavin always goes with him on games when an airplane's involved. Talk about boyfriend material. Swoon.

Mitch might be without his usual bestie, Gavin, but he's chatting and laughing with Tyler, at ease among the club members. He's been coming for months, though he prefers to read minor roles—I think he mostly comes to watch Millie be her fabulous, theatrical self. He's sweet, a welcome grandfatherly presence in a group that, besides a couple of Millie's friends who periodically show up, skews younger. Depending on their game schedules, we average a handful of professional athletes each time. Then there's Ren's theater buddies that he made in high school when we moved to LA, who tend to take this a bit more seriously and don't socialize a ton with the rest of us.

It's a motley crew, but I like that. I never feel weird or out of place, because . . . well, we're all a little weird and out of place. It's okay to be awkward or not talk to people without worrying you've offended anyone or gotten something wrong. For example, no one even cares that I stand alone in the kitchen, shoving Toast Skagen into my mouth and not talking to anyone, while I stare at the clock, becoming progressively more anxious as we approach the starting time for reading.

Because Sebastian is nowhere to be seen.

Ren's front door flies open, and my heart jumps, then plummets.

"Hiya, Zigs." Viggo kicks the door shut behind him, a giant tray of baked goods balanced on one flat hand.

My shoulders slump. "Hey, V."

"Wow, what a welcome." He toes off his shoes, still balancing the baked goods tray. "You look thrilled to see me."

I set down my Toast Skagen and brush the sourdough bread crumbs off my hands. "You just weren't who I was expecting."

"And who were you expecting?" he asks sweetly.

"Mind your business." I take the tray from him, inspecting it. "Wait, where are the—"

"Relax." Viggo eases a satchel off his shoulder and unzips it. "I remembered the *chokladbiskvier*."

"Made gluten-free?"

A lot of other things come tumbling out of his satchel—a couple historical romance novels, a tiny clip-on reading lamp, an ancient-looking granola bar, knitting needles, a ball of yarn, and a wad of papers that look sort of official and intriguing but which Viggo quickly sweeps up and shoves into his back pocket before I can try to read them—until he finally unearths a clear container bearing the chocolate meringue cookies I knew Sebastian would love.

"Made gluten-free," he reassures me. "Super easy. Just swapped gluten-free bread crumbs."

I pull out two twenties from the back pocket of my jean shorts—the ones Sebastian cut and distressed for me—then offer them to Viggo.

But my brother doesn't pluck the twenties from my fingertips like he has any other time I've ordered Swedish treats from his baking side hustle. This time, he curls his fingers gently around mine, folding them over my money. "Keep it. Figuring out a new gluten-free recipe that works was payment enough. Rooney's gonna love them."

I frown. "You sure? I don't mind paying you—"

"I said keep it." Viggo sets the container of *chokladbiskvier* in my hands. "And I meant it."

"Thanks, Viggo."

He pats my shoulder gently as he clocks Ren. "Sure thing, sis. Now, if you'll excuse me. Unlike you, Ren's gonna need to cough up some dough."

I smile, opening the container's lid to take a peek. The *chokladbiskvier* look beautiful, a glossy chocolate glaze covering the chocolate buttercream and almond meringue biscuit beneath. They smell incredible, too, just the way they have every time my mom's made them.

"All right!" Ren calls inside one hand cupped around his mouth, offering Viggo a thick wad of cash with the other. "Let's get seated and get started."

We've done this so many times, we tend to start without preamble. Reading an entire Shakespeare play is a full evening commitment, and Ren always starts us at seven sharp so we won't run late.

I glance around, hoping for some sign of Sebastian. He promised Ren he'd be here. He promised me, too.

Sighing, I stick the *chokladbiskvier* in the fridge to keep them away from grabby hands—also known as Tyler—and quickly finish my Toast Skagen while they start reading. I throw back a gulp of water, then dart over to my seat right before my first line and let myself fall into the familiar comfort of reading Beatrice's lines—a feisty, prickly heroine who I've always admired, whose snappy dialogue I've loved reading for years.

As Benedick's first line is about to come up, Ren lifts his eyebrows at one of his high school theater friends, Gabe. Gabe nods and glances down at his script, making me think he and Ren had a quick chat beforehand about being backup if Sebastian didn't show.

Mitch says his lines as Leonato, a larger role than he normally prefers to read, but one he already seems to be thoroughly enjoying, leaning in to Millie, who holds their shared script perched on her lap. After Gabe's quick repartee with Mitch as Leonato and Tyler, who's reading the Prince, I throw in my first jab at Benedick, whose next joke lands flat because Leonato and the Prince have moved on to another conversation.

"'I wonder,'" I tell Benedick—well, Gabe—just as I hear the door open, "'that you will still be talking, Signior Benedick, nobody marks you.'"

Gabe opens his mouth, but before he can speak, Sebastian steps inside on a cool night breeze. "'What, my dear Lady Disdain!'" Perfect, piercing sarcasm laces his voice. The door slams shut behind him. "'Are you yet living?'"

TWENTY-TWO

Ziggy

Playlist: "Bad Things," Meiko

"You were *perfection*," Millie says, squeezing my arm.

I smile. "Well, thanks, but look who's talking."

"Oh, psh." She waves a hand, laughing softly as Mitch helps her ease one arm into her cardigan, then the other. "I was no such thing."

"You were!" I tell her, handing her a container of leftovers consisting solely of Viggo's baked goods. Millie has a serious sweet tooth. "I've never heard a better Margaret."

"Flatterer," she says, winking. "Good night, honey. See you next month."

"Good night, Millie." I hug her, then hug Mitch. "Good night, Mitch. Drive safe, okay?"

I hold the door open, waving as those two, the last of the club members to leave, make their way to their car.

A laugh I haven't heard in a week, rough and low, makes me startle as I turn and shut the door behind me.

Sebastian stands in the kitchen, those beautifully inked arms elbow deep in sudsy water, working his way through a sinkful of pots and pans.

Ren's deep, booming laugh, like Dad's, echoes in the space and Sebastian's rough laugh blends with his. It makes me smile reflexively.

"I'm not lying," my brother says hoarsely. "I swear!"

"That is some next-level nerd shit," Sebastian tells him.

Ren sighs happily, wiping his eyes. "Oh, Christ, I'm crying."

I bite my lip and push off the door. "Having fun, you two?"

Another rumbly laugh leaves Sebastian. "Your brother is a massive dork."

"Well, obviously," I agree. "Though I don't think you have any place to tease about that, Sebastian, now that you've read your way spectacularly through a lead role in *Much Ado About Nothing* with a bunch of fellow dorks, now do you?"

A soft smile lifts his mouth as I stare at his profile, feeling those butterflies dance in my stomach. "My true colors are revealed."

Ren knocks shoulders gently with me as I step beside him and pull out the dishwasher rack to start loading it with plates. "You don't need to do that, Zigs. You had practice early today, you have to be exhausted."

"So did you," I remind him.

Ren shrugs. "I'm waiting up for Frankie anyway. I don't mind."

"Where is she?" Sebastian asks. "And when will she be back? I'm going to be scarce by then."

Ren frowns over at Sebastian. "Water aerobics. And in about half an hour. But why are you going to be scarce by then?"

"Because she's still pissed at me," Sebastian says.

"She isn't," Ren tells him, leaning a hip on the counter. "She's just got a lot on her plate right now, stressing her out, but you killed it this week. She was on a cloud about that ESPN article covering your comeback."

"Well, that's good." Sebastian rinses a pot, then places it on the drying rack. "I'm still not pushing my luck with her, though."

I finish loading the plates, then reach for the tray of dirty silverware, but Ren tugs it out of reach. "That's enough from you," he says, smiling. "I'll finish this. Go home. Get some sleep."

"I'm a big girl, Ren." I poke my brother's side, making him squeak. "I'll go to bed when I want."

"No tickles," Ren says sternly.

Sebastian glances up, watching us. "She's ruthless with that tickling shit."

"She is," Ren says, taking a step away from me. "Once she tickled Viggo so hard, he peed himself, then started hysterically crying."

I grin deviously. "That was a beautiful day."

"If it were anyone but Viggo," Sebastian mutters, "I'd say I feel really bad for him."

Ren laughs. "Yeah, as is often the case, Viggo really did deserve it. That man lives for pushing buttons."

Sebastian shuts off the water and dries his hands, then folds the towel neatly, setting it on the counter. "Can I drive you home, Ziggy?"

My heart jumps in my chest. After our busy week, barely talking, I'm as startled by his offer as I am thrilled by it. Which is pathetic, but it doesn't seem to matter that I know cognitively how ridiculous it is, to be this excited by an offer of a ride home—my body just won't get the memo.

"Sure," I tell him, shrugging. "If you don't mind."

"I don't." Sebastian claps a hand on Ren's back. "Thanks for inviting me to this. It was nerdy as shit—" Ren shoves him gently and Sebastian laughs. "And a hell of a good time."

Ren follows Sebastian as he sweeps up his copy of *Much Ado*, a worn paperback whose spine is cracked, which I find delightfully compelling. No fresh bookstore purchase for Sebastian. His *Much Ado* looks well loved.

Smiling to myself about that, I turn toward the door and lift my sweater from the coat hook.

Standing there reminds me of when Viggo walked in with all

the baked goods, jarring my memory. I drop my sweater, then turn back to the kitchen. "Shoot. I totally forgot!"

Sebastian and Ren frown as I rush past them, then yank open the fridge door. I pull out the *chokladbiskvier*, then hustle back over to Sebastian, all but shoving it into his chest. "Here. For you."

Sebastian glances down at the container. His brow furrows as he peers through the lid. "What is it?"

"Only the best chocolate cookies ever," Ren explains.

"Made gluten-free. I forgot to tell you about them. I kept them in the fridge so they'd be safe from Tyler. Well, and Millie."

Sebastian blinks at me slowly, that frown still tightening his face. "Thanks, Ziggy. I . . ." He clears his throat. "I appreciate it."

I smile. "Come on. Sooner you drop me off, sooner you get to enjoy them."

Ren throws Sebastian a hug, then me, watching us from the doorway as we walk to Sebastian's car. This one is sleek and sporty. Not the Bugatti, but still one that looks low and dangerously fun to drive—if one enjoyed driving, that is, which I don't. It's so darn nerve-racking.

As if he's just read my mind and lives to torment me, Sebastian holds his keys my way. "How about you drive us, Sigrid?"

I take a step back. "Oh. I don't think that's a good idea."

He arches an eyebrow and leans against the hood of his car, swinging his keys around his finger like he swung my panties around them that night at the wedding.

That reminds me—where *are* my panties? Does he still have them?

"And why not?" Sebastian asks, dragging me back to the present moment. He jingles the keys in my direction.

"That's . . ." I swallow nervously, putting another foot between me and the car. "That's a killing machine."

"It's not. It's actually a really relaxing car to drive. It's low to the ground, very responsive. I just thought you might want to give it a try."

"But I don't like driving," I tell him.

He stares at me, eyes flickering in the starlight. As he pushes off the car and walks up to me, his gaze searches mine. "Maybe it's not that you don't like driving. Maybe you simply haven't found a car that makes you fall in love with it. I'm just throwing it out there. There's no pressure to drive if you don't want to, Ziggy."

I bite my lip, torn.

"Well," he adds, grimacing in this silly way that makes me smile in spite of myself. "Maybe a little pressure. I want to sit in the car and put a hefty dent in these chocolate cookies while you drive me. They smell fu—" He clears his throat. "Freaking incredible."

I stare at him and tap my foot on the sidewalk, debating with myself. A big part of me wants to tell Sebastian Gauthier exactly where he can shove his fancy car keys and this sports car propaganda. But another part of me wonders if maybe he's right. Maybe this car, this drive, will be different from the rest. Maybe something I've spent my adulthood so far white-knuckling my way through might actually become something I enjoy. I won't know till I try, and what better time to try than the season of Project Ziggy Bergman 2.0?

"Fine," I mutter, plucking the keys from his hand. "But don't say I didn't warn you."

"Jesus Christ, Ziggy!" Sebastian grabs the oh-shit bar on his side as I whip around the turn, hitting the gas.

I smile, exhilarated. This is *amazing*. The car feels like an extension of myself. As Sebastian said, it *is* responsive—lightning fast and effortless to control. Two blocks away from Ren's, I sensed how much I loved this car, then turned away from my place and took us on a massive detour.

"I warned you," I tell him into the wind.

He stares ahead, wide-eyed, as I come to a stop at a red light, his hair wild and windblown.

He looks like he's just had a near-death experience.

Slowly, he glances my way. "Holy. Fuck."

He looks so messed up and upended, a little like the Sebastian I surprised on his balcony last month, with that messy hair and stunned expression. It makes something crack inside me, then spill, bittersweet and bubbly. I want to laugh. And I want to cry. And I want to laugh some more.

Thankfully, at least, for now, the laughter wins, bursting out as the light turns green and I hit the gas again.

Sebastian stares at me like he thinks I might have a couple screws loose. "What are you laughing about?"

"I don't even know!" I yell into the wind, drinking in the balmy Southern California September night.

Sebastian seems to relax when I decelerate a little, settling into the car's speed comfortably as I wind us down the road. "Sigrid."

"Yes, Sebastian."

He drags his knuckles across his mouth. "Would you . . . uh—" He drops his hand. "Would you want to go to a bookstore with me?"

I swerve a little, blinking his way, then back to the road. "What, now?"

He glances at his fancy silver watch, whose brand I remember him doing a magazine ad for. "It's not too late, is it? When's your game tomorrow?"

"No game tomorrow. Not till Tuesday."

"Even better." He pulls out his phone and starts typing. "Well, then, chauffeur—" He taps the car's screen and types in an address, making a GPS route appear. "Take us to Culver City."

TWENTY-THREE

Ziggy

Playlist: "Somewhere Only We Know," Rhianne

"It's . . . closed." I frown at my favorite indie bookstore, which I've been going to for years. They have a very impressive romance section, which isn't often the case in a general collection bookstore. Since I've been going there, special ordering a number of fantasy romance titles, they've happily broadened their inventory even more.

"Have a little faith in me, Sigrid." Sebastian throws me one of those devastating long-dimpled smiles over his shoulder as he opens his door. He's halfway out of the car when he leans back in and grabs the container of *chokladbiskvier*. "Now that I can eat these without risking throwing them right back up," he mutters.

"Hey!" I shove open my door and shut it, following him. "You're the one who dangled those keys in front of me. I warned you."

He rounds the car to my side and takes my hand, squeezing gently. "You did." His thumb sweeps across the back of my hand. I shiver as I stare at him and heat dances across my skin from where he's touching me. The wind picks up, cool and a little damp, thankfully giving me a reason besides the real one for my slip.

Sebastian tugs me gently toward the door. "Come on, you. Let's get inside and warm you up."

"But it's—"

"Closed," he says, his back to me as he pulls me along. "So you've said."

I try really hard not to stare at his butt in his dark jeans, but it's a lost cause. Hockey player butts—with the exception of my brother's, of course—are truly a thing of beauty.

With his free hand, Sebastian pulls his phone from his pocket and types something. Not ten seconds later, his phone dings. He leans in, reading his screen, then crouches, entering a code on the door's lock, which glows red. The lock beeps, then flashes green. Sebastian stands and turns the handle, then pushes open the door. "Ladies first."

"What is happening?"

Sebastian sets a hand on my back and nudges me forward. "The owners are big Kings fans."

I do a double take as he shuts the door behind me. "Wait, they just gave you the code to their bookstore?"

"I mean, I might have offered them very nice complimentary tickets to our first regular-season home game to incentivize them, but . . . yeah."

I peer around as Sebastian walks off and flips a switch, then another, brightening the store from the faint nightlights that greeted us. He doesn't turn the lights all the way up, leaving the space gently illuminated, the lanterns over each aisle dimmed to a soft glow.

"Sebastian, this is wild."

He turns my way and sets the *chokladbiskvier* container on the checkout desk. "I know you love books."

Sometimes, if I'm up at the A-frame at just the right time in spring, I catch that day when the wind knocks the blossoms off the first big old tree on the hiking path from the house. It feels like magic, like a moment from another world—so perfectly lovely, my heart can't hold it all in.

That's how I feel right now—like those delicate, perfumed petals are drifting not around but inside me, filling me with something too lovely, too wonderful to be possible.

"After your game," he says, raking a hand through his hair, tugging at it, "I was going to see if you wanted to come here, but then—"

"My brother blew in like an intrusive, albeit sweet and smiling, semitruck and invited you to family dinner. Then you bolted."

Sebastian drops his hand, nodding. "Then I bolted." He blows out a slow breath and peers up, shoving his hands in his pockets. "I didn't want to be an inconvenience with my new diet and—"

"Sebastian! We've got years of practice cooking gluten-free for Rooney; we could have fed you easily. And even if it took a stop at the grocery store for a few items, it would never be an inconvenience to make sure you could eat with us."

"This is new for me, Sigrid. I don't know how to ask for that without feeling like an asshole."

"But it's my family," I tell him. "We'd never see it like that."

"That's just it. Ziggy, what you have—with your family—it's so far beyond me. I have . . ." He glances off, shaking his head. "No fucking frame of reference for closeness like that, kindness like that . . . *love* like that."

My heart trips on that word. *Love.*

"But," he says, crossing the space between us, brushing knuckles with mine, tangling our fingers. "I'd like to try. Because, Ziggy, at your game, with your family, that was the best thing I've ever been around, except maybe you in your dragon towel turban."

I poke his side, but he catches my hand before I can get a tickle in. He links that hand with his, too, staring down at our fingers as he tangles them together. "I know they aren't perfect," he says. "Your family. I know there are ways they've fallen short of what you needed, but you have a rare good thing in your life."

I nod. "My family's incredible."

"They are," he says quietly, his thumbs drifting across my hands.

"And I . . . am so far from that. I didn't just bolt because of the fucking celiac. I bolted because all I could think as I stood there after your game, all of you looking at me expectantly . . ." He sighs. "*Expectantly*. That's the problem. I haven't done well historically, with expectations. And if I want to, I have a lot of work ahead of me before I can meet them and not be a disappointment."

Tears well in my eyes. "Sebastian, you wouldn't disappoint us."

"Oh, I would. If I kept doing what I have been. And I've been doing that for a long time; it is deep in my makeup." He peers up at me. "I've got a lot of issues. Dad issues. Stepdad issues. Mom issues. And I'm not saying that to deflect responsibility; I'm saying that to own it. My dad walked out when I was six and never looked back. My mom married a fucking sociopath who messed me up right under her nose, and she either didn't see it or wouldn't, and I thought the difference mattered, but the more I think about it, the more I realize it really doesn't. What matters is that I was an angry, hurt child who only felt in control of his life when he used that anger and hurt to make other people angry and hurt. I acted out and struggled, and I couldn't get a rise out of anybody—couldn't earn my mom's attention, couldn't provoke an outburst in my stepdad's anger until it became something Mom would notice and care about. My teachers were bribed and cajoled to go easy on me. My coaches put up with my bullshit because I was too good at hockey to kick off the team.

"I didn't get in trouble or get my ass handed to me like I should have. I just got told"—he hesitates, before he swallows roughly—"*over and over again*, what a disappointment I was. So I let it become a self-fulfilling prophecy. And I have been doing that for a long time. To punish my asshole dad and hopefully tarnish his professional hockey legacy with my sordid one. To humiliate my stepdad and show him I don't give a fuck about his approval, his adamant insistence that he'd break me, control me, that he'd have the final say. To maybe, just *maybe*, finally, get my mom to see how fucked up all of this has been."

He shakes his head, then finally peers up, sighing as he meets my eyes. "That's what I come from. That's how I've operated. I learned a long time ago to live with knowing I disappointed people who mattered to me. Then controlling how and when I disappointed them became taking back the power I never felt I had.

"It got tricky, when I signed with Frankie, and I respected her so damn much, her vision for using a professional athlete's influence to build a meaningful, generous life and legacy. I warned her who I was, what I was like, but she wasn't scared of me—hell, she scared *me* into straightening out some of my shit, doing things I'd put off that were good, that I wanted to do, that made me feel just a little bit better about myself, even if I kept them quiet. Then Ren dragged me kicking and screaming into friendship with him, and that guilt sank its claws into me, started gnawing at me, making me want to be more careful, to not do things so terrible they'd disappoint him badly or make him regret our friendship. I tried to commit forgivable sins, make less egregious slipups. I made peace with the fact that I had warned him and Frankie I was a lost cause, that they knew what they were getting themselves into, and I'd disappoint those two occasionally, which I have."

He sighs, brushing our palms together, back and forth. Slowly, he drags his gaze up to meet mine. "But, Ziggy, the thought of disappointing *you* . . . I can't stand it. I have felt so fundamentally unworthy of sharing air and space and even this small fragment of time with you, and for once I've just let myself sit in that, soak it in, and it's changed me. You've given me shit when I deserved it, grace when I didn't. You've seen parts of me that no one else ever has, and not only did you stick with me anyway, you saw possibility in me—you believed in me when you had no reason to."

I blink back tears and squeeze his hands hard. "Sebastian—"

"I'm almost done," he says quietly. "I promise."

Slowly, he starts to walk backward, taking me with him, toward the romance aisle, which makes me smile even though my vision is watery with the threat of tears. "I'm telling you all this because I want you to know that you're the best person I've ever known, Sigrid Marta Bergman, and I'm the luckiest to call you my friend."

He glances over his shoulder, then brings us to a stop. "This publicity stunt we've been pulling, I know it was your idea, that it's working, and you're getting what you want out of it, but I've gotten something so much more meaningful from it, because of you, and I wanted . . ." He releases my hands, then shoves his back in his pockets, holding my eyes. "I wanted to show you thank you."

I tip my head, smiling as I try really hard not to cry. "'Show me' thank you?"

He shrugs. "*Saying* thank you is fine, but it wasn't enough for this, for you. I wanted to *show* you. So here we are. The place is ours for as late as we want it—well, until they come in at eight tomorrow morning to get ready to open up. And not that I think you have a free inch of bookshelf space, but whatever you want here, it's on me."

"Sebastian," I whisper, my heart aching as it pounds, those magical blossoms drifting inside me, too much, too wonderful, too lovely. "Thank you." I step closer to him, until my hands go to his wrists, squeezing gently.

"Ziggy, don't—"

I set a finger against his mouth. "Sebastian, don't. Don't tell me not to thank you. I will thank you." Slowly, I lower my hand, making sure he's not about to start his usual self-deprecating nonsense. Satisfied that he's listening to me, I slide my touch up his bare forearms—warm skin, the shadows of his tattoos, which I finally let myself look at closely—stars and planets, plants and flowers, mythical creatures and bits of words, fragmented, lost, scattered across his skin. Gently, I take my hands higher, over his rolled sleeves at his elbows, up to his shoulders.

He exhales roughly as I bring my palms across his chest, until they both rest right over his heart. "Thank you," I whisper, holding his eyes. "For telling me, for trusting me with so much of yourself and your past. I can't . . ." Shaking my head, I bite my lip. "I can't imagine going through what you did, when you were little. You had to be so scared, so lonely, so hurt."

He tears his gaze away, peering down, but I duck my head until my eyes find his again.

Slowly, he lifts his gaze and holds mine. "I'm sorry," I tell him, "for all the ways the people who were supposed to love you and keep you safe failed you. I'm sorry that how you learned to survive hurt you and the people around you. And I'm . . . so damn proud of you for wanting something more. It takes courage, Sebastian, to want to be something more than you've been, to reach for a life beyond the safety and control you've built for yourself. I'm lucky to be your friend while you do that."

Sebastian sets his hand over mine and squeezes, hard and long, as he stares at me. "Thank you, Ziggy."

I smile, tugging one hand away from beneath his palm, lifting it to his hair. "My driving kind of messed up your perfect coiffure."

He smiles, too. "Well, fix the damage you did, then, woman."

I lift my hands to his hair, scraping through the wild waves until they fall how he likes, a little combed back, parted to his left, curled right along his jaw. His jaw that I brush my thumb across, savoring the sandpaper roughness of his scruff to his chin and the tiny dimple there. I press it with my fingertip and smile. "Boop."

He narrows his eyes. "Did you just *boop* my chin dimple?"

"And if I did?" I stare at his mouth, begging my body to behave itself, not to ruin this perfect moment between us by doing something as reckless as kissing him. "What are you gonna do about it?"

Sebastian leans in, pressing an index finger to my cheek, right in my dimple, then he gently taps the bridge of my nose, above my eyebrow. "I'm gonna *boop* every damn freckle on your body in retaliation."

I gasp.

"Oh, I know what you're thinking," he says, walking closer, making me step backward with him until my back hits the bookshelves. His hands wrap around me in time and soften the impact of the shelf, protecting me from its hard wooden edge. "There are a lot of those freckles, but I swear to you, Sigrid—and fair warning, I really mean it since, thanks to you, I've become a man of my word—*boop* my chin dimple again and just see where it gets you."

I stare at him, heart racing, searching his eyes. "A man of your word?" I whisper. "As in honest? You'll be honest with me?"

The laughter in his eyes dies. He stares at me as his thumbs rub gently along my sides. "I'll be honest with you, yes. I'll do whatever you want, Ziggy. You just have to ask."

I hold his gaze, deliberating, weighing, how reckless I'm brave enough to be. "Where are my panties from that night? At the wedding?"

Sebastian's expression morphs to surprise. "*That's* what you want to ask?"

I shrug, then set my hands on his shoulders, lacing them together around his neck. "I'm starting there. Now, kindly answer me."

"They're . . . in my nightstand."

"Your *nightstand.*" I lift my eyebrows. "Why are they there?"

He presses his tongue into his cheek. "Next question."

I frown at him. "You said you'd be honest."

"And I have been. I didn't say I'd answer every question you asked."

"You said you'd do *whatever* I asked."

He hesitates, then says, "There was a silent clause in there that you missed—it's a footnote. If you looked at the transcript, you'd have to squint real close, but it says, 'within reason.' That question is outside reason."

I sigh, defeated. "Fine."

His hands drift gently across my back. "Next question."

"Hmmm." I search his eyes, gathering my courage. "You've told me you just want to be my friend. You've told me not to ask you for more."

A muscle in his jaw jumps. His grip on my back tightens like it's a reflex. "Those aren't questions."

"I'm getting there."

He swallows. "Okay."

Slowly, I twirl my fingers into the tips of his hair, gaze locked on his. "Do you only want to be my friend because that's all you want from me? Or because it's all you think you *should* want from me?"

Sebastian's quiet for a moment, hands softly circling my back. "I only want to be your friend because you matter that much to me, Ziggy. Because I'm just learning how to do this well and trying to do any more than that sounds like pure fucking hubris, like Icarus flying straight toward the sun. Because this is how I can . . . *show* you what you mean to me without hurting you or disappointing you. Because if I hurt or disappointed you, I don't think I'd be able to forgive myself."

"But what if it wasn't hubris?" I whisper, my heart aching. I've never met someone harder on themselves, someone who believed in themselves less.

"But it *is* hubris," he whispers back.

I blink, tears filling my eyes. How do I get him to see the goodness that I see in him? How do I make him believe he's safe to be more than a friend to me *if* he wants that, to try and risk and allow himself to fail sometimes and pick himself up, knowing I'll be right here, every step of the way?

His face tightens as he registers the unshed tears turning my eyes glassy. I hold his gaze, and his words drift through my mind:

Saying *thank you is fine, but it wasn't enough . . . I wanted to* show *you.*

Those words . . . they're an important reminder, and they give me a little sliver of hope.

Sebastian is someone who needs to experience things, to *feel* them, not hear words about them.

I'll just have to show him this isn't hubris—it's life, and it's scary, trying to learn someone, to take care of them, to do right by them, when you're human and you're imperfect, with your own needs and fears and pitfalls, and you're bound to fail sometimes.

I'm not a terribly patient person. I like to set my eye on something and get it done. I've been that way with every soccer team I wanted to make, every academic goal I set, my checklist of adulthood milestones—college in three years, finally getting my driver's license, achieving financial independence, securing my own apartment. But for Sebastian, I can be patient. For Sebastian, I can wait until maybe, just maybe, one day he'll realize he's safe with me to want more, *if* he wants more.

I hope he wants more. Because I sure as hell do.

"Ziggy." His voice breaks. He lifts a hand, wiping my tears. "Please don't cry. I hate it when you cry."

"Too bad. You brought me to a bookstore after hours with nobody to bug me and all the time in the world. You opened up to me and trusted me. You 'showed me thank you' very, very well, Sebastian. I'm allowed to cry."

"Anything but tears," he whispers, wiping my eyes as new ones spill down my cheeks. "Please."

Biting my lip, I drop my head back against a shelf, our gazes locked. "Well . . . if I was allowed one more chin *boop*, I think maybe I'd stop crying."

He glares at me playfully, eyebrow arched, then sighs. "Fine."

I push off the bookshelf, until our chests touch, until our faces are inches away. Slowly, I lift my finger, smiling as I press it into his chin. "Boop."

He huffs a laugh, and I lower my hand, until it falls on his chest. My fingertips graze the skin at his open collar, the edge of a butterfly's wing resting at the hollow of his throat.

Air rushes out of Sebastian as his grip on my back tightens. I peer up and our noses brush, our eyes hold.

Be brave, Ziggy. Be brave.

"Question," I whisper.

A swallow works down his throat. "Answer."

"Do you want to kiss me right now?"

He stares at me, his eyes soft as they dance across my face. "Every day since I saw you. Now. Tomorrow. When I'm on my deathbed. Yes, Ziggy, but we're just—"

"Friends."

He nods slowly, his nose grazing mine, air leaving him unsteadily as his hands drift down my back. "Just friends."

"What about 'just friends' . . . who kiss?"

He groans. "That sounds like bad news."

"Funny," I whisper, rubbing my nose against his, "I've been trying to give myself an edge lately. A little bad news seems right up my alley."

"But I"—he exhales roughly, setting his temple to mine, his mouth brushing my ear—"am reforming. Bad news is the last thing a penitent should be seeking."

"A penitent seeks absolution," I tell him.

He nods, sighing when my fingers drift into his hair.

"Then let me absolve you. Let me tell you that this kiss can be between two friends who care about each other, who want to keep each other safe and make each other feel good. Let me tell you that in no way will you disappoint me or harm me in this. Enjoy me. Let me enjoy you. It can be that simple, I promise."

"Ziggy," he sighs, pulling me against him. His breathing's unsteady. I feel his heart thudding fast and hard in his chest. "You promise? Nothing changes after this?"

I wrap my arms around his neck, my lips brushing his ear. "I promise."

He doesn't hesitate, doesn't give me time, and I love it. He cups my face and devours my mouth.

I sigh as I taste him, as his lips sweep over mine, first gentle, then hard and desperate. I clutch his shoulders as his hands slide down my waist, then lower. He spreads his hands across the curve of my backside, tugging me closer.

A gasp leaves me at the exquisite relief of his body wedged against mine. He's hard inside his jeans, rubbing right up against my clit beneath my shorts. Pleasure pools warm and aching, a soft, steady pulse. Every inch of me melts into him.

I tug his hair, and now *he* gasps. I kiss him harder, teeth clacking, until he settles our rhythm—hips fused, rolling together, mouths moving, slow and decadent, hot, hungry strokes of tongue.

I could do this forever—kiss him, hear him, hold him—drink in every sensation of his body so connected to mine. Sebastian's hand goes to my hair and dives into my braid, cupping my head.

"Ziggy," he pants. "God, you taste so good. You feel so good."

I smile against his kiss. "So do you, Sebastian."

He shifts his hips and palms my butt, pulling us closer. Pleasure pools into a sharp, sweet ache between my thighs, in the tips of my breasts as they brush against him. My head falls back. My legs give out.

My hand darts out reflexively to catch myself, but Sebastian catches me first, and eases me down. Still, I manage to knock half a shelf of books to the ground. I squeak in horror. "The books—"

"Fuck the books, Sigrid."

"They'll get bent! Damaged!"

"I'll buy them all," he mutters against my mouth, yanking a thick one across the floor, then setting it under my head like a pillow.

I laugh at that, tugging him close. Sebastian crawls over me and settles his weight between my thighs, knocking off a new string of books from another shelf. They rain down on us but bounce off his back as he shields me, pressing kisses patiently down my neck. "That's a lot of books to buy," I whisper into his hair, before I kiss it.

"Worth every penny." He presses wet, hot kisses back up my neck and finds my mouth, working his hips into mine.

And then time just . . . slows. The air kicks on, a soothing hum. The lights above cast a saintly halo around this man who's so convinced he's the worst kind of sinner. Gently, I lift my hands to his hair, smoothing it back.

His gaze searches mine. Then, slowly, he bends his head and kisses me, soft and slow.

I wrap my arms around his back and pull him closer, until his nose brushes mine, until our chests brush. He sighs into my mouth as I glide my hands down to his backside, tugging him closer.

Propping himself up on both elbows, Sebastian smooths back my hair, framing my face with his hand. "So beautiful," he says quietly.

I tip my head as his gaze dances over my face. "This from the beautifullest person I know."

"Shut up," he mutters, kissing me.

"Like you don't know," I mumble back, but he silences me with another sweet, seductive kiss to my mouth, chased by a hard, wicked stroke of his tongue. He breathes my name as he gives me more of his weight, and I feel him hard and heavy, right where I need him.

Wrapping my arm around his back, I wrench him closer, until our chests touch. Our mouths fuse into deep, slow kisses. We move lazily at first, Sebastian with his hand tangled in my hair, his mouth open with mine; me with my hands skating over the firm muscles of his back, up to the silken thickness of his hair falling into his face.

"Sebastian." I call his name quietly as pleasure weaves through me, builds, and coils. I drink in his sounds, his broken, aching groans, each sharp, jagged breath.

"Ziggy," he whispers.

"Best. Kissing. Ever."

He smiles against our kiss. "Best kissing ever."

I wrap my leg around his and slide it down his calf, pressing my hips closer. His forehead drops to mine, and a moan leaks out of him, low and broken. Its raw, needy echo, the perfect nudge of hips, tugs that white-hot thread of pleasure right through me until it snaps and unravels into a thousand fine sparkling fibers. Release hits me, sharp, shaking, sweet relief that pounds low in my belly, between my thighs, in the tips of my breasts, up my throat, to the edges of my ears, where I feel his breath, harsh and hot.

I arch into Sebastian again as another wave rolls through me and drink in his rough groan, his hand tightening its grip in my hair, as he stills his body, heavy over mine. I feel every inch of him, hard and insistent in his jeans, and tell myself as soon as I'm composed enough from this earth-shattering orgasm to remember what my hands are and how they work, I'm going to make this man fall blissfully apart.

Slowly, he pulls back, peering down at me, smoothing back fine and now sweaty strands of my hair. His knuckles graze my hot cheek, flushed from coming.

I watch him, dazed, all noodle limbs and needy touches. Throwing my arms around his neck, I smile as he leans in and kisses me, sweet and soft.

"This," I whisper, "just might have ruined me for all future bookstore visits."

Sebastian's eyes crinkle. His torso starts to shake. And then he lets out the loudest, loveliest laugh I have ever heard.

TWENTY-FOUR

Sebastian

Playlist: "I Wish I Was," The Avett Brothers

My laugh becomes a gasp when Ziggy pushes me onto my back and slides her leg across my stomach, right over my cock that's so damn hard, I don't know how it hasn't busted the zipper in my jeans.

"Ziggy." I set a hand on her thigh, stopping her.

She freezes, propped on her elbow, peering down at me. "What is it?"

Slowly, I ease upright, and she sits up with me. Bringing a hand to her face, I trace my fingers across her freckles, then sink them into her gloriously disheveled braid. "I'm okay."

She peers down at my lap, where I am, by all evidence, very not okay. "What?"

"I . . ." Blowing out a breath, I stroke her flushed pink cheek with my knuckles again, then press a gentle kiss right to one of my favorite freckles, nestled in her dimple. "I'm okay."

Her head tips in that way she has, as she pulls back, not harshly, just curious, her eyes searching mine. "But you were really good to me—"

"Not good enough."

"Sebastian." She arches an eyebrow. "I'm the one who just orgasmed so intensely, I saw outer space. *I* get to tell you if it wasn't good enough, and I'm telling you it was."

"I'm glad." I lean in and press a soft, slow kiss to her cheek, breathing her in. "Then it was good enough for me, too. That's all I need."

She scowls as I spring up and stand, though not as gracefully as I'd like, given the pounding pulse in my cock. She thinks she saw outer space? I was about two hip nudges away from going off like a rocket. Calling to mind the last time I ate a calzone and literally thought I was dying, I was in so much pain, I find myself able to stand fully upright now, and offer her my hand.

Ziggy takes it, a little hesitant at first, before she lets me yank her upright. She lands with a bounce, tugging down her adorable dark green T-shirt, which rode halfway up her torso during our little session on the floor. When she settles it back down on the waistline of the jean shorts I cut for her, I see it again, the clever seventies-throwback smiley face doctored up with Shakespeare's iconic hairdo and goatee. Beneath Smiley Shakespeare it says, *Have a nice play.*

She stares at me for a second, our hands lingering together, fingers tangled. Her brow is furrowed, her gaze searching me, like an X-ray, running diagnostics.

I smile, because I can't help it. I used to be terrified of that stare. Now I think I just might crave it. Because it means she's trying to understand me. It means Ziggy might not like what I'm doing or get it, but she's willing to stay with me anyway.

Slowly, she turns toward the books scattered across the floor and bends. As she reaches for the first book, baring her ass in all its glory inside those jean shorts, she lets out a satisfied sound, low and smoky in her throat.

I crouch and start to pick up books, too, perhaps staring at her butt so much, I drop a few books that I try to pick up. I come very, *very* close to begging her to tear off those shorts, shove me onto my back, and sit on my face, but somehow I stay strong, cleaning up our mess beside her.

"Well." Ziggy sighs. She turns, bearing a towering stack in her arms. "Guess it's time to browse some books."

"So." Ziggy crunches down on one of the fucking incredible chocolate cookies she gave me, brushing away crumbs as they fall onto the book cradled in her lap.

I peer up from the book I've been leafing through, one of her favorite fantasy romances. We swapped genres. Ziggy handed me this "romantasy" as she called it; I gave her one of my favorite dystopian sci-fi novels. "So?"

"Why did you give your part to Gabe halfway through Act Three tonight?"

I set aside the book and angle myself toward her, brushing her leg with mine where we sit on the floor, leaning against opposite bookshelves. "It seemed like the considerate thing to do. I was supposed to be there on time to read Benedick, and I got there late, interrupted him with my entrance."

She smiles. "And a very dramatic entrance it was."

I make a theatrical bow. "But Gabe was on time, ready to read Benedick, and I know Shakespeare Club is a big deal to Ren's theater buddies. I figured it would be fair to split the part, given that."

Ziggy tips her head and pops the last of the cookie in her mouth. "Gotcha. Well, that's nice of you."

It's also not the whole truth. The whole truth is, I know that play. I know it very well. And I know Beatrice and Benedick have a damn good love confession in Act Four and Act Five, too, for that matter. I couldn't . . . I couldn't do it. I couldn't look at Ziggy, even though we'd be playing roles, and tell her I love her. I couldn't say that to her and have it mean nothing.

Not . . . that I plan on saying those words to Ziggy in the future and meaning them. But still, she's someone who means so much

to me after just a few short weeks in my life. She's someone I want
to cherish and be good to and enjoy the hell out of. She's my friend.

*Your friend, huh? Who you just made out with and dry-humped
right to the edge of a body-shaking orgasm?*

Yes, well. This is true. But Ziggy and I made a promise. We enjoyed each other like this, and now nothing will change. As she said,
there's such a thing as friends with benefits. And while I'd originally hoped to keep my hands off her entirely, that's been blown to
shit since the night on my deck, when I felt her up thoroughly,
when she kissed me so damn well, my legs gave out.

I have managed, however—and I plan to continue doing so—
to keep this new level of physicality one-sided. I can give her whatever she needs, when she shows me she needs it, make her feel
incredible, without taking anything for myself.

I can be good to her. That's all I want to be—so damn good
to her.

But maybe not so good as to let her eat all my gluten-free chocolate cookies. "Easy does it, champ." I drag the cookie container
back my way.

Ziggy gapes at me. "I've had *three*!"

"Three?" I crunch into another cookie. Jesus Christ, these are a
fucking dream. How they're gluten-free is beyond me. "Yeah, that
number's accurate if you multiply it by an *exponent* of three."

"You butthead." She shoves me in the hip with her foot. "I've
had three."

I grin, putting the book back in my lap as I pop the rest of the
cookie in my mouth. "Whatever you say, Ziggy dear."

She sighs, plopping her book back in her lap, too. It's quiet for a
couple minutes, nothing but the soft *shush* of paper as we turn
pages, the occasional crunch as I bite into another cookie.

But then, in a move of pure stealth, Ziggy grabs the container,
steals another cookie, then shoves the whole thing in her mouth.

"Woman!" I lunge for her, laughing as she shrieks around her cookie and bolts upright, taking off down the aisle. "Those are my gluten-free cookies!"

"That *I* special-ordered for you!" she yells around her bite, taking the bend of the aisle sharply and whipping around it.

I nearly catch her, rounding the aisle just a second later. "You'd deprive a chronically ill man the simple joy of eating three dozen chocolate cookies filled with buttercream icing and almond meringue biscuit? For shame."

She cackles as we round the bend back to my end of the aisle, where my cookies wait, like delicious little sitting ducks, poised for her to steal them all.

"Swear to God, Ziggy, if you take them—I love my chocolate cookies."

She hops over the container, then spins, flushed and smiling as she meets my eyes. I stare at her, warm and worked up, aching to tug her into my arms again and touch her, learn her, make her flushed and smiling for an even better reason.

Slowly, she bends and picks them up, then snaps the lid on.

"I'm glad you love the cookies." Her voice is quiet as she peers up at me. "Because there's lots more where they came from."

I take the container from her, peering down at the cookies through the lid, then back up. "Where did you get them anyway?"

"Viggo," she says.

I scowl. "Goddammit."

"What?"

"I don't want to like him. But I think I'm going to have to, if he baked these."

She smiles. "Viggo's a piece of work, but everybody always ends up loving him. You will, too."

"I don't love anything except hockey," I remind her.

Ziggy's smile widens as she reaches for my hair and smooths

her fingers down my temples. Then she spins her wrist, opening up her hand. A chocolate cookie sits in her palm. She picks it up, then offers me a bite. "Says the man who just admitted he loves these cookies."

I give her an icy look, softened by a grin. Leaning in, I take a bite of the cookie.

"Looks like," she says, "a few other things might have found a place in your heart." And then she pops the rest of it right in her mouth.

―――――――

Outside her apartment, Ziggy turns and faces me. "Thank you, Sebastian. Tonight was really . . ." She blushes, smiling. Starlight turns her hair cool auburn, makes her eyes sparkle like emeralds in a deep cave. "It was really lovely."

I clasp her hand, then squeeze how she likes, how she always squeezes mine. "It was." Our eyes hold for a beat too long. Ziggy blinks away.

"So," she says. "This week, your schedule"—we have a shared Google calendar now, because it made it easiest to plan publicity outings—"is bonkers. So is mine."

I nod. "Yeah. No time for angry yoga."

"Nuh-uh." She scrolls through her phone. "Poor Yuval."

"Poor Yuval what?"

Ziggy flicks an incredulous glance up at me, before refocusing on her phone. "They have a massive crush on you. I'm autistic— I never notice that stuff, and even *I* picked up on it. How haven't you?"

Because I couldn't give a fuck less what anyone wants from or feels about me, unless it's you.

I roll my eyes. "You're way off."

"I'm not, but whatever." She pockets her phone. "Okay, our

week's goofy busy. That's just that. But we'll figure out something soon. Hang in there while Lars makes you suffer. Ice that foot, okay?"

She wraps me in a hug, her usual, sweet, platonic Ziggy hug that still drives me wild, smashing her tits to my chest, tickling my face with her hair, bathing me in her soft, clean water scent.

"Ziggy?"

"Yes, Sebastian." She's still hugging me, or maybe it's more accurate to say I'm holding her hug-hostage, with my arms wrapped tightly around her, clutching her close, because it's easier to be brave when I'm not looking at her, when I feel her heart beating right by mine, her comforting presence pressed against my body.

"Would you . . ." I clear my throat, irritated with myself by how nervous I am. "I checked the calendar, and saw you don't have a game then, so I was wondering . . . Our first three preseason games are away, but would you come to my home game? The first home game next Sunday?"

I feel her smile lift her cheek against mine, before a sigh leaves her, tickling my neck. "You goober. Like you even had to ask. I was already going to be there."

TWENTY-FIVE

Sebastian

Playlist: "Eagle Birds," The Black Keys

"I like what I'm seeing, Gauthier." Dr. Amy Howard, our team physician, wraps her stethoscope around her neck and smiles at me. "Weight's back up. Trainers' report on your foot's recovery is glowing. Your vitals are excellent, with the exception of that elevated blood pressure, which I'm chalking up to nerves."

My blood pressure's up due to nerves, all right. It's my first home game after nearly flushing my career down the shitter, and lots of eyes are on me, watching me for proof that I've been worth the hassle, that I'm good enough to merit keeping around. I have a lot to prove. Then there's the fact that Ziggy's coming, that she'll be watching me.

That's the biggest culprit of all.

"You been following that gluten-free diet strictly?" Dr. Amy asks. I blink, wrenched from my thoughts. "Yes. Very."

"How's that going?"

"Fantastic. I feel like, my whole life, I've been squinting through a smudged, foggy lens and that diet's wiped it clean. My stomach barely ever hurts. Those aches that I'd get, they're spacing out. I'm following that diet very strictly, given how good it makes me feel."

She smiles. "I'm very glad to hear that. Give it more time. You'll feel even better. And keep up that good self-care."

"Will do, Doc." I slip off the exam table and tug on my warm-up jacket. "So all clear?"

She nods. "All clear. Good luck tonight. Score some goals like you always do."

"You got it. See you later."

I weave my way through the bowels of the facility, back toward the training room, where everyone's in casual athletic clothes, doing their typical pregame exercises before we hit the ice.

"Seb!" Ren waves me his way, where he stands down the hall, holding his phone.

I jog toward him, then stop. Ren turns so I can see the screen, and I smile. "Hey, Linnie."

"Hey, Trouble!" she yells. I thought she was just yelling at the stadium because it was loud, but I'm starting to think maybe Linnie just yells everything. "Good luck! I can't come tonight, 'cuz we're all puking!"

I grimace. "Uh-oh. All of you?"

Linnie nods solemnly. "I started it. Actually, Cade at preschool started it. He puked on my coloring book, then I came home and puked on Daddy. Then Daddy puked in the toilet, but it still got Mommy puking. Now my baby Theo's puking"—she leans in, big pale blue eyes widened dramatically—"*everywhere.*"

Ren sets a fist in front of his mouth. He looks a little green. "Linnie, can we maybe not talk about puking anymore? It's making my stomach feel weird."

"Sure," she says brightly, resting a cheek on her open hand, blinking at us owlishly. "What else do you wanna talk about?"

I snort a laugh. This kid is so damn funny.

"Well . . ," Ren frowns. "I don't know. Maybe how many spells you've cast today?"

"Ten!" she hollers, both hands up to show us, which means

she drops the phone. We get a shot of her ceiling, which is covered in glow-in-the-dark stars, before the screen jostles around, then settles on Linnie again. "The no-puke spell didn't work. Theo puked all over the wall. It looked like runny vanilla ice cream."

Ren dry-heaves.

I take the phone as he bends over, hands on his knees, and takes a deep breath. "How do you cast spells?" I ask.

"I'm a witch." She frowns at me with clear concern that I even had to ask.

"Ahhh, a witch."

Ren stands and takes a slow, deep breath, nodding. He takes the phone back from me and mouths, *Thank you.*

"How'd you become a witch?" I ask her.

"Easy. I just am. Like Aunt Frankie." She reaches off-screen, then returns with a Linnie-size version of Frankie's cane. "She showed me how to cast spells to get rid of scary things."

Ren smiles in that way he does whenever someone talks about Frankie. It used to annoy the shit out of me, when I was moody and pissed about life, but now I just feel an odd kinship to that total-fucking-goner look.

Which . . . I shouldn't. I'm the asshole with so much baggage, so many fears, I'm too chickenshit to ask for more than friendship from the woman I'm so gone over, I can't do a damn thing in a day and not think about her.

It feels like a band's squeezing my ribs since I took Ziggy to the bookstore last week, since I dumped my emotional mess all over her and she was so damn good to me, since we kissed and touched like that.

I've been pretty twisted up.

One moment I want to fucking run to her apartment and bang on her door and tell her I want everything she'll give me. The next, that bone-deep fear of all the ways I'm still so much of a disaster that I will sabotage anything good I might have with her takes over and makes me freeze up.

I have to be patient with myself. I keep reminding myself what Ren said about moving out of the shitty place I got myself into, when this whole thing started—when I crashed that car, then Ziggy crashed into my life:

It's going to take time. Good things, healing things, that lead to growth, are often like that.

Victories are won with patience, endurance, and tiny, incremental steps.

Those moments when I'm weak, lying in bed at night reading, thinking about Ziggy with those cookie crumbs spilling onto her book; cooking meals with all the ingredients she helped me buy; doing yoga with Lars and the team, wishing I was doing angry yoga with Ziggy instead, I think about there being a day when I feel like I've cleaned up my shit and gotten myself in order enough to be worthy of asking Ziggy for more.

And then I think about how I'd lose her entirely if I got lucky enough to have her as more than a friend, then blew it all to hell. If one bad day or choice could obliterate the richest, healthiest relationship I've ever had.

"You look like you're a little scared, Trouble." Linnie leans in until she's just pale blue eyeballs and a brown-black curl of hair on her forehead. "You need a spell to help you out?"

I swallow, then clear my throat. "Sure, Linnie. I'll take all the help I can get."

Ren grins as Linnie props her phone up, clutches her tiny cane, and leans on it, like Frankie does, saying some kind of incantation that sounds remarkably like the Swedish I've heard Ziggy mutter under her breath when I'm on her last nerve. I smile, too.

"There ya go!" She claps her hands together as the cane clatters off-screen. "All set."

"You're the best."

"Good luck, Trouble. Good luck, Uncle Ren. Score me a goal. No, two. No, three!"

"We'll do our best!" Ren tells her. "Bye, Linnie. Love you."

She leans in and presses her lips to the screen, turning the picture to a pink blur on a loud smacking sound. "Love you, byeeeeee."

The call ends.

"She's such a trip." Ren pockets his phone, then turns toward me. "Thanks for joining in on this. She was asking about you."

My stomach does a somersault. "She was?"

"Oh, Linnie is low-key obsessed with you. She keeps asking when Trouble is coming to Sunday family dinner."

I grin. "I'm not gonna lie, I love that she calls me Trouble."

Ren laughs. "Ziggy cracks up every time she says it."

My smile fades. I think about Ziggy, sitting at the table with her family, how good she probably is with her niece, if she's half as good with her as she was with the kids at the roller rink fundraiser. Like Ren, she got down to their level with every one of them, saw them, engaged them, genuinely kind and attentive.

I think about how much I actually might like sitting at that table with Ziggy and all those noisy Bergmans, the same chaos that surrounded me at her game filling up a dining room.

"Thanks for keeping her going with the spells questions, by the way," Ren says. "If she brought up puking again, I think *I* would have brought up my lunch." Ren shudders. "I really can't take puke. Talking about it. Thinking about it—"

"*Zenzero!*" Frankie hollers from down the hall, striding toward us like her badass self, cane tapping on the ground. She's in a long black puffer jacket, her usual black-and-silver sneakers, black slacks, and a heather-gray V-neck sweater. Kings colors. "I've been looking for you."

He grins, all heart-eyed, at her. I forget what the nickname she used means, but it makes him a puddle of mush every time she does. "Hey, love button."

"Don't pull that cute crap on me right now. Carl Clayton for ESPN, *the* Carl Clayton, just found me and said—hey, Schar." She nods to Kris, who walks by us, doing a double take.

He straightens like a private who's just encountered his commanding general, then smiles her way. Not all former staff just get to stroll around down here, but even if she weren't married to Ren, the collective nostalgia for Frankie's days here as their in-game social media coordinator, which predated her becoming an agent and my signing with the team, would be reason enough that she still mingles here from time to time.

"Frank the Tank. Good to see ya." Kris offers Frankie an elbow. She taps his back with hers. I glance between them, confused by the gesture.

"Cold and flu season," Kris explains, nodding toward Ren. "Bergman here said if he saw any of us touch his wife's hands with their grubby petri dish paws between now and playoffs, he would not be responsible for his actions."

Frankie and I turn toward Ren in tandem, wide-eyed. Ren blushes spectacularly as he scrubs the back of his neck. "Brutal but necessary, Francesca. No more repeats of last season's stomach bug."

"Oh, come on!" Frankie argues.

Kris takes signs of Frankie's ire as the rightful cue to make himself scarce. I start to back off, too, but Frankie grabs me by the jacket. "Not so fast, Gauthier. I want words with you." She turns back to Ren. "I did *not* get that bug from the team."

"Yeah, gumdrop, you definitely did. You came for burgers after we won, and slapped hands with Tyler, Arneaux, and Valnikov, all of whom started puking their brains out the next day."

"Wow, you remember exactly who she slapped hands with?"

"One day, you will understand," Ren tells me, then says to Frankie, "Puking their *brains* out, I tell you. Then, two days later, you were in the exact same predicament, vomiting left and right. I mean, you made spaghetti and meatballs and then, ten minutes later, tossed your cookies—well, your Italian, rather—so bad on the couch, we had to throw it out." Ren gags. "Oof, went a little overboard there. I'm making myself nauseous."

I rub my throat, coaxing down the knot set there by a wave of nausea. "Ya think?"

Now it's Frankie's turn to look a little green. "Ren, can we stop, uh . . . talking about . . . that?" She dabs her forehead, which is now damp with sweat.

Ren frowns, his gaze traveling her with concern. "Happily. I hate talking about puke." Hearing that word one last time seems to send her over, because suddenly Frankie grips Ren's arm and promptly empties her stomach all over the floor.

After my mini emotional freak-out during Linnie's call and the puke drama, I'm fucking euphoric to be out on the ice, my mind blank, my body weightless. This is the easiest place for me to exist. Just me and my skates, my stick and a puck and the goal to put it into, over and over. Sure, there are my teammates. There's the fun of bringing together some really beautiful hockey with them. But nothing beats that feeling—in my skates, flying across the ice, the puck and my stick like an extension of me.

The air's that perfect bracing cold as I play around with the puck, then take a slapshot on our goalie, Valnikov, that makes him yelp as he catches it with his glove right in front of his nuts. "Ease up, Gauthier. I'm trying to start a family!"

A few of the guys laugh as we weave around each other.

Ren skates toward me, looking a little pale but mostly himself. I skate up to him and stop on a small spray of ice. "You okay?"

"Yeah." He clears his throat, then glances over his shoulder, searching the box where his family sits, but no sign of his wife. "I'm worried about Frankie. She doesn't just puke."

"Don't start that shit again." I skate back, putting six feet between us in half a second.

He raises his gloved hand that isn't holding his stick. "Sorry."

Arneaux passes me the puck, and I flip it up onto my stick, messing around. "She'll be all right, Ren. I know you worry about her, and I know she's got her health issues, but you gotta trust her. If she says she's okay, she's okay."

"She used to lie to me about that," he mutters, taking the puck when I pass it to him and working it back and forth as he switches sides of his stick, "her being okay."

"'Used to' seems like a pretty important part of that sentence."

He peers up at me, pale eyes narrowed. He glances down at the puck and sighs. "Yeah, you're right. She doesn't do it anymore. She promised me she wouldn't, and she hasn't since. I need to trust her."

"Plus"—I nod up toward the box where his family sits, Frankie now nestled in among them—"she's not alone. They've got her." Frankie sets down what I know by now is a root beer with a straw in it—it's always her drink of choice when we periodically meet to talk business over a meal—and waves to Ren.

Ren lifts his glove, staring at her. "Yeah, they do."

My gaze travels his family's faces. His parents, who smile and wave, who I smile and wave back to. Viggo, who I scowl at when he sticks his tongue out at me like the child he clearly is. A couple I vaguely remember from the wedding—the man has dirty-blond hair and a beard; the woman, with curly waves that pop out of a bun on her head—offer a wave as Ren smiles at them. Frankie, who smiles around the straw in her root beer, eyes locked on Ren, then—

Oh, Jesus. My heart slams into my ribs.

Ziggy, all dimples and freckles, smiling wide as she waves. She's wearing the cutest goddamn fluffy black earmuffs I've ever seen.

I lift my glove and wave back, trying to remember how breathing works.

"How about you get us a goal or two tonight?" Ren says as he circles me, pulling the puck with him. "Just for the pleasure of hearing my sister whistle. You think you can make some sound? Just wait till you hear Ziggy."

TWENTY-SIX

Ziggy

Playlist: "You You," Odetta Hartman

Well. This is going to be a problem.

Watching Sebastian play hockey is a huge turn-on. He's a brilliant player, which I knew already from having attended Ren's games since Sebastian signed. But knowing him now, a month into what began as a mutually beneficial publicity stunt but became so much more, I feel this profound sense of pride and happiness, a connection to this person soaring across the ice that I didn't have before.

It's the third period, two measly minutes left, and LA's down one, thanks to some slipups on the defense and an unlucky flub on the part of Valnikov, the Kings' goalie. Even so, Sebastian looks cool and composed, unfazed by the pressure that's on him as he bends low, dark hair curling up around his helmet, watching Ren lean in for a face-off, fresh off Anaheim's latest goal.

I watch Ren win the puck, which he sends Sebastian's way.

Sebastian *flies* across the ice, feinting, weaving, lightning fast as he moves the puck, beating one player, then another. Ren's not as fast as Sebastian, but he's pretty darn close, quickly catching up to him. It makes me smile, watching them out there together. I bounce nervously in my seat, my hands clasped in front of me.

Whether it's two years of playing together or some kind of fundamental connection between them, Ren and Sebastian have moved the puck across the ice flawlessly all night, finding each other in the most improbable moments, in a way that steals your breath.

As Sebastian closes in on the goal, Anaheim's defender skates up to him, swinging his stick, trying to steal the puck. But Sebastian's too quick, pulling it between his skates, then through the defender's legs—a nutmeg, we'd call it in soccer—that makes the arena burst with excitement. As the defender spins, well and truly beaten, and the goalie angles toward him, Sebastian flicks the puck across the crease to Ren, whose stick creates a delicious *slap* as it connects with the puck, burying it in the net.

I scream—we all do—jumping up and shouting as the buzzer sounds and the light over the net whirls to life, flashing red. Frankie and I hug hard, jostling each other while we watch the Kings swarm Sebastian and Ren as they skate up to each other and embrace.

Over my brother's shoulder, Sebastian peers up, and my heart skips. His eyes find mine, and he grins, wide and sweet, not even a shadow of that sardonic smirk that showed itself so often when we first started all this.

I smile at him, too, bursting with pride. I know he's not mine to be proud of, but he's still my friend. I can't help it.

Reaching around Frankie, I knock my brother Ryder's shoulder. He glances my way, puzzled. "Heads up," I tell him.

After losing most of his hearing due to bacterial meningitis, Ryder wears hearing aids, and what I'm about to do will make him miserable if I don't warn him. He grins, reading my excitement, knowing what I want to do. After a quick maneuver with his hearing aids, he nods my way, giving me the all-clear.

Setting both pointers in my mouth, I let out a whistle that reverberates around the box, making everyone yelp and laugh.

"Damn, that was beautiful," Frankie says.

I smile her way as we settle back into our seats. "They work really well together."

"They always have. But Seb, tonight, there's a fire under him I haven't seen before."

"I think he's feeling better," I tell her. "Since he got his celiac diagnosis and he's eating right, not drinking as much. He's healed up and nourished himself. That makes a big difference."

Frankie rubs a hand across her mouth, then glances my way. "I think that's certainly part of it, yes."

"What else is?"

Suddenly, there's a ruckus, making me peer toward the ice. My stomach drops.

One of Anaheim's players is swinging at Sebastian, who's . . . doing much less than I'd like to defend himself. I've seen Sebastian brawl before. It's ugly—for the *other* person. He's as fast with his hands as he is on the ice. But tonight, there's no sign of that man.

Anaheim's player winds back again and tries to nail Sebastian in the side of the head.

Thankfully Sebastian slips it deftly, right as the ref skates in and tugs away Anaheim's player, sending him straight to the box.

"Well," Frankie muses, sitting back with her arms folded across her chest. Her eyebrows are nearly up to her hairline. "First time for everything."

"What do you mean?"

She lifts a hand Sebastian's way. "Seb didn't fight back. I've never seen him do that before." Sebastian spins and skates in a wide half circle, brow furrowed, exhaling heavily.

My stomach knots. "Is he okay?"

Frankie scowls at the Anaheim player slipping into the penalty box, then glances back Sebastian's way. "Yeah, he's fine. He's got a hard head."

"That's for sure," I mutter.

Coming full circle, Sebastian skates right up to where he was fouled, leaning down with his stick, ready for the face-off.

Anaheim's player skates up, leans in, too, and the puck's dropped. Sebastian wins it, pivots on one foot, and smacks the ever-loving hell out of it, right into the net. The buzzer sounds, the light turns red, and then, gloriously, the next buzzer sounds, heralding the end of regulation play. The game's over. The Kings won.

The whole place goes wild.

After I finally unearth myself from the pile of my family, who's jumping and hugging, celebrating like a bunch of goofballs, some sixth sense makes me turn back toward the ice, searching it.

Sebastian glides across its surface, popping his mouthguard out, stick down at his side, helmet off, clutched in his glove. He's watching the box, a small, lopsided grin tugging up one corner of his mouth. Our eyes meet, and I smile so wide, my cheeks hurt.

His smile widens, too, revealing those ridiculously deep, long dimples, a flash of white teeth. I raise my hands and mime clapping. His smile opens to a laugh that shakes his chest as he skates closer, then stops and takes a theatrical bow.

I snort a laugh.

One of the Kings' players swings by and nudges him on the shoulder, making Sebastian turn, before he glances back and finds my eyes. He nods toward where the team exits. He's asking me to meet him where the players let out.

I nod.

When I tear my gaze away, my entire family is staring at me, their faces a blend of curious and amused.

"What?" I pick up my coat, a new dark green wool number that, after some internet sleuthing, I found online in a tall. For once, I have a nice coat that doesn't stop halfway down my forearms. "Never seen two friends share a moment in the wake of a badass victory?"

Everyone goes back to picking up their things, talking among themselves.

Mom's smiling as she turns toward Dad and says, "Well. I

think this calls for some celebratory dessert and drinks at the house, don't you?"

———

Sebastian's flushed and glowing as he walks out with Ren, fresh off a postgame interview that Frankie is already meticulously watching online, tucked in a corner away from us, mumbling to herself.

His hair's pushed back more than normal, wet from a shower, revealing those wide, sharp gray eyes, the beautiful lines of his cheekbones and jaw. He smiles when he sees me, like he did on the ice—bright teeth and deep dimples. My heart spins like a top.

Wrapping my arms around him as he drops his bag, I let him twirl me. "You were incredible."

"I know," he says, laughing into my neck.

I snort as he sets me down, and I bring a hand to his head. "You okay?"

"Yeah." He shrugs. "This will probably shock you, but I have some experience with getting into brawls. I know how to make sure I don't get conked too bad."

"Coulda fooled me on that last part," Frankie says, walking up to him. She squeezes his arm, and gives him something shockingly close to a smile. "You did great."

His smile falters, like she's stunned him. He blinks at her. "I, uh . . . thanks."

Frankie frowns, then smacks his arm. "What's wrong with you? Why are you acting like that?"

"You complimented me!" He steps back out of her reach. "I don't know what to do with that."

"Take the damn compliment, Gauthier. Jesus! I'm not *that* hard on you, am I?"

Ren wraps an arm around Frankie's shoulder and kisses her temple. "Francesca. How you feeling?"

"Fine," she mutters, staring at Sebastian. "Except this one is making me think I've traumatized him."

Sebastian smiles at Frankie, his expression warming. "You haven't traumatized me, Frankie. I'm just . . . getting used to actually having earned kind words from you."

Frankie's expression softens. "Well, good."

"You were wonderful, *älskling*," Mom says, tugging Ren's head her way and kissing his temple.

Ren smiles. "Thank you, Mom."

"And you too, Seb." Mom wraps her arms around Sebastian.

He blinks over her shoulder at me, eyes wide, then slowly brings his arms to her back. "Thank you—"

"Hell of a game, son." Dad's in there next, bear-hugging Ren, then squishing Sebastian into his arms, just as Mom lets go.

Air rushes out of Sebastian.

I bite my lip and shrug as his eyes hold mine, crinkling with what I think is a suppressed laugh.

"Let the man breathe," Ren says, patting Dad's back.

Dad lets go. "You two." He points between my brother and Sebastian. "That was beautiful hockey."

"Thank you, Dr. B—"

"Sebby!"

A voice I've never heard before cuts through our conversation. Sebastian's shoulders rise, and his jaw hardens. He spins around. A woman who looks to be in her forties stands, tall and lean, built like a ballerina. His mother?

Her hair's dark like Sebastian's, but her eyes are deep blue, nothing like his. A man stands beside her, white-haired, wearing wire-rimmed spectacles, his posture as ramrod straight as hers. He wears an expensive-looking wool overcoat. He doesn't acknowledge us at all, though the woman slants us a glance before she rushes toward Sebastian.

"You were incredible, my darling son. I'm so proud of you."

Sebastian's stiff in her arms. I watch this exchange with growing unease.

"I think we'll be going," Mom says to me before she raises her voice. "Seb." He glances her way, still stuck in his mother's clinging hug.

"Join us, won't you?" my mom says. "We'll celebrate."

He swallows, then nods. "I'd love that."

"Oh, but, Sebby—"

"You're welcome, too," my mom says, smiling politely. "That is, if Seb would like you to come."

I set a hand over my mouth, sucking in a breath. My mother is such a badass.

With that, Mom slips her arm inside Dad's, then turns back toward Ren and Frankie, moving with the rest of my family, who came a little ways down the hall. Ren glances back toward Seb, his gaze darting between him and his mom, his brow furrowed with concern.

I wave him off. I've got this.

"Mom." Sebastian's voice is tight, like he's being strangled. When I turn back, it sort of looks like he is. His mother's still clutching him, whispering something in his ear.

"Catherine," the man says. If I thought Sebastian's voice was cold, this man's is arctic. He still has yet to look at me or my family, or more importantly, even acknowledge Sebastian. "That's enough now, don't you think?"

"Oh, Edward, I'm just happy to see him. I'm so proud of him." She pulls away, patting Sebastian's cheek. He flinches. "You've finally turned a corner, haven't you?"

Sebastian's gaze grows cold as he stares down at her. I feel him slipping away, like the sun dragged behind dark, heavy clouds.

I can't explain it, except that I just know he can't go there again, that he doesn't want to.

Right now, he's surrounded by two people who made him miserable, reminding him of miserable things, of how miserable *he* used to be. But I'm the friend who knows the person he's becoming, living the happier, healthier life he wants, surrounded by people who uplift that health and happiness.

I wrap my hand around his and step beside Sebastian, offering his mother my free hand. "I'm—"

"Ziggy," he says quietly, tugging me closer to his side, almost like he's protecting me. "My friend. Ziggy, this is my mother, Catherine, and her husband, Edward."

Her husband. He doesn't even call Edward his stepdad.

I exhale slowly, forcing a polite smile. "Hi."

"Hello . . . Ziggy." Catherine glances between us, but her focus is set on Sebastian. "Sweetheart, we thought we'd have dinner with you now. Can't your plans with . . . them"—she glances toward my family, her expression pinching—"wait? Another time?"

Sebastian squeezes my hand hard. That's when I feel it. He's trembling. I shift my grip inside his, until he loosens up, enough for me to thread our fingers together. Stroking his hand with my thumb, I huddle in a little closer. I want to comfort him the way he's comforted me. I want him to know I'm here—I'm not going anywhere.

"Not tonight, Mom. I didn't even know you were coming. I already had plans, and I'm not changing them."

That's a lie. There were no plans. Mom's invite came from an idea born at the end of the game. But I smile all the same, because I feel it—Sebastian choosing what he wants, what makes him happy, what's good for him. Because it sure as hell isn't this.

His mother's expression cools. She sniffs, eyes down on her cashmere sweater, which she tugs to her wrists. "Well, all right. Next time, then—"

"Why are you here?" Sebastian asks.

She seems surprised by his question, blinking, wide-eyed. "Well, that's a silly question—"

"It's not," he says quietly, patiently. "It's a very reasonable question, seeing as you haven't come to any of my games since—"

"You became an embarrassment to us?" Edward says coldly. "Or should I say, *even more* of an embarrassment. Consider your behavior, Sebastian—"

I flinch. Edward calls him Sebastian. Edward's the reason Sebastian hates his full name.

I feel sick to my stomach. I want to cry. I've been calling him the name used by this creep.

"It's been disgraceful," he continues. "Why would we subject ourselves to that kind of proximity to you, when all you've done is disappoint—"

"That's enough," I tell him, tugging Sebastian my way. He bounces into me, swallowing hard as I glance his way. Our eyes meet, and I wink at him. A small smile lifts his mouth.

"Excuse me?" Edward glares at me.

I turn back toward him and give him my own cool stare. "You're not going to talk to him that way, not in front of me."

Edward flicks an icy glance at Sebastian, eyebrows raised. "Well. I'll just be going, then."

"Edward." Catherine turns toward him, reaching for his hand, which he ignores, storming off.

She turns back our way, pivoting toward me, then back to Sebastian. "I just wanted to smooth things over—"

"There's no smoothing things over with us, Mom." Sebastian squeezes my hand, like he's shoring himself up. "And while I . . . love you, I don't . . . I don't know how to see you and him without it hurting. Really fucking badly. I need space and time from you. I need to deal with a lot of shit that he did that you either knew about and ignored or chose not to see."

Her eyes fill. "Sebby—"

"Please don't," he says tightly. "Just . . . please. Leave me alone right now. I'll be in contact when I'm ready to talk, but I warn you, you're not going to like what I have to say. And if you won't hear me out when I'm ready to talk, then we will be done, Mom, I promise you. I'm not doing this anymore, pretending this was all my fault, that *I've* been the only problem all these years. It took all three of us to be where we are today, and like hell am I going to keep messing myself up by lying to make you feel better. Goodbye."

He turns, dragging me with him.

I glance over my shoulder. His mother watches him as we walk away, her face hard, tears welling in her eyes.

"Seb—"

He shakes his head, silencing me. With his lead, we take a turn down a hallway, then quickly down another. Sebastian shoves open a door, drags me inside, then slams it shut.

I don't even have a chance to look around, to make heads or tails of where we are, before he wraps his arms around me and buries his face in my neck.

"Just . . ." His breathing is fast and unsteady. He squeezes me so tight, my breathing isn't very steady, either. "Just hold me, please."

I wrap my arms around him as he presses his face harder into my neck. He doesn't make a sound. He barely moves.

But I feel hot, wet tears on my skin. His.

Carefully, waiting for any sign it's unwelcome, I start to rub his back in big, gentle circles.

Sebastian melts into me, giving me more of his weight, his head heavier on my neck.

I'm silent because he needs me to be, and because sometimes there's nothing to say.

Sometimes there's only quiet comfort to give, time and space to hold for pain that reassuring words and paltry solutions can't touch.

"I need a fucking therapist," he mutters against my skin. Straightening, he wipes his eyes with his palms. "And a new fucking family."

I peer up at him with a brave face, trying to hold back my own tears, to be the steady one while he falls apart. My hands settle on his shoulders, squeezing gently. He lists into me again, dropping his cheek against my forehead. A heavy sigh leaves him.

"I think a therapist is a great idea," I tell him quietly, linking our hands together. "And while they aren't the tamest bunch of people to be around, and they'll probably—no, definitely—get under your skin at some point, you've already got a new family waiting in the wings, eager to love you, to be as much your family as you need them to be."

He looks at me curiously, brow furrowed.

I brush his hair back from those tear-wet cheeks and smile. "Mine."

TWENTY-SEVEN

Ziggy

Playlist: "Beige (unburdened)," Yoke Lore

If you'd have told me a month ago, as I sat at my parents' table, frustrated and lonely and stuck, that I'd be here tonight, candlelight dancing over my family's faces, (gluten-free only) crumbs littering the white linen that we rest our elbows on, I'd have laughed in your face.

Yet here we are.

I smile as I glance around the table, at my parents smiling our way, heads together. Willa grinning into her wine as she tries and fails to take a sip without snorting a laugh. Frankie, head thrown back as she cackles. My brothers laughing *so* hard. Ryder, wiping his eyes as he belly-laughs. Ren clutching his chest, a sign he's truly tickled. Viggo chuckling as he tips back in his chair and scrubs his face.

And to my right, Sebastian, elbows on the table, head hung as he laughs right from his belly, so deep and hard, his whole torso shakes. He glances up right at me and catches me staring. I smile, my cheeks warm from my glass of red wine . . . and maybe from something else.

Maybe from the pleasure of sitting beside Sebastian at my parents' home the past two hours, knees knocking beneath the table, eating dessert, sipping coffee (for him) and wine (for me). Maybe from the curious joy of seeing my mom pull Sebastian into another hug when we got here, then drag him into the kitchen, showing him all the gluten-free cookies we had, the *kladdkaka*, a rich flourless chocolate cake that is naturally gluten-free—we always have it on hand for *fika*, a traditional Swedish coffee break—before she led him to the living room and showed him embarrassing photo after embarrassing photo of all the kids growing up, lingering on my pictures, until a wide, delighted smile lit up Sebastian's face and he glanced my way, holding my eyes like he is now.

"How ya doing, Sigrid?"

"Fine, Sebastian—" I bite my lip, shutting my eyes.

He knocks my knee with his beneath the table. "What's wrong?"

"I . . ." Opening my eyes, I meet his. "I called you by your full name. I've been calling you that for weeks, and . . . *he* calls you that." I find his hand beneath the table and squeeze it. "I'm sorry. I didn't know. I would never have—"

"Ziggy." Sebastian leans in, voice lowered, soft, silver eyes holding mine. "You calling me that, it pissed me the fuck off at first, but that lasted like five minutes. Then I realized I loved that you called me Sebastian. You . . ." He shrugs. "It was like you scratched it out, his voice, those memories of how he used to say it, just wrote right over it with this pretty, loopy scrawl that swallowed up that shitty scribble beneath it." His gaze searches mine. "Remember, I told you I was okay with you calling me that. Don't worry."

"Are you sure?" I whisper. "Because, Seb, I'd never—"

"Sebastian," he whispers back. "Call me what you've called me. Don't change it. Don't change it just 'cause I lost it in a treatment room and cried like a baby."

"You didn't cry like a baby." I press a knuckle into his thigh. "You felt your feelings. It was good. Healthy. Natural."

"Well, then don't change what's natural with us, what you've been doing, okay?" I hold his eyes as his fingers find mine and tangle them. "Okay."

"All right, kids." Frankie stands slowly, yawning. "I'm wiped."

"Home we go, Francesca." Ren reaches behind his chair, where her cane sits propped on the wall, and sets it in front of her. "Love you, family."

Frankie takes it and gives him a smile, before blowing us all a kiss. "Love you, hooligans. Good night."

"Good night!" we call. "Love you!"

Mom stands from her chair as Dad stands, too, a little slow himself, following behind Ren and Frankie to see them off.

"C'mon, Lumberjack." Willa drains the last sip of her wine. "We should get ourselves to bed, too. Early flight home tomorrow."

Ryder nods, leaning forward, starting to collect dirty plates.

"Leave them, Ry." Viggo stands, then takes the plates from him. "You two hit the hay and get some sleep. I got nowhere to be in the morning."

"But you did all the baking," I tell him.

"A couple batches of cookies. It was nothing—"

Sebastian stands, taking the plates from Viggo before my brother even registers what's happened. Deftly stepping around me, Sebastian works his way down the table, fast and efficient, stacking plates, then scooping up wineglasses. I follow suit.

Viggo glares at Sebastian's back as he takes his towering stack of dirty dishes into the kitchen, sets them carefully on the counter, then opens the dishwasher to load it up.

I lean across the table, wineglasses clutched in one hand, and poke my brother's chest. "What are you scowling at him for? He's just cleaning up the dishes."

"Exactly," he mutters, frowning as he gathers the last straggling coffee cups. "I don't want to like him. But I think I'm gonna have to, *if* he's truly that dedicated."

"To the dishes?"

He reaches past me for the last cup and sighs heavily, frowning up at Sebastian. "Among other things."

I wrinkle my nose. "What are you—"

"G'night, Ziggy." Willa opens her arms to me.

I hug her back one-armed, clutching the wineglasses in my other, before Willa starts trundling up the stairs to Ryder's old bedroom on a loud yawn.

Ryder takes my one-armed hug next, then gently tugs my ponytail. "Night, Zigs."

"Night, Ry."

"Well." Mom steps up beside me and snuffs out a trio of candles on the table, pinching the flames between her fingers into three curls of smoke. I used to watch her do that as a kid, convinced she was a sorceress, and it was only a matter of time before she told me about my magical powers, too.

Turning toward me, she sets a hand on my back and rubs gently. "This was a nice evening."

"It was. Thank you, Mom." I nod subtly toward Sebastian in the kitchen, where he works his way through the dishes, taking the coffee cups from Viggo and shooing him away. "I really appreciate it."

"Of course, *älskling*." She smiles softly, her head tipped as she looks at me. "It was nothing."

"It wasn't nothing," I whisper against the lump in my throat. "Not to me."

Her smile deepens. "The ones my children love, I love, too. The ones who become their family are my family. What we did tonight, that's just what family does."

I nod, smiling. "Yeah. But that doesn't make it nothing. That makes it special. And good." Leaning in, I set my head against hers. Mom's just an inch shorter than me, so our temples rest together easily. She turns and presses a kiss to mine. "*I love you,*" she whispers in Swedish.

"I love you, too."

"Speaking of good, Sigrid." My mom kisses my temple again. "And special. He's one of them. You keep him close, *förstått?*"

I smile as I watch Dad join Sebastian in the kitchen, muscling his way in to help, while Viggo packs up the leftover cookies and cakes.

"*Förstått,*" I tell her.

Sebastian stands outside my apartment building with me, keys swinging on his finger. I need to stop seeing my panties twirling there instead and blushing every time he does it. "Tonight was . . . really wonderful," he says. "Thank you."

"Thank *you,*" I tell him.

He frowns. "For what?"

"For coming over, spending time with my family. I know they're a lot."

"They are," he agrees. "But the best kind of 'a lot.'" Slowly, he steps closer, clasping my hand, his thumb brushing my palm. "Thanks for sticking up for me tonight."

"Sebastian, you don't have to thank me for that—"

"Yes, I do. It . . ." He shifts on his feet. "It meant a lot to me."

I bite my lip, then nod. "Okay."

His gaze dances over me. "I meant to say you looked very lovely tonight, Ziggy. The emerald coat. The gray off-the-shoulder top. Stylish."

"Well, I've learned from the best."

"Ah, you figured out what you liked all on your own." He tips his head and steps back, still holding my hand. His gaze slides down my legs. "Damn, those look good on you."

He's talking about my jeans. Tapered leg, mid-rise. Just the right amount of stretchy. Exactly like my old favorites that he cut into shorts, whose tag he read so carefully that first night he came by my place for reasons that were beyond me then. When I came back from my run right before the game tonight, these jeans and two other pairs in dark and black washes were waiting for me in a box propped against my door.

"Oh." I turn a little, side to side, inspecting them. "These old things? Stop it."

He laughs. "I don't think I will."

I peer up, meeting his eyes. "You sent these, didn't you?"

"Who, me?" He makes a face. "I would never do something that—"

"Considerate? Thoughtful? Generous?" They aren't cheap, these jeans. I remember seeing the price tag when Mom bought them for me and nearly choking. I also haven't been able to find them *anywhere*.

"Shh." He sets a finger to his mouth. "Word might get out that I'm capable of such things, then what would I do?"

I smile. "You'd be exposed. Brutally. For the good person that you are."

"Ah, don't push it." He shrugs. "It wasn't a big favor to ask. That's one of the brand partnerships that I managed not to fuck up. They were all too happy to bring back that style for me. Just took them a couple weeks to get it together."

My eyes narrow. That means he's had this in the works for a while. Since . . . well, since I really didn't think he cared about me at all. It makes those butterflies in my stomach flutter dangerously.

"It was really sweet of you, Sebastian. Thank you."

"It was nothing," he says.

"Hey." I tug at his hand. "You just gave me hell for downplaying what I did when you thanked me. Don't turn around and do the same thing. You thoughtfully, single-handedly made it possible for me to have these jeans, the only ones I've ever found that work for me, and it was sweet and you deserve to be thanked for it."

"They're just jeans. You stood up to my awful family."

"Because you deserve to be stuck up for, to be protected from that, that, that *fuckery*."

"Sigrid!" he gasps.

I poke his side. "Be serious."

He sighs. "Must I?"

Giving him a look, I glide my fingertips along his. "For a moment, yes. Let's agree we won't downplay what we are or do for each other anymore, okay? I just want us to be us. I want us to be honest. You saw how busy we've been the past few weeks, how much less we've seen of each other. I don't want anything else like half-truths and omissions keeping us even further apart. Okay?"

A smile lifts his mouth. "Yeah, Sigrid. Okay." Pocketing his keys, Sebastian steps closer and threads his fingers tight through mine. His gaze drifts up to my hair, which he smooths gently away from my face before he meets my eyes. "I'm gonna miss you."

"Miss me?"

"Sigrid." He lifts his eyebrows. "You just said yourself how busy we've been. That's nothing to what's coming. Have you looked at our Google calendar for the foreseeable future?"

"Oh." I clear my throat. "I might have been avoiding it."

Because I know what's coming. Angel City's regular season is winding down, but the National Team has international friendlies lined up throughout the month, and my schedule's packed with a slew of new and prospective brand sponsorship meetings, interviews, and photo shoots. The irony is that these opportunities, in part made possible because I put myself out there in the public eye with Sebastian and got myself noticed, are the very things that are going to keep me away from him.

"Well, when you give up that avoidance tactic, you'll see what I mean." He sighs heavily, tugging me toward him. "C'mon. Hug me goodbye."

My chin bumps into his shoulder as I tumble into him, as he wraps his arms around me hard and buries his face in my neck. I feel him take a deep breath in, then hold it, before slowly exhaling. Slipping my arms around his waist, I rest my cheek against his shoulder. He already feels more solid, stronger, healthier. Tears prick my ears. "I'm gonna miss you, too."

"Bullshit," he mutters into my hair. "That's what professional hockey schedules are."

I nod against his shoulder. "Total bullshit."

"Two swears in one night." He *tsks*. "You really have turned into a bad girl."

I laugh, blinking away tears.

His hand comes to my back, circling gently. "We'll have some overlap," he says. "We'll still see each other. And there are these fancy newfangled contraptions called phones that we can use to stay in touch. You can text *and* call on them. It's incredible."

I snort a laugh, pulling away. I can't help but smile. "Like you'd call me."

His eyes hold mine. "I'd call you every day if you wanted me to, Sigrid."

My smile falters. "You would?"

"Hell, yes."

"Oh." I bite my lip. "Well, then ... consider yourself ... wanted."

His eyes flare like summertime sparklers. "You too, Sigrid."

"Okay."

"Take care of yourself, all right?" He hugs me to him hard, his hand cupping my neck, his mouth against my temple, where he presses the softest kiss. "Don't be *too* bad, at least, without me."

I smile against his shoulder. "No promises."

"Of course the fashionable Sebastian is fashionably late to his own damn birthday party," Viggo mutters, rearranging the gluten-free cookies, six different kinds that are spread across three trays. In the month since Sebastian's and my schedules picked up into pure, barely ever aligned chaos, Viggo's been a gluten-free baking machine.

"Give him some credit," I tell my brother. "He did just fly in from a game, oh"—I crane my neck, reading the clock on Ren's oven—"an hour ago."

"Excuses, excuses. Ren's here!"

"It's his house, you numbskull. Of course he's here."

Viggo huffs and tugs at his cravat. He's dressed—shocking no one, since he's obsessed with historical romance novels—as a Regency Era aristocrat, complete with a peacock-blue tailcoat and scandalously tight saddle-brown breeches. I keep snort-laughing every time he tries to bend or do anything but stand in a pair of pants that seem to be dangerously compressing the parts of him I prefer not to think about. Every time he has to move, he lets out a little squeak of discomfort that's giving me life.

I glance around at Ren and Frankie's place, decorated with creamy paper lanterns and spooky cobwebs, elegant black garlands, and balloons clustered together. Candles cover every surface and dance in the sea breeze that sneaks through the open windows and screen door leading out to the deck.

Sebastian's day-after-Halloween birthday bash is shaping up nicely.

Over two breakfasts at our usual spot the past month (the first, post–angry yoga; the other, post–another bookshop-browsing visit, this time, during regular hours, with no book casualties or other devious behavior, the memory of which *might* have made me blush head to toe when we visited the second time), Sebastian admitted to having a birthday that was barely a November 1, just-past-midnight arrival, which I argued basically means he's got a Halloween birthday. After some plotting with my brothers, Sebastian agreed to let the Bergmans host a costume-themed party for him the day of.

Plans have been in place for a few weeks now. Invitations were sent (by me). Costumes were mandated (not a big ask for this crew, who loves to dress up and goof off). And an all-gluten-free menu was decided on (thanks to Viggo, who bakes like a boss, also loves cooking, and was interested in being paid for said endeavors).

Now it's just a matter of waiting.

And not losing my elf ears in the dill dip again.

Swearing in Swedish under my breath, I pluck out my elf ear once again and move around Viggo to rinse it in the sink.

Viggo *tsk*s. "I heard that foul language, young lady."

I shove him in the butt with my foot, making him tip sideways and squeak in discomfort. "Hey, Viggo, why don't you try to bend over and pick up that dish towel you dropped?" I point with my chin to said towel lying sadly near his feet.

He glares at me. "I'm on a budget. This was the only size breeches Wesley could nab from the *Hamilton* production's costume inventory without notice, okay?"

I snort a laugh. "Can you even breathe in them?"

"Marginally." He cracks a smile as I laugh even harder.

"We're here!" Oliver shuts the front door behind him and Gavin.

I let out a complimentary whistle. They're both wearing tuxes that fit them like gloves.

Oliver's sporting a fluffy silver wig. Gavin's wearing a wig, too, but his is brown, sort of like a seventies shag, and his beard is much thicker than normal. I wonder if he grew it out precisely for this.

Lord knows, if Ollie asked him, he would. That man adores my brother.

Viggo and I tip our heads in tandem, trying to figure them out. "Who the hell are you?" Viggo asks.

I swat him on the shoulder. "Be nice."

Gavin rolls his eyes and gives Oliver a withering look. "Told you."

"C'mon, guys!" Ollie yells. Gavin takes the cheese plate from him and leaves Oliver standing in the hallway. "Sondheim and Bernstein! How did you not get that?"

Gavin mutters under his breath, but there's a smile cracking his stern mouth.

Viggo blinks at Oliver, then understanding dawns. "The lyricist and composer you love."

"That *everyone* with *any* taste in musicals loves." Oliver traipses into the kitchen, brushing Gavin's hands away from the cheese plate. "Don't even think about hiding the Brie from me, Hayes."

Gavin grins, then kisses him on the cheek, hard and sweet. "I would never dream of it."

The doorbell rings this time, which means it's not family.

"I got it!" Ren jogs out into the open living space from down the hall, wearing a dark gray suit with wide pinstripes, running his fingers through his hair.

His *black* hair.

I gape at him. "Oh my God, Ren. Tell me you didn't dye it."

My brother snorts, giving me a shake of his head as he stops in front of the mirror mounted on the wall in his foyer. He shifts his hair, and now I can see that it's a wig, albeit a darn good one. "Frankie said if I even looked at hair dye, she'd tie my hands to the bed, which"—Ren grins—"ya know, not exactly the disincentive she was going for—"

"Ay!" We all throw our hands up over our ears. "None of that!" I yell.

Ren laughs, then tugs open the door. What looks to be most of the Kings' team strolls in.

Tyler and Andy are dressed as Tweedledee and Tweedledum, Kris as the Mad Hatter. More pour in, hands filled with gifts and beverage contributions, even though I know Ren told them not to bother.

I wave hello, then turn back to kitchen prep, checking the heat on Viggo's Swedish meatballs, complete with gluten-free breadcrumbs, then gently stirring the gluten-free twisty pasta noodles that will go with them, which are a little finicky. We've learned from trial and error that cooking them extra al dente, before they're drained and tossed with oil, keeps them from sticking and turning to mush.

Frankie strolls out of the hallway, dark hair draping down her shoulders and back, in a killer black plunging V-neck dress that hugs her body.

I give her an eyebrow wiggle as she walks up to the island, reaches for a root beer gummy from a brimming black onyx dish, and pops it in her mouth. "Frankie. Wowza."

She shrugs, grinning. "Yeah. I look pretty hot. The dress makes my boobs look fantastic."

I peer at her boobs. Not that I've paid particular attention to my sister-in-law's breasts over the years, but I've known her for a long time, and I can't help but notice they kind of look . . . bigger? It would be supremely out of character for her, since, like me, she has a lot of sensory issues with her clothing, but who knows, maybe she braved a push-up bra for the occasion.

"You look amazing," I tell her. "Feel amazing?"

"Hell, no. I feel like dumpster garbage in August that waste management forgot to pick up. But I'll be fine."

"God, Frankie." I shudder. My sister-in-law has a vivid way with language that is both a blessing and a curse. "What's wrong?"

Her grin doesn't fade. She just chews her root beer gummy and turns toward Ren, watching him shut the door behind everyone, then herd them inside, into the main room. "Nothing."

"Nothing?" I'm so confused.

But then it doesn't matter what I'm thinking or what's being said, because the door opens again. And this time it's Sebastian.

Wearing head-to-toe black, a glittering onyx crown wedged in his hair that flashes silver as he turns his head and shuts the door.

My eyes widen. I drink in the details—the leather jacket and pants that fit his body as well as a second skin, the pewter stitching woven throughout that shimmers subtly as he moves, revealing a design as intricate as his tattoos. He rakes his hands through his hair below his crown, making those silver rings on his fingers sparkle.

And then his gaze finds mine. He smiles, slow and knowing. It's sweet, but it's also . . . sexy, that tiny tilt of his mouth, higher on one side than the other, the subtle arch of one dark eyebrow.

I watch him walking toward me, piecing it together, why he looks so familiar. Not just because he's my friend. Not just because by now I think I might know his face as well as my own. But because he looks like . . .

I gasp, slapping a hand over my mouth.

Sebastian Gauthier is dressed as a character from my favorite romantasy—an epically magical, dark and twisty, super-smutty Swedish fantasy romance. And not just any character—the villain. The irredeemable, horribly cold and brutal villain. At least, he seems that way, until his whole redeeming backstory and secret altruistic strategy reveal him as the hero in Book Three. I gave him Book *One* a week ago. He can't have read all of them. They're each nearly a thousand pages. There's just no way.

"Hello, Ziggy dear." Sebastian leans a hip against the kitchen counter, grinning wickedly. It's not his old sardonic smirk, nothing cold or aloof. It's playful and warm—no, not warm. It's hot as hell.

I swallow roughly. "Hi, Sebastian."

He *tsk*s, wagging one silver-ringed, inked finger. Oh God, I think I might implode from lust. I don't know what I'll do if he does one more sexy thing—

"No Sebastian here." He sweeps his hands down his body. "That's Rainer, Lord Ansgar, to you." He tips his head, staring at me, his smile growing. "And I owe you my apologies. What was I thinking, calling you Ziggy, when you're . . ."

Don't say it. I'll kiss you if you say it. I'll tackle you with kisses if you say it.

His smile widens to the devastating-dimples, bright-teeth smile that I can barely survive on the best of days. ". . . Tindra, Warrior Faery Queen, who thoroughly kicks my ass in Book Two."

"Oh God," I mutter against my bit lip.

Sebastian's grin sets those crinkles at his eyes as he pushes off the counter, then takes my hand, squeezing it in our way. "You okay? You're being very quiet."

I swallow, my heart pounding. I nod. "I'm okay." On a step closer to him, I set my hand on his jacket and trace the stitching up his torso to his collarbones, to the open throat of his collar, where his skin glows golden. Holding his eyes, I tell him, "Happy birthday."

His smile softens as he holds my eyes, too. "Thank you."

Impulsively, unable to stop myself, I throw myself into his arms and hug him, pressing a hard kiss to his cheek.

"Ziggy," he chokes out, strangled in my neck-squeezing hug, "watch out for the—"

Poof. The sound not unlike an umbrella being opened echoes behind him. Someone curses on his right as they stumble into the fridge. A tray of utensils clatters loudly to the floor. I pull away, wide-eyed.

Sebastian Gauthier—or should I say, Rainer, Lord Ansgar—stands in front of me, a rare and delicious blush heating his cheeks. Stretched out behind him, dark yet gossamer fine, woven with the same sparkling pewter thread as his clothes, are—

"Wings!" Viggo hollers. "He's got *wings*!"

TWENTY-EIGHT

Sebastian

Playlist: "All of Me—Cover," Noah Guthrie

That . . . did not go how I wanted it to. Ziggy blinks at me, deep green eyes wide, mouth parted in surprise.

"Wings!" Viggo hoots and does a fist pump. "I called it. Cough it up, honey bunch."

Oliver scowls at his brother, then pulls out a twenty and slaps it into Viggo's outstretched hand.

"Seb!" Ren yells. "You're here! The birthday boy is here!"

I'm tackled rather quickly by a rowdy bunch of hockey players. "Whoa," I holler. "Watch the wings!" Reaching back for the wings, I try to collapse them, but it's hard. The past few times I tested them since they were finished, I slipped them off, then closed them, but they're firmly attached to the jacket now, and I'm surrounded by a team of rowdy hockey players who are euphoric from a win yesterday and the prospect of letting loose tonight.

Taking pity on me, Ziggy inserts herself easily, right through the shovey hands and affectionate jostles. Her youngest-of-seven family experience is evident, her expression and touch unfazed by the chaos as she calmly reaches over my shoulders, placing her chest tightly against mine, baring her neck inches from my lips.

My mouth waters. I shut my eyes and breathe her in, rainwater clean and soft. I want to wrap my arms around her and run my palms right over her beautiful, full ass. I want to bury my face in her neck and lick my way up her throat. I want to sink my hands into that soft, thick hair, press her legs wide open with mine, and lose myself in her.

The wings collapse, and Ziggy leans back. "There." Her head turns, and our noses brush. Her eyes hold mine.

I swallow roughly. Ziggy does, too.

And then I'm dragged back by the team for a photo that Viggo takes, grinning like the self-satisfied schmuck that he is.

On a break between takes, I glance over my shoulder at Ziggy, who smiles at me, looking like . . . God, she looks like heaven. A pale, pearl-white gown draped down her body, a quiver's strap across her chest, arrows poking out behind it. Her hair's pinned half up, woven with tiny braids and revealing deceptively believable elf ears. It's so her, such a maddening twist of sweet and sexy, nerdy and naughty, I can't even take it.

She flashes me a wider smile, eyes holding mine, then brings a cookie to her mouth and crunches.

A groan leaves me as she licks her finger, then throws back the rest of the cookie, exposing the long, pale column of her throat.

This is going to be a very long night.

It's despicably late, even for a formerly "carousing" night owl like me. Frankie's passed out on the couch, snoring, as Ren closes the front door behind the last of the stragglers, waving and calling good night. A massive yawn leaves him as he turns and rubs his eyes.

"I've gotta go to bed," he groans. Dropping his hands, he spots Frankie passed out on the couch. "Poor Francesca."

There's something different in his smile as he walks toward her, then brushes a strand of hair off her face that's close to her open mouth. Gently, he scoops her up and adjusts her in his arms. Frankie's head lolls to his shoulder. "So fucking tired," she mutters.

He presses a soft kiss to her forehead. "I know, *älskade*. Off to bed we go." As he starts down the hall, he glances my way and stops. "Feel free to crash here tonight, just to play it safe."

"I didn't drink anything. But thank you."

He frowns. "You didn't?"

"Haven't for weeks."

His eyebrows rise. "I'm a jerk. I hadn't noticed you weren't drinking, Seb. I shouldn't have had alcohol here if you were try-ing to avoid it—"

"Don't think twice about it. I was absolutely fine." I nod my chin toward the hallway. "Now put your wife to bed and get some sleep."

He nods, smiling. "All right. Good night. Just text when you leave, and I'll set the security, okay?"

"Will do."

Just a minute after Ren disappears down the hall, Ziggy strolls into the main room, rubbing the shells of her ears, which are red and seem irritated. She glances up and does a double take, smiling at me. "Hey."

I stare at her, surrounded by the wreckage of a truly wonderful party—the first I've ever had that I can remember being happy at, let alone sober for. I have a thousand photographic memories stashed in my brain from tonight—I feel so damn grateful that she stars in most of them.

I feel so damn grateful for *her*.

More than grateful, I feel . . . Fuck, what I feel shouldn't have the name that it does. I don't let myself even think the word. I can't. Not yet. Not when I'm so far from where I want to be, from what she deserves.

"How ya doing?" she asks, tossing her abandoned elf ears onto the kitchen island. She slumps against the counter, all long, lithe arms and tired, lovely eyes.

"Exhausted," I tell her. "You?"

She nods, yawning loudly. "Exhausted."

"Ready to go?"

She tips her head, peering up at me. "Yeah. I am. Will you drive me home?"

"Of course."

Sighing, she pushes off the counter and grabs her elf ears off its surface before scooping up a duffel bag by the door, waiting for me as I gather up the leftover gluten-free baked goods.

Her smile is tired but happy when I open the front door and set a hand at her back as she steps outside. I lock the handle behind us, then text Ren we're gone so he can set his security.

Slowly, we walk to the car, and Ziggy flops into her seat.

And then I drive us in the quiet, because I like quiet with Ziggy, how we can simply be in it, together. It feels familiar and comfortable. Safe.

As I pull up in front of her building, I glance her way and feel my heart twist. She's asleep, her head resting against the window glass. Gently, I brush back a strand of hair from her temple.

"Sigrid."

"Hmm."

I smile as she lolls her head my way, eyes still shut. "Home."

She sighs. "Not home."

"If you'd open those big green eyes, you'd see you are."

She shakes her head. "Can't."

A soft laugh leaves me. "Well, I've fireman-carried you before. I can do it again."

"Mm-kay."

I push open my door, then round the car before opening her door and easing her out. Ziggy flops over my shoulder as I set her duffel bag on the other. I kick the car door shut behind me, then hit the lock button on my keys.

"I'm upside down," she mumbles, sounding a little delighted by this. I smile and squeeze her thigh. "No you're not. The world is."

I feel her head lift a little, like she's looking around. She drops her head, then swats me on the butt. "Liar."

"Have to stay in character."

She sighs. "You dressed up as Lord Ansgar."

"He's a total badass. I couldn't *not* dress as Rainer, Lord Ansgar."

I riffle through her duffel bag and find her keys, then let us into her building. A month of dedicated training and hockey has already made my body build back the muscle I lost this summer—I walk up the stairs steadily with her on my shoulder, open her apartment door, then let myself in with her keys again.

Nudging the door shut, I lock the bolt with my elbow, then walk toward her bed and lower her onto it.

Ziggy sighs as she flops back, arms above her, red hair fanned out across the bed. "So tired," she mumbles.

Gently, I tug off her boots, then loosen the corset-style laces at her stomach, up to the curves of her breasts, stopping myself before I touch them. She draws in a deep, satisfied breath. "Thank you, Sebastian," she sighs.

It feels so intimate, so . . . right, tugging off her shoes, loosening her dress. In that moment, I know if I could do this every night for the rest of my life, if I could ever be worthy of that, I would.

My throat feels thick. My heart thunders in my chest. "Sleep tight, Sigrid."

She licks her lips, then drowsily lolls her head my way. Her eyes open to sleepy slits as she peers up at me. "I miss you."

I swallow roughly. "I miss you, too."

Sighing, she shuts her eyes. "And I'm just gonna miss you more and more."

I clasp her hand, gently tracing her fingers, long and lovely, the soft curves of her nails. "I miss you more and more, too."

"Too much," she whispers.

I peer up at her, searching her face. "Too much?"

She nods.

"Ziggy—"

Her snore is soft and sweet. It makes me smile, torn. What does she mean, she misses me too much? That it's too much to ask, this friendship, this . . . dynamic, while I'm busy with the season? I want to shake her awake and ask her, but to what end? So she can tell me something that will crush me? So I can ask her for something I'm not prepared to give?

Slowly, I lift her hand to my mouth and kiss her palm, feather-light. Then I set it down on the bed and clasp it, stroking her warm satin skin.

"I'm too selfish to ask you to stop missing me, Ziggy," I tell her quietly. "So . . . please don't stop. Please hang tight. Just hang in there for me. I promise, I'm trying. Okay?"

She sighs, a soft smile lifting her mouth. "'Kay."

———

Breathing heavily, I'm bent low as I glide across the ice, not because I'm winded, but because I'm pissed and trying not to lose it. I'm pissed because we're losing. I'm pissed that my asshole absent father decided, now that I've cleaned up my act and I'm having the best season of my career, that he's interested in being in my life, despite my telling him he can fuck right off until further notice, and he's at my game tonight, like he has been a handful of other times the past few months, watching me up in that fancy box with the owners, laughing and schmoozing them, acting like they're best fucking buddies, all so proud of me; like he's had anything to do with me getting where I am, except for dumping half his hockey-inclined DNA into my makeup, then splitting when he got bored.

I'm pissed because it's been six months since that night I tucked in Ziggy after my birthday party and begged her to wait for me while I got my shit together, and it's felt like six years, for how hard I've worked to make myself good enough.

I *still* don't feel good enough.

I'm pissed about how much self-restraint it's taken, keeping my hands and lips off her, keeping my mouth shut so I don't say what I'm dying to say too soon, before the time is right.

And I'm really fucking pissed that it's been three weeks since I've last seen her. Between a rough stretch of away games and Ziggy's schedule, which has taken her around the country, doing publicity with the National Team and as an ambassador for Ren's charity, of which she is now a partner, along with Oliver's boyfriend, Gavin, and her sister-in-law, Willa, who's also a professional soccer player, we haven't done more than text or talk on the phone.

I miss her so damn much. Just like she said that night—too much.

Seeing her whenever I can, doing angry yoga together, grabbing breakfast, taking a quick road trip while she drives her favorite car of mine to a new bookstore, joining Bergman Sunday dinners whenever I'm home, have been the crumbs sustaining me over the past six months.

The past three weeks without her, however, the only thing holding me together has been talking and texting with her while traveling with the team, driving home, in my hotel rooms after tough games and tougher virtual sessions with my therapist, and hockey—the physical relief of pushing myself so damn hard on the ice, I have nothing left when I collapse into bed afterward. But it's getting harder to hold back that cold fury that used to settle into my veins when I played, when unresolved anger and pain pulsed through me, screaming for release.

I breathe out again, the way my therapist taught me, and pick up my head, receiving the puck from Tyler's win at the face-off, then flying down the ice. Seattle's defenseman charges toward me, and I fuck around with him because I can, leading him right as I swing my stick wide with the puck, then pulling it across me, faster than he can blink, and shooting.

Seattle's goddamn goalie saves it, though, and I grit my teeth, skating away, frustrated as I chase after another Seattle defenseman, who powers up the ice with the puck. He passes it center ice to his forward, who works the puck past our guys, then dumps it to a Seattle forward, who shoots and sends the puck right over Valnikov's shoulders, into the net.

I growl in the back of my throat as the buzzer blares and the light flashes red, skating back to center ice, breathing heavily, shutting my eyes as I try to hold it together.

And then that prickle at the back of my neck makes me stop dead. I straighten, then turn, glancing over my shoulder, right into the stands. I don't make eye contact with fans. I'm generally too hyperfocused on the game to even remember there are people around, watching us. But tonight, I look exactly where that sixth sense tells me to, the second row, halfway down the rink toward Seattle's goalie, where we've been attacking two out of the three periods.

And then my heart does something terrifying. I swear to God it just stops, for a second, like a hiccup in my chest.

Ziggy.

She's . . . here.

I blink at her, stunned. And then this . . . warmth spreads, right from the heart of me, out to every inch of my body, like she's the sun and just seeing her, drinking her in, has lit me up, head to toe.

She tips her head, a little furrow in her brow. Her smile slips.

Probably because I'm staring at her like a dipshit, wide-eyed, stunned, instead of smiling at her, waving, doing a damn thing to show her how happy I am to see her, how far beyond pleasantly surprised I am that she's here.

Slowly, finally, I lift a gloved hand. Her smile brightens as she waves back, making her black earmuffs jostle a little, her braid sway down her shoulder. That's when I just . . . feel it all leave me. The anger, the cold, aching sadness, like a poison leaving my system.

Staring at her, lost in her, finally, I smile.

TWENTY-NINE

Ziggy

Playlist: "Trampoline," Kelaska

Sebastian stares up at me, with this . . . smile I've never seen before, wide and free and so unbelievably beautiful. I used to find his face really tough to read. He was good at hiding what he felt behind that chilly, detached expression of his, those cool, gray eyes. But now, months of friendship under our belt, I know him better. I can tell when he's anxious, when he's tired, when he's preoccupied, when he's happy.

But this . . . this is new. This is something to pay attention to.

I stare into those lovely quicksilver eyes, drinking him in, and mouth, *Missed you*.

He sighs heavily and nods, then yanks out his mouthguard. *Too much*, he mouths back. My heart jumps. It aches.

But I'm used to that by now. It's been half a year, six long months, of my heart jumping and aching around Sebastian. And it's been worth it, because I was tired as could be when he laid me down on my bed after his birthday party, but I wasn't unconscious. I heard him—not just what he said, but how he said it.

Please hang tight. Just hang in there for me. I promise, I'm trying.

I almost sat up, grabbed him by the shoulders, and shook him as I told him, of course I'd hang tight, of course I'd hang in there, I couldn't possibly do anything else.

Because what I feel for Sebastian snuck up on me, quieter and stealthier than the best Bergman prank, and wove itself so deep into my being, I have no hope of extricating myself from it, even if I wanted to.

And I don't want to. Even though it's hard, knowing what I feel, yet wanting and waiting.

What's hardest—and each day it's a little harder—is wondering if I should be the one who finally gives us the shove. If I'm the one who has to ask for an end to the waiting, the hoping, the aching for more.

I've grown so much the past seven months, since I started my Project Ziggy Bergman 2.0, since I swore to myself that I'd be braver, speak up for myself, make the people around me see me for who I am. I've earned greater recognition and respect—on my teams, in my family, in my ambassadorships and brand sponsorships. I've told people off, defended myself, said hard things when it wasn't easy.

But this is the one thing I still don't know how to do. I don't know if or when I should tell him what he means to me, when he's begged me not to see him that way. I haven't known if I should ask him to move forward with me when he's pleaded with me to wait right where we are.

But then I had an idea. I mentioned to my mother heading up to the A-frame at my favorite time of year, suggested we visit the Washington State–residing Bergmans—Ryder and Willa, Axel and Rooney—take a little time away to rest. We could celebrate my birthday, which would fall on the weekend we were there. Mom suggested we make a whole week of it.

That's when I knew I had to see Sebastian first. Sebastian, who was coincidentally in Washington State, too, though earlier than we made plans to be. Sebastian, who I missed so badly it hurt, while I loafed around LA in a rare few days of nothing on my schedule, waiting for him to come back.

I put on my big-girl pants and bought a plane ticket. He didn't have to have invited me to want me there or be happy to see me. I could invite myself. I could show up and surprise him and . . . I don't know, maybe offer a little encouragement. And if it helped me feel less like I was crawling out of my skin with missing him, that would be a nice bonus.

So I got on a plane to see him play. That was that. And now here I am.

Our eyes hold for only a second longer, before the game that brought us both here wrenches him away. He does a quick double take as he turns back to his team and Ren bends over at center ice for the face-off in the wake of Seattle's goal.

Afterward, he mouths, poised to pop his mouthguard back in. *Wait for me?*

I nod, smiling. Doesn't he already know?

I'd wait for as long as he asked.

———

Sebastian's a vision, shower-wet hair and quicksilver-bright eyes, grinning wide as he jogs toward me and tackles me into his arms. I hug him back hard as he squeezes me so tight I squeak, and when I pull away just enough to plant my usual platonic kiss on his cheek, he turns, as if to do the same, which isn't typical for him. We do it at the same time, and our mouths bump in an awkward, not-kiss kiss. Sebastian practically drops me, then grabs my hand as I steady myself.

"Sorry," he mutters. His hand squeezes mine.

"Me too." I smile nervously. It's so weird, not having seen him for nearly a month, when for months on end we've seen each other, even if only briefly, at least every ten days, two weeks at most . . .

Not that I was counting.

Sebastian steps closer, then pulls me back into a hug, resting his temple against mine. A slow, heavy exhale leaves him as I slip my arms around his waist. "Take two," he whispers.

I smile against his cheek. "Take two."

"Missed you."

"Missed you, too."

"Why are you here?"

I pull back again, squeezing his shoulders, which are bigger than they used to be.

Everything's bigger on Sebastian. He's put on muscle, gotten so healthy the past six months. His eyes are clear, his skin glowing, his body tall, straight, and strong. "For you."

He smiles, though a little furrow settles in his brow. "For . . . me? You just came to see me play?"

I nod.

"You flew up here solely for that."

I shrug. "Why not? I mean, I'm crashing at the A-frame tonight, and I'll grab breakfast with the local Bergmans tomorrow morning, but I'm here for you."

He swallows roughly. "I'm . . . really glad."

I smile, dropping my hands down to his, squeezing gently. "Me too."

Putting an arm around me, Sebastian guides me with him so we're clear of other players and staff. I don't miss the man who couldn't be anyone but his father, seeing as he looks just like Sebastian thirty-some years down the road, trailing in the distance, laughing loudly with Mr. Köhler and other big names in the Kings management. I follow Sebastian's lead, not acknowledging him, and walk with him down the hall.

"So." He tugs me close, sticking his nose in my hair, how he does sometimes when we hug, like he's breathing me in. At least, when I let my imagination run, that's what I hope he's doing. Smelling me, simply because he likes how I smell.

"So."

"This A-frame here," he says. "Based on what Ren tells me, it sounds pretty idyllic."

"It is." I turn and face him as he brings us to a stop. "I actually wanted to, uh ..." I clear my throat and try to stay calm. "I actually wanted to invite you to come back up here to the A-frame, right after your season ends."

His expression shifts a little, something curious, and if I'm not mistaken, a little heated. "Oh?"

"For my birthday," I explain. "It's my favorite time of year, up here, in the spring. It's beautiful. And Mom said she'd throw a party for me. Make all the Swedish foods. We'll play board games—Scrabble is my jam—go on hikes, just rest and recharge."

Sebastian's expression shifts again, and this time I can't read it. "So ... all your family. Everyone will be there?"

"Uh-huh." I smile. "Big family celebration."

It takes a beat, but he smiles, sweet and affectionate. "That sounds great. I'd love to. Your birthday's the twenty-first. That weekend?"

"Well, actually, Mom suggested we spend the week there leading up to that, starting with the previous weekend, through my birthday weekend. People can just come and go as it works for their schedules. It makes it most accessible that way, for everyone."

His smile deepens. "I'll be there."

"Gauthier!" someone yells. "You're needed."

Sebastian glances over his shoulder and sighs. "Sorry. I have to run, but I could try to meet later—"

"No, go. And then get some sleep. You've got an early flight tomorrow, I'm sure, for that Vancouver game." I hug him once more.

He doesn't seem convinced. "But you came all this way—"

"I'll just say hi to Ren, then get going. It's a bit of a drive to the A-frame from here, and I don't want to be on those roads too late."

"All right." Sebastian's expression turns concerned. "Be safe, okay? Text me when you get there?"

"I will."

"See you soon, then." He pulls me in for one more hug, speaking against my neck. "Family dinner? Not tomorrow, but next Sunday."

"Next Sunday."

He pulls back, smiling at me. "Then, the Sunday after that, you get to show me this A-frame of yours."

I bite my lip as he turns and jogs off. I watch him until he stops at the corner, waving one more time right before he disappears.

I wave back, a little scared but a little *more* thrilled about what I've just done.

I don't like to think too hard about it, but I'm not clueless—I know what happens at the A-frame. I know Willa and Rooney, in their own ways and time, went up there, clueless as to what was coming, and came back irrevocably tethered to my brothers, wildly in love. I know hasty Bergman exits have been made when Frankie and Gavin showed up there, years apart, for the hearts they loved, bearing their own hearts on their sleeves. I've put the timeline together and figured out exactly where Freya and Aiden were when Theo Bergman MacCormack began. I watched Willa and Ryder marry there, Axel and Rooney renew their vows there, my parents kiss and slow dance in the kitchen.

I know good things happen at the A-frame. Love things.

I'm ready for that possibility. I want to kick that door wide open and welcome Sebastian right into the heart of it.

I just hope he wants that, too.

THIRTY

Sebastian

Playlist: "Save Me," Jelly Roll

Stepping out of my rental car, I shut the door behind me and stare up at the beloved Bergman A-frame. I smile. It's everything I imagined, and somehow even better. The tall, sloping original structure, floor-to-ceiling glass windows. A solid, sturdy porch. Then a generous, newer-looking addition to the left. Slate and dark, wet wood. Moss and ferns. Trees form a canopy over it, casting cool shadows on me as I hike my bag up higher on my shoulder.

Ziggy opens the door, and my heart trips in my chest. She's wearing a pale blue sundress speckled with tiny orange flowers, and her hair's braided—copper, auburn, and fiery red woven down her shoulder. Smiling, she jogs down the steps. "You're here!"

I rush toward her and hug her hard, breathing her in, trying to calm my racing heart. I can do this. I can be brave. For her.

Pulling back, I cup her face and smile down at her. I want to kiss her so bad, I have to bite my cheek to stop myself. "Happy Birthday."

"Not yet," she says brightly, trying to take my bag off my shoulder. I clutch it. "I've got this."

"Let me. You already insisted on driving yourself here, like a weirdo. I told you I'd pick you up."

She did. And I was a chickenshit who needed every damn second between the moment I told her I'd come here and right now to find my courage, to talk to myself the way my therapist has taught me—affirmations, grounding reminders.

Progress, not perfection.

I'm enough as I am.

My past does not define my present or my future. I believe in myself, and she does, too.

That last one, that's the hard one. Not because I doubt Ziggy's belief in me—I don't. I just have to believe in *myself*, to believe that's enough. That I'm enough for her to believe in, exactly as I am.

Wrapping an arm around her shoulder, I smile down at her as we walk up to the house. "I didn't want you to pick me up when you're supposed to be relaxing."

"A drive can be relaxing," she says.

I lift my eyebrows. "That so?"

"I mean . . ." She smiles sheepishly. "It isn't necessarily for me—"

"That's what I thought—"

"—unless it's that fancy car of yours."

"Sorry to disappoint." I nod over my shoulder. "That was the best they had."

Ziggy's eyes light up as she registers the fancy sports car rental I splurged on, knowing it's exactly the kind of ride she'd enjoy. "Oh, we're *definitely* taking a drive in that."

"Hell, yes, we are."

Something suddenly strikes me as I glance past my rental, around the empty clearing. There are no other cars. "Where is everyone?"

"Not here yet." She shrugs. "Some of them should be, others weren't planning on being here until tonight. Mom and Dad apparently slept in and got a late start. They left days ago, doing this whole romantic drive up the coast, stopping at wineries along the way and being cute."

I smile. "They are pretty damn cute."

"It's almost unbearable," she agrees. "Willa and Ryder live pretty close by, said they'd be here, but now, apparently, their ancient Subaru is giving them trouble, so they're getting that sorted out. Freya, Aiden, and the kids fly out tomorrow." She peers up, going through the list.

"Oh, Ax and Rooney live just a ways over there." She points down a narrow path close by the house that leads to a meadow, wildflowers swaying in the late morning breeze. "They'll show up when they show up. Sometimes Rooney naps midday, so I'd expect them for dinner. Ren and Frankie have Frankie's doctor appointment, then they're flying up tonight.

"And . . . Viggo, Oliver, and Gavin are waiting for their flight to board as we speak, so they said." She snorts. "Just picturing the three of them in a row together makes me smile. Ollie will have double reinforcements for his flight anxiety."

Right as we make it to the top steps of the porch, her phone starts ringing in her pocket.

Frowning, she pulls it out. "Sorry. I just want to be sure to answer in case—"

"Go ahead," I tell her, setting down my bag, then walking across the porch, leaning on the railing as I look around. The trees are bursting with lush green leaves the same color as Ziggy's eyes, many of them boasting soft, fluttering blossoms whose lush peach pink rivals her best blush.

I breathe in and smile. It smells like her here. Like clean water and open air and new beginnings.

"Viggo, seriously?" Ziggy snaps. "Why do I need to go looking for that *right now*?"

I glance over my shoulder, frowning in concern. *Everything okay?* I mouth.

She rolls her eyes, then mouths, *Just Viggo being Viggo.*

I snort, then turn back, drinking in the view—cool blue water stretched along the other end of the property, a wide, winding trail that looks well loved and worn, a bowing ancient tree whose cloud-white blossoms drift across the path.

Ziggy growls in frustration, then stomps inside, slamming the door behind her. I glance toward the door, half grimace, half amused smile. I feel bad that she's annoyed, but Ziggy fired up is always going to turn my crank. I love her feisty side.

Just as I'm turning back, something clocks me right in the side of the head. I look down. A soccer ball.

"What the *fuck*?" I walk to that end of the porch. This time I catch the next ball that comes straight for my face with a snap between my hands. I set the ball at my side and glare toward the direction it came.

This makes no sense.

Curious, annoyed, I hop easily over the porch railing and drop to the ground, following the path that I think the balls took. That's when another one comes straight for my face. I dodge it. Barely.

"Viggo!" I hear a voice hiss. "Stop aiming for his goddamn head!"

"You're not the boss of me," Viggo hisses back.

"Someone should be," says a voice I vaguely recognize. Enough of this bullshit. I stop walking and yell, "Hey!"

A hand claps over my mouth. It's surprisingly strong. I shove it off and spin around. Ryder.

He lifts a finger to his mouth.

I shake my head, so damn confused.

"Fashionable Sebastian." Viggo reveals himself from the crest on the path, pointing over his shoulder. "We'd like a word."

"Fuck off."

He sighs. "I had a feeling you'd say that. Which leaves me no choice but to—"

"Okay." Axel, the oldest and tallest brother, with his serious expression, who looks a little like Viggo but with Ziggy's sharp green eyes, steps out from behind a tree. "Enough of the *Godfather* shit. Just tell the poor man what you want."

"You've turned into such a softie," Viggo says to him, clearly exasperated.

"Jesus Christ, Viggo." Oliver marches up to me. "Would you kindly join us in the storage shed?"

Oliver points over his shoulder to a structure a little farther down the hill. Sighing, I drop the soccer ball to my feet. "Fine."

"Welcome," Viggo says, "to your first, and possibly only, Bergman Brothers Summit, Seb."

Oliver, Ryder, and Axel sit, slumped on boxes and upturned buckets, looking as displeased with this development as I am. It makes me feel marginally better.

"I'd say 'happy to be here,' but I've turned over a new leaf, and I don't blow smoke up people's asses anymore. So I'll be honest: I'm actually not one bit pleased I'm sitting in a musty shed with you fools rather than the woman I lo—"

I stop myself, clenching my jaw. They don't get to hear that word from me before Ziggy does.

Oliver's eyes widen. He sits up and smacks Viggo in the chest. "Told you! I *told* you! Now *you* cough it up, honey bunch."

Viggo scowls at his brother. "I didn't bet you money on this."

"I know!" Oliver says. "I mean your *dignity*. Cough up your dignity, because this is ridiculous. He's here because he loves her, because he's been spending the past half year trying to be a person he feels is worthy of Ziggy, which, ya know, long time and all for poor Zigs, who really does not like to wait, but still, kudos to him for the commitment—do it once and do it well, am I right?" he says to me, before turning back to Viggo. "After all that, he's *finally* here, and what do you do? You knock him in the head with a soccer ball and lure him into this damn shed to tell him something he already knows. Isn't that right, Seb?"

I swallow roughly, scared that I'm so transparent. Relieved that I'm so transparent. That someone who loves Ziggy sees how I want to love her, too.

"Yeah," I say quietly, earnestly. "That's right."

Oliver drops back against the shed's wall on a *hmph*, folding his arms across his chest as he glares at Viggo.

Viggo gapes at his remaining brothers, as if for moral support. "C'mon, guys. Help me out."

Axel shakes his head. "Nope. I was against this. There are great uses for Bergman Brothers Summits. This is not one of them." He stands, dusting off his thighs. "I'm going back home to my wife and the *quiet*. You are too goddamn loud."

With that, Axel slaps open the shed door and strolls out.

Ryder sits forward next, elbows on his knees, looking at me. "I'm uh . . . sorry for the *Godfather* move back there, but I just wanted the chance to say, before you walked in there—every time I talk to Ziggy, she talks about you. With so much love. She loves you."

My heart jumps against my ribs.

"I don't know what kind of love it is," he adds, shrugging, lifting a hand to his hearing aid curled around his ear and seeming to make some sort of adjustment. "But I know all kinds of love matter and are beautiful. Whatever it is that you two share, I just want to know you'll be good to her, the way I know she'll be good to you."

Now *that* I can respect. I nod. "I can promise that."

Ryder smiles, a bright grin behind his dark blond beard. "Excellent. Then I'll be going."

"Wha—" Viggo gapes at him.

Oliver pushes off the wall and stands, too. "I've said my piece. I'm out."

The shed door swings shut, listing a little on its hinges as the wind moves it. Which leaves me and Viggo. Just the two of us.

Sitting back against the wall, I cross my ankles, arms folded across my chest. "So here we are. I feel like we've been working our way toward this for a while."

"No you don't." Viggo stands and starts pacing. "You don't get to lead this meeting."

I glance around, eyebrows raised. "You see anybody else here? I'm just talking."

Viggo knocks back his ball cap and tugs at his hair, spinning and facing me as he slaps it on again. His eyes are tight, his face hard. "From one self-admittedly glib person to another, I really don't appreciate how cavalier you're being."

I sit up slowly, perking up to that. He's not wrong—at least, he's not wrong about who I used to be—brushing off what mattered to people, to myself, being flippant and sarcastic, hiding myself from earnest sentiment and genuine feeling. "Okay."

Viggo seems to deflate a little at that. He turns and half-heartedly kicks over a bucket. "I'm probably not the brother you thought you'd be left to talk with. But Ren's not here, so I have to do this—"

"Ren trusts me. I'm not worried about what he'll think of this."

I have no doubt that if Ziggy wants what I'm about to ask her for, and we tell Ren, he'll be nothing but happy for us, that he'll wrap us in that big wingspan hug and crush us to him.

Viggo drops onto a box, which lets out a little puff of dust as he lands. "You aren't?"

"I'm not." I lean forward, elbows on my knees. "But I am worried about you."

Viggo sniffs, glancing off. His jaw's hard; I can see that, even beneath the beard. "She's my baby sister."

I smile, oddly moved. "I know."

"She's . . . she's the best person, and if you hurt her, I swear to God . . ." He wipes his nose, then glares at me. "I worry about her, okay? She had a really tough time when she was younger."

"I know."

Ziggy told me around Christmastime, one night after family dinner at her parents', the fire burning, letting out soft hisses and pops, what she'd started saying months ago that first night we hung out—how hard middle and high school were, how much her mental health suffered, until she got her diagnosis, and even for a little while afterward. How Ren picked her up and took her to Betty's Diner, bought her as many milkshakes and fries as she wanted and just listened to her as she told him everything she was too scared and anxious to tell anyone else. How Frankie came into her life right around then, another autistic woman with a job she loved and clothes that felt good and a wicked sense of humor; someone who showed her it might be hard then, but it would get easier, that she'd find a way forward and learn to be happy in the life she was figuring out.

I loved Frankie and Ren before that already, but after that conversation, I loved them infinitely more.

Viggo stares at me with those intense, pale Bergman eyes. "Then you get why I'm protective of her. Why I worry about her. Why I try to protect her from everything I possibly can so it can never hurt her like it hurt her then." He exhales heavily. "I was right fucking there in school with her, and I didn't see it. I didn't see how they bullied her. They did it so damn quietly, so stealthily, or I swear to God, I would have done unspeakable things."

"You feel guilty."

"Really fucking guilty!" he yells. "And she knows that. I've apologized for failing her. I've told her how sorry I am that she was right under my nose, hurting so badly, and I missed it—" His voice breaks. He buries his face in his hands. "I missed it."

I stand, a lump in my throat, and plop down beside him. I set a hand hard on his shoulder. "She forgave you."

He nods.

"And told you there was nothing to forgive," I add.

"Which is bullshit," he mutters.

"Sure feels like it. It's hard to be given grace when you don't think you deserve it."

Viggo drops his hands, then peers over at me, his eyes wet. He's quiet, his gaze searching mine. So I take this rare instance of him actually shutting his yap, and tell him, "You and I are pretty much opposites."

He laughs emptily, glancing away. "How so?"

"For the longest time, I refused to carry anyone with me—on my shoulders, in my thoughts, in my heart." I shrug. "It made me feel in control. Safe. Which . . . I was neither of those things, of course. But I was coping as best I could."

I squeeze his shoulder. "Whereas you, Viggo . . . I'm pretty sure you carry *everyone* on your shoulders, in your thoughts, in your heart."

Viggo ducks his head and exhales heavily, tugging off his ball cap and chucking it to the shed floor with a *thwack*. "Goddammit."

"Because it makes your chaotic life feel a little more in control, and—here is where you are an infinitely better human than me— it allows you to feel like you're keeping the people you love safe. Because you have a devastatingly big heart, and I imagine it's pretty damn scary to possess that much emotional real estate."

His shoulders shake. "What the hell is happening?"

"I think maybe you're getting a taste of your own medicine?" I let go of his shoulder, then set my elbows on my knees, leaning close to him. "Ziggy talks a lot about you. Often, she's exasperated, but there's a through line in what she says, something I've picked up on."

"And that would be?" He rakes his hands through his hair and tugs.

"That you love your family and your friends and your books and everything you put your heart into so fucking much. Which I can only imagine is really beautiful sometimes, and really brutal other times."

Slowly he glances my way and sighs heavily. "Yeah."

I stare at him. "Maybe it's just time to . . . find different ways to take care of that big heart, to protect it. Ways that don't exhaust you and twist you up so badly, you don't even recognize yourself. Ways that allow you to live *your* life, not worry about everyone else's."

"Ah," Viggo says, "but then I'd actually have to figure out my own life."

I nod. "Fair. It's daunting to do that."

"Indeed."

"But . . ." I stand, shoving my hands in my pockets as I turn and face him. "As someone who's spent the past six months trying to do just that, I can say that it gets a little easier. And it's definitely worth it."

Viggo peers up at me, his eyes searching mine. Then he stands and scoops up his ball cap, dusting it off before he slaps it onto his head again. "Well." He rolls his shoulders back, mirroring me as he slides his hands into his pockets. "I guess all I have to say is . . . thank you."

I frown at him. "Thank you?"

He nods. "For turning the tables on me. For doing a shit ton of work to be a person worthy of my sister, though, let's be honest, no one's worthy of her."

"Fact."

He grins, wiping his nose, peering off. "Take good care of her, okay? Just be good to her." I smile. "I will, if she lets me. And if I fuck up, you can beat my ass."

"Splendid." He offers me his hand. I take it and tug him my way.

Viggo stumbles into me as if I've surprised him but accepts my hug. In fact, I think he might just hug me back. After a few seconds, he pulls away, adjusting his hat again. "Now, if you'll excuse me, I'm just going to go—"

"VIGGO!" Ziggy shrieks, so loud and shrill, I wince.

Viggo's eyes widen. "I'm just going to go run for my life."

The shed door whips open, and Ziggy stands, looking like a glorious, vengeful Valkyrie, chest heaving, her braid shredded to wild red ribbons framing her face. "What the *fuck* are you doing?" she yells.

The rest of the brothers who were here earlier suddenly appear behind her—Ryder, Axel, and Oliver, all looking pretty roughed up.

"We tried to hold her back," Oliver explains between pants. "But, uh, Ziggy, one. Us—" He points to his brothers. "Zero."

Ziggy rushes toward Viggo, hellfire in her eyes.

"Hey, you." I hug her, bringing her to a stop.

"I'm really mad right now, Sebastian," she mutters against my shoulder, her body stiff in my arms.

I rub her back in gentle circles. "I know. But we had a good talk."

"He put me in my place," Viggo offers. "Handily."

Ziggy pulls out of my grip and glares at Viggo. "I'm still gonna tickle you till you pee later."

He sighs bleakly. "I'm not gonna lie and say I look forward to it, but I accept my fate."

She spins around and looks at her brothers, who clearly tried to slow her down. "Don't do that again. Don't come between me and the person I—" She closes her mouth, her cheeks turning pink. "You know what I mean."

They nod solemnly.

She stomps her foot, her face flushed. "I'm so darn sick of this. No more babying me. Love me, but please see me as I am. A grown woman who can make her choices. And I. Choose. Him. Full stop. Okay?"

They all smile. She blinks, stunned. "That . . . was not the response I was expecting. What is going on?"

"Ziggy." I clasp her hand, squeezing. Gently, I thread our fingers together. "What do you say we go for a walk?"

THIRTY-ONE

Ziggy

Playlist: "Snow on the Beach," Brennan Lynch

Sebastian tugs me gently with him. I glance over my shoulder at my brothers one last time, puzzled as they smile then turn and start walking in the direction of Axel's house.

Spinning back around, I follow Sebastian, my hand tight in his, our fingers tangled together. My gaze drifts over him, and my stomach flip-flops. He's wearing the worn jeans from the night he came to my place and we ate cake on his deck, my favorite of his soft T-shirts, the silvery-sage one that I've wanted to steal since the first time I saw him wear it, except that then it would rob me of the pleasure of seeing it on him.

Bearing to the left, he leads me onto the main hiking path, straight toward the tree.

My tree.

Whose blossoms drift down in the air—small, white, snowdrift petals landing in a creamy carpet at our feet. I bite my lip, tugging against him, trying to stop him.

Suddenly, I'm very, very frightened.

I don't feel like big, brave Ziggy 2.0 anymore.

What if he isn't turning and looking at me under my tree for the reason I want him to? What if, in this time he's needed, he's realized more between us isn't what he feels capable of, isn't what he wants?

Trust him, Ziggy. Believe in him. Like you always have.

Sebastian faces me, brow furrowed, head tipped as he walks closer, sliding his hand up my arm until his grip wraps around my elbow. "C'mere, Sigrid."

I bite my lip harder, trying to breathe steadily. "I'm scared."

"I know." He smiles softly, drifting his other hand across my back as he peers at me, his gaze holding mine. "I'm pretty scared, too."

"You—" My voice catches. I suck in a deep breath, then breathe out. "You are?"

He nods. "I've been 'pretty scared' since the day I saw you."

"Since the day you *saw* me?"

"Oh yeah. First time Ren had me over, you were there, at his place—well, you were out on the beach right beyond the house—throwing the ball with that demon dog—"

"My puppy niece is not a demon dog. You watch your mouth."

He grins. "You were throwing *Pazza* the ball. The wind was whipping your hair around. And the way you smiled as you crouched to the sand with her, then laughed when she knocked you over, it just . . ." He blows out a breath, patting his hand over his heart. "Hit me. Right here. So, naturally, from that point, I avoided you at all costs."

I stare at him. "You . . . did that on purpose?"

He steps closer, his knuckles brushing my cheek. "Very on purpose. And I held off pretty well for a couple years, avoiding you. But to no avail. Little did I know what an acrimonious relationship you and underwear have or how damn good you are at breaking and entering. Before I knew it, you'd infested my dreams so badly, I went on a wild nighttime drive just to escape you and crashed my damn car. Then, when I was sulking about the miserable life I'd made for myself, you scaled my house, pushed your way into my life, and, Jesus, Ziggy, it was the best damn thing that's ever happened to me—every moment I've known you.

"That month, when all we did was spend time together. The past six months that have taught me what it is to make a promise and keep it, to want and yet deny myself, to ache and still wait, so I could stand here in good faith and tell you, I'm still fucking afraid that I'm not enough for you, that I *never* will be, but I've got this ruthless shrink who gives me these disturbingly healthy, hopeful reassurances, like that's my past talking, not the present I share with you, or the future that I want to.

"I've learned, working on myself, to believe what the shrink says, that I could either let my fear of inadequacy keep me frozen, where I've been, where I've kept us, or I could *live* with you in all my imperfection, trusting you with that fear. Once I wrapped my head around that, it was the easiest decision I've ever made because only one of those options lets me love you the way I want to, and all I want to do is love you. So . . . I'm here to tell you that all those fears I've already shared with you before, that I'm sharing with you now, they're here, but they don't get to come between us anymore. I'll face those fears every day so I can love you, so I can work to be worthy of your love.

"Because I *do* love you, Ziggy, more than I ever believed I could love anyone or anything. Because if only you loved me for the rest of my existence, that would be more than enough—beyond my wildest dreams and hopes. I'm not fixed. I'm not perfect. But I do love you with all of my heart, Ziggy, with every broken part of it that I'm piecing back together. I hope . . . if you don't now, one day, you can love me the way I love you, but if you don't, if you can't—"

"Sebastian." Tears stream down my face. Slowly, I cup his face, my thumbs stroking right down those lines where no dimples show themselves, but they will, if I have anything to say about it.

"I love you. I've loved you so many different ways since you said yes to my harebrained scheme and showed me in so many tiny, beautiful ways that you saw the brave person inside me that I was just learning to see and love and listen to, since you bravely opened up and let me in and took my hand in yours. I loved you, and I won't stop loving you. I want to love you as my friend, as my partner, as someone I'll discover life's possibilities with—within ourselves and out in this wild, wide world.

"I know I'm goofy and kinda weepy and extremely attached to fictional characters, and I haven't always thought there'd be someone who could want and cherish those oddball, sensitive corners of myself, but you do. You've shown me that, because that's how you love—in *showing*—and if I get to spend however long I have experiencing that love, showing you my love, too, I'll be the luckiest woman there is."

Sebastian stares at me, blinking away wetness in his eyes, before that smile I've been waiting for shows itself—bright, wide smile; long, deep dimples. I trace my thumbs down his cheeks. "I love you, my sweet friend. My Sebastian."

He presses his forehead to mine and sucks in a breath, his hands drifting up my back as he tucks me close. The wind kicks up, swirling my hair around us, making him laugh. Snowy blossoms rain down on us, making me laugh, too.

Under that tree, my tree, my wishing, hoping, too-lovely-for-my-heart tree, I set my hand over his heart—the one I never in a million years could have dreamed for myself.

His mouth brushes mine, tender, slow. I breathe him in as he pulls me close, as I wrap my arms around his neck, swaying us side to side.

"So." Sebastian smiles into our kiss. I smile back. "So."

"What do you say you show me that A-frame of yours after all?"

My family is a bunch of high-handed meddlers. But this time, I'm not mad about it. Because this time, it means I have Sebastian and the A-frame, all to myself. For the rest of the day and tonight, at least. That's what I need. Just us, here. Finally.

Sebastian sits across from me in front of the fireplace, which I lit because he asked me to, I think mostly so he could look at my butt as I worked, while he chows down on a sandwich. His *second* one. Thick, soft, gluten-free bread that actually tastes good, crunchy Bibb lettuce, Dijon, mayo, and chicken salad made with spring's first herbs that Rooney has coaxed to life over the years along the planters on the back deck.

I sigh and push away my almost empty plate, too full for another bite. Sebastian glances at my plate, chews, then swallows. "You gonna finish that?"

I smile, nudging the plate his way. "Go right ahead, *älskade*."

He pauses, sandwich halfway to his mouth, then lowers it. "What's that mean? Ren calls Frankie that."

A hot blush hits my cheeks. I didn't mean to say it; I've just been thinking it for months, every time I look at him. It's a wonder I hadn't blabbed it already.

I nudge his hip with my toe and smile, a little embarrassed, a lot in love. "It means 'beloved.'"

He looks at me in that way he has, that I've caught sometimes but told myself I was reading too much into, in my overactive-imaginative, romance-reader way—those thick, dark-lashed gray eyes, hot and hungry. Sebastian sets the plate down with a clatter. "Not hungry anymore."

"You sure? You were really hungry."

"I was." He takes my arm and tugs me toward him. "I am."

I crawl over his lap and settle down, setting my hands on his shoulders. He peers up at me, giving me that unruly dark hair to run my fingers through. "Ziggy."

"Hmm?" Light kisses his Adam's apple as it bobs in his throat. I bend and kiss it, too.

He swallows again, his hands wrapping around my waist, down over my backside. "I'm nervous."

I pull back, then tip my head. "About what, Sebastian?"

"Making love. I've never done it. I've had a shit ton of sex. None of it sober. Never with someone I loved. I'm . . . kinda freaking out. But the only thing that's not stopping me is that I've been dealing with an eight-month case of blue balls that might just make me lose my mind if I don't do something about it." He grins when I laugh, bright teeth, crinkled eyes, so pleased that he's pleased me. "And . . . ya know, the whole wanting-to-make-love-to-you part. That's a pretty big incentive to push past my fear, too."

I brush back those dark waves, trace my finger along the scruff of his jaw, over his chin dimple. "Boop."

He narrows his eyes at me.

"You and I," I whisper, before I kiss his jaw, his cheekbone, the slash of a scar across his left eyebrow, "will figure it out *together*. I'm nervous. You're nervous. We'll be nervous together. We'll touch and try and hopefully laugh a little bit, then we'll be us, together, however that feels right. That will be beautiful. That will be . . . more than enough."

His hands drift up my back. His hips shift beneath me. "I think we should do some figuring out together, then."

I laugh softly, then lean in for one more slow, savoring kiss. "I think so, too."

Sebastian leans in close, kissing me harder, his hands tight on my hips. I press my thighs into his waist, moving myself closer, against him. He sighs when I do that, a smile lifting his mouth. "You're gonna rock my world, aren't you?" he mutters.

"That's the plan."

"Excellent."

I squeak as he lifts us both to standing, walking me over to the couch, across the warm wood floors, which sunlight paints honey gold and glowing. Gently, he eases me down, then crawls over me, pressing his body into mine. "I liked what we did at the bookstore," he says quietly.

I smile up at him. "Me too."

"Then again, I'm going to like it every way with you."

"Why's that?"

"Because it's you, silly." He kisses my neck, then breathes in. "God, you smell so good, Ziggy. I need a little bottle of your scent so I can take it with me when I'm on the road."

I smile, kissing his hair, running my hands down the hard, flexing muscles of his back. "It's just soap and my skin."

"Damn. Well, guess I'll have to take you with me everywhere I go, then. Nothing to be done about it."

He crawls back up my body and kisses me, deep and hungry, his hips moving into mine.

"Sebastian."

"Hmm?"

"I want to be naked. I want you to be naked, too."

He pulls away so fast, I laugh, tearing off his shirt, revealing this body that I've seen heal and strengthen, whose every mysterious marking I'm going to learn with time and the tip of my finger traced across his skin.

I reach for his jeans' button and pop it open, then tug down the zipper. Sebastian breathes roughly as I do, as I sit up and tug them down with his briefs. He stands just long enough for me to drag them all the way down to his ankles, then steps out of them. He pulls me up to standing and reaches for my dress, then lifts it over my head. "No underwear," he rasps. "Or bra."

"The devil's fabric," I mutter as he sinks to his knees.

Gently, he kisses up my thighs. "I've wanted to do this for a long time, Ziggy."

I slip my hands into his hair, staring down at him as he peers up at me. "I've wanted you to do it, too."

Slowly, he slips his fingers between my legs. A sigh gusts out of him before he leans in. "Can I?"

I nod. "Yes."

His mouth is soft, searching, his fingers teasing me, curling inside. I arch up, burying my hands in his hair as he licks me, fast and expertly, learning to back off when I pull away, when it's too much, how to swirl and flick while his fingers work inside me.

"Sebastian," I gasp.

He groans, bringing one hand up my stomach, weighing my breast in his hand. His thumb flicks my nipple and I cry out.

"Don't stop. Don't stop," I beg.

He buries his face against me, taking his time, working his fingers harder, until heat finally hits me, a searing, pulsing flash flood that sweeps through me, makes me bow back and yell his name.

I collapse very clumsily onto the couch and Sebastian leans over me, eyes hazy, pupils blown wide. "Let's do that again," he mutters, kissing my stomach, then lower.

"Don't even think about it!" I laugh. "Get up here."

He crawls my way and kisses me, laughing into my mouth as I tug him closer and growl playfully, when he makes a motion like he's going to crawl away again.

Easing back onto the sofa, which is deep and cozy, a faded, worn cotton soft against our skin, he lies beside me, stretched out. His eyes dance down my body, his hands trailing gently in their wake, wonder painting his face. "Ziggy, how are you this beautiful?"

I blush, hot and swift, and smile, my fingertips gliding down his broad chest, the butterfly over his heart, the flowers and constellations stitched across his skin. "I was thinking the same thing about you."

"All these freckles," he says quietly, his fingertip tracing them, connecting the dots over my shoulders, down my chest, to the edge of my breasts, where they fade. I arch into him as his knuckle grazes my nipple.

I rest my hand on his shoulder, gliding down it, my fingertips taking their own journey, over planets and scattered words, open books and ancient symbols, tortured creatures and angels' wings, birds taking flight and broken vessels, spilling out on their sides. "I want to learn about them."

"I'll tell you," he says. "Just . . . not right now, if that's okay?"

I nod as I hold his eyes. "Not now."

"I want to touch you again, Ziggy."

I smile. "I want that, too."

Softly, Sebastian, drifts his hand down over one breast, then the other, tenderly lifting each, teasing my nipples. I sigh into his kiss, rubbing my thighs together. Gently, he drags his knuckles down my stomach, then splays his hand over my hip, parting my thighs. His fingers delve into my curls, over my clit, which pulses steadily. He strokes as he watches me, light and tender, then starts to swirl in soft, slow circles, lower, lower, just like he learned with his tongue. "Like this?" he asks.

I nod. "Yeah. Like that." A gasp tears out of me, then another, fast, aching breaths.

"Your sounds," he whispers. His eyes scrunch shut, his forehead pressed to mine. "You even sound beautiful."

I pant as he dips his fingers inside me, where I'm already so wet, so exquisitely close to release, then drags them back up, circling my clit gently. I whimper and arch my hips, throwing back my head as he curls one finger inside and strokes into me, another joining it, rubbing my G-spot. He sets his thumb over my clit and circles it steadily.

I stare up at him, smiling, wanting, finally free to give in.

Pleasure rolls through me, deep inside where he strokes, across my clit, where he circles it, over my mouth as it moves with his, through the tips of my breasts as they brush against his hard chest.

With the next stroke, the chasing roll of my hips, the building wave of release crests and slams into me. I arch into him on a hoarse gasp, shaking as he keeps going, as he whispers against my lips, kisses me.

"Inside me," I beg. "I want you—if you want—"

"I want," he mutters. "Condoms?"

"Tested and negative. On the pill."

"Tested and negative, too," he says, laughing as I begin scrambling beneath him, urging him over me. "You're really eager, aren't you?"

"Christ, Sebastian, aren't you?"

"No." He waves a hand playfully as his throbbing, hard cock slaps into my thigh. "Not at all."

I laugh and draw him close. I lift my finger to his mouth. He looks at me and opens his lips. I set my finger inside, and he sucks, licking it. "Such a good boy."

His cock twitches hard against me. "Fuck," he groans as I pull my finger away, wet and dripping, then rub it over my entrance, adding wetness I really don't need, but I want to be sure, so it's smooth and easy.

Staring down at his beautiful length, thick and hard, then up at him, finding those familiar, lovely eyes, I guide him inside me. I sigh as he rocks into me, on slow, shallow thrusts that become a little deeper each time, his eyes searching mine. "God, Ziggy." He grits his teeth. "God, you feel so good."

A moan leaves me when he strokes into a spot that's so exquisitely sensitive, it makes my toes curl. Gently, he turns me toward him so I'm nestled on my side against the sofa, my leg over his hip. "This okay?" he asks.

I nod. "Very okay."

Sebastian sighs as he eases back into me, his eyes searching mine. "You feel like a fucking dream."

I smile shakily, wrapping my arm around him, drawing him close. "So do you."

Tracing my hand down his hip, to his backside, I remember what I saw on that nightstand the night of the roller rink fundraiser. I know what it's for. I can't touch him there well right now, given how we're positioned, but I can tease him. If he wants me to.

He nods as I come close. "I like it," he says.

I bring two fingers to his mouth this time, and he sucks, holding my eyes as he rolls his hips into me. I reach around him, thoroughly enjoying the gift of long limbs as we tangle together and move, smiling and kissing, sighing, broken by laughs and gasps of pleasure. I rub him, right behind where he's hard and drawn up tight, then farther back, his legs shaking as he moves with me.

"Ziggy," he breathes. "I'm not gonna last."

I kiss him. "I don't want you to."

"Rude," he whispers.

I snort a laugh, but then my laugh becomes a groan as he grips my hip and rocks deeper into me, hard and quick.

"Come with me," he begs. "Please, Ziggy. I need you."

My eyes start to drift shut, but I force them open to look at him as he moves faster, his eyes locked on mine. "Ziggy."

"Sebastian." I breathe his name as his hips falter, as he presses me against the sofa and kisses me frantically. His mouth falls open into our kiss as he spills into me, as he presses himself deep inside me again, then again. On another faltering, fading stroke, I finally go over with him, too, loud and aching, curled into him as it racks me.

He moves into me still, slower, gentling. Panting, I pull him close and slide onto my back beneath him. Sebastian gives me his weight, heavy and hot, and drops his face into my neck, his warm breath fanning across my skin.

His chest heaves. Mine does, too. He clumsily props himself up on one elbow and brings his fingers to my tangled hair, smoothing it back from my face. Then, sweetly, he bends his head and kisses me. "You . . . that . . . so very good." He sighs and groans as he shuts his eyes. "What are words? I used to have them."

"I have a few." I smile and nuzzle his nose. "I love you."

"I've got those, too," he says quietly as he opens his eyes again and looks at me, right to the heart of me, fingers gliding through my hair. "I love you, Sigrid. So much."

"Not 'too much'?"

He grins and nuzzles my nose, too. "No such thing."

THIRTY-TWO

Sebastian

Playlist: "Share Your Address," Ben Platt

"Sebastian," Ziggy groans, her face smooshed into a couch pillow. She reaches for another pillow we stole from the couch and whacks me with it. "Down, boy."

I kiss my way across her back, freckle after freckle, smiling against her skin. "Sigrid. I let you sleep three hours."

She groans again, turning over, then stretching. Her frown up at me is adorable. I kiss the pillow wrinkle in her cheek and a freckle on her nose that I missed on my last pass.

"You're cute when you're pissed."

"You won't say that when you're dead," she mutters, rolling onto her side. I kiss her shoulder, her waist, her ass.

Her beautiful, round ass. I squeeze and bite it gently.

Ziggy yelps, then glances over her shoulder, eyes wide. A heated smile lifts her face. "What are you doing?"

"Savoring you. I have a lot of time to make up for, Sigrid. You have to understand."

Her smile deepens as she flops onto her back and opens her arms. I crawl over her and kiss her, slow and deep. My cock rubs against her, and I groan, breathing out slowly. "I can let you sleep more if you really want."

She lifts her eyebrows. "He says, *after* he wakes me up."

"Progress, not perfection, Sigrid. I'm a man on a journey of growth. Have patience with me."

She laughs, shaking her head. "You're lucky I love you."

"Yeah, I am."

Her laugh fades but her smile doesn't. I stare down at her, beautiful fiery hair bright as the flames beside us, their light dancing across her skin, the only light left in this day as night wraps around us.

Ziggy stretches out on the blankets and pillows we tossed in front of the fire, then brings her hands to my face. Slowly, she scrapes her fingers through my hair. And then she sits up, legs tangled with mine, and kisses me. Her eyes search mine, her smile deepening.

And then she shoves me onto my back.

I stare up at her as she swings one leg over my torso, then settles down, straddling me right over my aching cock. Air rushes out of me and my hips shift reflexively beneath her.

"Sebastian," she says sternly, arching an eyebrow. "Be a good boy."

I grin and pointedly shift my hips beneath her.

"Naughty," she mutters, leaning over me and pinning my wrists above my head on the floor. It puts her breasts right at my face. I kiss them, one soft, loving suck at each of her nipples. She bites her lip and rubs herself against my length. I chase the friction, the dizzying pleasure of it, moving my hips so my cock wedges in tight against her. She gasps against our kiss.

"Am I in trouble now?"

"Ooh, yes." She clutches my jaw, kissing me hard and deep, a tiny tug of my lip between her teeth that makes air rush out of me.

Ziggy's hand trails down my throat, feeling the sound as it rumbles beneath her touch.

Gently, she squeezes, making me throw my head back. I grip her hips. "Please, Ziggy."

She squeezes harder, bringing me dangerously close to going off with just a few rubs over me, which, given how a few rounds earlier went, isn't unprecedented, and I'm not ashamed about. My girlfriend's very good at whatever she sets her mind to, and she's certainly set her mind to this.

Ziggy lifts up her hips, grips my cock hard at the base, making me pant roughly as she eases me inside, where she's hot and wet and so damn tight, it makes my molars clack together. "Fuck me," I groan.

"Language." She swats my ass, then sinks all the way down, swift and efficient. It's a near-death experience.

"*Oh*, fucking hell. Jesus Christ, Ziggy."

"Naughty, naughty." She smiles against our kiss, then kisses her way across my jaw as she rolls her hips, fast and deep, so damn well that after only a few minutes, my knees draw up and I grip her hips, desperate with the need to fuck up into her.

"Nuh-uh." She catches my hands and sets them over my head again, leaning over me.

"Ziggy," I groan, arching my hips. "I gotta come."

"Says who?"

"Says *me*."

She grins. "Not yet, Sebastian."

I moan as she slides her hand down my throat again and presses the way I showed her I like. "Ziggy, I can't—"

She stops, holding her hips still.

I pant, my hips jumping as she leans and softly bites her way across my chest tattoos, over my nipples.

"I said not yet, Sebastian."

A cracked groan leaves me as I pulse inside her, so close to coming, so desperate for it. I love how good she is at making me wait, and I'm also about to goddamn lose it. "I'm gonna get you back so bad after this."

She grins against my skin, then gently rolls her hips, a testing tease that sets me off.

I gasp, scrambling against the floor, pushing against her hand that still holds my wrist. She lets go and is entirely braced for what comes. Flipping her onto her back, I sink into her, hard, fast, frantic punches of my hips.

Ziggy slaps her hands onto my ass, pulling me tight into her before she rakes her fingers up my back into my hair and tugs sharply. Her body clenches around mine, rhythmic, tight squeezes as she throws her head back. I bury my face in her neck and shout her name as I rut into her and come, so long, I lose my vision for a few seconds, dark, sparkly stars that fade as I blink dazedly, peering down at her.

Ziggy's chest heaves, her hair wild and tangled across the blankets as she shakes her head, stunned. "That . . ." she says. "Was . . . Words. I've got them. Just need a minute."

"And she says she's the Scrabble champion." I'm poked in the side. I grab her hand and pin it back, then settle my weight over her, kissing her sweet and slow. "Tomorrow, you're getting your ass whooped at Scrabble, Sigrid."

She rolls her eyes. "Dream on, Sebastian. Dream on. And besides, it's *today*." She points, floppy armed, to the clock over the oven. Her family will be here by ten sharp. Ziggy warned me if Elin Bergman says she'll be somewhere at that time, she is there at that time, so there will be no cushion.

I groan, dropping my head to her neck again. "Okay. Maybe we should finally sleep a little bit."

"Ya think?"

I yawn loudly, then curl myself around her, burying my face in her neck. I think I'll sleep like this. Ziggy is supremely cozy. "Set an alarm?" I ask through another yawn.

Ziggy's fingers comb through my hair. "I would, except I've got two hundred pounds of big, sweaty, sexed-up Sebastian draped over me."

I smile. "That's me."

She snorts. "It'll be fine. I never sleep late. We'll wake up in plenty of time."

―――――

We do *not* wake up in plenty of time. At all.

The sound of feet lumbering up to the porch, voices echoing as a key slides into a lock, wrenches us awake. Ziggy's eyes snap open at the same time as mine. For a moment, we share a mutual look of sheer, unadulterated panic. But even as we haul our bare asses up the stairs, sprinting for cover, I'm the happiest I've ever been.

There's no one I'd rather run headlong with into the next wild, uncertain moment of life than the woman who holds my hand.

THIRTY-THREE

Ziggy

Playlist: "It's a Wonderful World," Peggy Lee

"Ziggy Stardust." Dad wraps his arm around my shoulder, pulling me close, and presses a kiss to my temple.

"Hey, Daddy." I set a hand on his back and smile up at him. "Get enough to eat?"

He gives me a look. "You know I did. Your mother has a serious impulse to overcook, and I simply can't let it go to waste."

"There are a lot of mouths to feed," I point out. My gaze travels the back deck of the A-frame as sunset spills across it, in its delicious, homey glow. The Bergman brood, and even sweet Charlie, who's finally come around to Sebastian, fill it to the brim in chairs at the outdoor table, eating, talking, laughing. Some of us overflow into the yard, too, kicking a soccer ball around, goofing off with bocce balls.

Dad smiles, squeezing my shoulder once more, then letting go. Setting his hands in his pockets, he shifts his weight off his amputated leg and its prosthesis. I know better by now than to ask if he wants to sit. He'll sit if he needs to, and he won't if he doesn't.

"So my wily youngest daughter—"

"*I'm* wily?" I raise my eyebrows. "You meddlesome people are the ones who set us up for our A-frame . . . one-on-one."

I blush spectacularly as Dad coughs into his fist, grinning. He's blushing, too. "Well, Sigrid, it was all your mother's idea. She said sometimes people need time to come to their senses, but some-times, they need the time to come for them to see sense."

I laugh. "Sounds like Mom."

Like she's realized we're talking about her, Mom glances over her shoulder and narrows her eyes playfully. Dad smiles at her in a way that makes Mom grin deviously, then turn back to where she sits beside Rooney on her far side, with Frankie on the other who is lounging like a queen on the chaise portion, root beer float propped on her big belly as she sips from a giant bendy straw.

I'm going to be an aunt again in just a month from now, and I can't wait. Frankie's spectacular puke at the preseason game that Sebastian told me all about, and her odd comment plus fantastic boobs at Halloween, made a lot more sense once she and Ren told us the good news: Baby Zeferino-Bergman is on their way, this May.

"I like him so much," my dad says, breaking my thoughts. "He's a good man."

I peer up at Dad and knock shoulders with him, then glance out to the yard, where, beside a smiling Ren, Sebastian stands, handsome in a soft gray T-shirt and a pair of chambray shorts that hug his fantastic butt, gently tossing a bocce ball. He's got a blue ball cap on, tugged low over his dark hair, whose disheveled state I'm entirely responsible for. He watches me, gray eyes piercing and lovely, a pleased, hungry smile warming his face. I'm wearing that same smile, too.

"I know he is," I tell my dad. "But . . . not *too* good."

Dad gives me a conspiratorial smile. "What fun would that be if he was?"

"Precisely."

"Besides, he'd never survive in the Bergman family if he was." Dad nods to the yard, where Sebastian is now in a mutual headlock with Viggo, who shouts a laugh as Sebastian nails his tickle spot. They both collapse to the grass.

"Aunt Ziggy!" Linnie tugs at the soft persimmon sundress swinging above my knees.

I crouch to meet her eyes. "Linnie, what's up?"

"I want music." She bounces up and down. "Swingy music."

"Oooh." I raise my eyebrows. "Swing dance music?"

"Yes!" she shrieks. "You can twirl me."

"I'd be honored. Give me one sec."

Dashing across the deck, I pick up my phone, which is synched to the speakers mounted around us, and pick Linnie's favorite song, fast and happy, though what swing dance song isn't?

As the opening bars hit the air, Linnie runs toward me and I lift her up, earning her bright, squealing laugh. "Again, Aunt Ziggy!"

"Basics, first!" I set her down and hold her hand as we do the steps I taught her.

"Triple step," she hollers, moving to my right, then to my left. "And triple step *again*!"

I laugh. I'm sensitive to noise, but I love how loud this little girl is, her unbridled joy. I hope she never loses it. I'm going to do everything I can to make sure she doesn't. "Rock step!" she shrieks, hopping back on her heel, then forward.

"Hey now." Sebastian jogs up the stairs to the deck, spinning his ball cap backward so he can see us easier. "Who's swing dancing without me?"

Linnie gapes up at him. "Trouble, *you* know swingy dance?"

"I do," he says.

I gape at him, too.

"What?" He gives me a coy look, then lowers his voice, leaning in. "You said you loved swing dancing. It would involve me touching you a lot. I watched a few videos when I was in hotels for away games, because I was absolutely going to be prepared to swing dance if you asked me to. I even had plans to ask *you* to go swing dancing, but this darn hockey season got in my way."

"Well," I sigh dreamily, "you've got a little time until you're back for the playoffs. I suppose I could take you up on your offer until then."

Sebastian gives me a slow, knowing smile as he slips a hand around my back and pulls me close. "Sigrid. I plan to be dancing with you for a lot longer than that."

As the big band music swells in the speakers, I smile up at him and take his hand with mine. "How perfect." I steal a kiss, then let myself spin, free and safe in his arms. "That was my plan, too."

Sebastian

Playlist: "Somewhere Only We Know,"
Vitamin String Quartet

One year later

I watch Ziggy walk out of the water, waves lapping at her bare calves, wind whipping her hair, like the ocean itself wants to claim her. Every time I watch her wade through the surf, all I can think of is the night of Ren and Frankie's wedding, when she stood on that balcony like a water goddess in her seafoam-green dress, tall and fierce, wide eyed with wind-wild hair. How ready I was, even then, to fall to my knees and worship at her feet.

It's been one year since she told me she loved me, since I found the courage to confess my love, my fears, my hopes. Every day I wake up, praying it's not a dream that I'm about to be torn from, a cruelly captivating figment of my desperate imagination. Every time I hear her voice, see her bound across my threshold, hold her in my arms, I breathe a sigh of relief—she's real; *this* is real. She lets me love her. She loves me, too. In breathless, beautiful moments like this, I can barely believe it.

"Sebastian!" she yells over the roar of the ocean.

I smile, shielding my eyes from the sun with my hand. "Sigrid!"

She waves me toward her. Closing the distance between us, I walk quickly, bare feet sinking into the cool, packed sand. I slip an arm around her waist and kiss her neck, breathe her in, saltwater mingling with that cool, clean scent of rainfall that never leaves her. "What is it?" I ask.

She lifts her hand. A hermit crab. I shudder and take a step back. "Christ, Ziggy."

A laugh jumps out of her. "Are you scared, Sebastian? Of a tiny little blue hermit crab?"

I step behind her, wrapping my arms around her waist, nestling my chin into the crook of her neck. My eyes do not leave that unnerving, creepy, crawly invertebrate. "'Scared' is a strong word. I just . . . hold a . . . healthy respect for their pincers."

She glances over her shoulder, her smile deepening. Her eyes search mine. "Don't worry. I'll protect you from the pincers."

My tension eases. Heat fills me as I stare at her. Leaning in, I kiss her, soft and slow. "C'mon, Sigrid. Put the creepy crawly down and let's go back to the house."

Her eyes fall shut as I kiss her jaw, her neck, as my hands wander down her stomach, up over her breast. "What if I wanted to adopt it?" she asks quietly.

My hands freeze. I pull away, glaring down at her. "Ziggy, that's not funny."

She blinks up at me with big, sad eyes. "But, Sebastian, it's so cute."

"And it is not living in my house."

Ziggy arches an eyebrow. "Who said anything about it living at *your* house?"

My jaw clenches. I stare down at her. I've been dropping hints. Lots of them. And I know I need to be direct, that I should be brave enough to say exactly what I want. But I'm still working on my fears—that she might end up deciding I'm not enough, realizing that she deserves more. The thought of asking her to move in with me feels like dragging a knife down my chest and dragging my insides open.

I exhale slowly, steadying myself. "Your apartment has a no-pets policy."

She tips her head, smiling softly. "My lease is up next month. I was thinking it might be time to move on."

My heart jumps. "You were?"

She peers down at the hermit crab wandering across her palm. "Maybe I'll find somewhere that will let me have my own *Pagurus samuelis*."

I wrinkle my nose. "Your own what?"

"Blue hermit crab," she says, fingertip tracing over its shell. "*Pagurus samuelis* is its Latin name."

"And you know this . . . how?"

"I've got Ryder for a brother, Sebastian. I know way more Latin names for plants, animals, and insects than anyone should."

I peer down at the hermit crab, my nose still wrinkled. "But what about a dog? Weren't you saying you wanted a dog?"

A dog, I can get on board with. I had dogs growing up, and they were the only source of affection I had for a long time. I think about seeing Ziggy curled up on my sofa with a dog—*our* dog. Walking it with her, hand in hand on the beach. Opening presents on Christmas morning, selfies of us, bleary eyed, bed head hair, in our pj's, the dog sandwiched between us.

Ziggy shrugs. "I don't think it's fair of me to get a dog when I travel so much and it would have so little space in an apartment. Maybe someday."

She crouches down to the water, hovering above the waves as they roll beneath her, then gently lowers the hermit crab beneath the water, where it scuttles across the sand.

Sighing, she stands and dusts sand off her hands.

I stare at her, that graceful, striking profile—cinnamon spark freckles, long straight nose, copper lashes fanned across her high, sharp cheekbones—as she stares down at the water. My heart thuds, heavy and hard, against my ribs.

Say it, you coward. Ask her, just do it.

Ziggy turns and smiles at me, the sun's golden rays bursting like a halo behind her. Her eyes glow, tender and loving. She holds out her hand.

I take her hand and draw her toward me, slipping my arm around her waist, tucking her against me, chest to chest. Gently, I set her hair behind her shoulders, revealing her whole beautiful face.

"Reading date?" she whispers.

I swallow roughly, searching her eyes.

An idea starts to form as I stare down at her, remembering our many reading dates in my house's library, tucked into its quiet, cozy corner of the house, wall-to-wall bookshelves, floor-to-ceiling windows softened by sheers that cast it in a hazy, homey glow. I think about the mornings and afternoons and nights we've spent, curled up, side by side, on the sofa, legs entwined, hands wandering until our fingers locked.

Holding her eyes, I smile and tell her, "That sounds perfect."

———

"So." I tap the spoon on the side of the pan bearing homemade pasta sauce, then set it on the counter.

Ziggy glances up from where she tosses the salad. "So."

"You, uh . . ." I clear my throat, scrubbing at the back of my neck. "You were saying your lease is up next month?"

She nods, plucking up a piece of lettuce, tasting the salad. Frowning, she adds a drizzle of more dressing, then tosses the salad again. "Three weeks from now. That's right."

I stare at her, my heart pounding. It's been a week since my little epiphany during our walk on the beach. I've got everything ready. My plan is in place. I've practiced what I'm going to say. I hoped, by this point, I'd feel calmer, more at ease.

I do not.

If anything, I'm more terrified than ever.

What if she says no? What if I get it wrong?

As if she's sensed my worries, my fears, Ziggy glances my way again and smiles, swift and sweet. Then she leans in and kisses me, a fleeting, tender brush of lips that leaves me leaning toward her, wishing for more.

That's all I want with her—*more*. More time, more touch, more words, not that what we share is inadequate, but it isn't everything. It isn't her, living here, every morning and every night in my arms. It's drives and bike rides, traffic and waiting. It's the quiet panic that creeps in on those nights we're not together, and I miss her so badly, I can barely breathe.

Suddenly, the thought of waiting a second longer to ask her for everything I want, everything I need, is untenable. I'm afraid of how vulnerable this makes me feel; that's undeniable. But I'm even more afraid of letting another minute go by without her knowing that she means this much to me, that she's the heart of everything I want in my life. "Ziggy."

She peers at me, her hand gently cupping my face. "Sebastian."

I shut my eyes, leaning into her hand, and press a slow kiss to her palm. "I love you," I whisper against her skin.

She smiles, then leans in, gives me a soft, searing kiss. "I know. I love you, too."

Opening my eyes, I meet hers. "How hungry are you?"

She tips her head, her smile deepening. "Not desperately hungry. Why?"

My heart races as I search her eyes. I take a step back, flip off the heat under the pan, then clasp her hand tight in mine. "Come on, then. Dinner can wait. There's something I want to show you."

I tug her with me, down the hall, toward the library—fear, hope, love braided in my heart. I've been brave for her before. I can be brave for her again. She deserves this.

She deserves my honesty, my vulnerability, my trust.

She deserves the world. I hope she says yes, so I can spend the rest of my life giving it to her.

Ziggy

Sebastian stops outside his cozy library, the door unusually shut. I frown, perplexed.

Slowly, he turns and faces me, his hand gripping mine almost too tight, his thumb dancing across my skin. "Ziggy, I . . ." His voice is shaking. His hand is, too.

I step closer, set the back of my hand to his forehead, to his cheek. "Sebastian, what's wrong? Do you feel okay?"

He shakes his head, his eyes held on mine. "I love you," he whispers. "So much."

Emotion swells through me. I cup his jaw tenderly, my thumb stroking his cheek. "I love you, too. With all my heart."

A rough swallow works down his throat. Then he leans in and kisses me, hard and deep. I gasp in surprise, then pleasure, as I stumble back against the wall, dragging him with me. His hands sink into my hair. I wrap my arms around his waist and tug him close. His tongue dances with mine, and he breathes, rough and hungry, into my mouth. I drink in his sounds, his air, the weight of his body pressed against mine.

And then he tears himself away, light dancing in those quick-silver eyes, a flush warming his cheeks. He looks like one of my favorite romantasy heroes, preparing for battle, steeling himself for either a glorious, hard-won victory or a valiant, violent end.

"Sebastian?"

He clasps my hands, draws me with him, then he throws open the door.

———

I stare at the library, half of his built-in bookshelves curved around this side of the room empty, strangely bare. Sebastian clasps my hand tighter, drawing me into the room. "Where are your books?" I whisper.

He points over my shoulder. I glance that way, processing the stacks of books on the floor beside the now-empty corner. "They'll go there," he says. "In the new built-ins, once they're installed."

I frown, inspecting that end of the room. His desk is there still, sleek mid-century walnut; beside it, a hardy snake plant that Viggo gave him for his birthday; a modern metal floor lamp whose wide creamy paper shade hovers above the desk, but not much else. He rarely sits at that desk, rarely spends time on that side of the library. Where we stand, on this end, that's where we always end up, cuddling on the couch, surrounded by all his books.

"But . . . why?" I ask. "Why did you move so many of them?"

"They're not my favorite titles," he says, his thumb skating over my skin, his eyes holding mine. "I figured they could go on the less-used side of the room, by the desk, so I could make room . . ." He swallows thickly. "Room for *your* books."

My heart takes off, a wild sprint inside my chest. "My books?"

He nods, stepping closer. "Can't have you living here without your books, now can I?"

Heat floods my cheeks. Emotion knots my throat. "But . . . I'm not living with you."

He smiles, soft, unsure, an uneven tug at one corner of his

mouth, nothing of that magnetic charisma he shows the world. This is his fear, his hope, his love, born out on his face, just for me. "Well, I was hoping you'd want to live here."

I bite my lip, trying not to cry. "You were?"

"It's all I can think about," he says quietly, drawing me closer, into his arms, his hands skating up my back, delving into my hair, gentle, reverent. "Well, besides, thinking about being inside you, kissing you, holding you, watching you read and think and dream. And getting a dog with you. I might be able to work up to a hermit crab, but I think a dog is a good compromise to start, don't you?"

"Sebastian." I laugh tearily, so moved, so thrilled, so relieved. He wants this as much as I do.

"Sigrid." He holds my eyes, his hand cupping my cheek tenderly. "I still . . . feel so unworthy of this—you, the time we share, the happiness you give me. That's why it's taken me so long to ask, why I took the coward's way and spent months dropping hints rather than asking you outright."

I poke his side teasingly. "I don't speak hints. You know that. Hints fly right over my literal head."

He nods. "That's why it was cowardly. I knew that. I knew the chance that you'd pick up on what I was implying was . . . slim. But I think I just needed time to find my courage." He searches my eyes. "To work my way up to asking you."

Smiling, blinking through my tears, I tell him, "Sebastian, I would have said yes the moment I knew what you were asking."

He swallows thickly. "You would have?"

"To living together. Sharing a home. Getting a puppy. All of it, so long as it's with you—*yes*," I tell him, shaking my head. "One day you'll believe that I love you as much as you love me."

"Impossible," he mutters, drawing me tight inside his arms, tucking my head against his shoulder.

"Possible," I tell him as he nuzzles me, breathes me in, sighing heavily.

"Sigrid," he whispers. "Is this a yes now, too?"

I smile against the crook of his neck. "It's a yes now, too. A yes tomorrow. A yes . . . always."

His body goes unnaturally still. He pulls back and peers down at me. "Always?"

I stare up at him, searching his eyes. "Always," I tell him quietly, stroking his cheek with my knuckles. "But that's a conversation for another day, I think."

His grip tightens on my waist, in my hair. "Sigrid."

"Sebastian?"

"Always?" he asks again. His voice is thick, his eyes wet.

I nod, smiling up at him, the man I love with all of who I am. "One day you'll believe me. Until then," I whisper, leaning in, kissing him softly, "I'll just have to spend lots of time reinforcing the message."

He groans as I slide my hand up beneath his shirt. "You shouldn't have to."

"Shouldn't have to what?" I trace lazy circles around one nipple, then the other. "Show you that I love you? When you show me you love me, in ways I never believed someone would, every day?"

"Shouldn't have to . . ." His voice hitches when I scrape my fingers down that line of dark hair that dips beneath his shorts. "Shouldn't have to do so much because of my hang-ups."

"Hush." I kiss his neck, behind his ear. "I could tell you plenty of things you 'shouldn't have to do' for me, either, that you do, because it makes me feel safe and secure and loved."

"There's not a thing I shouldn't—"

"Exactly," I tell him, taking his hand, bringing it to my breast, pressing my hips into his. "We love each other how we need to be loved. It's that simple."

Sebastian groans as he thumbs my nipple, a shiver racking him as I palm him through his shorts. "I want to go clear out your apartment," he growls against our kiss. "I want every single part of your life here with me. Your countless books and your dragon print hair towels, your excessive athleisure wardrobe, every pair of cleats, and every hoodie of mine that you've stolen—"

"I believe you mean 'was gifted,'" I tell him breathily as he kisses my collarbone, licks across my skin.

"Live with me, Ziggy. Love me."

"I will," I whisper. "I do."

"I can't believe you're real," he tells me in between kisses, his hands wandering my body, "that *this* is real."

I smile against his kiss. "I can. And I'm so happy."

He pulls back, staring at me so intensely, goose bumps bloom across my skin. "That's all I want, Ziggy, is for you to be happy."

Tenderly, I slip my fingers through his dark, silky hair, dancing my fingertips down his neck. "I'm with you. Of course I'm happy. This is all I need."

"But—"

"If only you and I, this life we're making together, were all you could give me for the rest of your life, that would be all I'd ever need. This is *everything*. This is my happiness."

Sebastian stares at me, his eyes glittering. His sigh is a surrender, a relief, the sound of peace. "I . . . believe you."

I smile, searching his beautiful eyes. "Good. Now—" I sneak my hands beneath the back of his shorts, over his hard, muscly hockey butt, and draw him against me. "Let me reinforce, just in case."

"Reinforcement sounds wise," he mutters, cupping my face.

Our kiss is slow and decadent as he walks us back toward the sofa. Sebastian falls onto its tufted leather upholstery, dragging me down over him. I straddle his hips, bend over him, as he sinks his hands into my hair.

Our tongues dance, rough breaths, his pained groans, those whimpering moans he drags out of me as he grips my hips and grinds me against him.

"Sit on my face," he begs, sitting up, tugging off my shirt. He latches his mouth over my nipple, draws it in. I clutch his hair and gasp as he drags it gently between his teeth. "Please, Ziggy. Please—"

I stand unsteadily, yanking off my shorts, throwing them aside. Sebastian shucks his shorts and boxer briefs, kicks them away, drags off his shirt, too. I crawl back over him, straddling his waist again, crashing down on him, kissing him deeply. We both gasp as I settle onto him, hard and hot, wedged right against me, where I'm wet and aching.

"Fuck," he groans, working me along him. His chest heaves as he breathes, his arm tight around my waist, his fingers gliding through my hair. He falls back on the sofa again, grips my thighs, and drags me up his chest. "Don't make me beg any more."

I stare down at him, my fingers slipping into his hair. Our gazes hold. For just a minute, we look at each other, my hands in his hair, smoothing it back from his face, his fingertips tracing up my thighs, my hips, my backside.

Then, slowly, I lower myself onto him. My thighs clench reflexively as he thumbs my clit faintly, then licks up my center, feather-light and painfully slow.

My jaw clenches with the tease of pleasure. "We're going to play that game, huh?"

He grins deviously, those breathtaking eyes shining with mischief as he looks up at me. "Mm-hmm."

I arch an eyebrow. "Well, I'm just going to remind you, when you're begging to come, that you brought this upon yourself."

His eyes flutter shut as I reach behind me, grip his cock, and stroke down, then up, swirling over the head, squeezing how he likes. His hips rock up into my grip, but he doesn't stop those soft circles of my clit, those teasing flicks of his tongue that make me writhe, make my head fall back as I press myself into him, dying for more.

"Sebastian," I pant. "You're really going to regret this."

He smiles against me; I feel it as he finally sets his mouth on my clit, then sucks rhythmically. He slips one finger inside me, then another. I curl over him, gasping with relief, rocking against his mouth, his fingers as they stroke and rub me right where I need them to be.

Suddenly, he pulls his fingers away, starts kissing lazily over my thighs, my pelvis. Everywhere but where I want him.

I laugh, half pained, half amused, as I reach past him for the basket nestled beneath the sofa's side table, then pull out the small bottle of lube we keep there. We have a lot of sex in the library. "You," I tell him, squirting lube onto my finger, wetting it, "are being awfully naughty, Sebastian."

His mouth falls open, his kisses' momentum lost as I slip my finger behind his balls, over that tight rim, circling it, before I ease the tip just inside. "Fuck," he pants. "Oh, fuck, yes."

"You want to come like this?" I ask, working my finger deeper, until I feel the spot he loves, that makes him come undone.

He nods fervently, then tugs my hips closer, buries his face between my thighs.

I grip his hair, rocking against his mouth as I pump my finger, working him up toward release. He grips his cock with his free hand and starts jerking it, panting against my clit, even as he tongues it, circles it perfectly, entirely focused on my pleasure.

And then I ease my finger out in one gentle glide. I stand up on unsteady legs, stare down at him, wearing a triumphant, saucy smile. "That, my friend, is called retribution."

Sebastian swears, staring up at me wide eyed. "Get the hell back here, woman."

I flip my hair over my shoulder and smile wickedly. "Make me."

His eyes narrow, a smile pulling at his mouth. He springs up suddenly from the sofa like a jungle cat, and I squeal, startled, sprinting across the room. Sebastian grips my waist just as I'm about to round the desk and yanks me back against him. His hands slide down my stomach, over my breasts. He rubs my clit, kissing my neck. "You," he growls, "are an evil sorceress."

I smile, my eyes shut as my head falls back on his shoulder. "I've got to be just a *little* bad every once in a while. Besides, you started it."

"That," he mutters, spinning me and walking me back across the room, toward the tall rolling ladder that's anchored to the book-shelves across from the sofa, "is a very fair point."

I grin, tugging him with me as I fall back on the ladder. He sinks to his knees, throws my thigh over his shoulder and licks me, fast and earnest, sinks two fingers inside me, and strokes just where I need him to. I grip his hair hard, holding him close, drink-ing in the bliss of this sensation, of his sounds. He's got his cock in his free hand, jerking it roughly.

The sight of that sets me off, a rush of white-hot pleasure that pulses through me, aching, throbbing in my clit, in my tender breasts, my nipples, which I cup and pinch.

Sebastian groans as he feels me come, sinking his fingers in again and again, stretching out my orgasm. "Now," I tell him. "I want you inside me now, please, Sebastian."

He stands, panting, and wipes his face with his arm, licks his fingers clean. I stare up at him as he lifts my leg around his waist, as he hoists me higher, so I'm perched on the ladder, my free foot steadied on the bottom step, my butt nestled on a higher one.

And then he sinks into me with one sure thrust of his hips. I cry out, reaching up, gripping the handle of the ladder as he strokes into me, again and again. He buries his face in my neck, grunting, swearing, calling my name.

"Ziggy," he pleads. The ladder creaks. Every thrust inside me, air leaves him, rough and fast. I feel him thicken, feel him stroking into me, so deep, so intensely. Another orgasm looms on the horizon. "Oh God, Ziggy."

I grip his ass with my hand and clutch him to me, stop his hips against mine. He groans, his mouth falling open on my shoulder as I rub myself against his still body, the press of his pelvis against my clit as he grinds in slow circles.

"I'm gonna come," he moans.

"Wait," I tell him.

He shakes in my arms, bites my neck. "I can't," he pleads. "I can't wait."

"You can," I tell him, chasing the edge of release, feeling its first wave finally spill through me. "You will."

He groans, a hoarse, broken sound as he feels me clench around me. "Tell me," he pleads. "Tell me I can—"

"Come," I whisper into his ear.

He shouts into my neck, drawing back his hips and punching them into me, frantic, rhythmless, desperation etched into his taut body as he finally seats himself deep inside me and spills, so long and hard, I feel his release start to drip down my thighs.

He keeps rocking into me, keeps coming, muttering into my hair, against my shoulder, kissing my skin, saying my name, like a prayer, an invocation. I kiss his forehead and hug him tightly to me.

Finally, breathless, boneless, we both pull apart enough to look at each other. Sebastian's expression is smooth, calm, a sated smile lifting his mouth. "Sorcery, I tell you," he wheezes.

I smile, winded, weightless, so wildly taken by this man I adore. "Just love," I tell him. "So much love. Love for you. For always."

He holds my eyes, his smile deepening. "I love you, too. I believe you."

"Good," I whisper, stroking his cheek.

"But just to be clear . . ." He kisses me sweetly as he lifts me from the ladder. I wrap my legs around his waist, grinning when he hoists me tightly in his arms and walks me toward the sofa. "I could always use more reinforcements. Indefinitely." He kisses my temple. "Just to keep it fresh in my mind." He squeezes my butt. "My body." He kisses right over my breast. "My heart."

I cup his face and kiss him with all I've got, a laugh breaking out of me as we tumble clumsily onto the sofa. "Well, then," I whisper into our kiss, "that can most certainly be arranged."

ACKNOWLEDGMENTS

This wasn't the easiest book to write. The time in which I was drafting it coincided with what has been one of the most tumultuous yet healing seasons of my life, and for a time, getting into the emotional and mental headspace to write was difficult. Not unlike Ziggy, I've struggled with deep anxiety that cemented itself in my neurology while I spent decades as a masking, undiagnosed autistic, and sometimes that still manifests in stretches of profound self-doubt. Like Sebastian, only through the patience I've learned to give myself was I able to move through the incapacitating fear that kept me frozen, not magically cured but brave enough to do what I love even while I was afraid. Once I could crank out this story, I fell hard for these two. I hope, now that you've read their story, that you have as well.

I'm so grateful for the patience of my family as I quite thoroughly disappeared into another story. And I would have been so lonely without Sarah and Becs, cheering me on, delighting in my screenshot snippets, giving me Marco Polo pep talks; I'm unendingly thankful for their friendship and support. Finally, my own Dr. B, you encouraged me every time I started spiraling and reminded me that I could do this, "bird by bird, Coach." I promise now that this book is done, I will subsist on more than spoonfuls of peanut butter, too much coffee, and too little sleep (at least until the next book deadline is bearing down on me *guilty smile*). Thank you for the hope and happiness you've shared with me and made me feel safe to share with you, bird by bird. I can't wait to see where that takes us next.

This book's representation is deeply connected to my heart and lived experience. Bisexuality and pansexuality, neurodivergence and celiac disease (including fairly late diagnoses of these two). Though in some ways Ziggy and Seb are like me, in others they couldn't be more different. I'm thankful to these communities that I'm a part of, whose open hearts and shared experiences allowed me to lend nuance to Seb and Ziggy's characterization. Thank you also to Jen and Jackie for your wisdom, feedback, and insight as you read. No two people's experiences are alike, but my hope is that those with the identities and conditions represented in this story will feel seen, understood, and validated.

To my queer readers, however and wherever you are, you're queer enough, you're loved, and you belong.

To everyone out there who still feels sad when it's a pizza party, who misses Grandma's Thanksgiving stuffing, who wishes some days, they could just show up to that social function and eat what's there, I see you. While it's a profound relief to figure out what's making you ill and have a means to mitigate its damage, the method by which we do that is sometimes lonely and alienating, and it's okay to grieve and be sad.

To my fellow neurodivergents, finding your way in a neurotypical world, I hope you surround yourself with people who celebrate the authentic you that you're learning to understand and care for and be true to. It can be hard, and it can be isolating and discouraging, especially when relationships end or boundaries are drawn to protect yourself, when you feel awkward or uncomfortably different, when you're so drained by the prospect of trying to exist in spaces that are fundamentally inhospitable to how you operate and what you need. I hope you can be kind to yourself—stretching yourself in the ways and at the times it matters to you to figure out how it might work, then stepping back for self-care to refill that cup of yours until it's brimming with what brings you joy and love and contentment. You deserve that, no matter if it looks different from how any other person you know makes their way through life.

This book's themes—of hope in ourselves and others, in their and our possibilities, even in the wake of pain we've received or caused, of healing and seeking to grow into greater health and discover joy—are close to my heart, and I can vouch that they aren't easy. If you're on this journey, if you're on it with someone you love, know that I think you're doing something miraculous. You're brave. You're incredible for being right where you are. Don't give up on where your heart and the hearts of those you love dream of going. Belief in, hope in, seeing the best in people are the beats of the greatest love stories—not just with others but with ourselves—and it's one of life's greatest gifts. I hope you allow yourself to both give and receive what every one of us deserves: the chance to shape our lives into a story that we love, and a path that we are proud of.

The Bergman Brothers series, continuing with this book, portrays a big messy family, found family, and friends—imperfect people trying exceptionally hard to love each other well. There are rough patches and plenty of struggles along the way, but ultimately, their love is accepting, affirming, and profoundly safe. Some might say this isn't very realistic. To which I say, "I'd like it to be, and this is why I write." As Oscar Wilde said, "Life imitates Art far more than Art imitates Life." I believe stories affirming everyone's worthiness of love and belonging have life-changing power—to touch us, heal us, and deepen our empathy for ourselves and others. Stories have the power to reshape our hearts and minds, our relationships, and ultimately the world we live in.

I hope by now that, as it has been for me, this Bergman world is a haven for you, reader, where these intimate relationships with oneself and others, platonic, familial, romantic, and beyond affirm the hope for all of us—that we can be curious, open-minded, and open-hearted, without being judgmental; that we can welcome and embrace one another, just as we are, and become better, wiser, kinder, for having experienced all that is possible when we do.

Keep reading for a preview of
Viggo Bergman's story . . .

ONLY AND FOREVER

Viggo

Playlist: "Everybody's Lonely," Jukebox The Ghost

If there's one thing you should know about me, it's that I love a happy ending. That butterflies-in-your-stomach, rush-of-serotonin, breathless, euphoric, wrapped-up-in-a-bow happy ending. The last page of a romance novel as my eyes dance across *The End*. A shorefront view of the sunset, toes wedged in the sand, watching fading light spill glorious gold across cool blue waves, the grand finale end to the perfect beach day. The first bite of homemade pastry, finally perfected after countless recipe tweaks. And, of course, most of all, my family, side by side with their happily ever afters, crammed together at the long, worn wooden table in our home away from home nestled in the woods of Washington State, the A-frame.

My gaze drifts around the room, the sounds of everyone's rowdy voices and laughter sweetening the bittersweet. I'm surrounded by happy endings—my six siblings, their partners, their children, my still-so-in-love parents—and, given my love of happy endings, *I* should be fully, utterly, content, too.

But I'm not.

Because I'm still waiting for *my* happy ending. Irony of ironies, salt in the wound, unlike these lucky ducks, who, in six different ways, serendipitously tripped and fell, kicking and screaming, into meeting their perfect match, I've been *searching* for mine. And I'm the only one who hasn't found them yet.

"Viggo!" Ziggy, my baby sister, the youngest in the Bergman brood, calls my name from across the table, wide smile, freckles, and bright green eyes, flipping her long red braid over her shoulder. "Scrabble doesn't have to be so serious. Play already."

I snap out of my daydreaming and peer at the Scrabble board, tugging down my ball cap to hide my eyes. I don't like being caught in maudlin thoughts.

"'Scrabble doesn't have to be so serious.'" Ziggy's boyfriend, Seb, tips his head her way. "Did you really just say that? The woman who punched my thigh when I built a word off of the letter *u* and compromised her plans for her *q*?"

Ziggy blushes bright red, narrowing her eyes at Seb. "That's different."

His tongue pokes his cheek. "How so, Sigrid?"

I still can't believe she lets someone call her by her full name. Then again, if anyone could get away with it, it's Seb.

"You," she says breezily, plucking a cracker off the plate of snacks, "looked at my tiles. You cheated."

Seb grins. "Now, why would I ever do that?"

"Because you live to fire me up and suffer the consequences."

He sighs dreamily. "And what glorious consequences they are."

"Ew," I say miserably. "Stop with the double entendres—Oh, hell yes." Inspiration having struck, I lean in and spell out E-N-T-E-N-D-R-E.

Everyone groans around the table.

"With that double word square," I tell my sister, "I'll take eighteen points."

Ziggy grumbles as she writes down the score. Seb takes the opportunity to whisper something in her ear that puts a smile on her face.

I avert my eyes and try not to slip right back into my mope, but it's hard. Mom leans into the crook of Dad's arm, her hand resting on his as they talk with my oldest siblings and their partners—my sister, the firstborn Bergman, Freya, beside her husband, Aiden; my oldest brother Axel, born after Freya, holding hands on the table with his wife, Rooney, so at home in how they lean in together and talk and touch. My gaze dances farther down the table to Ren, the next sibling born after Axel, his arm around his wife Frankie, who sits, hands folded and resting on her very pregnant belly, as she makes some dry quip. Willa, wife of my brother Ryder, born after Ren and preceding me, laughs loudly at what she says. Ryder grins at Willa, his arm stretched across the back of her chair, softly twirling a coil of her hair around his finger.

So affectionate. So effortless. So romantic. My chest feels tight. Pain knots, sharp and sour, beneath my ribs.

A toe nudges me beneath the table. I glance up and find my brother Oliver, just a year younger than me, whom I'm so close to, not just in years, but emotionally, that we've operated like twins for as long as I can remember. Except now, he has his someone, too—Gavin, who sits, shoulder wedged against Ollie's. Our niece, Linnea, is perched on Gavin's lap as they color together, dark-haired heads bent over the page.

Oliver's eyes, ice-blue gray, just like mine, like Mom's and Freya's and Ren's, lock with mine. *You okay?* he mouths.

I swallow, then force a smile. *I'm fine.*

He frowns, which is rare for my sunshine-bright, often smiling brother. But he knows—he always has—when I'm low. And when he does, Ollie will go to great, often ridiculous lengths to make things better. This is just one thing he can't fix.

Oliver stares at me, brow furrowed. He doesn't buy my *I'm fine* line one bit. Which means it's time to redirect before he stubbornly decides to get to the bottom of it and try to problem-solve. I nudge my chin at the Scrabble board. "Your turn, Ollie."

He sighs, shaking his head, dropping the subject for now, and peers down at the board. A devious grin lights up his face as he brings his first tile to the board and places it beside the *e* at the end of *entendre*.

Tile by tile, they stretch across the Scrabble board, building a word that builds my sense of dread. E-S-C-O-N-D-I-D-O.

My brother lays down the last *o* with a jaunty snap. Sitting back, he smiles wickedly, then says, "Escondido."

I glare at him. "Yes, thank you. I can spell."

"You can't use proper nouns!" Seb calls.

"Yes, you can," Oliver and I reply in unison, locked in our mutual stare-down.

"Or more than seven tiles," Seb adds. He frowns in confusion. "How did you get so many tiles?"

"You get to sneak one extra tile per turn when you draw," Oliver tells him, still holding my eyes, "unless someone catches you, then you have to return it."

"Bergman rules," Ziggy explains.

To which Gavin adds, grumbling, "It's *mayhem*."

Oliver's smile deepens. "But it's awfully fun mayhem."

I glare at my brother. He's doing it on purpose, taunting me like this. As I once said to him when he was fresh off heartbreak back in college, it's better to be mad than to be sad. Oliver's going for that, poking me about Escondido.

While my trips from Los Angeles down to Escondido aren't a secret, to my family's dismay, their reason is. That reason is the only private part of my life, which is no small feat—I suck at keeping secrets, and my family's so close and communicative, secret keeping is basically unheard of. This is a secret I've kept because it's something I feel deeply vulnerable about—the biggest risk I've ever taken, the greatest dream I've ever let myself cultivate and try to follow through on, which isn't a strength of mine. My ADHD brain loves newness—new ideas to explore, new projects to kick off, new skills to learn. So many things bring me joy. I've never seen why I had to settle on only a few of them.

But this plan, this hope and its possibility, bring me a kind of joy that's eclipsed anything I've ever dabbled in before. So, step by step, I've worked toward making it a reality.

"Escondido?" Linnea, Freya and Aiden's daughter, four and a half, as smart as a whip and highly observant, lifts her head, those dark waves she inherited from her dad frizzy from hours spent running around outside. "Mommy says if she got a dime every time Uncle Viggo drove to Escondido, she'd—"

Freya leaps from the table and scoops up Linnea from Gavin's lap. "Bath time for you!"

Aiden bites back a laugh as he hands over their one-year-old, Theo, to my mom, who takes him with a raspberry to his tummy that makes him laugh. "I warned you she was listening," Aiden tells Freya.

"She," my sister says, tickling Linnea, who giggles, "was supposed to be asleep when we had that conversation."

"But spying on you is so much more fun!" Linnie yells.

Freya sighs and hitches Linnie higher on her hip before starting up the stairs. "You, little miss, are a troublemaker."

Linnie's giggle echoes up the stairwell.

"On the subject of Escondido, and while you have the family's attention," Oliver says, leaning his elbows on the table, "care to tell us why you've been regularly burning two hours' worth of gas each way, driving down there for the past year, Viggo?"

"Up until two months ago," Ziggy chimes in.

I blink at her, stunned.

"What?" she asks.

"How do you know where and when I've been?"

Ollie rolls his eyes. "V, we have mutually agreed phone tracking, remember?"

"To my continued dismay," Gavin grumbles.

I blow Gavin a kiss. He flips me the finger, safe to show his true colors since Linnie's made her exit.

Seb snorts, highly amused by this. I glare at him, then redirect my ire at Oliver. "Ollie, *we* have phone tracking, but since when do you share that highly classified information with the siblings?"

"Since Ziggy wanted to know where you were and what was taking you so damn long to deliver those gluten-free cookies for Seb."

Everyone at the table says, "Awww."

Ziggy turns bright red. Seb wiggles his eyebrows as he throws an arm around the back of her chair.

"So," Ollie continues, "I told her you weren't in Escondido. According to phone tracking, you were poking around Culver City. And, in fact, you hadn't been to Escondido for the past seven weeks."

"You two have a disturbing lack of boundaries," Axel mutters.

Rooney beams a smile our way. "I think it's adorable."

I scowl at Oliver. I used to think it was pretty adorable, too, but I'm not such a big fan now that it means my family knows my migratory patterns have changed. It means they're going to be sniffing around me even more, and if they happen to follow me, catch me at the—

No. I'm getting ahead of myself. My family wouldn't follow me. We're a debatably overengaged bunch, but no one's *that* far in each other's business.

Except maybe me. And I'm me, so I don't have to worry about following myself.

"Well then," Oliver says, setting his chin on his clasped hands, smiling sweetly. "We're all ears. Go on."

I glance around the room, my family's side conversations now brought to a stop. All eyes are on me.

As much as I want to confess and unburden myself, I can't make myself share this risk I'm taking, this hope I have that could fail and fall apart. Not yet, not when I'm already so raw from this family staycation that brought Ziggy's boyfriend here, declaring his feelings, making their relationship official and leaving me surrounded for the first time by *everyone* in my family being happily paired off.

"What can I say?" Scooping up a handful of pistachios and throwing them back, I tell them around my bite, "Escondido's zoo is killer. I can't stop going back."

Everyone groans and grumbles, going back to their conversations.

"You don't believe me?" I ask.

"No!" they all yell.

I snort a laugh, chewing my pistachios, as that bittersweet bubble of being loved yet lonely swells inside me. I adore my family. I'm grateful for them. And I also feel farther from them than I ever have before, because of how their lives have shifted while mine has remained fixed.

For now, just a little longer, I'm going to keep my secret.

Ding-dong.

The A-frame's doorbell ring echoes, silencing conversation once again. Ziggy shoots up from her chair and squeals happily. "They're back!"

"They" are Ziggy's childhood best friend, Charlie, and her partner, Gigi. Ziggy met Charlie Clarke when we were young, right after Charlie and her siblings moved to Washington with their mother during their parents' first acrimonious divorce (they have since divorced and remarried each other twice—it's a bit of a mess, according to Ziggy). Knowing my sister and Charlie's history, I wasn't surprised when Charlie showed up with Gigi earlier this week to celebrate Ziggy's birthday, which, in addition to enjoying a spring break of sorts, is why all the family's here. What *did* surprise me was when Charlie pulled me aside this morning over coffee and asked me for favor that sent me spinning sideways.

Charlie, my baby sister's best friend, looked at me with those big hazel eyes and asked me for a favor I couldn't refuse.

"My sister," Charlie said, "her life has sort of blown up lately, and I'm worried about her, so I'm going to try to bring her here. I have to do *something*, and I feel like if I bring her here, it might help. You Bergmans can make anything better. If she says yes, if she comes, will you help me?"

"How?" I asked.

Charlie smiled, bright and trusting. "Just by being you. Put a smile on her face for me. She needs someone to make her smile. If anyone can do that, it's you."

It was on the tip of my tongue to explain how much harder that was going to be than Charlie thought. But that would have required admitting something I was much too proud to admit:

I'd already tried to make Tallulah Clarke smile, years ago. And I'd failed.

"Did Ziggy mention," I ask Seb, "if Charlie and Gigi were . . . bringing anyone else back with them?"

Seb frowns at his tiles, rearranging them in their tray. "No. Why?"

I don't know how to answer that without giving myself, or the secret favor Charlie asked of me, away.

Seb peers up, clearly curious about my silence, and rakes back his dark, wavy hair; his frown deepening as his sharp gray eyes lock on me. "Viggo. Why?"

Ziggy grips the front door's handle and wrenches it open. I lean back in my chair, tipping it onto its two rear legs, craning for a better view.

In walks Gigi, then Charlie, talking loudly, laughing about

something I can't make out, as they shrug off their parkas and ease out of their boots. They step aside, like they're making room for someone else, like they're not alone.

Like someone else is there.

I lean back farther, trying to see past them. That's when I catch it—a full, soft shadow; a quiet throat clear.

Goose bumps bloom across my skin. And then, behind them, as striking as a sudden, silent storm, walks in Charlie's sister, the only other secret I've kept in my life:

Tallulah Clarke.

––––––––––

Tallulah Clarke is obviously not a secret to my family. They know her as Charlie's quiet older sister who kept to herself, who never had the time of day for us Bergmans during the years Ziggy and Charlie were best friends, before we moved to Los Angeles.

The secret is exactly who Tallulah Clarke was *to me.*

And so I'm not surprised that I feel my family's eyes shift my way, curious, as I stare at Tallulah with my mouth hanging open, eyes ridiculously wide. I'm too distracted by the sight of her, the jarring impact of seeing my first bitterly unrequited crush, to worry about my family's observation. Or to pay attention to exactly what my body's doing in its chair.

As I lose all sense of balance, the chair wobbles, creaks, and, like a felled tree, tips back in slow motion. I pinwheel my arms to try to stop myself from falling, but it's too late. I dive off the chair and land clumsily, managing to catch the chair right before it can crash to the floor.

Leaping up, I straighten the chair and shove it in against the table. My fingers curl around the top of it as Tallulah Clarke, seven years older than she was when I last saw her, steps to the side so Ziggy can shut the door behind her.

Jesus Christ. Tallulah is hotter than ever.

I didn't know Tallulah when the Clarkes lived in Washington State. She never came around. Charlie was picked up and dropped off by an au pair with a thick German accent or, on the rare occasion, by Charlie's mother; her siblings were a mystery.

Until, of all places, Tallulah walked into my very first class at USC.

I didn't know who she was until roll was called, until I did a double take at the name and pieced it together—Charlie's dark hair and wide eyes, her upturned nose. This was *the* Tallulah Clarke.

I watch Tallulah as she stands just inside the door of the A-frame, eyes down, shimmying a highly impractical rain-dappled jean jacket off her shoulders, toeing off even more impractical leopard-print flats. She wrinkles her nose when she sees mud caked on them.

I recognize everything about her that launched my body from awkward adolescent horniness to sexually aching, adult *desire*. I'd had wet dreams, fantasies, curiosities in high school, sure, but seeing Tallulah had obliterated all of that. Simply looking at her in class, being near her, was pure, lusty torture.

There's the beauty mark, right where I remember it—just above and to the left of her pouty mouth. Big, brown doe eyes fringed by dense, dark lashes. The promise of deep dimples in her round cheeks. Glowing, golden skin. And that body. That luscious body. Full, soft arms and thighs; wide, lush hips. The only stark difference is her once-dark hair, now dyed icy aqua blue, swept up in a twist on her head.

Her top is white, striped with marigold, the perfect complement to her warm skin. It's half tucked into cropped wide-leg jeans that hug her hips, ripped in all the right places. She always dressed like the child of Hollywood royalty that she is—stylish, artsy, all LA glam. That hasn't changed. Nor has its impact on me.

As if she feels me staring at her, Tallulah glances my way. Her eyes widen for a fraction of a second before they settle into that cool indifference that I remember all too well.

It bugged me then. And it bugs me now. Because—and I'm sorry, this will sound arrogant, *but*—everyone likes me. At least if I don't stick around *too* long or if they don't, if we don't spend enough time together for me to wear out my welcome and rub them wrong. When people meet me, I'm playful, charming, gregarious. I make them smile and laugh, I quickly figure out what makes them happy, then try to make them happier. To make them like me. And often, for a while, I'm damn good at it.

Except her. Tallulah was the one person who turned her nose up at me right out of the gate, my first and only semester of college.

It drove me up the damn wall.

Standing there, staring at her as she gives me another chilly glance, I feel the sucker punch *thud-thud-thud* of my heart whacking my ribs. Just like it did when she walked into my class seven years ago.

I can't stop staring at her, frozen by the memory of Tallulah as she answered quietly to her name beside me, as I turned toward her and pieced together who she was. Our elbows brushed, and electricity flew through my body so violently, I dropped *Mansfield Park* and lost my place. Tallulah glanced at the book, then up my body as far as my wide grin. (After having braces for the second time late in high school—losing and forgetting to wear my retainer after braces round one bit me epically in the ass—I'd just gotten them off and was very into flashing my once again straight, bright smile.) She gripped her chair and scooched it as far away from me as possible without being in the lap of the person to her other side.

I remember staring at her, crushed, offended, as she opened up her book bag, pulling out a thick novel made anonymous by a stretchy bloodred cover. Dark shoulder-length hair swept around her face, a curtain resolutely shut.

And that was that.

Tallulah and I don't have a history. Or, I suppose you could say, we have a very one-sided history. *I* was fascinated by Tallulah, by her gorgeous looks; her expensive-smelling, sultry floral perfume; her always covered mysterious, thick-spined books. But Tallulah didn't have the time of day for me. My pride was pricked. I could take a hint. I wasn't going to bother someone who didn't want to be bothered.

I can't lie—it stung. It felt serendipitous, that after our families had crossed paths in Washington State, though Tallulah hadn't gone to my school back then, here she was in Los Angeles, at my college, in my classroom. And yet, instead of looking as pleasantly surprised as I was by this turn of events, Tallulah looked thoroughly unimpressed.

I was insecure. I was just turning the corner from a gangly teen with braces, too lanky to fit the deep voice that had taken hold of my body. I'd started to feel like I was finally a little more put together—my body filling in from playing soccer and eating my way through the pantry, my braces finally off, a flattering haircut. College was poised to be even better than high school—I wouldn't be just an entertaining, albeit fairly intelligent, goofball—I'd be respected, admired, appreciated.

Tallulah swiftly took a crap on that.

So I shut up and kept to myself and stewed and pined and stewed some more. Days became weeks, as I wrestled with what the hell was happening to me. I'd never seen someone and felt my chest tighten, my belly do this disconcerting flip-flop, let alone with someone who quickly made it clear she thought she was better than me and my countless questions in our shared lit class and the Austen novels I couldn't stop reading and rereading, sensing something in them, searching for something more that I couldn't put my finger on. I didn't know what it meant, the way Tallulah made me feel. Until fall break, when my family made a long-weekend trip up to the A-frame, where I was poking around its bookshelves. I yanked out a small, worn mass-market paperback historical romance, and the back copy caught my eye.

Loathing. Lust. Unrequited, burning desire.

Burning. Desire.

Those were words I'd been struggling to find, feelings I hadn't known how to identify. I picked up the book, turned it over, dropped to the floor, sat with my back to the bookshelves, and started reading.

That was my first romance novel. A historical romance that poured out in detail what Austen often told in a few sentences or glossed over entirely. Heartrending confessions of adoration, intimate lovemaking, dramatic duels, kisses that lasted paragraphs and left my body hot all over. I devoured it, desperate to make sense of the wild power that a silent, chilly girl had over me. And I never looked back. I've been reading romance novels ever since.

"Viggo." Ziggy frowns at me as I rearrange myself, trying for a nonchalant lean against the chair, which wobbles again ominously before I ease off it. "What," she whispers out of the side of her mouth, "is wrong with you?"

I watch Mom hand my nephew Theo to Dad, then approach Tallulah as she smiles warmly, opening her arms for an embrace that Tallulah gingerly steps into.

"Wrong? With me? Nothing. Just tipped in my chair. Gave myself a little scare. Heh, I rhymed. Look at me, the poet."

Ziggy arches an auburn eyebrow. "You're acting so weird. And you keep staring at Tallulah." My sister tips her head, assessing me. "You've never met her before, right?"

My family has no clue I had a class in college with Tallulah. I wasn't about to go waltzing to family dinner on Sunday and announce that the woman I was having nightly filthy dreams about wouldn't even acknowledge my existence.

And then I left school after that semester, this antsy feeling that I wasn't where I was supposed to be tugging me toward something else, even though I didn't know what that was. Ziggy doesn't know about my equal parts interest in and resentment of her best friend's big sister, because I've kept that embarrassment to myself. No one in my family knows, either. I made sure of that.

Thank God. Because, after my track record of—with the most loving and benevolent intention, I might add—pushing and nudging my siblings into their romantic happily ever afters, they'd be all too ready to push me right into mine.

Relief buoys me up. My family doesn't know. I'm safe. And I have only one greater consolation than my family's ignorance of my long-ago crush on Tallulah: Tallulah's ignorance.

Because if she knew, this favor I'm about to do for Charlie would take it to a whole new level of humiliation.

Tallulah's eyes meet mine as she peers over my mom's shoulder. She frowns as she catches me staring at her again. I cover my blunder, flash her a playful, winking smile. The frown deepens.

Perfect.

I know how to keep it breezy, make things light. That's my bread and butter—deflect with hijinks and humor, divert with glib goofiness. I've done it so long, it comes as easy as breathing. Tallulah might have put me down with that arctic front, back in freshman year of college, but not now. I'll make it playful, keep it fun. It's a godsend in a way—with Charlie's favor guiding me, I have a plan, a strategy to cope with being around Tallulah again.

"Viggo." Ziggy elbows me. "Seriously, what's going on with you?"

"Nothing!" I smile Ziggy's way, hiding everything I'm desperate for her not to see. "I'm just being a hospitable Bergman."

My sister's eyes narrow suspiciously.

I'm saved from any further possible inquisition as she turns toward the table, where Seb's messing with her tiles, and gives him a heated, warning look.

Seb grins at Ziggy, but then his gaze slips past her as she starts arguing with Oliver, who wants to end the Scrabble game in favor of making s'mores outside, and I'm not so sure I'm clear of further inquisitions, after all.

Slowly, Seb stands and makes a pretense of leaning over the board, cleaning up the tiles as Ziggy relents and agrees to end the game. "What's that woman to you?" he asks quietly.

I bend and scoop up tiles, too, shimmying them to the crease in the middle of the board as Seb lifts the bag for me to empty them into. "Nothing."

He snorts. "Bullshit."

"I'm serious," I tell him sharply.

Seb peers up at me, eyes holding mine. "Sure. But when you're ready to walk what you so eloquently talk, you giant hypocrite, I'll be here."

And with that, he turns, tugs my sister his way by the waist, and strolls with her out onto the back deck, in the mass exodus of my family.

Leaving me with the last person I want to be alone with, standing just a few feet away.

Photo courtesy of the author

Chloe Liese writes romances reflecting her belief that everyone deserves a love story. Her stories pack a punch of heat, heart, and humor, and often feature characters who are neurodivergent, like herself. When not dreaming up her next book, Chloe spends her time wandering in nature, playing soccer, and most happily at home with her family and mischievous cats. To sign up for Chloe's latest news, new releases, and special offers, please visit her website and subscribe.

VISIT CHLOE LIESE ONLINE

ChloeLiese.com

Ready to find
your next great read?

Let us help.

Visit prh.com/nextread

Penguin
Random
House